Unwritten Rules

FAYE HOLLAND

First paperback edition: May 2025

Book design by Neptune Designs

Editing by Alexandra Snook, Bonnie Macleod, and Stephanie

Proofreading by Stephanie and JT

Assisted by Stephanie

Character art by Sheyenne Cannon (mossypaintandprint)

Formatting by Be Your Shelf Services

ISBN 979-8-9928562-0-0 (paperback)

ISBN 9798230839583 (ebook)

ISBN 979-8-9928562-2-4 (hardcover)

LCCN 2025904836

www.fayeholland.com

Author's Note

Thank you for giving my debut a chance! This was the product of many, many hours of love and endless murder boards I hung up in my room. Not to mention the endless mind maps on Freeform on my iPad.

Current Content:
Drug usage
Sexual assault
Death on page
Lots of blood (thanks Reaper)
Vomiting (if you're squeamish)
Open door sexy time
Mentions of suicide (off page)
Massive Cliffhanger (sorry)

If you find anything I did not mention, please let me know. It is my job to stay up to date, and anything that is brought up to me will be updated on my platforms and website.
www.fayeholland.com
@authorfayeholland

To my team, my Midnight Darlings, for being delulu with me.

To Stephy and Alexandra for keeping my sanity.

To my love, JT, for proofreading this on such short notice.

And to you, my reader. I hope you enjoy getting on Brent's bike and going for a wild ride.

Don't worry, you'll ride Reaper in his book. I know you'll want to.

Playlist

Take It out on Me – Bohnes
Two Sides – Mickemesk
love me – Ex Habit
Own It (Stripped) – Adelitas Way, New Medicine
Mind Games – Sickick
Moon – Austin Giorgio
Holy Smokes – Bohnes
Riot – Bryce Fox, Sam Tinnesz
monster – Layto
manic – Layto
Good F**King Music – Solence
D4MB – PLVTINUM
Take It Slower – Jiinzo
Granite – Sleep Token
Feel Me Now – If Not For Me
Dangerous Hands – Austin Giorgio
touchin' me – Chandler Leighton
Submission – Jiinzo
Immolation – Jiinzo
AFTER MIDNIGHT – benny mayne
SECRETS – Chri$tian Gate$
THRILLZ – Layto
Sex & Palo Santo – Jutes
…Baby One More Time – Crypto
redline – NUVILICES, Joseph Feinstein
MATCH MADE IN HELL – Dutch Melrose, benny mayne
hell of a good time – Haiden Henderson
Aftertaste (Sexier Version) – LORYANN
Problems – Jake Daniels
PRESSURE – Conquer Divide
She Got Me Like - Kode
Sweet Dream – Bohnes, Underoath
Body Language – Rayvus

Name: Brent Vaughn
Age: 21
Birthday: July 25
Sign: Leo
Height: 6'2
Eye Color: Grey blue
Hair: buzzcut but dark blonde
Distinctive Features: Body COVERED in tattoos,
wears rings when not playing baseball
MBTI: ESTP
Food He Hates: Waffles
Quirks: Rubs the back of his head when he's unsure
of something, always brings a zippo with him

Name: Fallon Montgomery
Age: 20
Birthday: April 19
Sign: Aries
Height: 5'4
Eye Color: light blue
Hair: golden blonde
Distinctive Features: always looks deep in thought,
wears gold jewelry
MBTI: ISFJ
Food She Loves: Sour gummy worms
Quirks: Fidgets with her jewelry when nervous,
obsessed with breakfast foods

1

Fallon

This year was going to be different. *I could feel it.*

That's what I told myself while getting ready for my first class as a sophomore at Willow Bay University—a prestigious institution attended by the richest of the rich, or the most fortunate scholarship winners. Last year was such a whirlwind with Kelly, and I was finally finding my footing.

I kept to myself, mostly. Starting a new school in my new house was a big change, but I was grateful for my best friend who became like a sister to me. She was the social butterfly, and I was the homebody—with a far too large an inheritance and a small dose of depression.

The campus I arrived at last year was so large that it was considered its own city, in a sense. Willow Bay was known for its vibrant campus life and strong community spirit. At least it was online. The mascot was a shark—whatever that was supposed to mean. I assumed it was because we were close to the ocean.

How shark-like life could be…

Kelly popped her wild, wavy, brown-haired head into the bathroom, breaking me out of my thoughts. Her honey-brown eyes were always perfectly lined with sharp black wings—she had mastered the art of makeup. "Hey, Fal, you excited for the fall semester? Oh. My. God. What are you doing?"

1

I leaned away suspiciously. "Uh, getting ready?"

She narrowed her perfectly smoky eyes at me. "Who are you and what the hell did you do with Fallon?" She came into the bathroom fully to pick at my hair, getting far too close to my face, and inspected my face with her eyes wide in disbelief.

I looked back at my reflection hesitantly, applying some lip gloss as a finishing touch. "It's sophomore year, and I feel like I can experiment a bit. Considering we have online classes and I only need to get ready three days a week, I didn't think it was *too* hard to get ready and dolled up."

We both looked at my reflection in the mirror. My blonde beach waves were straightened, and I applied makeup from a tutorial I found online. I looked back at her, somewhat worried.

"Do I look bad?" I asked.

She let out a laugh. "No! I think you look fucking hot! I think sophomore year *and* a boyfriend look good on you. It gives me a good feeling about things—they're *finally* looking up!" She gave a quick smack to my ass, giggling as she left me to my own devices.

"Me too," I sighed. "With some online classes, a house with my bestie close to campus, and a new look, this year is sure to be our best yet."

I placed my makeup in my to-go bag, which I planned to keep with me. My research on makeup may have seemed silly, but it made me feel better about being the weird, sheltered rich girl.

Unlike all the other nepo babies at school, I grew up with a mother who wanted to keep me down to earth and normal despite her immense wealth; she never let me know just *how* immense it was.

Kelly and I linked arms as we marched into the kitchen, excited for breakfast and the big first day. She whipped up a wonderful first day of school spread that included pancakes and a *lot* of bacon. When she cooked, it was *always* breakfast food.

I loaded my plate with a pile of each choice from the

smorgasbord of breakfast options. "Geez, you went all out this morning, Kel."

She beamed. "Only the best for my best!"

"Love you, dude." I giggled.

"Love you too, Fal. Oh! I totally forgot—well, almost forgot—to mention that there is a giant back-to-school bash on Friday. It's Greek Row shit, *but* I figured free drinks, dancing, and a good night out could do us some good. Make our debut as hot sophomores with hunky men to do our bidding."

I almost choked on my orange juice at the mention of hunky men. "Do our bidding? What are we, Mafia leaders?"

She threw me an evil grin. "We could be!" Her hair bounced as she nodded emphatically along with her train of thought. "I *really* want a boyfriend, Fal. I haven't dated anyone since high school. You have Garrett now, and I want to go on cute double dates!"

"Mhm"—I raised an eyebrow—"except for Jake, Ryan, Xavier, Trent... Shall I go on?" I counted the names on my fingers while she glared at me.

"Those *aren't* boyfriends," she huffed. "I want a *real* boyfriend. You know the type: doesn't cheat, likes to talk to me, doesn't just want sex, doesn't lead you on, talks to you in public, doesn't only text you at three in the morning..." She trailed off, listing many of the red flags from her previous hopefuls.

"I'm only teasing," I said, poking her in the side.

She perked right back up. "Well, in that case... I get to tease you about still being a virgin."

I rolled my eyes, toying with the eggs on my plate. "Don't even. For one: I'm only twenty. Two: Boys weren't on my mind with my mom being sick for so long. Then there's the issue of Sylvia being terrible."

"Somehow you always get an out whenever I want to tease you." She shoved a forkful of pancake into her mouth, mumbling about how good it was.

"Sorry, my dead mom gives me an out."

Kelly shook her head. "Yeah, but you and Garrett haven't done anything yet?"

I looked down at my plate. "We aren't exclusive, and I don't know that I want to have sex with him so soon. We literally just met."

"Fine, fine. You win." She waved me off with a hand and went about finishing her breakfast.

After breakfast, we decided to head to campus a bit early to take in the sights. I could never get over how big the campus was; it was like its own town, complete with a shopping center. Buildings scattered everywhere, with a mix of modern structures surrounding the classic architecture of the original campus built in the late 1800s. Just north of the campus buildings was downtown Willow Bay, where anyone over twenty-one went to party if they weren't on Greek Row.

And then there was Greek Row itself. Each fraternity or sorority house was situated on acres—yes, acres—of land, allowing each house to do whatever it saw fit with the property. They were all located to the south of campus, boasting forty houses, and were evenly split between the guys and the girls.

I read that they shared somewhere around six hundred acres of land between all the houses. There was a *lot* of money in Willow Bay.

A lot of legacies, too.

The original architecture spoke to the times—and the money—of the past. Founding families, new money families, and secret millionaires were among the students and faculty.

Money was no object here.

Kelly and I meandered into the science section of the campus as we looked over our schedules. Since we both needed the initial two years of base credits, we were able to take a few classes together. She was hoping to declare her major this year, while I've already declared Exercise Science.

I wasn't sure if I wanted to declare a minor or not.

Dance called to me, but I wanted to explore all my interests. My mother always encouraged me to do so, and I wanted to honor her memory by continuing to pursue my passions, even if I was going to take over her company, the Montgomery Group.

She never shared many details with me before she died, and I assumed it was to keep me grounded and down to earth. I only found out through the will that I was to take over a "luxury real estate firm" after I received a check for my initial inheritance.

I refocused on my schedule, pointing out a smaller building to the left of the main science building. "Looks like that's the building for our bio class."

She checked her phone and looked around. "We're crazy early. What should we do?"

"No idea." I shrugged.

Before we could make a decision, a girl in an all-pink outfit approached us with a bright smile and a stack of pamphlets. "Hiya, gals! Are you two rushing this year?"

I considered it last year, much to Kelly's displeasure. She *hated* Greek life and wanted nothing to do with it. I told her it could be fun, but she said she'd rather I stay a hermit.

I took a pamphlet, ignoring the glare I got from Kelly. "I've thought about it. Do you admit sophomores?"

Her smile widened. "Of course we do! Just between us, there are only two houses that don't—Beta Kappa Pi and Theta Nu. We try to avoid their Debby Downer attitudes."

With a look from Kelly that seemed to say, *How the hell am I supposed to remember that?* I tried to take a mental note of the names.

Looking over the pamphlet, I searched for dates and deadlines. "Is there a date on here?"

Pink Girl pointed out the date on the back. "Yes, ma'am! Phi Beta Lambda at your service! Please consider rushing us this year! We will also be at the big back-to-school bash, so come say hi if you see us. Happy first day!"

We watched her as she happily skipped away to another group of girls arriving on campus, probably giving them the same spiel she just gave us.

"Ugh"—Kelly rolled her eyes—"you aren't *still* on the sorority thing, are you?"

I shrugged. "It could be fun. I want to have a normal college experience with you. If we join, we could make some new friends. You might even find yourself that hunky man you were talking about earlier and start your little Mafia side gig."

She shook her head as I followed her inside, pushing past the large double doors. "If you want to check that out, go ahead. Personally, I have no interest. No major yet, and I prefer to play things by ear. Be a little spontaneous before settling into big decisions, yeah?"

Meandering down the hallway, we had plenty of time to kill. Since I'm always the early bird and Kelly tends to be fashionably late, we agreed to meet an hour early on campus. It was nice to take in the sights before everyone else rushed into the building; it helped me stay calm. With my anxiety, I would become physically ill if it spiked too high.

"Look"—Kelly pointed down the hallway—"I wonder what kinds of sugary goodness awaits in that vending machine."

"There better be sour gummy worms," I mumbled, hoping for my comfort snacks to ease my anxiety.

With our horde of snacks in hand, we found our classroom and made ourselves comfortable while we waited for biology to start. It didn't take long for students to trickle in, looking upset that school had started back up, while we entertained ourselves in the back of the room. The dynamics of the school seemed to reveal themselves as the classroom filled up.

People separated themselves based on their respective cliques. Greek Row students grouped together; what I assumed were scholarship kids sat together, while those who deemed themselves popular had their own section as well. It made me wonder where I would fit in—*if* I would fit in.

The professor walked in with three minutes to spare. "Good morning, and welcome to your fall semester. We will cover cellular biology to include, but not be limited to, membrane structure, cellular energetics, the cell cycle and growth control, and cellular organization. I know; it's fun stuff. If you are a science major, these *will* be important. If you are not a science major, congratulations! Your only task is to pass the tests and then forget everything you learn right after the final exam.

"Now, let's get to your first introductions. You will divide yourselves into groups for next week's assignments and will need to complete your project together as a unit. Before you create your groups of five to seven students, we will be going around the room. Please state your name, your major, and something about yourself. This can include where you are from, your hobbies, a fun fact, *et cetera*."

He pointed to a guy in the front row to kick things off.

The guy turned and waved. "I'm Shane. My major is: I have no idea. I'm from Houston, and I'm on the soccer team. Go Sharks!"

The intros continued until they reached Kelly and me. Kelly went first.

"Hey everyone, my name is Kelly, and I haven't decided on a major yet but I like skateboarding." Ever the extrovert, she beamed throughout her entire introduction.

I shifted in my seat. "I'm Fallon, and I declared Exercise Science as my major and am considering a minor. My favorite snack is sour gummy worms." *Stupid. So. Stupid.* My stomach churned.

After the last guy in our row introduced himself, everyone stood up and formed their lab groups. I looked at Kelly, hoping she would take the lead and get us a half-decent group.

"You two need partners?" A voice behind me answered my silent prayers.

Kelly stuck her hand out over my head. "Hi there, Shane! We would *absolutely* love to add you to our awesome lab group. Did you come alone or with friends?" She looked down at me with a covert wink.

He chuckled at her outspokenness. "There are three of us if you want to make it a solid five."

"Deal," she said, still holding onto his hand.

2

Fallon

"Fun class, huh? I think I could get into the whole science thing." Kelly bumped my shoulder with hers, wiggling her eyebrows as she popped the last piece of chocolate into her mouth.

Shooting her a knowing look, I said, "Shane, huh?"

"Ugh! I'm in love!" She threw up her arms, her long, layered brown hair flowing with the wind. "Next week will be the best week of my life."

My best friend, a skater girl through and through. She always wore edgy makeup, a graphic tee, and carried a board with her wherever she went. She also loved to post 2013-era-style photos to her social media. I loved her endlessly.

We became the best of friends at thirteen and fell into an effortless yin and yang of operations. She became my sister when she was there for me while my mother was at the end of her battle and eventually passed away.

Then, when I turned eighteen, I discovered that my mother had secretly left me a *significant* inheritance, in addition to her wishes for me to take over her company by the time I turned twenty-one. We had always been well off, but my mother—bless her—had hidden the fact that we were amongst the wealthiest people in the nation.

She left me a note.

I know that you know we had money. More than enough to be comfortable, but I never wanted you to be spoiled rotten. You have made me proud to be your mom, you have such a good head on your shoulders.

I just hope I've prepared you enough for the life that lies ahead of you now.

All my love,
Mom

When I turned eighteen, a lawyer handed me a few documents to sign and a check for millions of dollars. I knew next to nothing when I was handed over to my next of kin, Sylvia.

Slyvia, my aunt, hated my mother with a passion. She was always concerned with herself, her boyfriend of the hour, and money, *not* me. When I was legal, I was asked to leave—which wasn't a shock, since she refused to acknowledge me when she wasn't trying to hit me.

Wishing she was better, I lamented the heavy neglect that turned into full abuse whenever she drank. And she drank— often. Her life was "too important" to get screwed up by her somewhat estranged sister's kid. She often told me what she *really* thought of my mom. It wasn't fun.

Kelly was my rock through it all, when she could be. I had a tight leash. Thank God we moved in with each other the day my check hit the bank. Without her, I may as well have died.

"So," I started, looking at her with appreciation for her just being her. "Want to see what shopping we can do?"

She pointed behind me. "Looks like we might have some company for it."

Garrett, my maybe-boyfriend, appeared behind me, wrapping his arms around my waist and planting a kiss on my neck. "Company for what?"

I giggled, his kiss tickling me a bit. "Shopping! But! First, we need to check our schedules and map out our in-person classes to find the best spots to scope for your Mafia."

She waved a hand at me. "I say we hit the shops. We already have one here with us." She looked at Garrett, holding up her board. "Just know, I will take your girl on my sick board if you break her heart."

He nodded, smiling. "Noted. Also, Mafia?"

"One," I started, "I don't think we can both fit on that board. Two," I looked to Garrett, "she's building a Mafia-style cult. Keep up, babe."

"We'll make do," Kelly huffed, linking her arm with mine as Garrett dragged along behind us. She held up her lilac-colored penny board like it was a threat as we went.

Stomping along, Kelly discovered where her English class would be. We had one class together because she hadn't officially declared her major, which made her options for classes more open than mine. My classes were centered around the core credits required for a bachelor's degree in Exercise Science.

I was taking a physical education class: Explorative Exercise. We would be taken through a host of movement types. There would be dancing, skating, swimming, tennis, and any other activities that fit the scope of the class.

The sports science building was jaw-dropping. There was a lab dedicated to metabolic research and testing. The pod, where one could get the most accurate body fat data, was at the top of the list to check out. Ever since the pod came out, underwater submersion data had been tossed to the side.

Unsure of where I wanted to go with my degree, I picked it because it was the topic that interested me the most at the time. I'd spent a lot of my life choosing sports as hobbies, and my mother encouraged me to follow my heart in all things. Remembering the times we had, my heart ached at the thought of her not being able to share in this next era of my life.

Whatever you choose to do, follow your heart, and you'll know the path is right.

Science was my solace when I lived with Sylvia. It was simple and left room for exploration from my room. I was barred from participating in sports, so I studied them silently at night. Now that I was in college, I could let my mind run wild and free with the possibilities.

"Now that we've explored," I started, pulling myself out of my thoughts, "we should get off campus and do self-care in the form of shopping."

Kelly looked far too happy to go check out new shit to buy. "Walk or car? Or board?" She winked at Garrett.

"Seems like a good day to walk before the weather starts cooling off too much." He nudged me, pulling my hand into his.

A twenty-minute walk from the southernmost part of campus, the shopping center of Willow Bay looked like something out of a movie. Over the summer, they expanded the center into even more territory, and it looked like more and more shops would be opening soon.

There was major money in one spot; why wouldn't they expand?

It also wasn't just a shopping center. It was a place to display *and* flaunt wealth.

That, and grab some *really* good food.

Walking into the grand entrance, we were enveloped in an atmosphere of crisp, green money and heavy metal credit cards. The marble floors glistened with warm light radiating from the crystal chandeliers. Light music played overhead as we walked through, accompanied by the occasional light chatter of patrons and the clinking of glasses in a nearby café.

The centerpiece of the complex was a large water display. It was as if someone had teleported the world's most ambient waterfall indoors—water fell from the ceiling, cascading down a rock formation. The light sound of rushing water, coupled with the elite-looking clientele, completed the luxurious vibe. I felt like I didn't belong here, but my bank account said otherwise.

I looked to Garrett. "You sure you want to be dragged into all this?"

He asked me out on occasional dates and showed interest, but we never made anything official. I was gob smacked when a football player asked *me* out while we were on campus prepping our schedules before part of the campus closed for summer break.

We passed by after football practice had ended and he ran up to me, asking me out for coffee and for my phone number. His brown curly hair was dripping with sweat, his lightly tanned face had black stains all over it, and he looked a mess. His brown eyes were full of excitement as he handed me his phone. Nonetheless, I agreed to go on a date. Then another. And a few more after that.

But we weren't official. We hadn't even slept together.

"What?" He had a coy smile on his face. "And miss watching you try on clothes?"

"Ew." Kelly faked a gag. "I need some coffee first."

In the café, she ordered some blended version of coffee that was more of a coffee-flavored *milkshake* than coffee. I ordered my standard iced Americano with a packet of sucralose. Garrett copied my order.

"So, I was thinking…" Kelly trailed off.

"Oh no," I said.

"Oh yes. You need new clothes, and Garrett can be the judge of how hot you look—after my opinion of course. Sophomore year is going to look great on you."

Garrett looked at me excitedly, giving me a naughty smirk at the thought of me being out of my clothes.

Nope, not going there. I don't sleep around like that. Especially if I'm not an official girlfriend.

I sighed. "What are these new clothes even for?"

She grinned, a diabolical look in her eyes. "Parties and *parties.*"

"What about rushing?"

She clicked her tongue at me. "I don't want to rush. Can we hold off on that?"

"You're rushing? Which house?" Garrett butted in.

The look in Kelly's eyes said *nowhere*, but I said, "I have no idea. The options are wide open."

Kelly took a long sip of her drink, eyeing the stores we walked past. Luxury boutiques. Name brand stores. "Before we chat more about girls' clubs, I get to pick your outfit for the back-to-school bash."

I knew she was going to put me in something far too skimpy, but I obliged her anyway. "Only if you come with me to at least one event."

We entered what felt like seven stores in one: a massive luxury clothing boutique. The clothes ranged from casual to Met Gala-worthy gowns. How she could pick anything out in here was beyond me. It was a bit unnerving.

But she grew up in wealth, knowing more about the nepo baby life than I did. Sometimes, I trusted her far too much with that side of things.

Lobbing clothes at me instantly, I was shocked at how quickly she was picking things out. "How about this one? Oh! And this one. Here, try these two for good measure. And... this one."

Garrett had to start helping me catch the clothes she was throwing at me, laughing as we tried to catch them all. He was pretty to look at, and sometimes I wondered what he wanted from me. His brilliant smile directed at me said he was happy to be here—maybe it was just my anxiety again.

Taking some of the clothes to the fitting room—a closet with a curtain—I felt that some of them looked quite similar. After trying them on, stepping out, and spinning for my audience, I decided I liked the fifth outfit.

I slipped into the classic little black dress that seemed to subtly glisten under the lights. The material felt like butter against my skin and accentuated my figure. The dress had a plunging neckline with delicate straps and left enough to the imagination that I didn't feel completely naked.

Stepping out, Kelly and Garrett's jaws dropped to the floor. "Wow," they said in unison.

Trying not to blush, I tucked a strand of hair behind my ear. "I do kind of like this one."

"Cynthia!" Kelly called. "We'll take this one and this whole pile, thank you."

Garrett couldn't take his eyes off me even after I changed back into my normal attire—a basic cream cashmere sweater tucked into my navy pleated skirt.

We found a Japanese steakhouse where we could sit and eat lunch while keeping our shopping bags safe with the concierge. The one thing I could appreciate about being rich was the fact that I could have any service available to me, like someone watching my bags while I ate lunch.

It was still weird that I had that kind of *fuck you* money.

Hopefully, I wouldn't screw up and make my mom mad at me from heaven.

"I think my look is complete," I said in between bites.

"Now you're ready to look hot at parties with your arm candy over there." She giggled, kicking me under the table.

Kelly came from a quietly wealthy family. They stayed out of the news—out of the press. Her dad paid for everything she ever needed but never gave her too much. He believed that keeping her on a tight leash and restricting funds would tame her wild side, but she wasn't wild—she was a social butterfly. It was mostly about how she dressed; he punished her for being too "alternative" in her fashion choices.

His loss. She was never going to dress like the norm.

Picking up her phone from the table, she squealed. "It's Shane! I'm going to go meet him. I'll see you at home? I'll be there to help bring the bags in—swear!" She saluted me and ran out of the restaurant.

"You two are cute," Garrett said, poking my arm.

I tried not to blush. "Thanks."

"So, I wanted to know... would you be my date to the next baseball game?" He scooted into the seat Kelly had left empty, moving his food with him.

I wanted to, but I was worried that he would try to have sex

15

with me. It made me nervous to do it for the first time, but maybe getting it over with this semester would help me come out of my shell. He was a kind, attractive guy who seemed genuinely interested in me, and I couldn't imagine it would all be bad.

Shit, did that mean I'd have to tell him I was a virgin?

Putting my head on his shoulder, I tried to calm my nerves about exposing myself more. "That sounds nice. We should go get food after the game, too."

"I could be down for that," he said, playing with a couple strands of my hair.

We ate comfortably until I realized I needed to get ready for the party and get my bags thrown into my room. "Looks like I should be getting back to prep for this *banger* party. Take me home?"

After we met and I texted him, he replied immediately. I got the first crush butterflies, considering I'd never had a boyfriend before. We texted for a couple of days and scheduled our first official date, which made me even more nervous about entering the next era of my life. We agreed to be non-exclusive for a while after I shared some of my hesitations about getting into a serious relationship in college. Everything was fine.

He was kind and patient, which felt unexpected based on what I'd heard about other boys.

But what did I know?

He opened the door for me when we arrived at my house, and as promised, Kelly came barreling out of the front door to help with the bags.

"How's Shane?" I teased her.

"He'll be at the party. I'm so excited for us to double date. Thanks for taking care of my girl, Garrett! See you later!"

We waved him off and started our haul into the house.

The house we lived in was a very cute, quaint home that I purchased just far enough from campus to feel some separation. It was walkable, and one of the smaller neighborhoods in the Willow Bay area. We had enough space per house that each lot included a bit of outdoor space—space I wanted to fill with a garden and a natural pool.

Our neighborhood was an old one; it had been here longer than the school. The architecture was old and traditional, speaking to the careful craftsmanship of the Victorian era. I felt at peace here, with the non-symmetrical homes, steep roofs, and elaborate wood trim.

That was, when there weren't house parties on the street. It made sense later why the older couple was willing to sell at a lower asking price. They wanted to get the hell out of here.

I looked over at the latest house party—a predominantly male one—to see a bunch of them acting like fools in the front yard with beer and no shirts. Two of them were wrestling each other outside, and it wasn't clear if it was a play fight or not.

"What the hell are they doing?" I couldn't help but stare.

Kelly laughed. "Being a bunch of cavemen, obviously."

The two separated and reset their stances to prepare to collide again. The transition from wrestling to a fistfight had me leaning towards a real fight. The first guy with short, cropped brown hair took the first swing—a gnarly right hook—at the shaggy blonde and connected with his jaw. The guys around them cheered and hollered, encouraging the fight.

My eyes widened. "Dude, they're fighting for real."

The blonde one stumbled back and tried to correct his stance. He approached and attempted a few swings before landing an uppercut on the brown-haired guy. *That looked brutal.*

"Yikes," she replied, becoming engrossed like I was.

A dark, leather jacketed figure leaned over the porch railing, throwing something into the scuffle, a cigarette hanging from his lips. Under his jacket, he had no shirt on, and his body was *covered* in tattoos. He was clearly enjoying the chaos.

"What the heck is *that* one doing?" I pointed at him, trying not to stare.

She chuckled. "That one? Yeah, I can guarantee he's the one who started the fights."

I raised an eyebrow in a silent question.

Continuing, she said, "That's Brent Vaughn. I'm only half surprised you don't know him. Considering you didn't come out of your hole last year, it makes sense."

"Let me guess... he has a reputation of sorts."

"Yup. Total jerk. Pretty ruthless one, too. Once at a party, he was confronted for sleeping with someone's girlfriend—which he does often—and he pummeled the shit out of him for being confrontational. He's the star of the baseball team—the dark star, that is."

"Huh," I said, picking up the last of the bags. "Some guys just love to be chaotic."

I couldn't help but look back at him on the porch while crossing my arms. He was laughing along with his friends during the fight. A deep and carefree laugh at the violence made me wonder exactly how much chaos this guy enjoyed. He flicked ash from his cigarette, exuding *a cool guy* confidence.

He had barely any hair, which exposed the tattoos that extended up the side of his head and neck. It reminded me of a military boot camp buzz cut. Tattoos peeked out from everywhere, telling me that this man was inked up to the max. I couldn't tell how tall he was from here, but most people were taller than me standing at five foot four.

Kelly sighed as she opened the door. "So sad that those good looks are wasted on the assholes."

Before I stepped into the house, I turned to get one last look. *Call me intrigued.*

Brent's gaze flicked over to me, locking eyes with mine and holding me in place. He brought the cigarette back to his lips to take a long drag, daring me to look away as smoke leaked from his mouth and a smirk developed just enough to let me know he caught me continuing to stare at him. He raised an eyebrow and cocked his head, silently asking me what I was looking at.

I broke first and couldn't tell if I was intrigued or terrified after a staring contest with him. Forcing myself to move quickly, I all but jumped into the house to slam the door.

Last one, I thought, peeking quickly before closing the door.

He chucked his cigarette to the ground and pulled off his jacket, revealing a plethora of tattoos covering his entire upper body. He pulled that smirk back up and looked over to me, letting me know he was well aware of what I was doing.

"Want to start getting ready?" Kelly asked from deep in the house.

"Uh, yeah."

3

Brent

"Put this on," Reaper muttered, throwing a balaclava at me.

I grunted and slipped it over my head. *His obsession with masks is ridiculous.*

The Dictator—my grandfather—had me sequestered for *covert* jobs. He hated the so-called "stunts" I pulled, which were nothing more than basic fights that had been agreed upon.

Maybe.

Okay, *not* maybe.

Too many assault cases would do that to a guy.

"I hate wearing this shit. Plus, they know it's me." I picked up my bag, slinging it over my shoulder.

The toys would come out to play tonight for a man who betrayed the trust of the family business. I swore the Dictator ran the conglomerate like a Mafia, but who was I to judge? I was just a bastard who liked violence to him, which left me shoved into a job that suited my capabilities best.

The job was simple: Elimination.

Reaper was the best man for the jobs that dealt with pulling information—and teeth. His love of violence was second to none.

"How long is the ride, boss?"

Holding out a duffel bag with "work" items, I shook my head. "Stop calling me boss. We've been over this; it's weird. Just

Brent. The ride shouldn't be more than an hour. So, three hours max tonight, and I have a party to get to after this job. Let's not dawdle, shall we?"

One would think that after a couple of years of working with someone, we'd have the names down.

We didn't.

I mentally prepared myself for another dead body as I hopped on my bike, slipping the helmet over my head. Sure, I was violent, but the dead bodies? Not my favorite.

I preferred punching men in the face and having them put up a good fight with me. Even better when they rightfully accused me of sleeping with their girlfriends. They were desperate to prove their manhood by winning a fight with me... which they never did.

The ride was nice and smooth; keeping up with Reaper as he split traffic was always the fun part. He never cared about his reckless driving with anyone, while I at least had to try not to die. My grandfather's conglomerate, Chamberlain Industries, would one day be mine, as I was the sole heir. It died with him if I didn't get my hands on it.

We used a spot owned by an associate's real estate company for a lot of our less-than-professional dealings, and this site was no different. A place under construction and heavily monitored by us was the perfect spot to, well, execute.

Reaper hopped off his bike; the weight lifting off it made it look as if it gasped in relief. He was a beefy motherfucker who somehow became giddy at every job where he could get violent. His body looked ready to crush heads with his biceps and an insane amount of muscle. However old he was, he looked as if he had spent his entire life in the weight room with the goal of not fitting into door frames. Where I was built for speed, he was built for brute strength.

I wondered what his free time looked like some days. Other days, I didn't want to know.

"You read the file?" I asked him.

He shrugged. "I only saw the end result."

My hand went to my nose, pinching the bridge in annoyance. "We *need* names and information first. I need something to bring back to the Dictator or it's my ass on the line."

His eyes squint as he strokes his chin through his mask, kind of like how someone would stroke a beard... but I wasn't sure if he even had one; I've never seen the dude's face.

"How many names, and how much information before I send him to hell?"

"Just... whatever you can get. He's been working with some rivals for a while and I need to know who, what, when, and where. Can you manage that?"

Shrugging again, the giddy motherfucker skipped over to the door like a school kid across the playground. And to think *I* liked violence? Being named *Reaper* seemed to be for... reasons. All my thoughts ceased when he burst through the front door without so much as a warning.

If he wasn't so good at his job...

I shook my head and followed him in.

What I found was that Reaper had booted this man out of his chair and onto the floor, standing over him with his arms crossed. His bulky frame in skin-tight black clothing was intimidating the small man on the floor to the brink of tears.

"Woah! Augustus said that this was a business meeting!" He was screaming in fear of Reaper. *Honestly? I would too.* The fucker was scary.

Trying not to laugh at the scene of a grown man cowering in fear, I stood with my arms crossed in a similar stance. "This *is* a business meeting, but it's also an intervention."

He tried backing away, holding his hand out in a protective manner. "Wh-what is this about?"

I rolled my eyes. "Look, I'm going to make this easy for you. Give me the names, dates, times, or anything you have floating around in your noggin. Otherwise, Reaper here will pull them out of you."

His eyes bulged out of his head as he looked back to the

large, imposing figure standing over him. "I don't know what you want!"

Reaper set his boot slowly to his head. "John, I will count to three because I'm a nice man. Sometimes."

His boot pushed slowly.

"One..." His head was guided toward the floor.

"Two..." The ground and his head made connection with one another. Next, he'd apply pressure.

"And—"

"Wait! Wait! Jason! J-Jason Haines! He approached me about three years ago with a proposition."

I scoffed. "You fucking scum. You've been a rat for *three* years?"

"He said your grandfather was going down with some other woman and told me I could be useful and make it out unscathed! I don't know much more than that, I swear!"

Nodding at Reaper, he applied pressure to his head on the ground, making him cry out in pain.

Did Reaper just m—*never mind.*

"What did you do for him? Who else was involved?"

His pants were heavy, shallow breaths as he squirmed under the boot.

Not answering fast enough, Reaper bent down and yanked him onto the table with ease. He pulled out his KA-Bar from his chest plate and held it over his dick. "Want me to perform a castration, boss?"

"No!" he screamed. "They all spoke in code, and they had nicknames for everyone!" Breathing ragged, he had no time to prepare for Reaper stabbing him in the thigh.

Blood oozed from the wound and Reaper let out a low chuckle.

"What else?" I pressed. "I don't have all night and you're making Reaper angry."

"Look, I'm not the highest guy on the— OW!" He gripped his leg when the real pain hit from the knife being yanked out.

Reaper hovered the knife over his neck. "Take your pain like a man."

John grunted and gritted his words through clenched teeth. "Not the highest guy on the totem pole... I provided info... places and shipments... that's all."

I needed something else to go on—more information—or I'd be at the mercy of Augustus Vaughn, the Dictator himself. "More info or you die," I said flatly.

Holding up a hand to protect his fresh wound and a tear falling from his eye, he continued, "Names I heard were random. Rabbit. Rose. Stick. The codes for movements even more so. Tower. Green. Garden. That's all I know. They talked about a big plan in the works, but I never heard specifics. Please, that's—"

And... Reaper slit his throat.

"Goddamn it," I sighed, watching John desperately grasp at the wound as blood poured out.

"Well..." he said, "you said you didn't want to be late for the party."

Where did we even find this guy?

Without hesitation, he pulled out his cleanup kit from his bag and began his duties. John looked dead enough, and I hoped I had enough to brief my grandfather when I inevitably had to get back to him with his demanding timeline.

A scheme that had been operating behind the scenes for at least three years. Jason Haines. Weird codenames. Got it.

He started dragging the body off the table and into a bag that appeared from his kit. "I'll handle the cleanup, boss. Full write-up will be on your desk later tonight."

"Uh, thanks, Reaper."

"Fuck a pretty girl for me, will you?"

At least no day with him was boring.

Helmet on and bike started, I was off to my *normal* college life. I hoped to make good on Reaper's request because I needed to blow off some steam. One of my favorite ways to blow off steam, if I was being honest.

Greek Row was not my favorite place to be, despite being inducted into a fraternity by the demands of the Dictator. He said it would look better for me in the future, but I opted to live with a few friends in a neighborhood just far enough away from campus that I could have a reprieve from Greek life and the compound where he lived. A small room to myself filled with dark thoughts.

Nevertheless, I slowed to a stop in the driveway of the sorority house that was hosting the party this time. Beta Kappa Pi hosted most of the top parties on campus. The head of the house, Sloane, was a level ten clinger and, unfortunately, hosted a lot of the business events organized by her family. Seeing her often was truly annoying despite her being fun in bed.

And she was waiting for me, arms crossed, clearly in a pissy mood.

"Brent! Where have you been? You missed setup and I told you to be here early."

I hadn't even pulled my helmet off and she was already starting in on me. "I had work. You know I have *no* obligations to you, right?"

She stamped her foot as I brushed past her. "You could at least send a text."

I waved a hand in the air. "Yeah, yeah. Save it. I need a drink."

The party was in full swing, and a lot of people looked drunk already. I needed to get a buzz on and clear my mind.

"Brent! My man!" Josh waved me over to the counter where he was pouring shots.

Good, I needed a few. "Hey, man. Got any for me? I could use a double."

Handing me a freshly poured red cup full of vodka, we tapped our cups together and drank.

"First week treating you alright?" His eyes seemed glazed over with booze, which told me he'd been here a while.

"Yeah, how's the party?"

"Good, good! A few rounds of beer pong got me relaxed enough. We demolished this cute blonde earlier before her boyfriend took over and got me loaded." His head was bobbing to the beat and I could tell he should have called it quits on drinking for a bit. His being too drunk never turned out well, and since we both played on the baseball team, Coach punished us all if one of us made mistakes.

Last time, it was my fuck up and Josh was due for another soon.

"Nice, man. Hey, I'm going to go pop out for a smoke. I'll catch up in a bit. Don't do anything stupid," I said, pointing at him playfully.

My exit was interrupted by someone rudely bumping into me. I sighed, knowing this could turn south at a party with drunk students. He looked a bit drunk, and his eyes lit up as recognition washed over him. "Hey! You're Brent?" Words slurring, his face contorted into something that looked like anger.

"Yup," I said, emphasizing the "p" and expressing my annoyance with a grunt. I crossed my arms, looking him over.

I saw what he was doing before he even knew what he was doing. An arm wound up and aimed a punch directly at my face. Easily slipping past his sloppy punch, I caught his arm. "Whatcha doing?"

He spat in my face. "You slept with my girlfriend!"

A few eyes turned in our direction, and I heard a couple of chuckles from the back as I wiped my face.

"So?" I smirked.

Anger simmered behind his drunken gaze. "You're a— a bitch! That's my girl, man..." He tried to yank his arm from my grip.

"Nah," I said, shoving him back. "She wasn't your girlfriend. Sounds like it was just your turn, bro."

With that, he snapped and charged at me. Another easy slip —he was *far* too drunk for this. Shoving him to the ground while I chuckled at the sheer stupidity of our interaction, I left him in a mess on the floor as he muttered more insults and slipped out the back to enjoy a cigarette in peace.

Contemplating the meeting with my grandfather, I took mental notes of what I'd gotten out of John before his inevitable —too early—death. *Damn Reaper for being trigger happy.* Work had been picking up with whispers of traitors and rumblings of something I wasn't privy to just yet.

Nothing a cigarette couldn't fix.

I leaned up against the railing, flipping my Zippo out of my pocket along with a case of cigarettes. The nicotine settled the feelings in my bones and gave me a rush at the same time. *The best of both worlds,* I thought as I took my first puff, looking at the partygoers in the yard living their best lives.

A lot of these kids engaged in dirty business like I did—just without the death part. We all held our places in this filthy little world of the elites. Some of them were here for fun before joining the family business, while others were here to keep tabs on the rest. Not all was as it seemed at Willow Bay.

The back door opened, and that cute little blonde who lived across the street from me rushed out, looking like a hot mess. *Hmm, I wonder what has her flustered like that.* She adjusted her hair and outfit, looking as if she felt out of place here. She looked like the type of fun I was looking for tonight, but her posture conveyed something else that I couldn't quite put my finger on...

She took in the sights before settling her gaze on me. *Why was she staring at me?* She did that earlier, too. It wasn't *fuck me* eyes like the rest of the girls, but more out of sheer curiosity. Maybe my tattoos and overall vibe confused her. Whatever it was, I hoped she took full advantage as I raked my eyes over her delicious body.

I held up my cigarette case in her direction. "Want one?"

"Eh, fuck it," she said.

Blondie had a dirty mouth, too? *Just my luck.* I held her gaze as I lit up the cigarette that hung from her full lips. *I think I like this one.*

"Tired of the party?"

Her eyes didn't waver from mine as she dove into her

ramblings. "Not really. I bombed beer pong and then found my friend a soda she's been looking for." She held up a can of soda. "But she's with a guy, so they're probably sequestered somewhere. Figured I'd chill for a bit before I started looking for her again." She took an awkward drag from the cigarette, clearly having never smoked a day in her life. It was cute.

I'll see you around later, I thought, pushing myself off the railing and flicking my spent butt somewhere into the ether.

Her mouth shot open. "Hey! That's littering!"

I shook my head and laughed. "Look around, babe. Everyone is littering."

Knowing I'd come back for her later, I stalked off into the night to make a phone call. Blondie would have to wait for a bit, but I silently promised her I'd come back for some fun.

4

Fallon

My cheeks flushed with embarrassment from being a little tipsy and word vomiting on him. Who tells the campus bad boy, *Hey! Don't litter!* and recovers from that? I stayed on the porch a bit longer, hoping that no one else saw me, and tried my best to look like I was just enjoying a nice smoke break.

I'd never smoked before and had no idea how to look natural. I tried a vape once, if that counted.

After finishing the cigarette, I tucked the spent butt away for the garbage later and went looking for a bathroom to cry in from embarrassment.

Closing myself in a bathroom, I looked in the mirror. "I don't know if I can do this," I told myself. I didn't know how to fix the makeup that Kelly helped me with, but I would do my damned best.

Dumping the contents of my to-go bag on the counter, I found the compact to blot the oil off my face. I blotted and breathed, trying to calm my nerves after making a fool of myself in front of Brent. God, he probably saw that I was drunk and wrote me off as an idiot. *I am kind of an idiot*, I thought. I reapplied mascara and hoped it would be enough while taking deep breaths, willing myself not to hurl at the first party I went to.

I also hoped Brent would *not* be at the party when I went back in.

The party was still in full swing when I slowly crept back down the stairs. No one glanced at me; they were all consumed with themselves. Laughter and chatter filled the gaps where the music didn't, and I could almost hear distant cheers from another room. Probably more beer pong.

In every room, partygoers were dancing, drinking, or playing party games. Some dressed like I did in a glammed up mini dress, while others opted for more casual party attire. Heels and flats, dresses and shorts, and the men chose heavily varied levels of formality—board shorts all the way up to suits.

Wild.

A figure approached me. Garrett. His recently cut brown hair glinted in the lights, and he was dressed in blue chino pants with a cream linen top. He wore a dazzling smile.

"Hey, you." He pulled me into a small embrace, kissing my cheek. "Thought you ditched after beer pong. Sorry they made you drink so much."

"It's fine," I said, leaning into his warm touch. I was *definitely* drunk if I started thinking about how nice it would be to take him upstairs. *Note to self: No drinking around guys.* "I'm new to parties, remember? I'll need a big strong man like you to help me out." I shot him a little pout.

"Can this big strong man invite his girl to dance?" He held out his free hand to me, offering a dance.

"Maybe one or two..." I smirked as he pulled me into the space people were dancing in.

I swayed a bit to the beat and did a small spin while keeping hold of his hand.

"She can dance?" he asked.

"I'm interdisciplinary. I do favor classic dances like the tango, though. Did you know I participated in ballet?"

We continued to sway to the beat while I let him direct most of my steps. He seemed to have a natural sense of dance, but most wealthy kids had training in multiple areas to appear cultured. "Well, let's dance then." He placed a hand on the top of my hip and interlaced his other hand with mine.

As the bass pulsed in the room, he led me through a series of spins and dips, never taking his eyes off mine. His hands were steady as we glided across the dance floor, a laugh erupting from my throat.

"Wow," I breathed. "Why didn't you tell me you knew your way around a dance floor?"

He placed a small kiss on my lips. "Now you know."

I looked around, noticing that the dance floor had become even bigger since we started dancing, with bodies moving and thumping to the beat. Red cups in their hands and hands generally everywhere, this party looked idyllic. A true back-to-school bash.

Space buns caught my attention. *Kelly.*

"Hey," I turned to look at Garrett. "I see Kelly. I think I'm going to head off after I hand her this." I pulled the soda out of my small clutch and showed it to him.

"You sure?"

I nodded. "Yeah, I had fun, but I think it's far past my bedtime. Want to meet up before the baseball game?"

"I'd love that. Just tell me when and where and I'll show up. Maybe we can watch a movie?"

He pulled me into a hug and planted a deep kiss on my lips. I didn't think I could ever admit that he'd been my first kiss, but Kelly finally stopped calling me *never been kissed* around the house. "Yes, to a movie," I said, looking back to find Kelly's hair again.

Tiptoeing over and narrowly avoiding bodies, I pushed through the crowd to get to her. "Kelly!" I waved.

She poked her face through the remaining bodies between us and waved back. "Fal!"

We squeezed through the crowd and into a side room to get some air away from the masses dancing. I smiled and proudly presented my prize to her. "This was a tough find, and I had to play beer pong for it."

Slipping the can into her hands, she looked at it like it was water in the desert. *"Thank God. I have been... dancing nonstop. How's the party for you?"*

"I guess as good as it could be?" I shrugged. "Wait. You trailed off there. What *were* you doing?"

She had a devious smile on her lips. "Nothing..."

"Mhm." I stood with a hand on my hip. "Shane?" *Maybe a hit of something, too.*

"How'd you know?"

"I'm psychic."

Shane sauntered over, looking... disheveled. It was kind of cute how they both tried to hide their hookup adventures.

"Hey, Shane," I said in a singsong voice. "You two having a good time at the party?"

He rubbed the back of his head, smiling as if he had been caught with his pants down. "Yeah... super fun." He looked at Kelly, unsure of how to answer me.

"I think I've had enough partying tonight, and I don't think I want to get burned out so early on in my party adventures. We should start the 'Party Adventures of Kelly and Fallon' podcast."

She got excited and clapped her hands together. "We would secure all future riches with that podcast. It would be a truly epic venture. Will you be okay to get home?" She had a twinge of guilt in her features. She asked me to the party, and we were about to leave separately—I was sure she didn't feel great about that.

"Yes, of course! Just remember, I know where you sleep." I gave her a playful nudge to the shoulder.

"I don't know whether to be reassured or scared."

I threw her a wicked grin. "Yes."

We burst out laughing. One thing I loved about her was that she truly felt like a sister to me, despite not being related by blood. We stuck together like glue, and no matter what happened, we were there for each other at the end of the day. No abandonment, no worries, no drama. She was my soulmate in every way, and she reminded me of it every day.

I grabbed her hands. "You go and have some fun tonight. You have just as much right to enjoy your parties as I do to enjoy some snacks before bed and scroll through stupid pictures on the internet."

I gave Shane a once over. "Make sure she comes back alright? Or I'll have your balls."

Kelly blushed. "See you in the, uh, morning then? Since you're going to bed immediately?"

I nodded, sticking my tongue out at her. "Love you, dude."

"Love you more," she said, linking hands with Shane.

I waved her off and approached the crisp evening air that called to me. My phone dinged with a text from Garrett.

GARRETT:

what movie u want to watch?

ME:

something scary!

GARRETT:

theater or house?

ME:

i dunno yet

Tucking my phone away, I took in the sights. Outside was just as beautiful a view as the mansion. Acres of lush, green land. Trees galore. Bodies of water are scattered everywhere across the various properties of Greek Row. We lived in our own little slice of heaven, minus the college bros being, well, college bros.

The music died out as I walked away from the party, the sound of the bass trailing behind me. I stopped, pulled my phone back out to call for a rideshare, and found myself losing focus as my nose touched the screen.

A familiar voice came from over my shoulder. "Leaving so soon, babe?"

"Jesus Christ in heaven!" I clutched my phone close to my chest. "You scared me."

I spun around to face him. *Oh shit, I'm too close.*

35

He let out a low chuckle, thumbing out a cigarette from his case. "Want another?" he asked, offering it in my direction.

I looked at his case, noticing he'd restocked his supply, and it was full yet again. "Sure, I have some time to kill."

"Your friend ditch you for a guy?"

"Not that it's any of your business, but I decided to go home because I'm hungry and want *real* food." I inhaled the smoke, beginning to understand why people coupled it with drinking.

"Mhm. Driving home?"

I eyed him suspiciously. "No, taking a rideshare."

"Cancel it," he said coolly.

I scoffed. *Who does he think he is?*

"Wait here," he said, lighting up another cigarette.

This guy smokes a lot. I looked him up and down. "You've got all of three minutes," I said, sloppily pointing to an invisible watch.

He disappeared, and I decided to indulge him. Not that he knew I hadn't ordered my rideshare yet. I put out the second cigarette he gave me and carefully wrapped it in a napkin to keep in my purse.

No littering for me.

A loud revving sound came from behind the vehicles in the driveway, and a motorcycle slowly made its way to the curb.

Right in front of me.

The guy on the bike flipped up his visor, and I immediately recognized those eyes; they were the same eyes that had stared at me just a few days ago from across the street. Darkened blue in the night's dimming light—dangerous and staring right into my soul as if he knew my deepest secrets. Something sharp in them made my skin prickle.

Brent Vaughn.

On a motorcycle.

Handing me a helmet.

"Do you do this with every girl?" I stood taller, crossing my arms over my chest.

"You hungry or not?" He had a mild level of annoyance in

his voice. He probably wasn't used to being questioned, let alone being turned down.

I planted my hands on my hips. "You are *so* not coming to my house."

He flicked out his kickstand with a smooth motion of his foot and leaned back, mimicking my body language. "Who said we're going to your house? Not to offend you but"—he looked me up and down—"you don't seem like that type of girl."

He wore riding gloves, a leather jacket, and dark riding pants —the exact image you'd get if you searched *biker guy* on the internet.

And he was offering *me* a seat on his bike.

"Only if there's real food," I grumbled, snatching the helmet from his hands. "If not, I'm going to head butt you to death with this thing."

I slipped it over my head, feeling my heartbeat in my ears. *I'm not nervous. Just hungry,* I reassured myself.

Brent moved forward and patted the seat behind him, urging me to get a move on.

I slipped my leg over the side with *zero* grace and set my feet up on the corresponding spots for them. As I shifted around a little to get my ass in a comfortable position, it felt like I was sitting in a tiny saddle. It was a seat, but not the most luxurious one.

He snaked his hand back and snatched my arm, wrapping it around him. "You have to hold onto me, Blondie."

Revving the engine, we were off. The bike sped up with little effort and zipped us through town, a comforting hum keeping me grounded on my first official ride. Wind whipped past us, muffled by our helmets, as we picked up speed to merge onto the highway.

Oh shit, he's taking me somewhere to kill me. My first night out and it's to go get murdered. Kelly is going to have choice words at my funeral.

The large buildings became scarce as we made it out of Willow Bay and out into the outskirts of suburban living. The last time I'd been out of Willow Bay was to go to the airport. I'd never ventured out to explore the surrounding area before.

He was silent for the entirety of the ride; I gathered that words weren't his forte. After about thirty minutes on the highway, we finally took an exit.

We made a few turns here and there, finally slowing down on a gravel road that led to a building at the end. It held a flickering neon sign.

24 Hour Diner - Finest Pie in the USA

The bike rumbled as we slowed and parked in front of a diner that looked like it was straight out of 1952; the exterior was faded in various shades of red and blue. *This place sure had charm back in the day, I bet.* I dismounted and pulled off the helmet, shaking out my hair and hoping that it didn't smear my makeup. The last thing I needed was to look like a hot mess in front of this guy I'd already embarrassed myself with. Lightly combing my fingers through my hair, I sneaked a peek at my reflection in the helmet.

Good to go.

"Alright, Blondie. You in the mood for greasy food and the best dessert you've ever eaten in your life?" He pulled his helmet off in one swift motion, his buzz cut unaffected by it.

My legs wobbled as I took the first steps away from the bike. He chuckled and led me through the glass doors that jingled as they opened, alerting the staff to new customers.

"Well, well, *well.* Look what the cat dragged in." An older, graying waitress stepped out from behind the counter in a poodle dress and apron, a fresh pot of coffee in hand.

I was immediately greeted by the smell of fresh coffee, bacon, and pie. Red vinyl booths lined up under each window, and a jukebox in the far corner played chart-topping music from my grandparents' era.

"Go ahead and sit in your regular booth. I'll be by to—" she stopped and gawked at me. "Who's the young lady?"

"Fallon." I gave her a meek smile, looking to Brent for direction.

"That one," he said, pointing to a table.

I hurried over to hide in the booth. Squeaking the entire time, I scooted my butt into the seat and tried to make myself comfortable. The woman came over to drop some mugs and pour coffee, sliding us oily, laminated menus. "I hope you brought your appetite. We have the best cooking this side of the Mississippi River." She looked over to Brent. "Brent, honey, did you want your regular plate or are you going to try something new to impress the first girl you bring in here?"

He sighed. "I'll look over the menu, Miss Martha."

She looked back over to me and patted my menu. "Take your time, sweet pea. We're here night and day and if you have any questions, just holler."

"Yes, ma'am. Thank you." I smiled and picked up the menu as she walked away to browse through what might be causing those delicious smells throughout the diner.

"Don't worry about her. She always gives me a hard time." Brent quirked an eyebrow, clearly pretending to look at his menu, then over to me. "So, Fallon."

Did he just try to cover up the fact that Miss Martha dropped the bomb that he had never brought a girl in here before? *Probably.* Was I going to announce that? *No.*

"Hmm?" I looked up at him from the menu. I knew I hadn't given him my name, but hearing that he might have discovered it from an outside exchange gave me just a *hint* of delight.

He leaned over the table. His eyes, close up in the light, were piercing. They were a deep grey blue that held a circle of hazel. His hair was short, exposing the tattoos that crept up the sides of his head. I didn't even want to look at that jawline, which flexed in different ways depending on his facial expression. The brooding aura he held seemed to have sharpened over time.

"Pancakes or waffles?" he whispered to me. "Your answer will seal your fate on if I leave you here."

5

Brent

She was cute when I annoyed her. I planned to keep doing it. "Pancakes," she scoffed. "You can leave me here all you want; it would just take me longer to wait for another ride." She challenged me with a cocked eyebrow, taking a sip of her coffee.

"Hmm. Would hate to inconvenience that *boyfriend* of yours. It's a good thing you chose right."

Martha, the wonderfully patient woman that she was, came back around since we were the only souls in the diner this late in the evening. The drunks wouldn't be stumbling in for another few hours, leaving me alone with my new plaything. "Any questions, sweet pea? Would you like to start with something?"

I caught the look in Martha's eye as she glanced between us, and I knew I would be getting an earful later.

Blondie tapped the menu. "I was just looking at the breakfast sampler. I'd love to get it, but I'll need three extra pieces of bacon."

Martha looked completely infatuated with her as a smile spread across her face. "A girl who knows how to eat is a girl after my own heart. I'll get that right on for you, sweet pea." She looked over to me. "And you, Brent?"

"Whatever she's having," I replied, briefly looking over the menu I'd seen a million times before for dramatic effect.

She snatched the menu from my hands, and I looked up at her as if she'd offended me. Fallon gave an overly polite performance, handing her menu back with a sly smile on her face. "I'll get those plates right out for you two lovebirds," she said, walking away in her typical dramatic fashion.

I caught Fallon silently admiring Martha, probably hoping she could be as blunt with her as she was with me.

Leaning back, I lounged on my side of the booth, spreading my arms across the seat. I needed to decompress and chill after the day's events. For good measure, I propped my foot up right next to Blondie's thigh on her side of the booth. Some entertainment was needed to help me fucking relax.

She shoved my foot.

I grunted, peeking through my closed eyes. "I'm trying to get comfortable here, Blondie." I let my head fully relax against the seat behind me, the vinyl squeaking under its weight.

"What puts your comfort over mine?" A slight hint of fight was in her voice.

I tried not to laugh. "Get as comfortable as you like. I have a few suggestions if you're willing to listen."

She leaned over the table. "Can I ask you a question?"

Good lord, she didn't know when to stop. "You just did, babe."

"Then, I have another," she huffed.

"Shoot."

She hesitated for a moment, and I thought I heard her gulp. "Why are we here? Like, together?"

"You said you were hungry. I know a place with good food. Simple." *What's her point?*

"You play baseball, right?"

I could feel her leaning over more. *Was she staring at me?*

"Mhm."

She pushed my foot further until it fell off the seat entirely. I peeked at her from my relaxed position, noticing that her body language was fully invested in me. *I guess I'll oblige,* I thought, sitting back up to face her.

42

"Nepo baby or scholarship?" she prodded.

What were we playing, 21 Questions? "I could ask you the same thing."

"Touché." She took another sip of her coffee.

I accepted her challenge. Girls never gave me much of a fight, and she was just interested enough that I could probably have her eating out of my hand in no time. I figured I would hit her with something she least expected.

"Not everyone on the sports team is a scholarship recipient, and not everyone at the school is blessed with nepotism. Are you beating around the bush, trying to figure me out? If so, you'll have to give up just as much information as you'd like to pry from me. Starting with my question. Does your boyfriend know you're here?" I laid my chin on my knuckles, propping my head up on the table, and looking directly into those bright blue eyes.

Those eyes looked like a deer in headlights before she recomposed herself, without breaking eye contact.

"Fine. Deal," she shot back. "As for my love life, I don't have a boyfriend."

"Then who's the sucker following you around like a lost puppy?"

"None of your business," she spat.

"Are you a nepo baby or scholarship kid?" I raised an eyebrow.

"Nepotism. You?" I wondered if she would lie about herself. I knew who she was, but that was neither here nor there. So far, she has told the truth.

"Same." I took a sip of my coffee, clacking my rings on the handle. Her gaze shifted to my hand, probably curious about them. I wore two rings on my right hand and one on my left; she took full notice.

Her eyes narrowed. "Why did you bring me here?"

"For the food," I replied between sips of bitter coffee. "Why did you come?"

"For the food," she parroted.

Martha saved my life by interrupting us with several large

plates of food. She looked between us and furrowed her eyebrows in confusion. "You two look like you're in a heated debate. I hope it's not about bacon or sausage, because I brought both." She set them down and gave me a warning glare.

It was true that I had never brought a girl here, and Martha knew my reputation. I wasn't a good guy by any standard. Explaining *why* I brought Fallon here would be a future Brent problem. I waved off the look Martha gave me.

"Thank you, Martha," we said in unison.

"You're welcome, my darlings. Eat up, and I'll bring some pie afterward."

Fallon took in the full display of food and looked like a kid in a candy store. A wave of softness came over her face as she looked at everything displayed in front of her, and I wondered how much she actually liked diner breakfast foods. Her eyes grazed over it all—pancakes, bacon, eggs, sausage, and hash browns were prominently displayed alongside fruit and Texas toast.

She immediately started. Shoving a piece of bacon into her mouth, she asked, "What year are you?"

"Junior," I replied, poking around my plate to stack up my fork with a large bite.

"I'm a sophomore."

I looked up at her. "Yeah, I know."

Her eyes grew suspicious. "And *how* do you know?"

"It's tattooed on your forehead." A grin appeared on my face while I took a bite of the food.

She grunted. "Asshole should be on yours."

"Tell me about yourself," I said, meeting her eye contact again, gesturing for her to go on with more information. I wanted to know more about my new toy.

"Nuh uh. You first. You said it yourself. Question for a question." She pointed her fork at me like she wanted to stab me.

"I grew up with my grandfather." How many questions did she even have?

We sat in my favorite diner, going back and forth, spilling

tidbits of information about ourselves in this cat and mouse game. She thought she was the cat, but really, she was the mouse.

"I grew up with my mom until she died. Then I lived with my shitty aunt until I was eighteen."

Curious. "How did she die?"

She looked at me with warning. "You first on the info spill."

Bringing up my childhood trauma, I said, "My mom dumped me on my grandfather as a baby, and then she killed herself."

Her expression was a mix of surprise and empathy. "Oh, I didn't realize... My mother passed away from cancer. I'm sorry to hear about your mom."

"Yours too," I said, keeping my cool by taking a sip of coffee. It wasn't every day that I told the world I was a bastard whose mother had killed herself. Never meeting her was bad enough, but the Dictator never spoke a word about her to me. It was just something that was never talked about.

Martha had been with my family for a long time, and she was like my mother. So I considered my biological mother a moot point since I couldn't ask her any questions anyway. The table grew silent as Fallon devoured most of her meal, and I didn't press any further. Couldn't scare her away on the first date after all.

Trying to lighten the mood, I used my fork to block her from taking the last sausage link. I picked it up and took a bite out of it.

Her mouth fell open in disbelief that I had taken the last one. She tried to play it off by going for the grapes, but I offered the other half from my fork.

She reached to take it off with her hand, but I stopped her. "Nope, give me that mouth."

"I am *not* letting you put a sausage in my mouth, you heathen," she seethed.

I chuckled. "It's that or nothing, Blondie." My lips curled into a smile, trying to hold the fork back out to her.

"Then I don't want it," she said, waving over at Martha. "Miss Martha, can I get some pie, pretty please?"

She hollered back over the counter, "Which one, sweet pea?"

"An assortment!" A true smile spread over her lips.

Martha made haste with bringing out some initial pieces of pie. I've eaten almost everything here at one point or another, but always wandered back to my usual plate. "These are our most popular, and Brent's personal favorites, but I'll be back with a sample of all we have so you can decide for yourself." She flicked her gaze at me in a curious manner. Again, I knew I'd have to deal with the twenty-one questions about Fallon later.

She hurried away and Fallon looked back at the table, a sadness washing over her face. Did she hate these flavors?

"What are you pouting about?" I flicked the sausage I had teased her with onto her plate, hoping her awkward, sad face would stop.

She sighed and pushed out her bottom lip even more. "I can't bring this home. We rode on your motorcycle."

That's what makes you depressed? "You can get delivery next time, you know?"

Her eyes lit up. "Next time?"

I finished my coffee before responding, waving Martha back over for a refill. "Oh, yeah. You'll turn into a proper addict for this place."

The rest of the pie, as promised, appeared on the table while my coffee got a refill. "Hope you enjoy, sweet pea." Martha didn't bother to look at me whatsoever.

Fallon's gaze flicked between me and Martha, probably wondering what the backstory was. It looked like she wanted to ask, but decided against it. Not asking was the better move—I didn't want to share my life story with the girl I had just met, especially knowing that Martha would hound me about it later.

Pulling out my wallet in an effort to appear like I was at least making good on a first date, I asked, "What's the damage?"

Of course, Blondie reached into her purse as well. Martha looked between the two of us once again and held up a hand.

"It's… on the house tonight." She disappeared into the kitchen, probably to spill the news about the *infamous* Brent bringing a girl to the diner on a random evening. It was out of character for me, and I would have a nice round of questions to try to skirt.

Fallon laid three hundred-dollar bills on the table before diving right in, taking a bite of each piece of pie laid out before her. I flipped through my bills and matched her bid.

"Baller," I challenged her.

"Could say the same about you," she scoffed, taking a bite of the blueberry pie. "Looks like Miss Martha can enjoy the morning off after we terrorized her."

Laughing, I also took my fork to the piece of blueberry pie. I let her eat her fill of whatever her heart desired and hoped to God that Martha wouldn't come back around to yank me into the back for an interrogation.

After a beat of comfortable silence watching her eat, I glanced at the time on my watch. I needed to decompress before Reaper got back to me with who knows what in his report. At least I could count on him for a good cleanup job. The Dictator would be expecting me soon with the information we gathered.

I leaned forward, closing the distance between us just enough to drop my voice to a low, husky whisper. "Ready to go, Blondie?" I wrapped a strand of her pale blonde hair around my finger, holding eye contact with her. She looked nervous to be that close to me, and her breath shortened just enough for me to notice.

It was cute until she pulled back and tried to compose herself, rubbing her newly formed goosebumps. "Only if you promise me delivery next time."

Cocking my head to the side in curiosity, I gave her a half smile. She held out her pinky to me in an attempt to seal the promise. Oh, if she knew the things that were included in the promises I made… I latched her pinky with mine and promptly dragged her out the front door—without giving Martha the chance to flag me down.

"Hey!" she protested, pulling her finger from mine.

"I needed a smoke," I said, catching her pinky with mine again. She wouldn't get away from me that easily.

Popping a cigarette in my mouth one handed, she watched me with her mouth open again. If she wasn't careful, I'd take full advantage of it right there in the open parking lot. She watched me with such strange curiosity as I lit it up and took a long first drag to clear my mind of the day's events.

Little did she know, I didn't plan to leave just yet. Anytime I went for a bite at the diner, I liked to *truly* clear my mind at the nearby cliffside. Some days I contemplated jumping off and other days I just liked the view. *Maybe I'll jump off and drag you with me*, I thought.

Still holding onto that soft little finger of hers, I dragged her across the parking lot and into the forested wall that had a trail leading to my serene cliffside. The thick foliage concealed us, and she quietly trailed behind me while the only sounds were the crunching beneath our feet and the crackle of the cigarette I was smoking. *What? No smart-ass comments?*

We made it. The clear opening with that view from the cliff was something I loved so much. The expanse of the night sky opened up, with stars scattered across the black like a million tiny lights. Below us, there was very little light pollution to detract from the gorgeous wide-open sky.

This was my favorite spot in the whole world, and she better not ruin it.

I let go of her and stepped closer to the edge—today made me want to jump. I finished off my cigarette and flicked it over the edge, turning my head up to the sky to beg the universe to ease my stress.

I took a deep breath of the cool night air. "It's peaceful up here."

She only made a low grunt in response. I supposed she was nervous about being at the cliff's edge with me; I *did* consider throwing us over the edge. Her head tilted up to view the sky with me, and we sat in silence for a while.

Did she know what my day was like, that I needed to come out here and settle my thoughts?

Not looking forward to going back to the place where my grandfather resided, the urge to jump became stronger. The briefing and report from Reaper weighed heavily on my mind. Something about this betrayal involving a powerful man made me sure it would lead to a predicament.

Content with the time I spent in silence, I flipped around with a devious look on my face and grabbed her hand again.

"What now?" she protested.

Saying nothing, I dragged her back to my bike. What I wanted to say was "Let's fuck in the forest," but she might have jumped of her own volition.

"Let's get you home, Blondie." I plopped the helmet on her head and wrapped my jacket around her body. While I wasn't the most gentlemanly man on the planet, I wasn't going to let her freeze to death in that skimpy dress after the temperature plummeted over the last couple of hours.

6

Fallon

We pulled into the surprisingly quiet neighborhood at about four thirty in the morning. I hoped Kelly would still be out with her newest boy toy, Shane, so she didn't catch me walking in from being on the back of a motorcycle with…

"Hey." Brent whacked my thigh. "Are you sleeping back there?"

"Huh? Yeah. The ride was peaceful."

"We're here. Time to go inside." His tone was short, cold even.

Okay, jerk. "Wait. How did you know where my house is?"

He flicked out his kickstand, got off the bike, and slipped off his helmet. "I *literally* saw you the other day."

Fair enough. I pulled the helmet off my head, feeling the brisk air on my face. "Do you live at that house over there, then?"

He shrugged. "Sometimes."

"Sometimes? Are you in a frat or something? Have your own — Never mind." I waved my hands as if dispersing my questions into the air. "I don't need another repeat of earlier."

"Smart girl," he whispered, lighting up another cigarette while leaning on his bike.

He held the smoke in for a moment before releasing it into

the air, his face tilted up to the sky. He turned his head slightly and offered the cigarette to me.

Solidifying my status as a new smoker, I accepted. I copied his movements, looking up at the sky and releasing the smoke. At least the swirling smoke was cool to look at.

I handed it back to him. "I hope you don't have cooties."

"What if I did?" He smirked, popping the cigarette back into his mouth.

"Then I'd have to make good on my offer and head butt you to death."

"Kinky." He laughed, smoke leaking out of his mouth.

"You're insufferable." *And an asshole. Why does he have to look so hot but be such an ass?* I slipped an arm out of his jacket, but he stopped me and put my arm back in.

"I'll take it at the door."

I cocked my head at him. "Uh, you're *not* coming in."

Saying nothing, he gripped my arm and marched me to the front porch like I was a child being sent to my room. We stopped maybe two steps from the front door. *At least he didn't throw me at the door.*

He was facing me, and the air seemed to thicken as we stood there. We were quiet enough that I could hear my breathing and heartbeat. His gaze turned intense, boring into my soul as it held mine with an expression I hadn't seen on him before. His eyes seemed to challenge mine, his eyebrow slightly raised in a challenge of what I would do with him on the porch.

Taking a step closer, he closed the distance between us to just mere inches. His hand reached up slowly, and I swore I saw a millisecond of hesitation before his fingers gently grasped my chin. The grip was firm, yet gentle.

He was testing my boundaries.

My breath caught in my throat, and my eyes widened as his gaze flicked down to my lips. Slowly, his thumb stroked my bottom lip, freezing me in place. The tension was almost unbearable as he leaned in, making his intentions crystal clear.

As his lips just started to brush mine, the door opened with a sudden whoosh of air, breaking me out of my trance.

Kelly stood in the doorway, arms crossed, one eyebrow halfway up her forehead in equal parts amusement and curiosity. She cleared her throat, shattering the silence of the early morning.

"Is our guest staying or leaving?"

I blinked the tension away and stepped back. My cheeks flushed hot, a mix of embarrassment and frustration. *Please don't tell me it's sexual frustration.* Brent straightened himself, the smirk returning to his lips as he released my chin, his thumb brushing my bottom lip once more before dropping his hand. He flicked his gaze to Kelly and nodded to her before looking back to me.

"Leaving," he said, his voice reverting to his typical nonchalant tone. Though, his eyes might have told a different story. They looked me up and down, silently devouring me as I stood in his jacket. He didn't ask for it back. Instead, he presented a full, cocky smile. "Try not to miss me too much, Blondie."

My heart stopped as he turned on his heel, leaving only in his T-shirt.

I turned back to Kelly, my pulse still racing and a warm feeling brewing in my belly, and let my breath out slowly.

Her arms were still crossed and she wore a mischievous smile. "Guess I can't call you a virgin anymore."

"Oh my God!" I shoved her through the door and slammed it. I hoped that, to any god in the universe, Brent would *not* hear what came out of her mouth.

I stood behind the closed door, panting and holding my chest, wondering what the hell my night had turned into. Was I about to kiss Brent Vaughn?

Better yet, was he about to kiss *me*?

"Did I just see you standing on the doorstep about to swap spit with Brent Vaughn while wearing his jacket, or am I hallucinating? Aren't you dating Garrett?" Kelly's voice pulled me from my thoughts as she stood, looking back and forth between me and the front door.

We both shared a look of total disbelief.

I held up my arms in the extremely oversized jacket and shook the sleeves around like an idiot. "I don't know! Help!"

Kelly folded over in laughter, her eyes appearing to well with tears. "What now?" She had to steady herself against the laughter. "Do you just... wear it and hope he comes asking for it back?"

"Yeah, because that wouldn't be awkward at all or raise any questions," I replied, still giggling from the entire night. "Do I go over there and give it back and act like nothing ever happened? Or do I, like, leave it on his bike like a creepy love note?"

She snorted and came over to check out the jacket. "Hmm, you could keep it as a trophy. For, you know, conquering the bad boy of the school."

We devolved into another fit of laughter.

"Okay," Kelly tried calming herself. "I need to know exactly what happened and who you're going to choose. I need minute by minute details *and* how big his dick is. Is it bigger than Garrett's?"

I ran my hands through my hair, blowing out the anxiety from my lungs. "Ew, no. I didn't sleep with either of them. But I don't think you'd believe what happened. I don't even think *I* believe it."

We fell asleep on the couch after I told her every detail of the evening, minute by minute. I'd experienced it all and I wasn't sure that it wasn't all made up—the night was *that* unbelievable. Brent Vaughn takes you out and *nothing* happened? *Yeah, right.*

A knock came at the door while Kelly and I were drinking coffee shortly after waking up. I rushed to open it, not realizing I was still in my skimpy pajamas. Getting rid of Brent's jacket was fresh in my mind, and I hoped we could pretend that last night never happened.

I swung open the door. "Oh, thank God. I— Oh! Garrett! Hello!"

"Hello to you, too. Were you expecting a delivery or something?" He stepped in, placing a kiss on my cheek on his way in, holding a bag of something.

"Something like that. Must have had the days mixed up!" I feigned a laugh and looked back to see Kelly in her pajamas giving me a side-eye glance while sipping her coffee.

"Yeah," he said, looking between me and Kelly. "I have some food if you're interested. Are we still going to the baseball game? I didn't hear back about the movie, but I figured you needed rest."

Oh shit, that's right.

"Yeah, yeah. Let me just put on some clothes." I started down the hallway, trying to shake my thoughts away. I didn't realize what time it was.

Garrett leisurely trailed behind me. He got cozier by the day, and I wondered when he'd eventually ask me when we were going to have sex. With everything feeling like I was heading into a dramatic reality TV show episode, I wasn't sure I could deal with it.

I stopped at my bedroom door and raised an eyebrow at him.

"Can I come in?" He gave me a quick once over, finally noticing how skimpy my pajamas really were.

Kelly is going to have a field day with me later.

"Only if you promise to be a good boy." I opened the door and let him inside.

He plopped onto my bed. "Are you still down to hit up the diner for food after the game? The snacks there aren't going to be filling and I don't really want to eat twelve pretzels in lieu of a real meal," he chuckled softly, looking at me like he was waiting for me to undress in front of him.

"Yeah," I said, slyly hiding Brent's jacket in my closet while he looked away to take a mental inventory of my room. "I love diner food. What should I wear?"

Stretching out to lay on my bed, he got cozy with a clear view of the closet. "Something warm. It'll get cold later."

Almost diving into my closet, I shoved Brent's jacket under a large pile of dirty laundry to cover my ass in case he came in. I felt frantic as I glanced around to find an outfit that would be suitable for both a baseball game and a diner date.

Deciding on tailored high waisted navy-blue trousers and an ivory cashmere sweater, I quickly slipped into them. My choice in clothes was relatively simple, except for the new wardrobe Kelly duped me into buying. Wearing these clothes made me think of my mom; her style was similar, and I wanted to keep her close to me.

"Something like this?" I stepped out of the closet holding up my nude-colored loafers.

"How do you always look so good?" He strode across the room to get close to me and admire my outfit up close. The way he admired me made me nervous.

Trying to hide my reddening cheeks, I bent down to put on my shoes. "I get my style from my mom."

He brought his hand to the side of my face when I straightened back up. I tilted my head up toward him and he leaned in for a kiss. Unfortunately, the vision of Brent flooded my mind as I kissed Garrett.

His other hand gripped my waist and pulled me closer to him as his kiss grew hungry. I tried to focus on Garrett—here and now—and how his thumb slowly caressed my jaw as our mouths moved, but that asshole's face loomed like a dark shadow.

Relief washed over me that nothing went further and that he didn't press me for more before we left and made our way to the sporting complex.

The students were buzzing, and the energy was high before the baseball game. We had seats near the dugout where the players could see us in the crowd. Dread grew in my chest, knowing Brent could easily pick me out of the crowd.

I spotted him easily. Number seven. Even warming up he held that same cocky swagger he used when he went anywhere. *The dark star of the baseball team.*

Garrett and I got cozy with snacks and drinks before the

game started. The team lined up for their usual pre-game routine, Brent's gaze landing on mine. I knew that he knew that Garrett didn't know about last night, and an evil grin only Brent could have, appeared on his lips.

"That's Brent Vaughn," Garrett whispered into my ear. "He's a beast and the best shortstop I've ever seen."

I nodded along with him, a faux smile plastered on my lips as I watched a group of girls flocking to greet Brent specifically before he went out for the official start. Knowing I was watching, he leaned over and kissed a few of them on the lips and smacked some others on the ass. *Yeah, a beast,* I thought, fighting hard to keep myself from rolling my eyes.

We were playing against another strong team, but our players seemed to have a competitive edge and laser-like focus. I didn't quite understand baseball—or sports in general—but I knew that we had some solid players on our team. It dragged on for a while, and Garrett was completely involved in the game. *America's favorite pastime,* I thought, sucking down what was left of my soda. We were up in points, and while I hated to admit it, Brent *did* seem to be a great baseball player.

"Wow, what a great game," Garrett said, his attention snapping me back to reality. "I'm happy you came with me." He leaned in to kiss me, and I got more into it than I should have— for show.

"Me too." I kept letting him kiss me.

He finally pulled away. "Let's go get some real food, babe."

He took me to his favorite diner and told me about the nostalgia surrounding the place. He and his brothers would come here after games with their dad back in the day, but their dad became too consumed with work, so they started going by themselves to keep up the tradition. It was a cute story, and I wondered when I'd be able to chat casually about my mom again. I kept her memories bottled up like a dirty secret from others, wanting only to have her to myself.

She was all I knew. Then, I was thrown into a pretty abusive situation with Sylvia.

"I'm telling you, we have this next football game in the bag. Hudson has no idea what's coming for them." He was cute when he talked about things that excited him—a little sparkle in his eye as he spoke.

I kept up a soft smile, holding his eye contact despite my mind wandering back and forth between the diner with Brent, my mom, and Garrett in front of me. Taking small sips of my coffee, I tried to make myself look more animated than I felt. Kelly might have been right.

"You've basically started your own soap opera," she said.

How much more drama could I get myself into?

We turned at the sound of yelling coming from outside. *Maybe I shouldn't ask those types of questions to the universe.*

A group of guys stood around while another approached. One guy specifically cursed up a storm, pointing his finger at someone in the first group.

As I stared more intently, the group looked like... the baseball team. And the guy was yelling at Brent. Because, of course, he was. And, *of course*, Brent looked as cool as a cucumber as it happened.

The guy took a swing. Brent backed up a few steps, laughing as a cigarette hung from his lips.

"I'm going to go see what's going on out there," Garrett said, easing himself out of the booth.

"Wait." I grabbed his wrist. "Don't."

He gently pulled my hand away from his. "I'll be fine. Remember, I get tackled all the time."

"Tackled! Not sucker punched!" I chased after him.

Garrett was already out the door. "Everything good out here?"

"Go back inside, Bradford," one of the baseball guys called out.

The man screaming at Brent had a few guys backing him. Then he and Brent were on the ground instantly, throwing punches and grunting like cavemen. The rest of the group erupted into flying fists, shouts, and taunts.

There were shouts from inside about calling the cops. Brent rolled off of the guy, blood dripping from his bottom lip. He looked up, right at me, with a deadly smile spreading across his face.

Garrett stepped in front of me, blocking my view, and pushed me back toward the door. He turned around to face the fight, only to get sucker punched square in the jaw. Brent grabbed him and threw him into the fight, where he took a few more hits after taking down one of the other guys.

What a mess.

Luckily, the fight didn't last much longer, and Garrett slowly backed out, looking as if he hoped that would be the end of it. Men were scattered around everywhere, some on the ground, some still trying to fight. The baseball team was victorious after they brought down a few more opponents while the others who were still standing retreated, leaving their beaten teammates behind, probably hoping the baseball team wouldn't follow them.

Brent fist bumped one of his teammates to his left. "Fuck yeah, dude."

Garrett looked like he had taken a few too many hard hits, but he still came to inspect me. His eyes were filled with concern as he searched my face. "You okay? Did anyone touch you?"

"No, I think I'm fine." My eyes weren't quite focused on his face.

"Sorry to crash your date, Blondie," Brent called out as he and the team entered the diner. "I'll cover the bill, don't worry."

Garrett was still looking at me, but my eyes caught Brent winking at me from inside as he picked up a piece of my bacon and ate it.

"Let's get you home."

7

Brent

I hated working in this shit job for my shit grandfather. *The Dictator*. He was a demanding asshole who wanted answers, and I was not prepared for another beratement about how I was a failure as a grandson once again. Those got tiring.

Reaper left an oddly complete write up for me that made it look like we did a proper job without him prematurely ejaculating into his panties. He got so stab happy some days, but on others, he kept his cool. You never knew what to expect.

Maybe he needed to get laid, too. I didn't know what kind of life he lived outside of working for us, but I didn't need to know —or want to.

The file was a professional write up describing the information John presented to us. There was a comprehensive profile on Jason Haines and his involvement in business espionage, hostile takeovers, and other illegal activities. It wasn't anything I hadn't seen before, but he had been circling us for three years or more, and I could understand why my grandfather would be antsy about getting his information back quickly.

I wasn't informed about the top-level business dealings—I wasn't considered trustworthy enough. *My volatile nature is my undoing.* His words, not mine.

What surprised me was the meticulous nature of the notes, as if he had been taking meeting minutes, which made me feel confident enough to present the information.

Being ushered in by one of the regular muscles, my grandfather sat at his desk in his typical Godfather style. *You'd think he ran the Mafia the way he acts.* A lit cigar in his hand, he motioned me in with his typical lazy hand gesture.

I tossed the report from Reaper onto his desk and sat in my usual interrogation chair.

"Good work." He barely glanced at the pages before dropping the file back down. "Now, tell me something other than this bullshit."

"John *was* a rat and had been for three years under the direction of Jason Haines. He talked about wanting the pay and cuts of goods from him. Too bad he sacrificed himself for table scraps. I'm unsure of their meaning, but they used codes for movements like 'Tower,' 'Green,' and 'Garden.' We're still trying to understand what these words mean, but I'm sure we have some men who can sniff this out."

He scoffed and threw his stapler at me. Just like when I was a kid. "Not this shit, you idiot! You know I have fucking eyes on everything! What the fuck are you doing with the Montgomery girl?!"

"What?" *I'm with a lot of girls, what the fuck does he care?*

"That fucking girl you drove out into the middle of nowhere to visit Martha! You seriously can't be *that* dense to think she wouldn't tell me. I am going to ask you again: what the *fuck* are you doing with the Montgomery girl?"

My head hurt like a bitch from the Dictator beating me while screaming at me. As I entered my room, the silence was louder than usual. I tossed my jacket onto the chair—only, I didn't. Right. The "Montgomery girl" still had it.

Things got a little more interesting after he finished beating the shit out of me. He told me to stay away from her while he dealt with business he didn't want me fucking up, but that was the last thing I planned to do. The memory of her standing on her doorstep, swallowed up by my jacket played in a wicked loop in my mind. It was far too large for her frame; the sleeves practically made it look like she had no hands. Only, in my imagination, she was completely naked underneath my jacket.

She looked deliciously innocent, though.

Fuck, she probably was. Especially after the beating that I just received. One of the guys had to rip the old man off me before he fucking shot me. *The bastard pointed a gun at me! And for what?! I wasn't going to scare her off like he thought I would.* He droned on about his plans and how we needed to move carefully. To which, I eventually tuned him out before leaving.

I did, however, like the idea of my jacket draped over a chair in her room, where she could see it regularly. Did I? *Maybe I do.*

What confused me was her hesitation towards me. Girls didn't hesitate with me. But she wasn't most girls, was she? Those big blue eyes widened when I leaned in... fuck that innocence was *so* tempting. She was *so* close, too.

She lives just a few houses away...

I ran a hand over my head, feeling the fresh buzzcut I got a few days ago. I laughed, remembering what her friend had said to her at the door. *Guess I can't call you a virgin anymore.* Was she really a virgin? Who, at twenty, was a virgin?

Part of me wondered what would have happened if her friend hadn't opened the door. I couldn't predict it, and that was a first for me.

You're overthinking it—moving too fast. She's got her little distraction of a boyfriend and an inability to say no. But that smart mouth...

A knock on my door yanked me out of my thoughts of the day. I didn't even need to guess who it was.

Sloane.

She always had a way of showing up when I least wanted company. Pushing myself up off the bed to open the door, I saw her leaning against the frame in her typical catlike manner. The smirk on her lips reeked of trouble.

"Hey, you," she purred, pushing through the door as if it didn't exist. "Saw your bike in the driveway. Thought I'd stop by."

She lived nowhere near my house. "Sloane. I'm not in the mood. I'd like to relax for once."

"Since when does that matter?" She crossed her arms, giving my space a once over as if she was looking for something. Her gaze lingered on my empty chair, which normally had a jacket hanging there. She didn't seem to notice.

I stayed planted in the open doorway as she approached me. She was hot, confident, had everything going for her, and knew how to get exactly what she wanted. Too bad for her, I wasn't interested. Not anymore.

Her fingers trailed down from my chest to my pant line. "I missed you," she whispered into my ear.

Grabbing her wrist before she could grip my dick, I said, "Not tonight."

She blinked, and her smirk disappeared from her lips. "What the hell, Brent? You're not one to turn me down."

Pulling her wrist from my grip with a sharp yank, I put space between us with a sidestep. "I just told you no. What part of that do you not understand? I. Don't. Want. You. Here."

"You? Not in the mood?" She crossed her arms, eyes narrowing at me. "That's ridiculous, considering I can't get you off me half the time. What? Is there someone else now, or are you just playing hard to get?"

Her words didn't necessarily sting, but they were annoying. We weren't together and I wasn't about to explain myself to some pretentious princess. I laughed. "Clingy much? I just need some fucking space. I work, you know."

And, also, fuck your attitude.

"Space?" she scoffed. "Since when do you need space?" Her voice dripped with disbelief, and her mouth was left open in confusion.

I didn't answer her. I met her gaze until she sighed in defeat. "You know what? What-the-fuck-ever, Brent. You are *so* not worth this much effort."

The door was half shut when those fucking words snapped me. *No one* fucking tells me that and just walks away.

I grabbed her wrist and spun her around to face me.

"What?" she asked, challenging me. That half innocent voice pissed me off even more.

She wasn't about to leave thinking she'd gotten the better of me.

The moment my mouth was on hers, I regretted it. I hated that I let her get under my skin like that, but I wasn't about to back down. She placed a firm hand on my chest and backed me up to the bed.

Straddling me, she started pulling off her top. Seeing her expose herself to me like she'd done a million times did absolutely nothing for me. "This is more like it," she groaned into my mouth.

"Don't fucking talk."

I flipped her over to where I was straddling her and pulled her pants off.

She narrowed her eyes at me. "You're lucky you're cute, Brent."

"Yeah, don't get too comfortable."

Below me, I didn't see Sloane. *I saw Fallon.*

I woke up with a rotten feeling in my stomach. *Was this what regret felt like?*

No, it was just a bad hangover—nothing I hadn't dealt with before. That, and I only slept for maybe three hours.

I heaved my tired and beaten body out of bed, nabbing a shirt from the floor. My room was a complete mess because of the way Sloane liked to have sex. Trying to blur those thoughts, I looked around and sighed in relief when I saw that Sloane had left. I rubbed my face and eyes, hoping to wipe away at least *one* bad decision.

I made too many bad decisions, but I loved doing it.

The whole situation was really fucking stupid. First, my grandfather beats me senseless and tells me to stay away from Fallon because she's Maria's kid and I shouldn't *taint* her with my bastard ass. Second, I shouldn't have let Sloane stay, but I really wanted to get fucking laid and she was far too easy to get into bed.

Fuck, I wanted to punch something.

My fist connected with a *thud* and a *crack*, breaking through the wall and leaving a nice, gaping wound.

I turned to grab my jacket—only to realize it wasn't there—and threw the chair across the room, breaking my lamp into multiple pieces. My room became even more chaotic, just like my mind.

Whatever, I'll fix it later.

The cold flooring on my feet was a welcome sensation as I shuffled into the kitchen. I pulled a bottle of water out of the fridge to freeze out my insides, pushing away whatever feelings I was having down with the liquid.

"Hey, bro!" Josh walked into the kitchen. "Sounded like a hell of a time for you and..." he trailed off.

No one could keep up with who I brought into my room.

"Just some chick," I said, grabbing some leftovers from the fridge.

He laughed. "Well, save some chicks for the rest of us, dude." He smacked my back as he went to prep the coffee pot.

"Yeah, I'll try." *Try to forget Sloane was ever here.* Sitting at the island, I dug into the Styrofoam container of cold Chinese food.

Josh filled two cups of coffee and came to sit next to me at the island. He was a good guy, just a bit on the naive side of life. *If only I had some of the same luxuries.*

"You coming out to the field today? Coach said it was mandatory."

Of course he did. "I think that's what mandatory means."

8

Fallon

Brent was quiet after our excursion. I didn't expect him to come running back the day after looking for me or his jacket. Everyone knew what kind of guy he was—and I didn't exactly put out for him. Maybe he called it a loss along with his jacket. Whatever the case may be, it has sat on a hanger in my room for the past few days, waiting to be picked up by its rightful owner.

This wretched jacket was part of my daily routine for a few days. I'd take a shower and come out to stare at it. The first two days, I thought it would disappear from existence as if we had never gone out together, but it was still there. Staring back at me.

Kelly burst into my room to see me staring at the jacket. *What's privacy?* "Are you still looking at that thing like it's an alien invader?"

I sighed. "Yes, I am."

"It's not going anywhere, you know. Also, those stupid sorority plans you had…"

I stood straight up. "Yep! We're going. Fuck that jacket and its owner."

"I don't know why I even came in here to remind you," she huffed.

"Because you love me and feel bad for me."

With one last glance at the leather jacket, we were off to Greek Row.

"What do you want to do for Thanksgiving this year?" Kelly asked while she drove us out of the neighborhood to look for the right sorority house on campus.

"We could take a trip somewhere? A beach?"

Her eyes lit up. "What about Greece? I hear the men there are hot. Oh! Italy?"

Last year, Kelly and I went to her aunt's house to avoid seeing her dad, but the family drama followed us there—it was catastrophic drama involving her parents. I didn't have anyone I wanted to visit since my mom was gone—my family all wanted a piece of the Montgomery Group pie. It seemed that my mom was prudent in keeping her distance from them.

And since she left me with everything, I did the same.

"Are you sure you don't want to spend the holidays with your new boy toy?" I poked fun at her, knowing she probably didn't want to put a label on anything.

"Uh, no. We aren't that serious, and, bitch, I am *not* leaving you alone for the holidays. Out of the question."

I laughed at her faux stern look. "What if I gave you permission?"

"I said no." She whacked my shoulder. "Anyone who comes into my life knows that *you* are my family and come first in all things."

Trying to imagine her telling that to a husband, I couldn't help but laugh even more. "If you get married, you can't put me above your husband, Kel."

She furrowed her eyebrows and stuck her tongue out at me. "Watch me! Our podcast will live on even when we are old and gray!"

There was humor there, but also space to mourn for our future selves. Not being roommates—doing everything together —would eventually come to an end. Everything came to an end at some point in time.

"Also," she added, "when did you become such a nihilist? Is

that jacket giving you bad vibes or something? You know what? That's it. I'm going to burn sage throughout the house."

"Isn't sage used to ward off bad spirits? I'm not sure it will, you know"—I waved my hands in the air—"disperse bad vibes."

She pointed a finger at me. "One more word about bad vibes and I'll do it!"

We drove into view of a few houses hosting rushing info sessions, and I wanted to tour at least a few of them. Look at all my options and whatnot. I'm sure my mom would have encouraged me to try these things out, like she did with everything else in my life.

...If I could handle that much pink. Kelly may have been onto something when she gave me pushback on the idea. The amount of pink I saw surely ran the paint company dry.

Hesitantly, I looked back at Kelly as we stepped out of the car. "Do you remember which houses we were supposed to avoid? The two that the one girl was talking about?"

She looked at me like I had asked her an advanced calculus question. "Babe, they all sound the exact same to me. Alpha, beta, kappa, gamma, blah blah. I don't think I *could* remember, even if you held a gun to my head."

Hopefully, we don't run into any unfriendly encounters, then.

The first house we approached was pink, naturally. It had a Texas-themed vibe for the party, likely featuring some southern bombshells inside.

And a bombshell, I was not.

We entered anyway, deciding to make the best of the day we planned. A girl ran out. "Hi, y'all!" She had a *really* overdone southern accent. "Welcome to Kappa Pi Delta! We are here to help you scout out houses to rush. Oh, don't you two look so cute!"

I mustered a small smile and a wave. It was awkward. "We're just browsing today. I'm not completely sure if I'll rush this year."

"Oh, honey! You are welcome here, whatever year you're in." She came a little closer and lowered her voice. "Just between you and me, avoid Beta Kappa Pi and Theta Nu. The former being worse than the latter."

"I think another girl who invited us to rush week told us the same," I whispered back.

"Don't let the scary stories frighten you, darlin'. Lots of the houses out here look out for one another, just as the good Lord intended women do." She ran her hand in a gentle circle on my back and gave us a wide smile. "Now, tell me all about yourselves!"

We left the *very* southern house as quickly as we had come, armed with a somewhat confusing series of directions to Phi Beta Lambda—the house we were originally invited to during the first week of classes. Kelly looked even more weirded out by the way all the girls seemed to have a cult-like manner about them.

"I think she meant this way, but I don't know if I could handle another, uh, rodeo." She pointed in the direction of two other parties that were going on.

I shrugged. "At this point, I don't mind just exploring and getting free food and drinks. I am somewhat terrified of coming into contact with Beta Kappa Pi. Did you hear what those girls were saying about that Sloane character?"

"That she's a ruthless she-devil? I mean, you can't know for sure until you meet her, but if she runs the most prestigious sorority on campus with an all-star legacy, that means business." Since when did we swap our outlooks?

"Maybe you're right, but stop being so optimistic. It's weird. Just like the scary stories about some girl here on campus."

At another house, we decided to enter the party and ask around about which house it was. Inside the entrance, it became apparent with a sign reading *Phi Beta Lambda*. Easy enough.

This house—thank God—had *far* less pink everywhere and more real-life colors. The girls didn't feel like they were in weird cult uniforms, and no one had the same creepy updo to their hair. The only ones holding some form of uniform were the group of eight girls running the party.

"Hey, I know you two." A girl in a pink shirt came running up to us, waving and smiling.

It definitely felt less weird in this house. "You invited us on the first day of classes. We decided to pop by and see what you guys were all about."

She beamed at us, taking us by our hands. "I'm Veronica! Let's go to the main room. We're having snacks!"

Kelly looked over at me, questioning what the heck this girl was doing dragging us along with her. I nodded back at her with a *just go with it* look.

We chatted and socialized with normal people this time around. The snacks and drinks were delicious, and I was happy I didn't have to scrounge around for dinner later. A few girls started murmuring and making shushing sounds as the door behind us slammed open. Standing there was a girl with highlighted brown hair, dressed in cream heels, a baby pink mini dress, and a sash that signified her sorority name: *Beta Kappa Pi.*

One of the members of her entourage stepped out from behind her, wearing baby pink shorts and a sheer top. "We have an important message for the heads of every house." She stood frozen as if that was her only job and it was awkward to see a bunch of girls in the same completely see-through tops, their boobs on full display.

Hazing, maybe?

The only one not wearing the same top was the girl in the sash. I assumed she was the leader of her own little cult. *Her boobs must be sacred*, I laughed to myself.

Another girl came out to stand next to the first. "Beta Kappa Pi will be hosting tonight's afterparty and all are invited, no matter their house, creed, or financial status."

Kelly and I exchanged glances. "What a weird way to invite people to a party," I whispered.

Veronica was the head of Phi Beta Lambda, and as the head, she piped up in response. "In the spirit of rushing, thank you,

Sloane, head of Beta Kappa Pi, for your kind and generous invitation."

She waved her hands to her house members in encouragement to speak up. In unison, they announced, "Thank you, Sloane."

Kelly and I made a quick exit, feeling a little freaked out from the interaction. She gave me a weird look when we got home and barreled into the kitchen. "I guess I stand corrected on that Sloane girl. She seems like an absolute nutcase on a power trip."

"I've seen that happen one too many times. I feel bad that those girls had to walk around with their tits on display, though. It has me questioning what the fuck sorority life is like and maybe... I don't want to join after all. I can say at least I tried!" I set my bag down on the entry table and pulled off my shoes, my feet sore from walking in heels all day.

"Leftovers?" Kelly asked, holding up some containers from the fridge. "We have some... Asian, Italian, and good ol' fashioned American cuisines to choose from."

She spread them across the table, laying out plates and silverware as I sat in the chair. "I love me some good, cold leftovers in shitty takeout containers. I will say, I am morbidly curious about this party."

"Ha!" Kelly exclaimed, scooping food onto our plates. "That's a funny joke considering I've never heard those words come out of your mouth."

"Everyone will be there. It might be good to mingle and meet some new people."

"Wait." She set her fork and knife down. "You want to see Brent again! Oh my God, don't tell me you're going to wear his jacket and hope he's there."

My face turned red. "Holy shit, no! I would *never* do that."

"You didn't deny wanting to see him," she taunted in a sing-song voice while biting into some pasta.

I rolled my eyes. "If I wanted to see him, I could march down the street to his house and knock on the door. Besides, I'm somewhat seeing Garrett." My head was leaned into my cupped hand while I pushed some form of breaded meat around in circles on my plate.

"I still don't believe you didn't sleep with him."

"Dude"—I flicked my eyes over to her and scowled—"you interrupted him *trying* to kiss me. We didn't even do *that*, but I don't think it matters now. He is *not* the type I should be getting myself involved with. The whole time, I was convinced he was going to murder me in the woods. With everything going on, I haven't told Garrett I went on a date with Brent, but we aren't exactly exclusive; he could be going on dates for all I know."

My phone buzzed on the table, and I was grateful to get out of the conversation with Kelly. I didn't recognize the number, but the area code...

"Hello?" I tried to steel my voice despite my anxiety.

"Fallon, hello. It's Mr. Evans. We need to start discussions on your transition process into acting CEO this weekend." His voice was firm and left no room for argument.

I felt my heart sink into my butt. I knew what this meant despite knowing they'd come knocking for me eventually. When I turned eighteen, the rule was that I would step into her shoes when I turned twenty-one. Wishing I could hold off just a little longer, I sighed. "This weekend? I have schoolwork... and other... stuff."

Great, very convincing. Very CEO.

"Yes, well, you have had plenty of time to romp and play. You will make time for a meeting with the board this weekend. Also, drop the exercise major—you're becoming the CEO. You need something relevant. I didn't think I had to micromanage your behavior, but it seems we will be needing an intervention this weekend."

My mother wouldn't have said that—unless she would have... Maybe I didn't know all of her facets as well as I thought I did. I knew her as a mother, not as a businesswoman. "Yep. Got it."

There was a slight pause before his voice came back through. "You will be taking on *major* responsibilities. Responsibilities for which you are completely unprepared, whether you like it or not. Your mother has left this company to you, and by default, us. We are here to help you, so please don't act like a petulant child. This isn't something you can say no to without harming the empire your mother built for you; you have employees and their livelihoods to worry about now."

I tightened my grip on the phone, a tsunami-sized wave of emotion crashing over me. *What a tangled mess I've found myself in.* "Fine," I said, firming my voice. "I will be on the call this weekend."

"Good. I will send you the information you need to attend. And, Fallon?"

My heart stilled. "Yes?"

"Don't do anything reckless or stupid. I know how you young people are. This is my personal number; feel free to reach out if you need anything. See you this weekend." The line went dead.

Kelly leaned forward after intently watching the entire time. "Who was that?"

I sighed and sank into my chair. "Montgomery Group. I'm set to start my transition early. It's like they knew the perfect time to call me was when I've been sucked into some drama. Oh, also, I have to hit up my advisor because I am now a business major."

"Welcome to the world of the wealthy, babe." A strange look played on her face while she stared blankly at her plate. Whatever was on her mind, it seemed bothersome.

"I guess," I said, trying to fake a chuckle.

Her head turned to look at the clock, and she dropped her fork, standing up with urgency. "I just decided that we are going to that party. Come on, let's get you dressed."

"Uh, no. Did you not just hear about my phone call?"

She grabbed my arm and dragged me into my room, opening the closet to throw absolutely everything out of it in search of the outfit she wanted me to wear. One that would get me the most attention.

She held up a couple of things. "Oh yes. Put these on."

A strapless taupe-colored tulle dress was shoved at me, along with white bowtie-backed heels. I held up the little dress and wondered what it would even cover on my body. I cringed. "Are you sure I should wear this... *thing*?"

"Duh." She moved to leave my room to dress herself. "It's the afterparty, of course."

I shimmied into the dress and stood in front of the mirror. Fidgeting excessively, I adjusted the hem of the dress about fifty times. Wearing dresses like this was foreign to me—too flashy and form-fitting. It felt as though I were an imposter pretending to be someone I wasn't—a fish out of water.

If you're going to flop, at least do it with some sparkle, I thought. Smoothing the fabric over my hips, I took one last glance in the mirror before heading out.

"Here goes nothing," I said to myself.

9

Fallon

I found myself standing in the middle of a crowded party, feeling out of my depth, with my red plastic cup as my sole companion for the moment. I tried to feign the confidence I'd seen Kelly wear on multiple occasions, but my smile felt fake.

Maybe having a social life wasn't for me.

A hand grabbed my arm and tugged me out of the room.

"Where are we going?" I asked.

Kelly smiled at me. "To the bar, silly."

There was a very familiar baby-pink dress leaning against the counter, with a half-empty glass in her hand. Sloane looked impeccable while surrounded by her entourage and swooning freshman wannabes who hung on her every word. What kind of power must one possess for people to cling to you like an idol?

The sight of her scared me, if I was being honest.

Kelly ignored her as she flagged down the bartender, but Sloane perked up at seeing us. Her gaze landed on us, lips curling into a vicious smile.

"Hey girls," she drawled, clearly drunk as she pushed herself away from the bar. "You two look like quite the dynamic duo. Are you rushing this week?"

I tensed, not wanting to reply to this girl. Kelly gave her a faux polite smile. "Maybe."

Sloane took a long swig from her glass, eyes narrowing while she focused on Kelly's outfit—a plaid mini dress that suited her style, not the trends of those around her. "Nice dress," she sneered.

"Yeah, thanks." Kelly turned away to get her order in with the guy making drinks.

The group of girls started giggling, turning back to their circle and holding their hands in front of their mouths to whisper to each other. They kept glancing back at us. Amidst the whispering, I swore I heard, "She's trying to rush as a scholarship student? Gross."

"Ignore them," Kelly said flatly, handing me a glass of something.

We clinked our shots together and I knocked mine back. It burned. "What even is this?" I shot a look at the bartender.

He shrugged. "A blazing nipple?"

Kelly laughed. "To the blazin' nip!"

I hope no one is lighting their nipples on fire.

We grabbed a couple of extra drinks and made our way out to the main dance area. Kelly pushed me into the center of the dance floor and spun me around, our hands linked while we twirled in a circle. "You're killing it tonight, babe!" she yelled over the music.

I blushed, downing some more alcohol. My nervous energy faded; that or I was drunk. Dancing with others around and trying to avoid stepping on toes was not my scene, but I wanted to make the best of it.

There were some giggles behind me. I turned to see the groupies trailing behind Sloane as she swayed her way through the bodies. Was she Godzilla? *She looks like it.* She was positively drunk, holding a half-empty glass in one hand, her eyes locked on something. A cruel smile spread across her face.

She stopped a few feet away from Kelly and me, almost unable to keep her composure. "I just decided something…"

I shot a concerned look at Kelly, and she raised an eyebrow; we both remained silent.

"This dress is absolutely hideous. Take it off!" She started stumbling while some of the girls behind her played along with her antics, egging her on.

Kelly chuckled and rolled her eyes. "Relax, she-devil. Pink is more your color than mine."

Why was Sloane singling out Kelly? I pinched the bridge of my nose. "Hey, guys, we can just enjoy the party. Everything is fine."

"Ew, you stand up for this loser?" One of the girls sneered from behind Sloane.

What the fuck reality show had I been dropped into?

Sloane wasn't laughing along with the rest of her crew. Her face was twisted in anger as she lifted her drink. "You two are such a disgrace to this school. Who even lets in scholarships anymore? I mean, why? It's just like—" Her hand flung the liquid out of her drink before anyone could react. "*Oops.*" She laughed.

The drink splashed across Kelly's chest, soaking her dress. I gasped and stepped in front of her, hoping no one else would throw another drink at her—well, me. Kelly looked down in total disbelief before she tried flicking excess liquid off her. I was speechless.

"You bitch!" Kelly snapped, stomping away. I assumed it was for the bathroom to dry off.

Before I could speak, Sloane slinked away. It was more of a stumble, but it was a solid attempt. I watched as she left, and a familiar figure moved through the crowd, heading toward her— Brent. He grabbed her arm and pulled her away from her group.

Call me a voyeur, but I couldn't help watching. They moved farther away from people, and then she pulled her arm from his grip, yelling at him that he had no right to intervene. He told her that she had had enough to drink while looking *heavily* annoyed with her.

"Are you going to punish me for being a bad girl?" she cooed, looking at him through her lashes.

"Hey, babe." A voice caught my attention.

I spun around. "Oh! Hey, you."

Garrett looked around to see what I was looking at. "What are you doing?"

"Oh, uh, Kelly had some bitch throw her drink on her, and I'm watching her stumble away like an idiot." I couldn't stop fidgeting with my hands.

He leaned down to kiss me. I let him. It was nice to empty my brain for a moment amidst the drama unfolding in my life. "Kelly going to be okay?"

"Yeah," I sighed. "She's probably toweling herself down in the bathroom."

"Dance while we wait?"

He twirled and danced with me for a bit until I saw Kelly come back downstairs and make a beeline for the bar. She was rapidly typing away on her phone.

I didn't think much of it. She usually scrolled through social media when she was bored and probably wanted a few minutes to decompress and dry off. Most likely, in need of another drink, too. Her facial expression still seemed strange to me, though.

I tried to refocus on Garrett and the moment we were in. Dancing with him felt normal and natural. It was the typical way college kids dated—they went to parties, danced, and hung out. At least, *I thought* they did. What wasn't normal was how Brent put me on the back of his bike after being weird with me on the porch. Plus, it seemed like we were both seeing other people.

Maybe he did want to kill me but backed out at the last second. Or he just realized you weren't an easy lay. Stop being so paranoid.

I wanted to have a normal sophomore year and do normal sophomore things. That meant I *needed* to have a normal boyfriend and go on dates with him, which is what I was doing. *I think.*

Garrett leaned down so I could hear him over the music, his breath so close to my neck that it tickled and sent a shiver down my spine. "You look beautiful tonight."

I swallowed the nervous lump forming in my throat. We were dancing so closely. He put his hand in mine while the other drifted slowly to the small of my back, pulling me in closer. The room felt smaller, and his face was inches from mine. *Too close.*

He wanted more than I did, and it was clear. Before this semester, if someone had told me I would have been this close to *two* men, I would have laughed in their face. I never focused on boys; my mom grew sicker by the day during my younger years. They were the *last* thing on my mind, really.

The only thing I had any experience with was a kiss that happened on a dare in sixth grade. If you could call that experience.

We danced for a while, but my eyes drifted back to Kelly at the bar. I couldn't help but think that she acted weirdly today. Not her usual weirdness. It felt distracted. She was still standing there at the bar, but she wasn't texting anymore. Her body language looked strange and defensive as she focused on a taller male figure speaking to her.

Who is she talking to? The person wasn't Shane. The way they spoke seemed off to me, considering how she was standing. Kelly leaned in closer, looking to keep their conversation private. Whatever it was, it gave me an odd feeling in my stomach.

Garrett's voice cut through my thoughts. "Think you want to head outside for a bit and get some fresh air?"

I blinked, refocusing on the man in front of me. He looked relaxed, with an easy smile. His hair was slicked back for the party, and his outfit was a bit dressier than last time. "Yeah, sure," I breathed, trying not to think too heavily about Kelly.

The stranger was still standing close to her when I took one last look. *She looks fine enough, right?*

We left the dance floor and escaped onto the patio into the cool night air. He looked more handsome under the lighting on the porch, but he pulled us into a quieter spot near the garden. The party's conversations and music faded into the background.

Garrett was tall with a nice footballer's build. His curly brown hair was definitely charming and matched his honey brown eyes. Some days, I wondered why this stunning man with a nice smile hung around me. *Stop overthinking it.*

He leaned against the wall and took one of my hands in his. "I like you a lot, Fallon. Hanging out over the summer was one of the highlights of my break."

Oh no.

I turned my head away and tucked a strand of hair behind my ear. We had chemistry, but was I prepared for what he wanted to say? "Me too. My roommate was the one who convinced me to get out more. Since, you know, I kept to myself for a while after my mom…"

"I know." He reached up, cupping my chin, turning my face back to his. "I'm glad she did. I might not have met you otherwise."

His hand was warm on my chin. I wanted to lean into it more, but something made me want to hold back. "Me too." I smiled.

He moved closer. "So what do I have to do to make things official with you?"

Never in my life did I think there would be someone asking me to be their girlfriend. I wanted to have a boyfriend, but again, *something was holding me back.*

Gut feelings were something my mom told me to listen to. Our intuitions knew things that we didn't. When my mom told me she had a gut feeling about a situation, she would sit down and think it through. I wondered if that's what made her such a prudent and successful woman—by using her intuition to guide her through things.

Would I be the same, or would my lack of experience be my downfall?

I hesitated for a moment. "I… Are you asking me to be your girlfriend officially?"

He held my hand in an ironically serious way. He looked serious, too. "I guess I am. We've been on multiple dates, and from what I've seen of you, I want more."

After we met, we talked about school, our interests, and general information about ourselves, but I never thought a deep emotional connection had formed. We were very casual in our dating, especially since the dates never went beyond surface level conversation and perhaps some kissing.

Sure, his smile was infectious, he was insanely hot, and he made me laugh about absolutely nothing, but were we at a point to get serious?

A silence stretched between us for the first time. The sound of the wind, the leaves, and the distant party filled the air. I smelled the garden, the pool, and the faint scent of cigarette smoke. I breathed.

He raised an eyebrow. "You don't have to respond now; I know I put you on the spot. Why don't we go back to your place and hang out?"

Should I just get it over with?

It was safe to say that the car ride was awkward. Kelly turned me down when I suggested going home early and gave off strange vibes, but she had a drink thrown on her. I couldn't say I'd be in the best mood with a dried cocktail on my dress, either.

He walked me to my door with a nervous smile on his face. Maybe he thought I'd reject him. I didn't want to reject him. I wanted to get to know him on a deeper level before we made things official. My mom never had anyone after my dad left, and she told me to be very picky with the men I let into my heart. And money.

10

Brent

The bass of the party's music pounded in my bones as I navigated through the crowd in the dark. Bodies were everywhere, and everyone was wasted out of their minds. My ears bled when Sloane's voice cut through the crowd. She was giving some girl a hard time, swaying as she spoke.

I took a closer look, and Fallon was next to the girl Sloane was laying into. Her laughter was a bit *too* loud, her movements *too* unsteady, and I could smell trouble. She was beyond drunk.

"Take it off!" she yelled. I couldn't hear much else, but it didn't look good.

There was some extra commotion and then she threw her drink onto Fallon's friend. *Goddamn it.*

"You bitch!" She swiped at her dress and left quickly.

Fallon was frozen in place, looking far too adorable with her wide eyes. She looked shocked and unsure of what to do before Sloane spun around and walked away. Well, stumbled.

I waited for her to get far enough away to snag her by her arm.

"Hey, baby," she drawled.

"Sloane," I hissed, motioning for her little minions to leave her to us.

With Sloane, everything was predictable. Her family status

solidified her attitude: spoiled. She did what she wanted, when she wanted, and with whom she wanted. I hated her family for being the business connections in the twisted little world we lived in. She never had to worry her head about much since she'd probably get married off to the highest bidder. It sometimes made me feel bad for her, and I understood why she lashed out. *Only sometimes.*

I dragged her farther from the crowded room while she struggled, finally pulling her arm out of my grip.

"Can you not? You said I'm not yours! You can't come in here and do what you want with my arms!" *Thank God I spoke drunk-Sloane.*

I sighed and folded my arms over my chest. "You've had enough tonight. You need to get home."

Her face softened, looking almost sensual. "Are you going to punish me for being a bad girl?"

With some heavy coaxing and promises of things I knew she'd forget in the morning, I convinced her to leave. She lived only a few houses away, and getting her into bed guaranteed that she would fall asleep immediately.

She did.

I plopped into the chair at her desk and took a breather. I was *not* supposed to be a drunk escort. If anything, I planned on snatching Fallon again to force her to come with me for some answers.

Why did my grandfather forbid me to canoodle with her? No idea. All I knew was that she was Maria's kid, and my grandfather loved Maria like a daughter. Since his only child ended her life, I couldn't blame him for forcing the title on someone else. *We all have our own demons.*

But then, why the beatings? He fucking pulled a fucking gun on me—he had a temper, sure. It had happened multiple times before, but telling me to stay away from Fallon like this only pushed me closer to her.

I planned to have that girl eating out of my hands whether she—or the Dictator—liked it or not. Fallon was a part of the family, anyway. The Montgomery family was intertwined with the Vaughn family in more ways than one. What was an extra thread?

Sloane looked to be asleep, and I took that as my cue to leave. My focus was on Fallon and getting back to the party. I hoped to find her in the chaos that was a sorority afterparty. *She is mine.*

Sloane had a habit of trying to bring other people down to make herself feel better, a symptom of the life she lived. I didn't like it, and that's why I never wanted anything to do with her, despite her desperate attempts to hold on. She mocked me and told me I had commitment issues—which was true—but maybe she was just a girl who needed to stop flinging herself at me. She was just a bit of college fun like the others were, and I wasn't here for anything but work.

So was she.

The music inside was too loud to hear myself think. A smoke break before finding Fallon was in order. She looked good in that dress she wore, and it frustrated me how she brushed me off. I shrugged off the thought in the brisk night air out back, where I found a secluded spot to light up. The smell overpowered the stench of beer and sweat, calming my nerves like it always did.

What was it about her? Those innocent eyes? The way her lips wanted mine, even though she denied it? Whatever it was, I liked it, and I wanted her.

Speak of the devil, I thought, hearing her voice nearby. Curiosity got the better of me, and I decided to eavesdrop. Leaning closer, her voice became clearer.

"I… Are you asking me to be your girlfriend officially?" She didn't sound sure of herself, which meant there was room for me in her life. Hell, maybe she'd turn him down because I'd already weaseled my way into her brain.

She was really something, though. She had a baseball star and a football player paying attention to her all in the same week. I was so intrigued by her, and it pissed me off that I couldn't get a read on the girl.

They said something else I couldn't make out from their

hushed tones, but he didn't sound like he was too enthusiastic about it. *Did she reject him? God, I hope so.*

"Why don't we go back to your place to hang out?" he asked. *Doesn't sound like a rejection to me.*

Well, that was frustrating, but it made sense. I moved slightly to see if I could get a visual on them. I was already eavesdropping, so I figured staring wasn't any worse. I could hear Reaper, egging me on in the back of my mind. The fucker would probably be jerking off to this shit.

In view, his mouth was on hers, and she took the kiss with more want than she let on. No hesitation like she had with me. *Challenge accepted, Blondie.*

I was done watching. I finished my cigarette and crushed it under my boot.

Maybe I wasn't done because I found myself in our neighborhood, sitting on my porch, wanting to catch her coming home. If she ever did. The night was quiet, except for the occasional passing car or distant music. I leaned back in my chair and lit up a cigarette, letting my thoughts drift to more important matters.

The Dictator started rolling around in my mind with his orders and the jobs he had planned out for me. We had other matters to put to bed, things looking messier with each job we went to. I made a mental note to ask Reaper about what he knew, since I was usually just told to go and execute. They never trusted me much, even though I would *supposedly* inherit the company at some point.

If he'd just trust me more. *Oh, but he can't. I'm just a nuisance to him.*

A car slowly rolled down the street, and the headlights made me cover my eyes. I scooted down to avoid being seen but remained in a position where I could easily see what was happening. It stopped at Fallon's house and parked. My vision readjusted as I saw Garrett and Fallon walking to the front door.

I bet she'll lock lips with him and think of me. I wanted her to.

The question of whether she would burned in the back of my mind.

Why am I being so creepy? Usually, I would just dip out if they were too challenging. *But not with her.*

Fallon and Garrett stood at her doorstep. This time, I couldn't hear their conversation, but I wanted to. Was she rejecting him or accepting him? I plotted something and stashed it in the back of my mind for later while I watched their body language. They were standing too close for the second time tonight. His hand found its way up to the left side of her face, caressing her jaw.

It was pretty much a movie in slow motion as they kissed again. Long and drawn out, I felt my stomach do something… weird. *I didn't want this to happen.* The way her mouth moved with his for too long before they pulled away made me want to punch him. He said something else to her before he turned to leave, and I watched as her eyes tracked him longingly as he walked away.

Does she look at me like that?

She closed the door after he drove away and I stood up, contemplating my options. I could march over there and kidnap her, but that would make me late to see Reaper.

Unsure of how long I *actually* stood there, I headed to my bike to show up late anyway.

Reaper was in my wing of the house when I arrived, lounging in my favorite chair and drinking my favorite bottle of whiskey. He wasn't a very patient man.

Where did that fucking cat come from? It sat in his lap, purring like a fucking engine.

"What the fuck are you doing?" I asked.

He shrugged. "Hanging out. Want some?"

"Considering that's my fucking alcohol, I feel like our roles should be reversed. Doesn't matter. What did you find out this week? Dictator is being ridiculously cryptic, and then he beat me within an inch of my life after he found out I went out with the 'Montgomery girl'."

His facial expression was hidden behind his mask. This time, he wore a plain black ski mask. I didn't complain; he once wore a silicone horse head. The shit he wore on his head was *so* strange, but I was in no mood to comment on it. The only thing I ever saw was his green eyes and—sometimes—his thick brown eyebrows or his mouth. When his eyebrows were visible, I could usually guess his facial expressions.

"Your fault for being late." He threw back his glass and poured another. "As for the girl, she's Maria's heir. Mr. Vaughn had a close relationship with her." He stroked the cat in his lap and lit up a cigar from *my* stash. He had no boundaries, but at some point, I got used to it. "Do you think…"

"Ew, what the fuck? That I just tried to bang my aunt? No way in hell. He probably sees her as another Maria. Whatever is going on with her, I'm not allowed to know."

He shrugged. "The dirty side of the business has been in rocky waters from all these men we've been taking out lately. He probably wants to get to her first. I've been here a while; he sang the praises of Maria daily. They were strong partners in crime. The whispers, though, are about some 'girl' and how her being brought in needs to happen sooner rather than later. I assume that's your fuck buddy."

If only she was my fuck buddy. Well, I wanted more from her than that. She was interesting and mouthy—two things I had never encountered in the girls on campus or around me in general. They all wanted to drop their panties for me as soon as they saw me, but she didn't. And, damn, if that didn't piss me off.

I leaned back in the chair, taking a swig of the drink while digesting his words. "What else is in these whispers? Dictator doesn't tell me shit and you're some of my only ears here."

"You know them." He cracked his neck and puffed on one of my expensive Cuban cigars. "I receive orders and I'm happy with it, but there *is* something fucked going on in the dark side of the world. More stabbing for me and fewer questions to ask. If I were to take a guess based on what I hear, there are more snakes in the grass than you'd think. We have old business connects turning into wolves for Maria's company. Hence, your little fuck toy needing to come in now." He turned his attention to petting the cat and swiping around on his phone. For someone who was just a hired gun, I kind of liked him. He was straightforward. If he ever let me see his face, maybe we'd even be friends.

It made sense that there were people interested in Montgomery Group. Hostile takeovers happened all the time— especially in our part of society. It was always cutthroat, and you needed to stay on top of your game to play it the right way. But what was with all the movement recently? Wouldn't it have made more sense to act after she died, and not five years later? There were too many questions to ask in one night, so I shelved them in the back of my mind for further exploration later.

Reaper laid his head back in *my* chair. "Enough talking about boring fucking shit. Tell me about that blonde girl you railed. Does she have a friend for me?"

"Big boy can't find his own bitches?"

He threw *my* glass at me. "Fuck you. If you weren't my boss, I'd kill you for that."

"I'd like to see you try, loser." I laughed, dodging the glass.

"I have a few files of some men we were assigned."

"And?"

He laughed. It was a cold and startling laugh that only a trained killer like him would have. "We have assignments, dickhead. Stabbing? Don't mind if I do."

I sighed, knocking back the rest of my drink. "You couldn't have led with that?"

He tossed me a set of keys and a bright pink ski mask. *Fuck this guy.* "Giddy up, pretty boy. We're going killing tonight and getting some more info. You need to at least know why Gramps doesn't want you fucking that pretty girl."

Blondie flooded my mind. Those blue eyes and wicked smirk appeared, taunting me with that attitude. For her, I'd definitely kill a few people. Hell, maybe a lot of people. Intriguing didn't even begin to cover what she was. A brat? Surely. A puzzle? Mine to solve.

She wouldn't see it coming, but I'd have her begging on her knees for me soon. Dictator and her so-called boyfriend be damned. No one has ever stopped me from doing what I wanted to do anyway. Not even the law. And she had no clue...

"Fuck. You. I'm not wearing this shit."

His laugh filled the halls as we made our way out into the night. Answers were what I was going to get. And maybe, just maybe, I'd earn a seat at my grandfather's table since he decided I was only good enough for his dirty work.

~

"What the fuck is Jason Haines planning?" Reaper smashed the guy's head in with each word. Clearly, he had a personal stake in getting me laid.

The screams of a grown ass man echoed through the room, and I secretly got some sick enjoyment out of it. I hadn't been laid in a minute, so watching some torture would put some pep in my step until I finally landed Blondie in bed. *Which I will, very soon.*

I sat back and watched Reaper continue his oddly satisfying assault, his fists connecting with increasingly wet thuds to Chris's body. Blood was inevitable. The guy was relentless when it came to getting information—and me a love life, apparently. "Alright, alright," I said, pulling him back a few inches. "Let's not kill him just yet."

Reaper brandished his KA-Bar at him, waving it around. His eyes were crazy behind his mask, and he was in shark mode from smelling all the blood around us. Whoever fucked this guy's head in the past did me a favor when I needed him to pull out every brutal stop.

Chris was panting heavily, his chest rising and falling rapidly. His nose looked busted from how smushed and crooked it was, with blood trickling out of it, dripping down into his mouth.

Whatever didn't go in his mouth went down his neck and painted the front of his shirt crimson. I was sure I saw purple beginning to appear around one of his eyes. *Damn, Reaper could bludgeon someone.* "Okay, I need a break." His voice was pathetic, almost pleading.

I raised an eyebrow. Did he seriously think he could ask favors? "You get a break if you give me information. Otherwise, my colleague here will continue."

His hand went to his chest to steady himself. I saw so many self-comforting or defensive maneuvers from the guys we tortured, yet they all ended up looking the same—pathetic and begging for it to stop. "All I know," he struggled to get out between breaths, "is that they hired someone to track some girl they kept calling *Rose*. She needs to create a downfall before next year for some power transfer. It sounds like they're planning a hostile takeover of the underworld right now. A lot of power struggles are happening; a lot of new players are entering the ring."

Reaper stabbed him in the leg. I sighed and wiped my hand down my face.

"What?" He looked back at me, yanking the knife out as quickly as he stabbed it in.

I shook my head. "Anyway, what else do you know? What type of tracking, what does this *Rose* character look like, and what do you know about the power struggles in the underworld?"

"She—AH!" His body jolted as Reaper stomped on his injured leg. "She's just some kid! I don't know! Surveillance! I don't know her or what Jason is even talking about! I wasn't even supposed to be there that early…" He clutched his leg, and tears streamed down his face. I didn't blame him; it looked painful.

We learned that Chris was a higher-level runner hired by Jason himself and was given to us by one of our rats via Reaper's information extraction methods. Naturally, we nabbed him and brought him with us. Reaper loved a good kidnapping before torture and killing, and I'd never seen him happier.

I nodded at Reaper. He took my direction and stabbed the other leg. Every time he stabbed, it was like ripping a wet pair of jeans in one go—a thick crunch almost. He screamed—again—and begged us to stop. "We stop when you offer up more information," I said, leaning over to inspect the stab site.

"Or if you die." Reaper laughed.

"I don't know! Please." The low, pitiful begging wouldn't work.

This session had gone on for too long, and I was pretty sure he had said all he really knew. We'd never know, and all I knew was that I wanted to lay in bed and sleep for ten hours. I unholstered my gun from my waistband and pointed it at his head as Reaper looked at me like a proud father. "I'm tired. Now, what the fuck aren't you telling me?"

His hands went up in that typical defensive position. "That's all! I've given you a play-by-play of my entire time there, including anything I heard from Jason and his girlfriend."

"What is his girlfriend's name?"

"She's called Rabbit! I don't know her name!" His tears flowed freely from his eyes, mixing with the blood dripping from his facial injuries. It was sort of pathetic, really.

"What. Else." I positioned myself to push the muzzle into his forehead. The pad of my finger came to rest on the trigger, ready to send this idiot to his maker. I preferred it when Reaper did the killing, but I was sick and fucking tired of not getting what I wanted to move up in the ranks under my grandfather. The game had changed and I needed to prove myself.

And take my anger out on someone who wouldn't land me in handcuffs.

"Nothing," he sobbed. "I swear to you. Please I—" *BANG!*

My ears rang for a few seconds. I noted to start bringing some earplugs with me in case I felt like getting festive. Saving your hearing was worth it.

Reaper looked over at me, his eyes wide as he rubbed his

96

ears. Shocked, maybe? "Damn, boss. I thought I was going to kill him."

"You take too long," I said flatly and shook my head. Putting the gun back in its holster, I turned on my heel to walk away and shake off my frustration.

Fallon was connected to something; I could feel it. The puzzle pieces felt like they fit together somehow, and I was scrambling to catch up with the others who saw more than I did. She's the Montgomery girl I needed to *stay away from*, there is a girl named Rose being surveilled, and there seems to be even dirtier business in the underworld than I could have dreamed of. My sources weren't providing what I wanted, so I decided to start pushing them more.

Something, somewhere, was fucked and I couldn't figure out what it was. My next plan of attack was meeting with the Dictator and begging for a better position within the company or cleaning myself up enough to prove that I could work well with others. Anything to bring me in closer.

I was tired of being seen as the black sheep—the disappointing bastard who showed up on his doorstep about two decades ago. The face that reminded him of his deceased daughter. I planned to prove myself or die trying by getting him the information he sought—even if I didn't know what his meetings were about or what knowledge he possessed.

I also needed to devise a plan to catch Blondie off guard— *perhaps some light kidnapping.*

"Reaper?" I asked into the room.

"Yeah, boss?"

"Find out what you can about what he just said and make him disappear."

11

Fallon

Homework began early in the semester, considering I had chosen to take online classes to get more out of my weeks with Kelly. They started early with their reading assignments. Fall was the perfect season for having free days to explore and late nights to scramble to finish classwork. I loved Halloween, and I would *not* be missing out on the adventures of spooky season.

Every year, we had a tradition of visiting corn mazes, exploring haunted houses, enjoying scary movie marathons, and indulging in a lot of candy.

No exceptions.

"How are your assignments going?" Kelly poked her head over her laptop.

"I finished most of my work, but I got a head start so we have time to dick around this week without worrying about some of these assignments. This year is going to be crazy since I have to play catch up with my classes now that I *must* change my major because some businessman told me I'm *obligated* to." I shoved a sour gummy worm into my mouth.

"Geez. Sorry I asked. I was going to say English was hard, but I will respectfully keep my mouth shut about the difficulties of my classes around you." Sarcasm dripped from her tone before she laughed and threw her pencil at me.

I closed my laptop in defeat. I wanted to be an Exercise Science major, but duty called, and I needed to be a CEO babe. Turning off the music from the Bluetooth speaker, I shoved the laptop aside and sighed.

"I also need to tell you something. I needed time to process it, but I think I'm ready now."

She closed her laptop slowly. Her mouth was wide open in surprise. "Are you pregnant? Is it Brent's?"

My eyebrows furrowed in confusion. How would it have been Brent's? Or anyone's? "How would I even know I was pregnant if I supposedly had sex less than a month ago? Don't people usually find out after, like, six to eight weeks? Also"—I threw a pillow at her—"I didn't have sex with *anyone*, let alone that fuckboy."

"Then what else could need that much time of contemplation?" she retorted.

Good point. "Garrett asked me to be his official girlfriend at the party."

"Did you tell him that you have a hankering for a bad boy in the form of Brent? Or did you say yes?"

I tried to play it cool but ended up hiding my face behind the sleeves of my oversized sweater. "Ugh! I am *so* inexperienced. The only thing that ever happened to me before this year was a kiss as a dare in sixth grade. But I told Garrett that I would think about it. We hung out a bit in his car… and then he dropped me off and we almost had a full makeout session on the doorstep."

It was true. I hadn't done much, and I didn't know how I felt about it. Secretly, I wanted to get my virginity out of the way so I could stop stressing out about it. There were some opportunities last semester, but I couldn't bring myself to do it with a random.

"Do you think you'll actually sleep with him at some point?"

Maybe, but I would be surprised if it were anytime soon. "I haven't given it much thought. However, when we kissed, I got some fuzzy feelings."

She giggled. "At least we know he turns you on."

I fully buried my face in my sweater-covered hands. "I feel

like a teenager." My voice was muffled by the fabric. I looked back up at her and said, "I need some air since it's getting hot in here with all this talk. Want to come to the back porch with me?"

She agreed and we sat on the porch while I refocused my thoughts on potential holiday plans and future landscaping endeavors for the yard. My mind drifted back to the board of directors and Evans telling me how my life would look in the very near future. The meeting was an introduction—I got some names I wouldn't remember along with the faces of a bunch of stuffy-looking men in suits. They wanted to bring me up to speed with the goings-on in the business as soon as possible.

I didn't want to change my major. I didn't want to be told what to do. Despite my mother leaving me everything, I knew nothing about businesses—or how to run them. She left me a broken-down car. And I was *no* mechanic.

To say I was nervous would be an understatement. What would running an international company like the Montgomery Group be like? What was expected of me? Would I succeed, or would I run the company into the ground, destroying everything my mother had built for us?

Those were questions for me to address later. I shook them off and tried to bring my thoughts back to the present. To sitting with Kelly on the porch. "Do you think we should put in a hot tub?" I pulled out my very own pack of cigarettes and a pink lighter I had purchased when no one was looking.

Maybe I did want to impress a man. Attention felt nice.

"Since, um, when do you smoke?" Kelly gave me an incredulous look. She never saw me smoke a day in my life—or do anything edgy, actually.

Since Brent, I thought. I wouldn't tell her that, though.

Ignoring her question, I offered the cigarette out to her. It felt like I was mimicking Brent in a way. "Want one?"

"You should try weed sometime, since you're *quite* the bad girl now." She took it from my fingers and brought it to her lips, drawing in a long puff.

"Very funny. I'm changing topics now. I wanted to get some

work done out here and a hot tub installed so we can host some of our own parties."

"Only if you hire the hottest contractors so we can watch them work."

"Deal," I said, scrolling through my phone to find some contractors on a services app. It looked like there was some availability within the next week. *Hot contractors, here we come!*

I swapped apps to look at some travel websites. We talked about heading to Europe for a vacation, but I was feeling like we wouldn't be able to head out until after Christmas with the business shit I was being thrown into. Despite that, I looked into some places that offered full itineraries.

"What do you think about this?" I showed her my phone. "It's a six-day trip spanning France, Germany, and Italy."

"Now *that* sounds fun." She released a puff of smoke, looking out into the yard. She seemed to be lost in thought.

She disappeared after we hung out on the porch and went into her bedroom—she had a weird look, but I didn't think too much of it. She reappeared hours later while I was back to my homework.

"Hey girl, I'm off!" Kelly adjusted her earring while running out of her bedroom. She had her pinky looped through a pair of heels while she tried to fix the hoop into her ear.

She was always off to some place with someone. I looked up at her over my laptop. "What's the adventure this time?"

Before she could answer, a knock at the front door pulled both of our attention to the foyer. I popped up and went to look through the peephole. "It's Shane," I whispered, plastering a mischievous smile on my face.

Kelly was such a maneater. That, or he had a great stash of nose candy. Kelly had a preference for the rich-kid substances on occasion—I told her it was no good, but she was in her wild-child era.

I opened the door to see Shane standing awkwardly with a bundle of flowers. He also dressed up from his standard casual attire. Kelly stumbled back into the hallway to ready herself just out of our direct line of vision.

"Wow," I said. "Are these for me? You shouldn't have." I held out my hands and took the flowers from him.

He gave a nervous laugh as I took them. "Is Kelly ready?"

She was poking her head out from the hallway with a thumbs up, finishing the buckles on her heels. "Yeah. Come on in. She might be ready, or it could take about a year for her to come out. I'll go put these in a vase."

Holding up the bouquet for her to see, I shuffled into the kitchen to arrange the flowers properly on the dining table. It was bittersweet to see a man come over with flowers; it made my heart squeeze for her. I secretly wished I hadn't holed myself up when I lived with Sylvia, but it was to protect myself. I had plenty of time to get flowers from a man.

"Almost... Ready!" She called over to Shane as she ran back to her room. He patiently stood in the foyer in wait.

I wondered what her plans consisted of. She kept a lot to herself, despite being my best friend. I never pried beyond what she was willing to share. Frankly, with the things I *did* hear, I didn't feel the need.

She finally appeared. Frazzled, but ready. I showed them both out and called out after them, "Don't do anything I wouldn't do! Love you, dude!"

I shut the door and sighed. *Ah, the house all to myself.*

Never mind. My phone rang in the kitchen. I hurried to look at who was calling and instantly wanted to cry. *Evans.*

"Hello." *Kill me.*

"Hello, Miss Montgomery. I would like to announce that we have heard you have not changed your major, and we are going to assign you a bodyguard as our new emerging CEO." His voice lacked personality.

"Is a bodyguard necessary?" Did my mom have one? Did I even know about them? My life was turning into a weird mess, one day at a time.

"You are the sole heir to your mother's company. I would

expect you to thank me for sending James, your new bodyguard."

He was serious, and his tone never deviated from being stuffy and devoid of personality. Speaking with members of the board made me curious about my mother's life—the one she never shared with me or bothered to mention. *She left it all to me, but why did I feel so blindsided by everything?*

"And you didn't think to send me one when I was younger?" It was a fair question.

"We tried. Your aunt was your guardian and told us no—she sent over the paperwork for her refusal."

Sylvia. The bane of my existence. I've always wondered what else she could have gotten up to while I lived with her. Outside of drinking and attempting to sleep her way into money, she treated me oddly. Sure, she was cruel and hit me when she was drunk, telling me to go back to my room, but she was always acting... strange. There was always a creepy smile plastered on her face, something straight out of a horror movie.

Maybe she was possessed by the devil.

"She *what*?"

"She was your appointed guardian, after all. We will discuss it when we meet formally in the boardroom. Be on the lookout for James in the morning. He will bring paperwork for you." *Click.*

I'd been assigned a bodyguard and had mild anxiety. Somehow, Sylvia still haunted me even after she had kicked me out of her house. When would the drama end? Last semester was far better, and I wanted to go back.

Back to just Kelly and me hanging out at home. Back to no boys around. Back to scary movies and popcorn nights. In reality, I wanted to go back and talk to my mom again so I could ask her all the questions I had. She left me far too soon.

There was no way to go back or change the past. All I could do was enjoy the memories—and try not to puke.

I plopped down on my bed, resigning myself to the thought that I wouldn't be doing any more homework—or thinking. My brain was too overloaded and didn't feel like a sponge anymore. Instead, I grabbed the remote and flipped on the television in my room to watch some low effort, mindless content.

The sun was right in my eyes, and I looked over at the curtains. Brent's jacket was hanging next to the window, staring at me. *Yes, I put it back up there.* What was I supposed to do with it? Would he come back for it?

I got up and ran my fingers over the smooth leather, wondering what adventures it had gone on or the girls it'd seen. The jacket was well-worn and had just the right number of creases to show it was used but loved. A few creases here and there. It had been through a lot, and I found myself relating to it in a way. *Looks like we've both been through some things.*

A thought hit me. "You know what? I'm going to return you to your owner. You've had a fun stay at my house, but I think it's finally time for you to go home."

There was no time to talk myself out of it. I pulled the jacket off the rack and stomped my way over to the living room while the sleeves slapped back and forth. He was going to get his jacket back so there were no ties left. I didn't want him holding this over me somehow.

I swung open the front door, and the cold air hit me. Was this a bad idea? Probably. Was I going back? Nope. The jacket was going back to him—goosebumps and cold be damned.

My eyes adjusted to the dim light outside as a figure stepped onto my porch.

"Hey, Blondie." His voice was just as smooth as the first time I spoke to him—he dripped silk and charm on all the girls most likely. It was irritatingly charming when he used that godforsaken nickname.

I froze in my tracks. "What the hell are you doing here?"

"Me? Out for an evening stroll. You?" His tone was too casual. How was he so nonchalant about everything? He probably wouldn't flinch at a dead body, given how at ease he was all the time.

"I'm bringing your stupid jacket back." My voice was a mix of irritation and exhaustion.

He crossed his arms and smiled. In the low light, I saw where the tattoos crept up his neck and ended at his jawline. His hair was cut short in a buzz cut, allowing everyone to see them. Brent was tatted to the max and his face always said *try me*. "Yikes. Lots of attitude tonight, babe."

This guy is ridiculous. I stepped fully outside and closed the door, standing as tall as possible. There was no way I'd let him see me shrink away from him even though he looked down at me from his height. He was a tower of a man; probably over six foot. I held his jacket in one hand with the other on my hip. "Here." I held it out while looking him in the eyes.

The jacket jutted out into the empty space between us, and he looked at it like it was a foreign object and cocked his head. "Took you long enough."

I grunted in frustration. "You could have just taken it with you the other night."

He pushed the jacket back at me. "Where's the fun in that?" He took a step closer, and I could smell him. He smelled like trouble today: sandalwood and warm amber with a hint of cigarette. It was a crime that he looked and smelled *this* good, considering his reputation. "Seems like I have been running through your mind for a while."

"Yes. Like a petulant child." I flared my nostrils in an angry huff, shoving the jacket back out at him again.

Unmoved, he looked me up and down, his gaze lingering longer than necessary. "So... dressed like that"—he paused, clearly staring—"you decided to come to my house and return my jacket?"

I glanced down at my pajamas—*skimpy*, consisting of a spaghetti strap crop top that could easily pass for a bra and too short satin shorts. I clicked my tongue and realized I must have looked ridiculous.

He was testing me. Trying to force my hand somehow. *What was his angle?* I found it hard to believe that the moment I decided to return his jacket to him, he just so happened to be waiting for me on my porch. It was a little *too* strange to be an innocent coincidence.

Did this guy read minds?

We locked eyes and the tension held between us felt thick. Palpable. For some reason he made my heart race and adrenaline course through my veins. "Yes," I said, shaking those thoughts away. I tried to cover myself in a feeble attempt to reclaim some semblance of modesty. It ended up in a weird attempt to cross my arms over my chest.

He mimicked my stance and folded his arms. An eyebrow raised, he played a teasing smile. "I like it when you dress like this for me. Do you dress like this for that *boyfriend* of yours?"

I ignored that. "Last chance," I snapped, holding the jacket back out. "Take it back this time, or I'm turning around and going back inside."

He chuckled and leaned against the porch railing. That deviant smile still played on his lips. His demeanor was nonchalant as usual and it annoyed me. What kind of guy was always playing these types of games? A fuckboy, that's who. One of his fingers found his chin and he gave a faux pondering expression. "Dealer's choice, then. The first option is getting my favorite riding jacket back. The second option is getting to watch you walk away from me in those skimpy little shorts of yours."

Anger coursed through my bones at his disrespect. My face reddened in a mix of embarrassment and rage. He really thought he could do and say whatever he wanted. "You're a disgusting asshole. Take your shit and get lost."

I threw the jacket at him with all the force I could muster.

He caught it easily. Instead of leaving me in peace, he stepped closer, our bodies barely a foot apart. I looked up at him as he towered over me, and his face wore that annoying smirk again. *If he weren't as hot as he was, I would probably stab him.* "Careful, babe. You're going to hurt my feelings." One of his hands came up to his chest in a mocking fashion.

"Unlikely." I moved my foot to take a step back but realized I was backed up to the door. There was nowhere for me to go unless I opened it and slammed it in his face. "You have your favorite, and probably overused, jacket back. Now, shoo." My hands flicked away from my body as if that would make him leave.

He wouldn't leave. Even if I thought he would, I had a feeling that he'd just be back again anyway. It was like he had to finish his conquest before moving on to the next girl, but he didn't realize I wouldn't give it up for him that easily. Garrett didn't even get an answer from me about whether I wanted to go exclusive with him or not.

In a move that felt typical for his type, he leaned in and placed a hand on the door behind me, his face directly above mine. His voice dropped into a low whisper that sent electricity through my spine and down to my toes. "You know what? I have a better idea: you come with me."

Breath didn't come easily to me when he was this close. I tried anyway. "I'm... not going anywhere with you." *Lie.*

His eyes darkened, his playful tone turning serious. "You sure? Because I'm not really asking." The space between us became almost nonexistent, and his face was inches from mine. Just like the first time we had this rodeo. And there went my breathing again. "Go change, Blondie. Otherwise, I'm taking you just like that." Hungrily, his gaze traveled down my body and lingered on my barely-there pajamas. "Not that I mind. You look so damn good in these." He snapped the strap of my top.

My heart pounded so loudly in my chest that I was sure he could hear it. I could hear it. Maybe the neighbors, too. There was *no way* he was going to drag me away in basically my underwear! "You're off your rocker," I hissed.

Bad idea. He seemed to like it.

"Maybe," he whispered. Those lips were dangerously close to my face. He moved his eyes from my lips up until he met my gaze; his expression was unreadable. "But I'm dead serious, Fallon. You should get dressed, or I'll haul you off in your irresistible little shorts. Your choice."

In the same moment he went to snap the waistband of my shorts, I turned to open the door and run through it, hoping to get through and slam it in his face. Before it could latch closed, his hand shot out and stopped my attempt to lock him out. The door halted in place, and I met his eyes with a challenge to try me.

He really thought he was going to cart me off like some prize. "Do you want to play this game?" His voice was low, daring me to try him.

Giving him my best angry glare, I tightened my grip on the door. *As if I could overpower him.* "I am not going anywhere with you," I groaned, struggling to push at the door.

A dark smile played in the crack of the door. *He looked like a serial killer.* With little effort, he pushed the door open, his eyes never leaving mine. He was asserting a sick form of dominance tonight. "You can try all you want to hide from me, but we both know you're not going to. Even if you locked me out, I'd still get back in to get you, dragging you out kicking and screaming."

Who the hell did this guy think he was? Did girls really like this shit? I pushed back with what my little arms could give me, and I secretly hated myself for eating gummy candy and not working out. If I were more fit, maybe I would have stood a chance. *Or not.* No dice; the door didn't budge. The intensity in his eyes showed he wasn't planning on backing down any time soon.

I gave up and released the door with a huff. He pushed his way inside, and I backed away quickly, keeping a close eye on his expression. He looked like the Big Bad Wolf coming for dinner.

Half running, half stomping, I made my way back to my room while making a feeble attempt to cover my ass with my hands. I locked the door. No way was he going to see any more of me. Throwing on a sweater and jeans haphazardly, I wanted to get my clothes on as fast as possible in case he made good on his word to break into locked areas. What nerve this guy had. Kidnapping—*really?*

When I poked my head out from behind the wall, I caught

him standing casually just inside the door. He was taking in the surroundings and looked far too comfortable in my house. Before I could psych myself out, I walked back into the living room, leaving a couch's worth of space between us.

His eyes flicked over to me and sparked in approval. *Good to know you approve of my clothes on too, asshole.*

He closed the distance between us, holding his jacket out. "Here," he said, spinning me around and draping it over my shoulders. "If you're going to be—unfortunately—clothed..."

I looked over my shoulder at him, confused by his sudden change in demeanor. First, he tried to kidnap me while wearing what appeared to be underwear. Then, he was being a gentleman by putting his jacket on me to keep me warm. *Sour, then sweet. Just like the candies I ate.*

Before I could process any of it, he scooped me up in one swift motion, slinging me over his shoulder like I weighed no more than a sack of potatoes.

"Brent!" I yelped, pounding my fists on his back and kicking out. "Put me down!" It felt pointless to struggle. He had a firm grip on me and patted my ass as he closed the front door behind him.

All he did was laugh while he carried me down the walkway. His *car* came into view and the realization hit me that he had planned this. I was just dumb enough to want to bring him his stupid jacket back at the same time in a twisted coincidence. He reveled in my resistance and slaps to his back—he loved it.

He wanted me to fight back more.

My ass found itself firmly planted on the seat of the passenger side and he strapped me into the seatbelt. We were off before I could get my bearings. The twisted game he was playing with me started once again.

12

Fallon

"We're here," he announced, slowly sliding his finger down my thigh, tapping my knee. His voice changed again—becoming more playful.

I glanced around, taking in the scene of a creepily lit parking lot. Lights flickered in the dark, and the shadowy silhouette of the back of a building in front of me convinced me once again that he might try to kill me. This guy was always taking me out to secluded and almost frightening places. "I knew you'd murder me eventually," I sighed.

His laughter was warm and genuine—unlike the parking lot where we sat. He climbed out of the car in one smooth motion, the creak of the door breaking the silence of the night.

He opened my door. *Odd*, but gentlemanly. I didn't want to leave the warm, safe car to meet my demise, but the cold air spilled in. The fresh air mingled with his cologne, bashing me in the face with fresh and warm, masculine scents. He was lucky that he smelled good.

A hand appeared in front of me, urging me to get out.

"After you." His naughty grin reappeared, and his eyes changed back to their normal mischievous glint. He was laying on the charm like it was molasses. If I had a choice, I would have stayed in the car.

Conceding, I took his hand firmly. *No softness for him.* I tried not to focus on the firm grip he had or the warmth of his fingers while he pulled me out of the car and laced his fingers with mine. Handholding? For Brent Vaughn?

I forced myself to think about the cool night air against my neck and the faint scent of trees around us. *Not* on the warm feeling in my stomach. No, I listened for the distant hums of cars and life around me instead of the man who had me out here all alone. Not the nervous energy I had brewing, nor the way he was looking at me.

Why did he look at me that way?

"You wanted to haul me here in my pajamas?" I asked, *definitely* not focusing on the fact that we were holding hands and walking quickly toward this dark building.

"Yep," he replied coolly, gripping my hand a bit tighter.

"Where are we?" I fidgeted with my necklace with my free hand, wondering what awaited us inside.

He flashed a teasing smile over his shoulder. "You'll see."

The building was dark—like, dark, dark. It could have been abandoned for all I knew. Confusion washed over me as I wondered what the hell plans he had made for the night. The door creaked open, revealing a too dark hallway.

The entire place was pitch black.

I'm so dead for real this time. Kelly, I am so sorry.

I thought I smelled... popcorn?

He dragged me through a series of endless, dark hallways while our shoes squeaked on the linoleum. He stopped to present me with a final door and opened it to reveal an empty ice-skating lobby illuminated by a single flickering light.

The door to the rink opened, and an even cooler air washed over me. Nostalgia crept in, and for a moment, I could vividly remember my mom.

The vast open space awaited me. The ice, perfectly smoothed by a Zamboni, awaited.

I felt like I was home for a moment.

Brent broke the silence. "Just the two of us here tonight."

"I guess I'm too embarrassing to be seen with you around other people." I let a smart-ass remark slip while I took in my surroundings. It happened when I wasn't paying much attention to someone talking. I was focused on the feeling of good times.

The smell of a skating rink remained the same, no matter which rink you visited. They all just felt the same. And I felt like I was a kid again with my mom.

God, how I missed her.

"What's your skate size?" He brushed off my remark. Nothing could break that ironclad ego of his.

"It's been a while. Maybe a six, maybe a seven." I shrugged.

He disappeared into the hallway without another word. I almost didn't notice with how entranced I was in the space.

Part of me wondered what his angle was. Out of all the girls he could possibly set his sights on, why me? It wasn't like I was some standout girl on campus—just another face in the crowd, blending in without much effort. Maybe some people wondered if I got in on a scholarship, especially if they didn't know my name, and that was fine by me.

I thought back to the first time I saw him—or at least thought I did. He was goading that fight in his front yard like some typical bad boy movie cliché. I didn't think he truly noticed me, but with those looks he gave me, it was confirmation enough. Then, the campus-wide back-to-school bash, where he lurked in the shadows until I stumbled outside. The cigarette he gave me led to my willingly getting on the back of his bike for a night out.

It wasn't like me to do that. Not to mention Garrett. Two men vying for my attention? *Wild.* One of them asked me to be his girlfriend, yet I was out with the other one.

So, unlike me.

But Kelly encouraged adventure and hot guys.

I just didn't think a hot guy would include the notorious campus playboy, Brent Vaughn. He was a *use her and lose her* type of guy.

The lights flicked on with a loud hum and my thoughts dissipated.

"Miss me?" His voice came from behind, dripping with the same charm he wielded like a weapon.

I grabbed the skates from him forcefully and plopped down on a bench to try them on. No way was I giving him the satisfaction of a response. He was far too cocky in his confidence. He played the cool guy routine way too hard—there was no way girls fell for it.

If they did… *Ew.*

"Let's see what you've got." He stepped out onto the smooth ice, gliding backward with an ease that felt almost like a taunt.

I took my time easing onto the ice and found my footing, as if it were only yesterday that I was last on the ice. Despite bouncing from hobby to hobby, I *always* returned to skating. Sitting still was never really my thing.

The sound of the blades slicing through the ice felt like a lullaby from home. It reminded me of Mom. She always encouraged me to try anything that caught my eye and even joined in on some lessons, despite her complete lack of coordination.

I started slowly, allowing the rhythm of the blades on the ice to calm my nerves. I could feel his eyes on my back as I made my rounds to shake off the residual tension. I wondered what we were doing here tonight. What we were doing here together. What were his intentions?

"I think I'm warmed up," I called out across the rink. I shrugged off the anger and frustration that had characterized my life lately. *The ice is working its magic.* Depending on how Brent behaved, staying calm could still have been an option.

He was still there, watching me from the sidelines. The expression on his face—the cool guy look—wasn't there anymore. Was that a curious look painted on his face?

Whatever it was, it made me feel weird.

What did he want from me?

It didn't take him long after I slowed down to push off and skate directly toward me. His movements were practiced like he had spent a lot of time on the ice. Pretty funny for a baseball player if you asked me. The way he moved on the field and the ice screamed athlete. That, along with major confidence—well, cockiness. He had a certain way about him.

"Someone is full of surprises," he said on his way over.

"Am I?" Facing him, I pushed off to skate away from his approach. I knew his intentions toward me, and I wasn't going to let him get there.

He leaned into his movements to try to catch up. "I didn't take you for a pro."

"My mom let me take lessons." I pulled myself into a small spin to divert my path away from him. "I was encouraged to explore my own interests in life. She even joined me a few times for my lessons."

"She sounds great." His voice dropped lower, softer than his usual tone.

"She was." He matched my pace, gliding up next to me. I looked up at him for once, meeting his softened eyes. "What about you? You're a baseball guy. I didn't think they were too good on the ice."

"I am a baseball guy, but there's a lot you don't know about me."

"Care to elaborate?"

That arrogant-ass smile came back, lighting up his face. "Question for a question?" He shifted to skate backward, taking my hands in his.

"Is this how you usually impress girls?" I challenged.

His eyes focused on mine. "Only the ones who won't fall for my boyish charm."

I rolled my eyes. "You think you're so smooth, Brent."

Ignoring my comment, he pondered to himself for a moment. He took the question for question game seriously. "What is the biggest secret you're keeping?"

He thought he was so funny, didn't he? "Nice try, buddy."

"Had to try." He shrugged.

It was my turn. "What is it you want, Brent? Like, in life or anything else?"

117

The pace between us slowed down as if I had caught him off guard. "Do you think about this a lot?"

"If I have to answer, you do too."

He nodded.

"Yeah," I sighed. "I think about what my mom wanted for me before she died. About my best friend, Kelly, moving on with her life at some point. Where I would be after that and what it is that I want for myself in the future."

It wasn't a lie. I did think about it *a lot*. What would happen when Kelly moved on? I never made extra friends or found any stability in being alone. My mom left me her entire empire, and I had no idea how to handle it.

Brent picked up the pace again and I caught a moment of his eyebrows furrowing. He was searching for the answer. "What does Brent Vaughn want? For so long, I think it's been about living up to my grandfather's expectations. I think a simple answer to my endgame question is to be free to make my own choices."

I poked him. "Is that why you're so broody all the time?"

"Ah, ah." He waved his finger at me, eyes flashing with intensity. "My turn. What do you really think of me, Fallon?"

"Hmm." I tapped my finger to my chin. "I think you're a big oaf." Laughing, I skated away from him.

My feet were tired, but I persisted in skating for a few more rounds. Question for a question died out into silence, and I watched him in the comfortable ambiance of the music that played in the background.

I plopped down onto a bench and pulled the skates off. My feet burned. The last time I was on the rink was far too long ago. It made me feel good to be back out here—my mom would have wanted me to.

Then again, I didn't feel like I truly knew everything about my mother. She kept a lot from me and left me with things I wasn't aware of.

Brent sat beside me and leaned into my shoulder. His chin dipped low, brushing my ear. "Hungry?" Shivers ran down my spine. His tone was far too sensual for the question he had just asked.

I pulled back and eyed him.

He clapped a hand to my thigh. "Let's go, Blondie."

We drove away from the rink and into the darkened sky. I caught him looking over at me from the reflection in the window multiple times. It still confused me as to why he was showing such interest in me. I wasn't special in any way.

And putting this much effort into sleeping with someone? *Weird.*

Brent chose the place to eat. A drive-in fast-food joint where I was ready to order the entire menu. After his little kidnapping stunt, a scant breakfast, and skating around for a while, I was ravished. I went for two fully loaded double cheeseburgers, a large tray of tater tots, onion rings, and a chocolate peanut butter milkshake.

When I broke the trance I was in while ordering from the menu, I saw him looking at me more amused than ever.

I stifled a laugh. "What? I told you I was hungry."

He matched my order with a laundry list of his own and looked over at me. "Can't have your tiny ass out eating me."

The neon lights mixed with the moonlight across the dashboard as I got cozy in the passenger seat. The atmosphere between us felt changed in some way. Maybe it was the food being delivered; maybe it was something about astrology. I didn't know.

He leaned over to lower the music. "Can I be honest?"

Suspicious. "Sure." I'd already eaten half of my first burger before he'd even eaten more than a few fries.

"I have never seen someone your size eat so much food." His tone was light and his eyes were curious. It was like he was sizing me up, trying to get a read on me. If it wasn't him, I'd assume it was someone trying to get to know me.

But it was Brent. His reputation stated that he had ulterior motives.

I shoved an onion ring into my mouth and chewed it slowly.

"I didn't have much for breakfast before *someone* came to my house and rudely kidnapped me. Can you believe they were trying to take me in my pajamas? Not cool." The last of my burger was inhaled before I crumpled up the wrapper and tossed it into the bag.

My second burger came out immediately. I didn't lie; I was so freaking hungry.

He started in on his burger. "Wow, the *audacity* of some people."

We shared a genuine laugh between us. There seemed to be more and more of them coming as I spent time with him. It made me wonder when he'd try to take my pants off.

Internally, I smacked myself on the forehead. Stupid, stupid. You should be out with Garrett right now. You are playing with serious fire right now. Oh God, what would my mother think of me?

"So"—he turned his body as much as he could in the car to face me completely—"besides food, what else do you enjoy?"

Was he seriously asking me questions like it was a genuine date? *Odd.* I took a sip of my shake to buy myself a few seconds. "Music. My hobbies. Good company."

"Good company? Like me?" There he went again, smiling like it was his strongest weapon.

I sighed dramatically. "You wouldn't be so bad if it weren't for the whole kidnapping thing. Don't let it go to your head, Mr. Big Ego."

He leaned back to get comfortable. "I wouldn't dream of it, babe." A small tilt of his head had him looking at me again. "How many boys are you currently torturing besides me? I *think* I know of one other, but you're such a little man eater."

I focused on the milkshake in my hand. That was awkward, considering I'd never slept with anyone and could count on one hand how many people I had kissed for real. *It was one.* "Says the womanizer."

"Touché."

"How many women are you teasing?" If he wanted to play, I could play.

"She's such a feisty one, isn't she?"

I glared at him. I could be feisty. I bet there was a tutorial online about it.

"Lucky for you, you don't know the first thing about me." I dipped my tater tot and popped it in my mouth.

He eyed my choice of condiment. "I know you prefer honey mustard now. I know that you're a good ice skater. You're incredibly shy. You touch your necklace when you get nervous. Which, around me, you always are. Shall I go on?"

My milkshake was suddenly the most interesting thing in the world.

"I didn't hear a rebuttal. I rest my case."

Then, my tater tots became the most interesting thing. "Why do you have such a reputation?"

"Because people love to talk. They love drama and things that don't bring light to their own shitty lives." He pulled the straw from his soda up to his lips, challenging me to continue the conversation. "Why do *you* care so much about my reputation?"

I think he liked throwing me off kilter. "Who said I cared about it?"

"You did. Come on, do you really think I can't tell your heart rate is hammering in your chest?" He leaned in, stroking his finger up my neck to my jawline. "That I can't see the suspicion behind your eyes? Or that you're curious about what it would be like with me? Maybe... you secretly like my reputation."

His hand deserved the smack I gave it before I quickly adjusted myself in the seat. "No." *Maybe.* Heat quickly rose to my cheeks, and I avoided eye contact. "And that's more than enough."

"I already got my answer. Last question: Where do you want to go next time?"

Next time?

Was this man trying to court me?

Not only was I asked to be someone's girlfriend, but I was also now being asked out on a date by the type of man I swore I would stay away from.

What would my mother think of me?

That was a question, and I had to answer it per the rules we set indiscriminately. "I've never played baseball."

Something lit up his face. Excitement? Surprise? Both?

He took my free hand in his and brought it to his lips. "I thought you'd never ask. I'll show you how to play baseball so well that you'd be sought out by the MLB."

"You won't be the star of the team after I'm done with you."

I ate everything I ordered with ease and tucked the trash into the bag. It was a habit to ensure I never made a mess anywhere. A habit I picked up in the name of self-preservation. Some might have called it a trauma response, but I was no therapist—nor had I ever seen one.

There was a small moment of softness on his face when I looked up. He pulled my hand into his and gently clasped them together. "Ready to go?"

All I could do was nod. Inside the car felt far too comfortable. The music too well picked. If I were to guess, he wanted to woo me before trying to get me into bed. The *why* question still lingered in my mind. Especially when he started tracing circles on my hand with his thumb.

After what I imagined was a struggle with the thought of kidnapping me again, he put the car in drive, choosing the long way home. I leaned against the window to enjoy the cast of fleeting lights on my face.

"Falling asleep on me again?"

"It's been late each time you dragged me out," I mumbled. "You can't blame me for being tired."

"You know, they say if you can fall asleep in someone's presence, that means you're comfortable with them."

That had to have been the funniest thing I'd heard all year. "Guess you're cozy with a lot of girls, then."

"Fucking and sleeping are different."

I kept my eyes closed with my face turned toward the window. There was no need for me to see his expression to know I had struck a chord. The big, bad playboy got offended when it came to relationships.

That information would be useful to have in my back pocket.

"Ah, yes. One requires a certain level of *depth*."

Despite his irritation at my response, I felt an odd sense of ease, like the first night on the back of his motorcycle. Minus the wind.

The car stopped at the curb, and we both looked at the glowing porch light. The shiny beacon told me Kelly was home.

Brent put the car in park and turned to me. "Does the light mean that your friend is home?"

My eyebrow perked up on its own. "It means that it's too dark for me to be outside."

A deep chuckle escaped him before he leaned in closer. "How about a kiss before you go in, then? Over here since she interrupted us last time." He nodded in the general direction of my house.

He was amusing; I'd give him that. He also made me roll my eyes a thousand times during each conversation. "You're something else."

"You wound me." He dramatically grasped his chest like he'd been shot.

His ego probably took a few hits when he was with me.

"Oh, you'll be fine." I slapped his shoulder.

He persisted, leaning over to me and making his lips pucker. It was funny to watch happen in real time. The infamous playboy begging for a kiss? *Peak comedy.*

I placed my finger to his lips. "I'll think about it."

"Fair enough." He pulled back, wasting no time getting out of the car and opening my door in record time. He offered his hand and walked me to my door.

Again.

At the front door, he looked down at me. "Night, babe," is

what came out of his mouth as he grabbed my face in his hands. Then, this insane man *kissed my forehead*.

I blinked.

"See you around, Blondie." His tone was the usual nonchalant and irritating one. I had no time to respond as he marched down the path and back to his car. He was clearly pleased with himself.

The door opened to reveal Kelly glaring at me once again. "Spill. The. Beans," she said, pulling me inside.

13

Brent

I never thought I'd turn down an opportunity to get laid. But there I was, telling Sloane no again. It was hard to avoid the clingy brat.

She was blocked from my phone—too many drunk texts and calls. Also, far too many nudes. Those weren't as bad, but I didn't want those to show up at an inopportune time. Fallon was mine to claim, and no one would deter me. Not even myself.

Unfortunately for me, Sloane was persistent and showed up wherever she thought I would be. She wouldn't take no for an answer.

And if she found out who I was pursuing, Fallon would be put under a sniper's red dot. Sloane and her family were brutal in this life we lived. They had the power to kill without question, and Sloane always wanted to weasel her way in to make a nice business deal for her family. It was all about money and power.

On top of that, Fallon was set to take over her mother's company, according to what the Dictator told me—along with advising me to stay away from her. That left an open spot for a hostile takeover or just the total destruction of the company. It made *some* sense why he didn't want me around her, but I wasn't going to pay that any mind.

I would, however, protect her as much as possible in our

world. It was abundantly clear she was completely innocent. Sex had nothing to do with her innocence. When we spoke, she had a childlike wonder about things—an excitement that I wished I had for the world. What was also apparent was that her mother told her jack shit about the life we lived and waded through. What piqued my curiosity was *why* she was ignorant to our lives. Fallon was sorely unprepared for a life amongst the elites, and she had no one to teach her the ropes.

Until she met me.

"Look, Sloane, I am going to be late for practice, and you continually coming to my house or places that you think I'll be is just draining at this point." My front door was cracked open just enough to let me speak to her, but I kept the lock chain connected. I knew how she was.

"You act like you have an option here. I can make one call to my parents and your grandfather will have your ass. The time for your silly little games is over." There she went, making threats again, believing her family had real influence over mine.

Maybe it did. Maybe it didn't. I never tested her like this. "Making threats isn't how you get cooperation." That was a lie. It was definitely how I got cooperation.

What I meant was *making threats doesn't bode well for romantic partners*, but my point was still made from the look on her face. She would get wrinkles too quickly from how often she twisted her face up like that.

Botox would start early for her. *If it hadn't already.*

"It's the only way you'll listen to me." She crossed her arms, her too small purse falling off her shoulder and down her arm. That seemed to anger her even more as she shoved it back with a huff.

When Slone didn't get her way, everyone needed to prepare for a toddler-esque temper tantrum.

Did I mention how much I hated the elites?

"No." I rubbed my face and sighed. "You must be thinking of your other boy toy."

She leaned up against the door frame to bat her eyes at me.

The softening of her face looked better than the twisted expression. "Don't you worry. My daddy will convince you."

Thank God she left.

"Who was at the door?" Josh walked out into the kitchen, freshly out of bed.

I poured myself a cup of coffee, needing the caffeine. "Just a girl who can't take a hint."

"Lady killer." He laughed.

"Lady *avoider*," I mumbled.

He held up a carton of eggs. "Want some?"

"Sure."

"So, what's up with the lady avoidance? Never knew you to turn down pussy." He turned to me after setting up the stove, his eyes wide. "Are you going *monogamous*?"

I waved him off, diving back into the cup of bitter coffee. "Nah. Sloane's just a level ten clinger."

"I don't know, man. I wouldn't cross her."

"Yeah, yeah. I have other shit to worry about."

"Like?"

Like the information I discovered about Fallon. Like the quest I sent Reaper on. Like the overwhelming number of rats that kept popping up. "Work and shit. My grandfather has me working more than ever. Then there's keeping up with baseball and classes." The classes part was a lie, but everyone made the same comment.

"What's it like to be the grandson of the richest man since ever?"

He asked me that a lot. Being from a family that could afford just enough, Josh couldn't comprehend that there were zero obstacles if you had the funds. "Tiring," was all I said.

"I could imagine. You're going to take over for him one day, right?"

"Right."

"Alright, everyone! Lace up and start your laps!"

Practice for baseball was one of the few places where I tried to clear my mind. Exercise and pistol whipping have taken up much of my time lately, aside from keeping tabs on my girl. I was protecting my grandfather's investment in her mother in a way. Though he wouldn't see it that way.

Stay away from the Montgomery girl.

No thanks. That made her more tempting.

If only I could just feel how soft those lips were for once...

"Vaughn! Pick up the goddamned pace!" Coach blew the whistle, making everyone turn to watch my slow jog. "What the fuck is up with you today? Does baseball mean nothing to you?"

I hastened. "Sorry, coach!"

He shook his head, disappointed.

"Late night?" One of the guys taunted.

"Yeah, your mom knows how to tire a man out. I loved tag teaming her with Emily, too."

Whoops, Oliver didn't like that too much.

Oliver was the hot-headed one. I never liked him much on or off the field. He was uptight and didn't blend well with the team. Despite being a decent pitcher, the guy didn't have much else going for him. The team hated his attitude.

"Hey, it's not worth it," one of the guys whispered to Oliver as he turned around and stopped in his tracks.

I prepped myself. The anger was already visible in his body movements as he stalked towards me.

"No. Fuck you!" His spit landed in my face.

Well, that was lovely. I needed a shower anyway. "Not into dudes, sorry."

I ducked a fist coming in my direction; it was sloppy. It was always sloppy when they were emotional. Considering I mentioned his mom and girlfriend in the same sentence, I understood his outburst. I just didn't care.

We played a cute game where he attempted punches, and I dodged them. I really wished he would put up a better fight.

"What the fuck is your problem, Brent?"

I caught his hand and twisted it, giving him a cruel smile. "The better question"—I shoved him to the ground—"is what isn't my problem?"

Practice was over. Coach blew the whistle, and my punishment was being sequestered away from the guys with a *stop starting fights* speech. Since the Dictator was richer than God, nothing happened to me.

Or any of the other rich brats here.

"Can we at least keep the fights to somewhere else? I'm trying to run a fucking baseball team, here." Coach looked like he was at his wits end with all of us.

My face conveyed disinterest. "If they can keep their pussies from crying, sure. I'm not the one prone to these emotional outbursts. If you noticed, I didn't throw the first punch."

He wasn't looking too happy. The stress lines on his face had grown deeper. I wagered that being an employee here, under constant pressure and threats, would age a man faster than milk left on the counter. "Brent..." he sighed.

"Yeah, yeah." I waved him off. "Don't fret, Coach. I'll leave. I'm sure I'm due for another earful here soon. You can tell everyone I was kicked out of practice again."

He didn't argue.

That's how things always happened for me. Cops tried not to arrest me despite my scenes being public and sometimes caught on tape. The school let me skirt by with less-than-ideal grades. Fear of the Vaughn name was everywhere.

I flipped my phone out of my bag right on cue.

"Yes, sir?"

"Stop fighting at baseball practice where people have cameras."

"Yes, sir."

The irritation at my being a disappointment was loud in his silence. "Report to work later. You have things to do. Try not to need me to bail your ass out."

Click.

My next move was to text Reaper to meet up. He never liked working with the other guys we had on the top cleaning crew.

Here we go to work again, I thought.

And, of course, he just responded with a picture of a cat wielding a knife. He was not normal.

14

Brent

"Nice face."

Reaper chuckled. "I hide mine so you don't feel so bad about yours."

"One of these days, my grandfather will give me the green light to shoot you."

"He already gave me one for you, but I felt too bad about how ugly you are."

From the intel he gathered about Jason Haines, we found ourselves staking out a warehouse on orders from the Dictator. Why he sent me out like a henchman would forever irk me.

What we knew was that Jason Haines was planning something. What that something was? Either I was kept out of those conversations, or we just didn't know. The rules of the game changed consistently, and it was a struggle to keep up.

We sat out there for hours looking for signs of anything. It was basically like watching paint dry in a refrigerator.

Reaper shoved something into my ribs. "Mint?"

"No, and keep your voice down."

"Your breath smells bad."

An SUV pulled into the lot, and two men with briefcases shuffled out. I focused the rangefinder on what they were carrying—locked cases that most likely contained money, drugs, or goods unable to be traded in the daylight. Trench coats and locked cases at one in the morning? Yeah, nefarious.

"Code combos to get into the cases. Two out and one driver."

Reaper yawned in response.

My bet was that Jason wasn't going to handle this on his own. Too dirty for his prissy little fingers. He was the bane of my grandfather's existence. When Maria received her diagnosis, someone spilled the beans, and Jason was there to try to replace her as a mentee and gain access to the cushier side of the top one percenters.

Why continue to be middle class when you can sit next to God Himself?

Only that didn't work. Augustus Vaughn *hated* Jason with a passion for being a lazy opportunist and called him far too many names. Jason then left with a chip on his shoulder and a vow to destroy the family line.

Which included me.

"I can't hear shit."

I slapped him. "Shut the fuck up."

"Like they can hear us."

"At least lower your fucking voice."

A small group formed near the entrance of the building. Like Reaper said, I couldn't hear shit. Voices were obscured, and my best bet was to catch some lip reading with my view.

The men who arrived handed over their locked cases to the overly dressed guards and said what looked like *for the boss*. Too bad they didn't just say *Jason Haines* to make my life easier. The smaller one took the first case inside—to check it, I supposed.

Standing awkwardly, one was smoking until the first came back out with a nod to take the other case back. We waited to see what it would turn into. The second case came back with the same nod of approval. The two suits nodded at each other before handing over a duffel bag to the trench coats to send them on their way.

"Looks like a regular business deal to me. I'm hungry."

Bang!

"Mhm."

The suits gunned down the trench coats. Hostile deal?

The only reason for gunning down a business deal is if you had the upper hand over another company and wanted to tip the first domino. Make them think you were coming in guns blazing. In reality, their plan had been set in motion a long time ago. Was the attacker Jason? Or was Jason the one being attacked?

If only we had the proper intel to know what the fuck was going on.

Feeling a step behind in every situation was getting really fucking tiring.

The driver stepped out and calmly walked over to the suits, shaking each of their hands. There was no good view of him in that big ass jacket, with the hood up and a hat obscuring most of his face. Casual body language told me this had been a large setup.

I hesitated to speak or look away from the view. "Think we can ID the two dead guys?"

"Can try. Unless they burn the bodies."

"Why would they—"

He pointed to where they were drowning the dead in a liquid from a red canister. *Well, fuck me sideways.*

Flames. The bodies went up in flames after the driver tossed a match onto them. They weren't even good enough for a lighter. Just a wooden match. With them up in flames, our opportunity to figure out who they were also went up in smoke.

I slumped in my hiding spot. "I am *literally* never going to get this shit right."

Reaper clapped a hand to my shoulder. "Probably not, but I bet there's a good burger out there with our names on them."

Go do the job. Come back and report. That was the majority of my time spent working under the Dictator. We had a regular group of specialized cleaners who trained me after I found myself in one too many situations that *would* have landed me in jail—if I were anyone else.

Maybe he had a plan for me by training me under these guys. Maybe he didn't. Maybe I was just a nuisance and doing the dirty work wasn't a complete waste of time for my grandfather.

The Dictator. The man was one.

"Thanks, Martha." I nodded as she set our plates down.

She gave me a sideways look with a raised eyebrow before turning away and walking to the back of the kitchen.

"Damn, what did you do to Miss Martha?" Reaper rolled up his mask to expose his mouth.

"You never take that shit off, do you?"

"Nope."

There were only three times I'd seen him eat; this was one of them. What I saw was five o'clock shadow and tanned skin. Some tattoos peeked out from his neck, too.

He changed topics. "How's that little new—*not* aunt—fuck buddy of yours Mr. Vaughn said not to touch?"

How was she? I would have given anything to know what my little Blondie was like in bed. Soft skin against mine, those sweet lips screaming my name, and every part of her melting in my hands? Soon, I'd get there and memorize every inch of her with my eyes, hands, and mouth. She just needed to let me in long enough to realize I wasn't who she thought I was.

"Bratty." I shoved a fry in my mouth.

"Aren't they all? Anyway, I received confirmation that the Haines team is running surveillance on her. She's the one they've been looking out for in their rise to power. Don't ask me how I know; just trust me on the intel."

I waited silently for him to continue.

"This is where you say, 'Great job, Reaper!' and give me brownie points."

I kicked him instead.

"Feisty. I like it. Next time, make it harder, daddy. Jason and his people—or girlfriend lady—have been keeping a close eye on her since she left whatever family member she was holed up with until she turned eighteen. I did more recon on *that* info and found out via *our* intel that this aunt of hers forged some paperwork, putting you and your grandfather in some deep shit. Montgomery Group is scrambling to address the legal nightmare and digging into who may have been a rat on that end of things. Someone decided to play chess with their hostile takeover."

My fists over-clenched so tightly that my burger fell apart in my hands. "So, she's also involved in the shit we've been fighting for the last however many years?"

He didn't seem too bothered as he funneled onion rings into his mouth. "Yeah, pretty much. Except, from what it looks like to me, she doesn't even know the game she's a part of. She's more like a cute little deer just prancing around until the hunter takes his shot."

Great.

"Then why didn't the Dictator want me near her?" Scaring her off wasn't a good enough excuse, and I cringed at the other motives he may have had up his sleeve.

He shrugged. "That's not a question for me, boss. I put *my* neck out to get you this info. Do me a favor and don't let me get cut this time."

The tone in his voice said he was serious for once, and it made me wonder how many times he'd been burned before. I knew nothing of his past, but the fact that he *hides his face* tells me it's probably not a great one. "I doubt he'd even listen to me, even if I told him the words he wanted to hear verbatim."

"When are you bringing that little girlfriend of yours back around?" My coffee cup got a refill from Martha while she gave me a stern look. As if I'd made Fallon run for the hills after I brought her here. If anything, *she* deserved the stern look if I found out she told my grandfather about me bringing Fallon here.

Reaper looked me up and down, his eyes a little curious. "She's your girlfriend-not-aunt-fuckbuddy now?"

"Your what now?" Jesus, one of these days Reaper's lack of filter might give Martha a heart attack.

I waved off Reaper's comment. "She didn't run for the hills if that's what you're asking."

Everyone seemed to have a vested interest in Fallon. The innocent little rich girl, who seemed to hold the key to everything, was at the very center of a large elite game. I wondered if she knew how important she was.

I wanted to show her.

"If you bring this Belushi around her, she might. You, Mr. Mask, need to mind your manners." A scolding from Martha. No man was safe from one—not even Reaper.

He held up his napkin to wave his white flag. "Sorry, Miss Martha, I'll mind my tongue."

She cleared the table, and we agreed that we had no idea what had happened at the warehouse earlier. The information we received was solely to observe a business transaction and report back on who did what and who might be involved.

"We need to figure out who that driver was," I said, settling into my car seat and starting the engine.

Reaper strapped in and gave me an unsettling look. "Let me tell you about what else I found out that I couldn't talk about in the diner."

15

Fallon

I stared through the back window into the beautiful oasis that had been carefully curated for us by the not-so-hot construction crew that came in over the past weekend. Kelly was disgruntled there weren't more hotties available to work with their shirts off. Despite the lack of eye candy, I was enamored with our newly installed hot tub and the nearly completed natural pool.

"These guys really knocked it out of the park over the weekend." I took a sip of my hot coffee, snuggled in my favorite new pink robe.

Kelly stepped up beside me in her plushy blue robe. "The waterfall by the pool is going to be epic."

"It'll be especially great for whoever lives here next." A silent lament that not all good things last. School wouldn't last forever, and Kelly would eventually move on.

She sighed longingly. "Can we just stay here for, like, ever? No men, just us besties until the end of time?"

"I wish," I scoffed. "I bet Evans would drag me out of here, kicking and screaming, to the concrete jungle of New York. You might want to look into getting a cat."

I turned my attention to the bag I had packed with my laptop and books, hating that my future felt so... predetermined. By a bunch of men in a boardroom. By my mother. If she were still alive, would I still be facing the same future?

I shoved off the what ifs. She wasn't here anymore. She left it all to me.

As for the boardroom suits, they were simply doing their jobs. All very corporate, but still their jobs. Everyone had a family to feed.

The meeting on Sunday morning went by far too quickly. My path to leadership was laid out very bluntly—there was no mention of the shenanigans that Sylvia got up to while I was under her care, but I figured that was a conversation for a different time. I was to take on meetings, listen to my bodyguard, and expect someone to *drop by* to deliver paperwork and bring me up to speed.

The drop-ins were also their way of micromanaging me and ensuring I wasn't acting out of line.

The meeting also wasn't *just* a meeting. It was an intervention.

"Remember how those stuffy men told me I needed to change my major to something more *appropriate* for an up-and-coming CEO?"

She didn't break her gaze away from the hot tub. "Yeah, why?"

"Well, I need to go get dressed and get to campus so I can lament my freedom of choice in my life with my advisor." I set my cup down on the counter and threw my robe off onto the couch. "I am going to need some serious ice cream therapy after today."

Kelly mimicked my movements dutifully. "I am coming with you. Homework be damned!"

~

The student center was one of the largest buildings on campus, making one of those warehouse stores look like a boutique experience—minus the warehouse vibe. It spanned into more wings than I cared to keep track of, and the map for this place was so large that you'd need a guided tour each time you came in. The wealthy loved two things: their architecture and their unnecessarily large buildings.

It was built to look elegant, to impress both the parents who paid for it and the scholarship kids who attended. The rest of us probably didn't care as much. The neutrally bland color scheme said *I have money and no personality*. With an entrance that resembled Grand Central Station, I could have easily mistaken this place for an actual train station.

My stop?

Academic advising.

I smiled awkwardly at the receptionist who looked like she didn't care about her job. She was half scrolling through social media and half looking at me, expecting an answer. "I have an appointment with my advisor, Mrs. Matthews."

She flipped out a tablet. "Name?"

"Fallon Montgomery."

"Student key card?" She *still* hadn't given me proper eye contact.

I handed it over the counter and wondered what made her feel so lifeless at work. Would I turn into someone who didn't even give another person a second glance? Or even a first? With the respect my mother instilled in me, I also wondered if she embodied that at her company.

Sarah, or so it said on her name tag, pointed to a door as she went back to scrolling on her phone.

The hallway was narrow and long, lined with office after office. It felt too much like a conveyor belt in here, transporting the students from idealistic young adults to whatever was spat out on the other end. My room came up when I saw the sign for my advisor.

"What can I help you with today, Miss Montgomery?" At least there was a smile on the other side of the door.

I itched my arm and fidgeted with my bracelet. "I'm here to see about changing my major."

145

Before my ass even hit the seat, she was quickly typing up a storm and had several sheets of paper printed out and displayed across her desk. At least she was efficient. "Before you do, let's go over the sophomore requirements for your undergrad in the first two years. You did more than full-time last year, knocking out a lot of classes right off the bat. I'm impressed that you maintained a perfect GPA while doing one point five times the recommended full-time hours."

She turned back to her desk to click clack away at her keyboard before printing even *more* papers to spread out in front of me. I aspired to type that quickly.

"These three classes align with your currently declared major. It looks like you are taking two out of four on campus—math and biology. Your online classes may be affected, which will have you spending more time on campus than previously expected." She was drawing circles, doodling across the page in advisor-style notations while my insides churned.

"Can we look at all possible options?" I was already reeling from this entire semester, and we were nowhere close to midterms.

Mrs. Matthews was perched and ready at her computer. "Of course! What are you thinking of changing to? Will you declare a minor as well?"

I fidgeted again. "I'd like to see my options for something business related."

She clicked around, printing out more pages to spread out and markup. She rattled off a bunch of majors that sounded like no fun at all. "We offer a general business degree that encompasses all aspects, or we have accounting, finance, marketing, international business, and business administration. There are some other niche majors if you are looking to pinpoint something within the business realm."

The inside of my lip was going to be minced meat by the end of this conversation. "What happens if I can't change my classes this semester?"

The reassuring look on her face told me that she'd handled

many a situation like mine before. Parents demanding that their kids change majors after finding out they were pursuing something unrelated to the family business felt like a normal occurrence here.

"Your major change does not have to happen this semester." She smiled—a warm smile. "Here, if you look, you can finish this semester as is. These two classes here can be applied to your extra credit classes—free credits, as they call them. With your overtime work last semester, I think this puts you in a fine spot to finish this one out as planned."

That sparked a little bit of hope inside my chest. That I would still get to feel like myself for one more semester before I was forced to concede and continue with the plan laid out for me.

"So, no immediate change is needed?" I asked.

"No immediate changes needed," she said, collecting up the scattered papers on her desk into a neat pile. She paperclipped them for good measure. "Come back closer to when classes are about to open, and we can build out your schedule. Now, do you have an idea of which major you were considering changing to?"

"The general business degree." I wanted to scream and cry that my life was ending, but I began to realize that I was a nepo baby. I'd just been shielded from that fact for a long, long time.

What the hell did my mother expect me to do as basically a declawed cat? My stomach flipped in my chair at the thought. There was a big world out there of which I was blissfully unaware.

"Shall I get you squared away with a redeclaration?"

I nodded in response. If I had tried to speak, I might have cried.

It felt as though I held my breath through the rest of the conversation, admitting defeat and coming to terms with what my life truly was. I was Fallon Montgomery, heir to the Montgomery Group International Real Estate Firm. What that even meant was beyond me. Mrs. Matthews—bless her soul— attempted to soothe my very apparent anxiety the entire time. By the time I left the office to find Kelly, it was as if my perspective on the world began to change.

Not all of it did, though. Kelly waited patiently, sprawled across two chairs with her nose in one of those weird farming simulation games. Last time I saw her playing a game, it was a horse simulator.

"Hey, babe." She looked up at me, tucking her game into her bag. "How'd it go?"

"I am ready to go get ice cream now and learn how to grow up." I held up the paper stating a major change that I would eventually have to submit as proof to Evans when he came calling about it again.

She threw me a wicked grin. "Before we do that, a little birdie told me that the football team is going to start practice soon. If we want to be sad with ice cream, we could at least watch hot and sweaty men running around."

We settled on getting bucket-sized bowls of frozen yogurt. It was conveniently on the way to the sports complex. I brought my body weight in cheesecake, birthday cake, and coconut flavored frozen yogurt to my seat in the stands to eat something yummy while watching something yummy.

"I read somewhere that froyo is *actually* better for you than ice cream. We are being super healthy while these guys work out." Kelly plopped down next to me with a spoon in her mouth.

Sure enough, all the guys ran around the track mostly in shorts. My overly large bucket of cold dessert, mixed with this sight, *was temporarily* distracting me from the cold corporate reality that awaited me.

"Does it count as a cold plunge if we eat ice cream out in the cold?" I pulled my large coat over me, briefly considering that this may not have been the most well thought out plan.

"Yes! Dual health benefits!"

Everyone's phones around us started pinging rapidly. So did mine. So did Kelly's. We exchanged a glance while pulling out our phones.

"What the hell could that be? Must be some emergency

thingy…" she trailed off, unlocking her phone and scrolling to find the source. Her jaw went slack. "Fal, look at this."

I leaned over to peek at the massive group text that had been sent out.

> Six of your daddies are going to jail. Let the games begin.

My eyes almost popped out of my head. I was so done with this semester. Not only was I going to learn how the wealthy operated while paying catch up, but I was going to play some fucked up version of whodunnit.

Frozen yogurt wouldn't solve this type of problem.

"Does it say who it's from?"

She shook her head. "Nope. This semester is going to be a *wild* ride. I remember when something similar happened when I was younger. It wasn't like this per se, but someone was bent out of shape about something, and a few families had to deal with some pretty heavy legal trouble."

Did this happen often or something?

We looked up to glance at the guys on the field, huddled together while holding their phones. They whispered amongst themselves while pointing at their screens. Would we know whose families were involved, or was this a domino effect to get people to out each other?

The bleachers shifted slightly under the weight of someone sitting down next to me, their thigh brushing against mine. I looked up to see Brent with his confident, irritating smirk.

"Wild news, huh?" His voice was lower and edged with a more serious tone. I didn't think he had a serious bone in his body before today, but I have been learning a lot in the span of a couple of weeks.

I nodded, giving him a suspicious sideways glance. "Uh huh."

He leaned in closer, lowering his voice to a whisper near my ear. A shiver ran through my body before I could try to suppress

149

it. The effect he had on me was more than irritating. "Want to get out of here? Just you and me?"

With our two escapades permanently etched in my brain, I didn't dare to delve into questioning his motives. Lucky for me, I didn't come alone, and I sure as hell wasn't leaving without Kelly.

She was still fixated on the screen, furiously typing away and swiping around unbothered by the interaction I was having. Her brows were furrowed, which meant that her attention was tunnel focused. I turned back to Brent and shook my head. "Nope. I'm with her and I'm sure as hell not ditching. If it's truly a matter of life or death, you know where I live. Don't bother me otherwise." I jerked my thumb to my right in Kell's direction.

He stared at me for a moment, his expression blank. Probably because he wasn't used to hearing the word *no*. For a second, I thought he might try to pull another kidnapping stunt by telling me to come with him or else, but he didn't. Instead, he sighed and leaned back, stretching his arms across the seats behind him. He looked slightly defeated. "Alright, babe. Chicks before dicks. But"—his eyes darkened—"don't be surprised when I take you up on that offer. I'll be seeing you later."

Excuse me, what? I raised an eyebrow at him, wondering what the hell he was on about. He sighed and stood up like it was the hardest task he had faced to date. He threw me a wink before disappearing into the shadows, as usual.

Kelly began giggling. "Babe?"

I held up a hand to stop her right there. No way was I about to talk about Brent. "Don't even. We're going down *there* to find Garrett and see what's going on since it looks like practice is over because of that wild text."

Our footsteps rang out on the metal bleachers, propelling the sound into the otherwise eerily quiet area. The noise settled down after the text, allowing only for hushed conversations. The air was visibly thick with tension, and I could see Garrett standing off to the side with a few of his teammates. Clustered together and whispering amongst themselves like the rest of the campus, I assumed.

"Bet you they're talking about *this*," Kelly said, holding up her phone.

I tried to remain casual. It didn't feel like it was working, but I tried anyway. "Only one way to find out."

Garrett made eye contact as we approached the group. He forced a smile before backing away from the guys. "Hey, Fal. Kelly." He nodded at us. His voice was also not quite right, much like that smile he was forcing.

Bad sign.

"Hey, you." I smiled back, ignoring the weird looks from his teammates and his odd tone. "You guys look like you got some big game-winning secret going on."

One of the guys shifted uncomfortably. Garrett shot him a look before turning back to me. "I wish. Some crazy news is spreading through campus like wildfire." His voice and body language felt strange. "Apparently, some students' parents are caught up in some scandals. Money laundering, embezzlement, organized crime. You name it. Some people are going to lose it."

Kelly and I exchanged a knowing glance. Her eyebrows shot up when she read my mind. "For real? That sounds like an insane movie plot!"

She overshot it with her terrible acting skills.

He shrugged, and his eyes couldn't quite meet mine for a moment. "Yep. Pretty crazy. No names have dropped yet, but the gossip train has a way of getting information out. Legal teams be damned when you have a large number of young adults running around together. You two should be careful, as people might be on edge."

I nodded along with him as if I was absorbing the information. "Thanks for the heads up. We'll try to stay out of trouble."

"Maybe we should head back home?" Kelly nudged me with her elbow. It was a sign that said she wanted to gossip about *everything*.

"Probably a good idea," he agreed. My chest tightened with nervousness at the sound of his voice. The words were weighted differently.

I gave his hand a small squeeze. "We'll be fine. I'll shoot you a text later so we can plan a real movie night this time."

He smiled, but it never made it past his lips. "Sounds like a plan, beautiful."

"Start blanket shopping now," I called out as Kelly all but dragged me away.

He never replied, going back to low conversations with his friends.

Kelly and I sighed in unison once we were safely locked in the car. Our shared look said everything.

"One," she started. "Garrett was definitely off. Two, he knew *way* more than what that message told us. Three, Brent suddenly acting like a bestie is not normal."

I couldn't help but laugh at the last part while backing out of the parking space. "Agreed. Garrett's hiding something or, at the very least, withholding insider info. He mentioned crimes that make me wonder what his sources are and how connected he may be to the wealthy web of shit these families get into. As for Brent, I don't know what to say about that man. He does as he wishes, and I don't even know what to do with him."

Kelly clicked her tongue and pulled out her phone. "This year is turning out to be wild. We need to keep an eye on this."

While playing Nancy Drew to solve the mystery sounded fun, she could do that on her own and report back to me safely tucked away at home. "I just have this weird sinking feeling in my stomach."

She was busy typing away and delving into a mystery, but I was fixated on the road, wondering if the boogeyman was going to jump out at us.

Because why wouldn't he?

16

Brent

"How many girls do you think you could fit on your motorcycle, anyway?" The bleach-blonde one twirled a strand of hair around her finger, giving me *fuck me* eyes the entire time.

"Just one," I replied, leaning back and stretching my arms out behind the two who sat on either side of me. There was always a crowd of three or more girls cozying up and competing for me to dick them down. I was a conquest to them just like they were to me.

Some of them wanted to fuck the campus playboy.

Others wanted to *save* me or *fix* me.

Far too many of the latter.

College was supposed to be a few years of good times and learning the ropes of the company before taking on whatever the Dictator planned for my future. I was supposed to be the shining star in his international conglomerate, overseeing operations and managing subsidiaries. Instead, I was a tatted-up biker who just so happened to be okay-ish at baseball.

Was I bitter? A little.

I wanted a chance to prove to him that I could be more than a punch-happy grandson with mommy issues. That chance rarely came when I found myself set up for failure on botched intel jobs and sent out to eliminate threats to the family business.

Did we run a fucking Mafia or what?

Remember, as the potential future head of Chamberlain Industries, you're not just inheriting wealth; you're inheriting a legacy of innovation and leadership that impacts millions of lives around the world.

"Potential." Which meant he didn't see me as worthy.

"So, the car then? How big is your bed?"

I grazed my eyes over the group of girls, wondering who I'd choose *if* I had to. "Sorry, girls. Only one... or two at a time."

The bravest of them made a show of being touchy. My arms, legs, and damn near my dick right on campus. I shifted to give my dick some room; my pants were tight.

For a split second, I thought I caught sight of soft blonde hair making its way across the courtyard. In that second, I swore I saw her. *Blondie.* The way her hair swayed in the wind had me thinking back to when I had her so close, but she felt so far away. The thought of Garrett having his grubby little hands over her more than I did...

I clenched my jaw, forcing myself not to think about it. It wasn't her walking across campus, and I didn't know if that made this situation better or worse. I imagined her seeing me, stomping up to me, and calling me a player, spouting off about my reputation again.

"Brent?" One of the girls leaned in closer, her perfume noxious. "You okay, baby?"

"All good." I forced a grin. My regular smirk that had every girl I could ask for eating out of my hand. She was still touching me, circling her fingers dangerously close to my dick. With everything I could want, why the hell did a pang of... whatever that feeling was hit me so hard? "Just thinking about our next baseball game win."

Ever since I first laid eyes on her, Blondie had been messing with my head. She was different. She didn't give a shit about appearances, getting what she wanted without remorse, or anything that would interrupt her optimism. I tried to tell myself that I didn't care, but it only pissed me off more.

The girls chattered about the baseball game before my phone buzzed in my pocket. While I was happy for a chance to get away from the groupies, I was not pleased about the name on the screen or the amount of time left to answer before consequences would be doled out.

He had *impeccable* timing for an old man. I stood up and brushed off the clingiest one. "Gotta run, ladies."

I felt their eyes all over me as I walked away to answer the phone. "Yes, sir?"

"Your driver is waiting." *Click.*

"Yep. Love you too," I muttered into the abyss he'd never hear me from.

"Sit down."

His office was like something out of a 1920s mafioso playbook. Antique dark furniture. The decor. And, of course, the cigars. The air told me that it wasn't just another stern talk he was going to dish out to me. A couple of lawyer types stood around, adding to his aesthetic and intimidation factor.

I did as his cold and commanding voice said and plopped my ass in the chair across from him. Whatever was happening, his expression did not look good.

"A matter of importance," he started, seating himself behind his large desk, "is why I brought you here. There's something to be aware of. Something dangerous that could impact everything, including your future. I caught wind of... certain situations involving some of the wealthiest families. There's a federal investigation underway, and multiple hands are in the pot. The news is already leaking, and I expect it to blow up at any minute. When it does, things will get *very* ugly."

I glanced around the room at the men standing nearby and eventually landed my gaze back on my grandfather. My eyebrows pinched together in confusion because that was definitely the vaguest thing he had ever told me. "What does this have to do with me?"

He smacked his hand on the table, annoyed that I didn't understand his coded language. He never filled me in, and I flew blind most days. "Everything, you insolent brat! You are not just a student attending the prestigious Willow Bay University. You carry *my* name. With that name comes weight. You need to buckle up and prepare for what's coming. I want to see no more of these outbursts or this philandering behavior to which you are so privy. Keep your fucking eyes open. You have *far* more to lose than most of those other kids."

My thoughts snapped to Fallon. She was *the Montgomery girl* I was supposed to stay away from. But, considering how intertwined her company was with ours, I wondered if the circumstances regarding her would change. She was out in the open, with red dots covering her body, with who knows how many people would love to take her out, just to have a piece of the pie. She was tight-lipped about her life, never letting on more than she wanted people to know. Did she even know what her life would become the moment she stepped up to the plate?

"Understood. I would like to step up and take on more responsibility to be of service to the company, sir."

"We could—" Lawyer man was cut off by the Dictator throwing his whiskey glass at him.

"Shut up!" His voice was sharp. "Until you can prove to me that you are even fucking worth your first name in *pennies*, don't you *dare* go getting these fanciful ideas in your head."

He made a quick hand motion to one of the other men who was not covered in a drink, beckoning him to come to the table.

The man opened a briefcase containing documents. *Files.* More files for me to shamefully take with me to the basement as the lowest tier of employee. The name sounded familiar, but I was not here to ask any questions about the who or what of my assignments.

"Take this to your men and find out what you can about this woman. Give me something useful, don't fool around looking for a wet hole, and keep your fucking hands to yourself, and maybe, *just maybe*, I'll give you the time of day to ask me a fucking question."

I wondered if he hated me for his daughter's decision to take her own life. When she came back, she was still a teenager, and I had just been born. He still took me in and raised me. Fed me. Clothed me. But when it came to love, he fell short.

To him, I was a waste of space. An irritating thorn in his side.

To me, I was the sole heir to his kingdom. And I would show him that I was even stronger than he had ever been.

Let the Games Begin

Six of your daddies are going to jail. Let the games begin.

Whispers and snippets of conversations floated around campus. Each group checked their phones one by one.

A group by the fountains huddled, whispering conspiratorially.

"Did you hear about that girl who was seen with Garrett the other night?" she whispered. Her voice was a mix of intrigue and concern regarding the latest scandal to hit campus.

"Yep!" her friend replied, leaning in as close as she could get. "Turns out, she's *the* Fallon Montgomery. As in *the* Montgomery Group. My roommate saw her name on some of her class materials yesterday. She's been keeping a low profile for some reason, and maybe this is connected somehow. That won't be the case much longer, though."

Fallon Montgomery was indeed the sole heir of the Montgomery Group. The elites kept everything tied together in their little world of business, safely sectioned off from anything and everything that could bring them down. She might be the first to fall victim to federal investigations, or she might not. Whoever fell first didn't matter.

It would be better if they all fell at once.

Someone else chimed in on the conversation. "*And* she's been hanging around Garrett quite frequently. With this news—and the rumors we've already heard—you have to wonder what else could be going on. Are their families connected or in cahoots?

Shouldn't she be leading her dead mom's company at some point? Garrett's family has never smelled too great; they've got white collar crime written *all* over them."

17

Fallon

Kicked back and relaxed, Kelly and I were mid-binge fest watching our favorite horror movies. A knock on the door startled us both, sending popcorn sailing across the living room floor. We looked at each other, surprised that we could be so easily jump scared like that.

"This had better be a masked murderer and not Brent at ten or I swear..." I mumbled, getting up and surveying the new popcorn decor.

"Or you'll what? Sleep with him?"

I threw the empty bowl at her and went to check the peephole.

It was covered until I opened the door to see Brent leaning on the doorframe—in a different jacket. His face looked twisted, more serious than usual, and I wondered if he was here for an *actual* life or death reason.

There was no humor or teasing in his demeanor. "Can I come in?"

I stepped back and gestured for him to come in. "I guess I'd better make good on my word, then. Welcome to my humble abode."

He stepped through easily, unlike the last time when he had forced himself in.

"Kelly." He nodded, sizing her up. Was he... making eyes at Kelly? There was no way that just happened.

Maybe I saw something that wasn't there. Like a ghost.

She raised an eyebrow and looked over at me before responding to him. She was just as shocked to see him here as I was. "Good... evening."

I bit my lip to hold back a smile, and she shrugged at me. Our own little secret exchange.

"Since you're here, I hope it's about the life-or-death clause I mentioned earlier. Care to tell us what is such an urgent matter that you're here after bedtime?"

He looked over at Kelly before turning his attention back to me, as if he was asking to talk alone. "Garrett. And it's more of a private conversation." His eyes darkened, and his jaw was set firmly.

My hand went to my hip, knowing I wouldn't be keeping anything from Kelly anyway. "Whatever you tell me will immediately be relayed to her, but with a more dramatic flair. If you want to save me the time of re-explaining, just spit it out."

He sized me up to gauge my level of seriousness. We had a close friendship. We were sisters in every way but blood, and I made sure people knew that loud and clear. There was nothing kept secret between us, and I didn't expect that to change now.

Before he could explain anything, I realized he had mentioned my love life. *What an asshole.* He always poked his head where it didn't belong. "Wait. Garrett? What are you doing coming around my house in the middle of the night telling me it's life-or-death *and* that it's about my boyf— Garrett?"

Of course, I almost said boyfriend. *Good going.*

His nostrils flared as he took a deep breath. Annoyed with me. "There's word going around campus. I was *trying* to mind my own business, but I couldn't help overhearing the many, *many* whispers about the text that went out. *Your* name caught my ear, and it was all about you and him. Fallon *Montgomery* and Garrett *Bradford.*"

He paused, waiting for me to say something. He had the nerve to *tap his foot* at me.

"So?" I threw my hands up and gestured to say *What's your point?*

"As in *the* Montgomery Group. As in, you conveniently left out that you're the heir to Maria's throne, and I had to find out from a third party." He crossed his arms, waiting for me to answer his interrogation-style questions.

While it was true that I didn't boast about my name and legacy, it's not as if I kept it a secret from everyone. People had every opportunity to look me up or find out who I was. My mother kept a lot of it a secret from me for most of my life; I never wanted to have that same level of secrecy. That didn't mean I had to flaunt myself everywhere as if it made a difference.

Sometimes people didn't make the connection. If they found out my last name, it was common enough that they may not make the connection, but among the hyper wealthy and elite groups… it made for *interesting* conversation.

Last semester, I kept my head down well enough, but being seen with Garrett meant I was bound to be found out. *If* you could call it being found out.

I countered him. "How do you know my mother well enough to use her first name so casually?"

"Because your company and my company are good, *good* friends."

I gritted my teeth. There was *no* way I would end up working with him in the future. *No. Way.* "What does *that* mean?"

"My grandfather, Augustus Vaughn of Chamberlain Industries, knew your mother, worked with her, and spoke very highly of her." He sighed and rubbed his face. "Look, Blondie. This isn't the point of why I'm here. You may get dragged into some shit that, one, you're not even aware of, and two, that you don't *need* to be dragged into."

I shook my head and looked over at Kelly, who seemed ready to start back up with a fresh bowl of popcorn to watch us go back and forth. "What I'm asking is this: Why do *you* care? You and me? We've hung out in very clandestine ways, and you seem to care more about being full of yourself than about caring for other people. Is the point of all this to make me feel like you care about anything other than yourself in some weird way to get me to sleep with you?" I backed up to sit on the couch ledge. "Unless it's just a way to keep things contained for your own family's business. If we're as connected as you say, this could just be you trying to cover your ass."

Sometimes, I wondered how much of my mother I had in me. If I had some of the business savvy mindset she had. Or if I had some of the discerning powers that led her to become wildly successful. If I did, honing them would be on the agenda to succeed in the world I was oblivious to.

"The rumors have already started, and things like this can take a swift turn for the ugly if you're not careful. I can't tell you what to do, but these people around you are cutthroat and will aim straight for your jugular. Look at me." He held his arms out and turned in a circle. "I appear harmless, don't I?"

I shared a look with Kelly. What did he mean by *harmless*?

"Okay... humor me. What did they say?"

He sat himself at *my* dining table, daring to enter further into *my* house. I followed him out of pure curiosity about this interaction. Part of me wondered if his grandfather had sent him over to size me up, to see if I was actually capable like my mother.

He set his elbows on the table and steepled his fingers. "No one could believe that *you* were Fallon Montgomery—"

Kelly cut in, her mouth full of candy. "That *was* the point of her keeping her head down."

"Sure. That's fine to avoid causing a scene, but what I'm hearing is that he's using her as a meat shield for the upcoming legal issues facing his family. Did you not know that he's one of the *six* families being targeted?"

Kelly sat at the table with us, fully ready to enter the drama herself. "I *did* tell Fallon that when we talked with him that he mentioned a lot more than what that text said."

I sighed. "Since you're offering up information, I'll fill you in on my end. We went to the field today to watch the boys practice when that text was sent to everyone. You showed up shortly after, and you know what happened while you were there, But when you left, we went to talk to Garrett since the guys practicing looked done after the scandal hit everyone. All the guys were acting suspicious, and Garrett said that 'money laundering, embezzlement, and organized crime was involved when the text *never* mentioned any of that."

I needed something to eat if this was how the evening was going to go. Leftovers were in the fridge and were calling my name while my stomach grumbled. I just snatched the pack of sour gummy worms I left on the table instead.

"Then we left," I continued. "We had a moment of 'that was weird as hell' before theorizing that he, or someone there, might be hiding something. Whatever it was, he knew more than we did and wasn't forthcoming with the information. It was just generally *odd*."

He let my words sink in for a moment, looking around my house like he'd never seen it before. Like he didn't force his way in not that long ago. "Do you know his family at all? The Bradfords?"

"No. Why would it matter?"

He looked concerned. "You know absolutely nothing about being wealthy, do you? You are in the top one percent of everyone in this country, Blondie."

"My mother raised me right, if that's what you're asking." I sat back, challenging his accusation.

He placed his palms flat on the table. "In this life that we *all* share"—he looked between Kelly and me—"status is everything. Who you associate with is everything. What benefit does Kelly's family have for you that makes you friends with her?"

She looked shocked.

"That's not why we're friends," I stated flatly. He was

bringing our friendship into it by suggesting that it had to have some benefit other than the fact that we loved each other and wanted to associate with each other. We lived together for God's sake!

He looked between us, not believing there were any benefits beyond just friendship. "Great example: Your mother was a rare talent, and others will expect you to be just as good as her, if not twice as much. This includes not holding a relationship with a man that could threaten your throne."

"I haven't heard you speak about your father, and I suspect there is a valid reason for that. Garrett may know who you are, but you don't know who he is. It's a dangerous game you've been playing with him this semester and you will be caught in the crossfire. No one like us stays safe for long."

Brent Vaughn, the playboy, telling me what life was like. The guy who plays baseball and gets into fistfights for fun? *No way.*

He had to be bonkers.

Or sent by his grandfather with a threat or something.

I held up a finger. "As the known player of the school, are you telling me that *I* need to be careful about my associations? That sounds like the exact opposite of what you do."

He probably thought I was dense, judging by the expression on his face. He had to close his eyes and breathe before responding to me. "Do you know my grandfather?"

I pursed my lips, unsure of what answer he was looking for. Augustus Vaughn was the top dog of everything in this country. I'm sure he had politicians in his pocket like a mobster would. If Brent was in line to inherit such a large conglomerate, why was he such a... *him*?

"I had a meeting with him earlier this week, and he told *me* to keep my head down. Something big must be in the works. Can't be good if your name is circulating like this."

Kelly broke the intensity with the sound of her stomach screaming for food. "Sorry. I'm *super* hungry since my popcorn is all over the floor. Can we order some food?"

"Might be more productive with food." He pulled his phone out. "What are we in the mood for, girls?"

"Pizza and garlic knots. Oh! A brownie thing. Maybe some regular breadsticks…" Kelly was quick to answer. She loved her pizza.

She might also be very, *very* stoned at this point, given how red her eyes were.

"The pizza needs to have as much meat as possible on it, or she likely won't eat it in her, erm, current state."

He typed away on his phone and laid it face down on the table, leveling his gaze with mine. "I'm game for a sleepover. I ditched the Dictator's tail, so you two are stuck with me for the night."

Oh joy. He also called his grandfather a *dictator*, which led me to believe that they must have had a strained relationship of sorts. But that was a question for another time.

"So, you ordered the food knowing we'd be relying on you to stick around to see it get delivered. Devious plan."

I stood, planning to change my clothes, and he stood up with me. Kelly looked between the two of us as if we were her own personal reality TV show, and she was enjoying our weird little game. When I made a move to step away, it was clear he wanted to follow me, and Kelly just watched. I was happy that at least one of us was having a good time, even if she was stoned out of her mind and anything would provide her with that level of entertainment.

"Any *wild* secrets about her boyfriend?" I gestured to Kelly, hoping to distract him so I could leave and put on comfier pajamas. It didn't work.

"Who's her boyfriend?"

She perked up. "Shane Jones."

"Nope. Don't know him," he said bluntly.

She missed the point because she was that far gone. "Babe, I don't think you need to worry. I was being facetious."

Brent ignored her. "Is Garrett your boyfriend *officially*?"

He followed me after I turned away to walk toward my room.

I wanted to cover myself up if he was going to stay here. He saw me at my worst when he demanded I come with him, but we were in my house—at night. A small bout of anxiety started brewing in my stomach, and I hoped it would go away with some food.

"Not your business," I called out as I closed—and locked—the door.

The doorknob jiggled vigorously, and emphatic knocking began. He realized I had locked his ass out so I could change and have some privacy. This guy was a piece of work. Plus, his jacket was still tucked away in my closet, and the thought of him coming in, looking at it, and thinking it was my prized possession was not the goal. Unless he forgot about it.

How many girls had he given it out to so carelessly? *Ew. Don't think about that.*

"Babe, let me in. We still have other things to discuss."

My ugly sweatpants, stained and with odd holes in them, would have to do. The matching oversized hoodie—also stained —would make a perfect pairing. The look? As unsexy as possible around Brent Vaughn, horn dog extraordinaire.

"Not your babe!" I shouted back.

He had this weird habit of leaning face first into the doors I opened. He stood there, looking as though he was trying to seduce my door into unlocking for him.

It also appeared that he'd found his mischievous grin again, as it was plain as day on his mouth.

"Oh, wow." He looked me up and down. "*Love* this look for you." He twirled one of the strings of my hoodie in his finger.

"Great. I'll just change into something even uglier."

The door was stopped by his hand. He barged in this time, closing and locking it behind him. "Why didn't you tell me your mom was Maria?"

"Why didn't you just ask who I was?"

"Question for a question?" The smirk on his lips told me that he had turned on his charm.

Fuck.

"Not in the mood. I will give you one piece of information: my mother raised me right. She made sure I didn't act like you or any of the other nepo babies out there because she wanted me to have a *brain* and be able to think critically." Which she did; other people just saw another side of her.

He closed the distance between us while I looked for other, even uglier clothes that wouldn't turn him on. The guy was a freak, and he made me want him to be as turned off as possible at all times. Because I had to face the fact that he was in my room with the door closed and *very* close to me.

Those things combined were not good. Especially when it came to Brent Vaughn.

My heart betrayed me when I looked up to see him standing in the closet doorway, looking down at me. His eyes were full of hunger, and it was *not* for pizza and garlic knots. That look had surely made all the girls he encountered swoon, but I decided it was too cliché for my taste.

Sure, he buzzed his hair, had tattoos that lined his body up to the sides of his head, dressed far too well for his own good, and smelled like sex with a rockstar…

But that didn't mean I had to fall for it.

"What are you digging around for, babe?" His voice dropped back to that natural, sultry tone he possessed. The warning and urgency disappeared when he started thinking about me changing my clothes. About being out of them. I saw that look. He wanted me out of my clothes.

"Something even less sexy than these, since you seem to get off on my regular ugly clothes." I refocused on my rummaging to find something more stained, stinky, or holey. Anything. "And I'm *not* your babe."

He ducked away from the pair of pants I threw at him, laughing up a storm. "So, she prefers Blondie to babe."

"Neither, actually." I wondered about going through my laundry basket to find what I was looking for. "Can I pass?"

His large frame barricaded the door—because of course it

did. He wanted me stuck in here, begging him to let me out. "Can I kiss you finally?"

My hands swiped up and down, showing him my ugly attire. "Does all *this* really do it for you?"

A fingertip traced beneath my chin, drawing my gaze to meet his. I watched his pupils dilate, dark pools expanding as the air between us filled with tension. "I want to finally feel those fucking lips on mine."

Looking anywhere but into his eyes was all I could do. "Why?" I stuttered. "I'm clearly not your type. I'm just a challenge you can't help but persist at. You can't tell me I'm wrong."

His head followed my gaze, his eyes blazing with intensity as they stared into my soul. The distance between us disappeared, and I heard his breathing become shallow. My nerves fried on the spot, and my heartbeat was out of control. It had to be an adrenaline rush I felt—the nervousness that everyone experiences in unfamiliar situations or whatever.

Whatever it was, I was sure he could hear my heartbeat.

"Just let me kiss you, damn it." He grasped the back of my neck to pull me into him. The low, breathy voice sent tingles down my spine and in *other* regions.

So, I obliged and shoved my mouth into his. If it *was* happening, it would be *my* move.

And it was nothing like kissing Garrett. His lips felt like a lightning strike—exhilarating and terrifying at the same time. Unless I was a dumb virgin—which I was—I would say that it felt urgent and needy. It set my body on fire.

He was a lightning strike.

Like that first night when we stood at the edge of the cliff, overlooking the city and gazing at the stars.

Like when he pulled me onto his bike out of nowhere.

Like when he threw me over his shoulder to take me somewhere he somehow knew I'd want to go.

It felt like I was waking up.

Shoving my hand to his chest, I separated us. We were out of breath from the urgency of the kiss and the hands roaming *everywhere*.

Jesus Christ in Heaven, what the hell was I thinking?

I wiped my mouth with the back of my hand and pushed my way out of the closet. "Happy?"

A hand clasped over my wrist. "Wait."

"What?"

His phone pinged, and we both looked down.

"Looks like food is here."

18

Fallon

Two whole pizzas disappeared almost instantly between an athletic baseball player and a stoned skater chick. How those two managed to eat almost an entire pizza *each* was a mystery to me. They even ate breadsticks and garlic knots. My meagre three pieces couldn't compare.

Brent broke the silence first. "Where's my bed?"

"Fallon's room. You two seemed cozy in there anyway." She'd been eyeing me suspiciously since I ran out with beet red cheeks when the food was delivered, wearing a different hoodie —Brent casually walking out behind me.

I choked on a garlic knot. "No way! He can sleep on the couch."

"Mhm," she grunted. "I'll wear earmuffs tonight."

My food fell right out of my mouth.

"You ruined a perfectly good garlic knot, you ass!"

Buzz!

Kelly's phone and mine buzzed in unison on the table. A notification from a social media app I hadn't opened in months appeared. And then another. And another. My heart sank into my butt when I saw the headlines and tags.

Montgomery Group Heiress Identified?

I didn't want to continue reading. Who knows what would

be hidden in the sea of mess—gossip on the internet was always a hundred times more brutal. *Bring me back to classic tabloids!* I held my phone out to Kel; she picked her own up with her eyes bulging out of her head.

My stomach churned as I scrolled through the posts, tags, headlines, and comments. Garrett's family was accused of fraud, money laundering, and organized crime—the same things he'd mentioned to us. My pictures were also plastered all over it, identifying me as Garrett's girlfriend and the sole heir to Montgomery Group International Real Estate Firm. There were incorrect connections between our families and businesses. I was being dragged into the mud.

Everything my mother worked for was coming into question. There were speculations about how dirty our company was. The way instant responses to news occurred was terrifying.

My face drained of all color as I looked at all of this. "Fuck me," I breathed.

"This can't be real, right? You're everywhere, and there's, like, federal investigations and speculations about your mom's company." Kelly looked how I felt.

Brent moved his chair over to look at my phone.

I was too shocked to speak and just handed it over to him.

"What do we do?"

I shrugged. Nothing like a heart wrenching scandal to sober Kelly up. It felt like a wake-up call, and I was wide awake at midnight.

Brent turned my phone around to show me a text that had come through.

GARRETT:

Meet me tomorrow? We should talk about this.

How much farther my heart could have dropped, I didn't know. My body felt like it was going into an adrenaline-fueled shock. I didn't know what to think or believe about what was happening. How quickly my world turned upside down.

How did they have these pictures of me? Someone had to have been following me.

Evans would have my head on a platter by the morning.

Brent's demeanor changed in my periphery as he watched me digest the internet meltdown and Garrett's message. "I'm definitely not leaving now."

That bodyguard who would be showing up anytime now was more than justified.

Confusion, anger, and feelings of defeat started to overtake me. "I don't think that's a good idea."

"What? I came here to tell you about this, and it just so happened to blow up while I was here."

Everything felt like too much. "I don't want you to stay. It's no good for you, and being seen with me after this is probably not good for either of us…"

"Blondie."

"Please stop." I stood up, shaking. "We don't—we can't. You're the infamous womanizer. I'm newly identified. None of this makes sense or even feels right to me."

"My wanting to help you means nothing?" He mimicked me again, standing up and inching closer to me.

We had two dates—*if* you could call them that. He just wanted to see if he could bed me. I was just a fun little challenge for him. There's no way. He's just looking out for his own company, right? Just purely selfish, that's all. "You're seen with a new girl almost daily, Brent Vaughn. You cannot expect me to believe that you have *only* pure motives coming over here."

He huffed, clearly entertained. "This is your only excuse whenever I talk to you or even *look* in your direction. A guy like me could never want to help anyone in his life. Sure, I'm only here to mess with you. Bend over then, I'll show you."

Excuse me, what?! *Bend over?!*

I've never wanted to punch anyone in the mouth before. That all changed when he came into my life. Having a normal semester was impossible in the current climate, but *this* was so uncalled for. Him and his dumb, stupid motorcycle.

179

"Is that what you say to them all? The group of not one, not two, but *five* girls the other day? I see you around, and I wish I didn't. You crashed my date with a fight, for God's sake! I wish I hadn't taken you up on that stupid motorcycle ride at the party. You're just no good."

Nothing made sense, and everything felt like a game. Brent wanted me to let my guard down around him long enough to add a notch to his belt. Garrett suddenly became a stranger overnight. What was next? My best friend turning on me? *Overwhelmed* wasn't a strong enough word for how I felt.

My entire world crashed again as nausea washed over me. It wasn't enough that my mother died of cancer; I had to navigate the world she left behind with no guidance of my own.

The distance between us closed again, charged not with lust but with irritation. "You want to question *my* judgment? At least I know when people want something from me. Those girls want one of two things from me: My dick or my money. From day one, you've done *nothing* but judge me, and don't think for *one second* that I didn't see that look in your eyes. While I spent time trying to learn more about you, you spent that time to look down on me. You think you're so smart despite being just like the rest of us. Being naive in experience and sex doesn't absolve you of not being as innocent as you want us to think you are."

Not being as innocent as I want them to think? He must have been out of his mind to think that I was playing games with him. Something was broken in his brain.

He smoothed out his shirt, physically composing himself. It made sense that he got worked up easily if he was always inciting fights. "We went out on dates—two of them! We never even made it past almost kissing, and you *still* think that I'm in it for pussy. If that's what I wanted, I would have quit a long time ago."

I bit the inside of my cheek, looking for anywhere else to look. Kelly was trying not to look while focusing intently on her food. Embarrassment flowed through my body freely like water. My composure was faltering.

"Just for the record," he said, voice softening, "I did *not* pressure you into anything. I asked you for a kiss all of maybe *two* times, which you just obliged me in your fucking *closet* of all places."

My cheeks were bound to become permanently red at this rate. I wanted to hide inside myself from how exposed he was making me feel.

It was annoying that he might have made sense. I was angry that my life had been turned upside down so quickly, spiraling into chaos. I was furious that I had poor judgment in choosing men when I thought I was doing as well as my mother hoped I would. A man being let into my inner circle, into my life, and turning out to be no good? It was my mom picking my dad in another life. Since her death, it was like I wasn't trying to live at all. Hiding away and sheltering myself more than she ever would.

Everything felt like a mountain I couldn't climb.

All I saw was my biggest fears coming to life.

And a world I knew nothing about revealing itself to me too late in life.

I was an escapist. And even worse, I was scared. Putting my head down was my way of dealing with things. Especially when it came to the second half of my teens. Why face my name—my legacy—when I could lie to myself and pretend it wasn't real?

I stared at the floor while my vision blurred. Processing some of the things he said—the truth—was not what I wanted to do. Fire was all over my face and down my neck from the intensity of it all. Life had punched me in the gut.

The movie finally ended, and I still wasn't tired enough to go to sleep. I forced myself to lie down, but my eyes just wouldn't shut.

Emotions were high all around. Everything felt dark and grim. I fought hard to escape that feeling. When I lived with my aunt, things were bad. She called me some of the same things, but worse.

"*Spoiled rich brat!*"

"You and your mother have always looked down on me. Now, look at you!"

I could almost see her hand above me again, telling me how shitty I was, ready to hit me.

Sleep wouldn't come to me, so pizza it was. The plush carpet barely made a sound as I padded through the house and into the living room. Brent was wide awake, sitting on the couch when I came in.

"Hey," he whispered.

"Hi," I replied, crossing into the kitchen. My head was still reeling from earlier, and I felt the urge to distract myself with whatever pizza was left.

I rummaged through the fridge to pull out a box of whatever was left.

"Can we chat?" He was right behind me.

Nodding my head, I shoved a breadstick in my mouth.

He rubbed the back of his head before taking a brownie out of the box I offered up to him. "It felt too charged to try to remedy the situation earlier, so I've been sitting here wondering how to apologize."

"Didn't think you got so offended so easily."

He chortled. "Could say the same about you."

No one said anything else as we ate in silence at the table. What would we say? It was true we didn't know each other so well, but we knew how to effortlessly push each other's buttons. We'd only observed each other for the short time that the semester had been underway. Me, judging him. Him watching me in whatever weird way he did.

I may have been quick to misjudge him, but I didn't have to like him. Tolerating him would have to suffice.

I sighed into my cold piece of pizza. "I can't sleep."

"Same."

My fingers idly poked at what was left in the box, hoping it would spark some inspiration for something—anything. The only light in the house was the dim glow from the kitchen nightlight and whatever moonlight filtered in through the window. It was perfect for winding down and sleeping, but my body was not cooperating.

His usual smirk appeared across from me. "What is it, Blondie?"

"Please stop with the 'Blondie' stuff." I shook off a shiver that ran down my spine. *The cold*, I told myself. It *was* cold as hell inside.

"You look like you want to ask me something." He ripped off the end of another breadstick. "I can see that look you get on your face. Right here. Yep, that spot. It does this cute little thing —it shows your brain working overtime."

He made me want to roll my eyes whenever he opened his mouth. "I'm going back to bed. It's cold and my feet hurt."

His interest perked up at the word "bed" and I knew I'd fucked up. "I'll join you. I don't mind being a space heater."

Him? In my bed? No way, no how. That was asking for danger *and* death. I couldn't handle being in my room with him for two seconds before shoving my face into his when he taunted me. If he were in my bed...

"No funny business."

Surprise painted his face. He looked genuinely floored. "And here you were, yelling at me about how I was just going to make you a notch in my belt."

"Don't make me take it back."

"Alright. Let's go," he said, holding out his hand to mine.

Surely, I would regret that. I regretted it when I sat down on my bed and pulled my legs up to my chest. My room, invaded by *him* of all people. Again. That closet over there was where I kissed him. *I* kissed him, and that was my choice to make.

"Earlier," I started, "I didn't mean to outright attack you."

"Wow," he gasped. "You're apologizing?"

I shoved him a little. "I can take that back, too."

"Fine, fine." He held his hands up and settled in next to me. "I've also never been this challenged by a girl and it made me angry."

Yeah, right. "That can't be true."

"You're like this maddening, impossible little puzzle."

I laughed and shook my head. "Sorry that taking someone out on real dates is *so* hard on you."

We laid back in bed and stared at the ceiling. The situation we were in was completely new to me—both business-and personal-wise. Being pursued by the biggest player I'd ever seen was bizarre in itself. Add in some strange corporate, elitist drama, and you have a situation I should have put on my bingo card for this year.

"Everything feels like it's crumbling right now," I muttered.

"Welcome to the life of never-ending shit."

Not being able to look at him while talking was better; he always stared *into* me while we talked. "It feels like my mom is dying all over again. I don't do well in these situations. Escapism made me feel better when shit hit the fan, but I'm guessing I won't be able to escape this time. That's the part that is freaking me out and making me feel trapped. And don't even get me started on my aunt..."

"And here I was thinking we were so different. Your escapism looks different from mine, but it's still escaping all the same."

"By being a man slut?" I laughed and kicked him.

Having a heart to heart with the punchiest man I've ever seen was also not on my bingo card this year.

"If that's how you want to label it. The baseball star. The playboy. The guy no one wants to mess with because he'll kick the shit out of you. My grandfather didn't earn the title of *Dictator* for no reason. He expects rigidity. Excellence." He let out a sigh and looked over at me, the softness in his eyes coming through. "So why give a damn about anything? You're the first one to put up a challenge, and it's different—I like it."

"Different? Weren't you just saying—"

"Yes, different. You sat and had food with me. Despite your protest, you came out with me a second time. Normally, I get hit up, it's a quick fuck and I dip."

I cringed.

He continued, "If they did want more out of me, it was always *after* I fucked them. You don't even seem to want to come within a ten-mile radius of me half the time."

Looking at him, he was just another egotistical guy. Tattoos. Short hair. Leather jacket. The guy who rode a motorcycle to get girls to drop their panties, smoked like it was his second language, and fought like he had nothing to lose. Like he didn't care about anything or anyone, keeping everyone at arm's length, except when it came to the girls who *did* drop their panties.

To think he criticized my discernment skills. *Asshole.*

"I've never really thought about getting my rocks off. That's never happened anyway."

Propped up on his elbow now, he stared at me in the dark. "It's because you want something real."

"If only people were real," I sighed, flopping my arms out. "Your jacket is in my closet, by the way."

His hand found its way to my arm, his touch somewhere between comforting and seductive. A fine line to walk. The warmth of his skin on mine sent a shiver through me.

"I'll be sure to let the groupies know that they can't have it," he murmured.

Carefully, I laced my fingers with his out of curiosity. It sent a message of sorts—a welcoming one, perhaps. He considered it for a moment, looking down at our hands linked of my own volition. He could assume whatever he wanted. He was warm and comfortable, and I wanted to enjoy a little of that for a moment.

"Question for a question?" Knowing I'd regret asking, I added it to the growing list of regrets anyway.

He didn't answer with words. The pillows were brought down, and we propped ourselves up while he looked at me suspiciously.

To start us off in an insane manner, I asked, "So, have you ever slept with a virgin?"

His eyes went wide, the disbelief abundantly clear on his face for the second time today. "Damn, went straight to it, Blondie." He breathed out slowly, tracing soft circles on my hand with his thumb. A touch that sent a warm pulse through my skin. "If you must know, yes... Have you ever touched yourself?"

I started this, so why was I shocked? My cheeks heated up, and I hesitated to answer. "Um, can I pass?"

He shook his head, a devious smile playing on his lips. "Nope. You asked, now you answer."

"Fine," I muttered. "Here and there, but I feel like I have no clue what I'm doing with some of the shit I bought. Aside from me, have you ever been on a date that didn't end with hooking up?"

He paused for a moment, weighing up his answer. "A couple of times," he finally admitted. His voice dropped low, almost seductive. "Have you kissed anyone but me?"

I bit my lip. "I'm sure you know of one, but outside of him... No." Saying it out loud made me feel like I was stripping myself bare in front of him, exposing it all. "Did you expect me to sleep with you at all?" This question was going to give me something I didn't know I wanted.

The space between us shrank as he shifted closer to me. "Not at all. You intrigued the hell out of me, and I wanted to figure out why." His eyes darkened as he asked, "What's the craziest thing you've ever done?"

Our conversation ignited a warmth low in my belly that I didn't want to think about, but I initiated it all. Thinking about the crazy things I've done—which I could probably count on one hand—I only remembered everything I've done with him. "It's a tie between getting on your bike or kissing you in my closet." I tried to keep my voice steady, despite my hummingbird heart fluttering in my chest. "What's the craziest thing the infamous Brent Vaughn has done?"

He answered quickly and without hesitation. "Getting interested in you. What's the first thing you thought when you saw me?"

I laughed, remembering the warning Kelly had given me

about him. "Kelly warned me about you after coming back from shopping. It's funny because I thought to myself, *This guy looks full of himself,* as I watched you instigating fights in your own front yard. When did you see me first?"

He started playing with my hair while a thoughtful smile rested on his lips. "Some time earlier than that. I saw you in the neighborhood and was *very* grateful to have you as a neighbor. Why did you kiss me in the closet?"

I slapped his chest. "You wouldn't stop talking about it! Why did you *want* to kiss me?"

"Because," he said, moving his hand up to grip my chin, slowly swiping his thumb across my bottom lip. A spark of heat shot straight through my body, warming up the inside of my thighs. "You talk back so much; I wanted to know how sour your words tasted, but when you kissed me, you were as sweet as honey. Can I do it again?"

My room shrank a million times. The tension in the air so thick I could taste it. The pull between us so magnetic—even if it was temporary—made me want to do something that I'd regret in the morning.

"I—" My words caught in my throat. What did I say to that? My brain was malfunctioning. "What if I want more?" The words slipped out before I knew what I was saying.

"Blondie..." his voice was so guttural and deep that it had me gripping his arm, digging my nails in.

Oh, hell. I just did myself in, didn't I?

With fresh goosebumps prickling my skin and unfiltered thoughts slipping out, I felt drunk on whatever was flowing through my veins. "Why do you call me Blondie?" I breathed.

He was barely containing himself but obliged me with my extra question. Our faces were dangerously close together as he focused on my lips with a hunger that scared me. "Because I love watching you *squirm.*"

My lips parted in surprise, and I found my nerve. I took his lower lip between mine and grazed my teeth across it, feeling him shudder. My heart pounded so loudly that it had to be apparent to both of us. The rush in my ears told me adrenaline was taking over, and lust filled my bones.

In the moment it took me to take a single breath, he flipped me over and pinned my hands to the bed. "Don't play with me, Fallon." His tone was deathly serious.

"I'm not playing. What if I want more?" I challenged him from my very disadvantaged position, my eyes grazing every inch of his body.

Oh. My. God. What was I doing?

He released my hands from his grip to peel his shirt off. *What a fucking body.*

I was probably drooling.

"This what you want?" He pulled my hands to his chest, and it took all my strength not to ogle for longer. He lowered himself to my ear and nibbled on it. "Now it's my turn."

"Dear God," escaped my lips in a pant.

A vicious, low laugh rumbled from his throat. "I love this side of you, but tell me… what does 'more' mean *exactly*?"

I was hot. Everywhere. I managed to find my voice despite how mousy it sounded. "More—fuck." I couldn't concentrate. "It means I want… to have sex with you."

There it was. Out in the open. My V card was his for the taking.

He nuzzled into my neck, trailing soft kisses from my ear to the point where my hoodie prevented him from going any farther. "Show me."

I shakily snaked my hands to pull off my hoodie. I was bare in a small bralette he'd seen earlier. No big deal, right? We were both bare-ish on top.

A delicate bite to my neck forced an arch in my back while my entire body tingled. "Brent," I gasped.

"Fallon," he replied. His voice was full of merriment. With his mouth on my skin, I was set ablaze.

This was nothing like touching myself or anything my imagination could conjure. He was down to my belly, gripping my sides with just enough force to hold me in place. The tingling from his touches had my body begging for more, reaching out each time he pulled away.

Then he was gone. I looked up to see him undoing his belt. My eyes went wide. Oh, shit, he was taking off his pants.

Do I take mine off, too? What are the rules of engagement?

"Cold feet?" he asked, stepping out of his pants that had dropped to the floor. He was in nothing but his boxers, and I was sitting there like a true lost virgin.

Scratch that. In his boxers with a *very* apparent boner.

I stuttered. "I, uh, do I take mine off too?"

He broke into a full, gorgeous smile as he let out a snort. "Fuck, you're so cute," he said, shaking his head and pushing me back onto the bed. His mouth collided with mine in full passion.

Radiating. I was radiating. Our mouths moved in sloppy, hungry kisses as I desperately pulled his body into mine. "Here," he breathed into my mouth. "Let me help you."

Wiggling around, he gently pulled my sweats off while I let out an excited giggle. He flipped me over, so I was on top of him this time, grabbing at the back of my neck to pull me back to his mouth. He was starving for my mouth, and I was fully straddling him. Just two small pieces of fabric between us...

I leaned into what felt right, my hips slowly rocking as we continued to make out, earning groans and harder grips from his hands. He started rocking into me, and I knew this was my tipping point.

"Ready for more?" he growled into my mouth.

"Uh huh," I breathed back into his.

On my back again in an instant, he was pulling off my underwear and positioning himself between my legs. *Oh, fuck.* He gingerly rubbed my thighs, attuning me to his touch. He kissed the inside of my thigh sweetly. "I want to warm you up. I want you to lay back, look pretty, and tell me if something doesn't work for you. Got it?"

Warm me up?! I'm warm! Hot. On FIRE.

"Okay," I whispered.

And just like that his mouth was on a very sensitive spot, tongue circling around my clit. I'd seen this acted out before, but oh my God, it felt like an itch being scratched that I didn't know I had. Slowly, he slipped a finger inside and gauged my reactions. I was breathing heavily, panting, and trying not to scream with joy.

"How's my Blondie doing?"

How *wasn't* I doing with him eating me out? I didn't know what to say, so I said, "Great."

Wow, it's great! Can you tell I'm a weirdo?

My eyes rolled back when he started moving his finger upward with his mouth still firmly planted and his tongue moving. It felt so fucking great; I didn't lie about that. "Yes, very great," flew out of my mouth, and he chuckled.

A second finger slipped in, and I bit my tongue so I couldn't make a sound about it. Two fingers moving in and out slowly, I felt a build-up brewing inside of me. The way he worked his tongue in sync with the way my body reacted wouldn't have me lasting much longer. He ramped up the intensity as if he could feel what I felt and kept hitting the spot just right. A puddle. I was a puddle. In a pool of pleasure that I never wanted to escape.

He kept going to take me to my breaking point. *Oh, fuck!* There it was. It was so close to claiming me and I groaned and begged for more. "Yes," I breathed.

Moaning in response, he held that spot, pushing me over the edge.

Did I scream? I hoped not, but I knew we weren't being discreet in any way whatsoever.

I was sensitive and pulsing. He slowed down while my body spasmed out. *Holy shit.*

He moved back up, helping me out of my bralette and slipping out of his boxers. "I'll be gentle," he said, kissing my collarbone.

On top of me, I watched in full view as he stroked himself a couple of times. His gaze never left mine as he glided the tip up and down at my entrance before smoothly pushing himself inside me. It was a full feeling I desperately wanted to keep, and *fuck*, it felt so good.

Slow, steady strokes started us off as he leaned back down to take my lips with his again. My body responded strongly to every thrust with a moan of pleasure. With every move he made, my hips followed suit.

"Tell me what you feel," he whispered. "I want to know everything going on in that pretty little head of yours."

"I—erm," I started, stuttering. "I don't know what I'm supposed to say."

"I know." He kissed me again. "Try your best." He picked up the pace once he felt me relax with him inside me.

All I knew was that I didn't want it to end. I gripped him harder. "I have *no* idea how to describe how good this is. I want more."

"More?" His tone was teasing, daring me.

I nodded.

"Say it again," he demanded.

"More," I pleaded. "I want more."

He flipped me onto my stomach and pulled my hips back. "Put that pillow under your belly."

I did as he told me and found myself semi-bent over in a lying position, with my ass in the air. My hips were gripped firmly, and he slid back inside me. We both groaned. A breath came low into my neck. "Ready?"

"Yes," I moaned.

The pace was quicker, but it was just too good. Too, too good. "No wonder people do this a bunch." I laughed. It was absolutely nothing like silicone.

A small laugh escaped him as he gripped the sheets next to my head. "You think?" he said, placing a small kiss on my head.

I instinctively pushed back on him with every thrust, my body begging his for more and more. Fuck me, I needed more. "Harder."

His body quivered above mine, and his groans grew deeper.

Was it as good for him as it was for me? His body responded to mine as mine did to his. The thrusts were harder, more desperate. I got flipped back over, and he plunged deeper, faster, harder. In the trance of watching him above me, the expressions he made told me it was good for him, too.

We were completely lost in the moment. The heat between us made the cold feel so far away. The breaths and moans between us filled my room, as did the sounds of my laughter at being such a weirdo. Him inside me and the kisses…

"Fuck," he muttered. "I'm going to come."

A growl came from his throat while he pulled out, spilling his cum all over my stomach. "Wow," I sighed, body going slack. "Spectacular."

He scrounged around for a towel in my room while I laid there with it all over me. Once he had one in his hand, he knelt next to the bed, gently wiping me down. "Let's get you cleaned up." He couldn't stop smiling and shaking his head.

"What?" I sat up.

"You're just so fucking cute. That's all."

He climbed into bed after tossing the towel into the hamper and held me close as we both drifted off to sleep. Future me would be having words with past me.

19

Fallon

"Fallon? Are you awake in there? Some guy named James is here and says he's your bodyguard or something. I have breakfast when you're ready, but it looks like Brent already left."

Knock! Knock!

I shoved Brent as he spooned me in bed. "Brent," I whispered while tapping him. "Get. Up!"

He shifted and moaned, stretching his arms out before clasping them around me again.

More rigorous knocks. "Fal? You alive? I'm coming in because you *never* sleep all day."

I was wide awake and jumping out of bed. "Hold on! I'm awake!"

Brent didn't budge like the sleeping dude he was while I was scrambling to cover my naked body. There was no way to hide the evidence if she came in, and I was furious at Brent for not locking the door behind him.

Kelly poked her head into the room. "I made panca—" Her eyes caught sight of the other body in my bed, and me clutching a blanket around my naked body. Red-handed. "Oh. My. God," she said before closing the door and scampering away, giggling.

"I'll be right out," I hollered at the door.

Mental facepalm.

There were four of us at the breakfast table, sitting as awkwardly as people in our situation could. Eggs, bacon, pancakes, and maple sausages covered the table in a large family style spread. We all looked around uncomfortably while taking small bites of food, wondering who would break the silence first.

Brent decided he would be the one to do it. "Breakfast is great, thanks, Kelly."

"Uh huh." She gave me a sideways glance and kicked me under the table. "Did you two *sleep* well?"

I kicked her back. "Perfectly fine, *thanks*." Subject change time. "So, James. You're my new bodyguard?"

He looked startled that I had acknowledged him and nodded. "I also brought the documents Mr. Evans would like you to review. Don't worry, I will guide you through the process and instruct you on the roles you will be taking on during your transition."

Brent looked between James and me, taking in the information. "You're taking over your mother's company in your sophomore year of college?"

"Why, going to run back to tell Augustus Vaughn?" I avoided his contact after my newfound attitude slipped through the cracks.

James startled for the second time, realizing Brent Vaughn was at my house after spending the night—and fucking me. That news was *not* something I wanted circulating, but I anticipated a lot of discussion about it at some point. The complications kept rolling in for me day by day, never allowing me to come up for air.

And I'm kinda sore. *Awesome.*

"It's probably good news for him," he replied after downing a glass of orange juice. "Your mother and my grandfather worked closely, and I don't expect things would change with you stepping up to lead the company."

"Are you not in line to inherit?"

From the way his jaw tensed when I asked the question, it seemed like it was a sore spot for him. If he wasn't set to inherit the company, why was his grandfather deemed *the Dictator* and so hard on him?

"So…" Kelly chimed in. "Is the hot tub good to go for use? I want to go soak away this knot in my back and have cute date nights with Shane."

"Yep." I popped the "p" for emphasis. "What documents have you got for me, James?"

"Nothing urgent that cannot wait until later in the day." That had to be code for private.

The drama that unfolded just hours ago made me dread seeing the outside world and everyone in it looking at me differently. "I don't know about you guys, but I'm not excited to be on campus today."

"You're uber famous now, Fal."

"Don't remind me, Kel."

Brent leaned into our conversation. "Need a ride?"

"And be spotted with another guy? No thank you. Kelly and I will go together." I glanced at him, feeling like I was seeing a different person. He had a contented look on his face, one that typically held either a devious smirk or an uninterested expression. His regular laid-back demeanor was replaced by sitting unusually tall—his chest puffed up more than normal.

Maybe he was playing the big man in town since Kelly—and James—found us out. Not that it would have been hard to figure out we slept together.

"Damn right. Chicks before dicks. Sorry, Brent." Kelly poked her tongue out at him.

If only things could feel as simple as they did at the kitchen table this morning, but it wouldn't last long. My depressingly short reprieve.

The drive was quiet, and when we arrived on campus, it felt like being transported into an alternate reality. A crowd of students gathered around us as soon as we stepped out of the car.

Fall time was upon us. The leaves were turning, all the green foliage turning brown. The air was cool and perfect for a stroll.

Too bad I wasn't able to enjoy it.

"Why didn't you tell us you were Fallon Montgomery?"

"What's the story with you and Garrett Bradford?"

"Come sit with us for lunch!"

All of it was brutal, and they wouldn't stop. Bodyguards could only do so much to keep the crowds at bay, but my life had turned into a tabloid story, and the internet spread it like wildfire. I expected that Evans would soon be all over me at some point to start doing damage control. A true PR nightmare for a soon-to-be-christened CEO.

So much for going to classes and keeping my head down. Those days were long gone and would never come back, no matter how much I begged or pleaded with the universe.

Welcome to elite life, Fallon Montgomery.

Class was more of the same, but I was grateful that my schedule change wouldn't go into effect until next semester. There was only so much time I needed to spend on campus for my online classes, and students taking pictures of me and whispering would quickly become tiring. I hoped it was a fleeting story that would be overshadowed by the next hot drama to sweep the campus.

It got worse when the professor announced that no one should take pictures of me and asked everyone to stop making noise. All eyes were on me for the entirety of the class. If someone had warned me about the fame attached to my mother's company, I could have at least tried to be mentally prepared for it all.

The head of Beta Kappa Pi, Sloane, made her appearance, linking arms with me and acting like we were the best of friends. "Hey, girl!"

"Hello," was all I thought to say. She was the top girl at the school—at least that's how she made it seem. My instant fame and the fact that I was set to inherit a prominent company must have looked attractive enough to her that she wanted me in her circle.

She sat and crossed her legs, flipping her hair over her

shoulder. "You are *the* Fallon Montgomery. I wish you had told me sooner, babe. You are ever the elusive girl, but I am *so* excited to meet you. Did you know you're third on the list?"

The girls around her started nodding and chattering. Her tone was odd, fake.

"List?" Yet *another* thing I was unaware of.

"Yes, silly." She giggled. "The rich list, of course. Being in the top ten is an honor, but top three? Ugh, I'm jealous! We have no time to waste. I'm sixth, by the way. But someone of your calibre is needed in our sorority, and we need to find you a man in the top ten."

I have no fucking idea what this girl is saying to me.

She pulled me down by my arm, forcing me to sit with her so she could show me her phone. A list on the screen was shoved into my face. "See? Montgomery is number three. That means you're the third richest family among, kind of, everyone. Number one is my boyfriend, Brent Vaughn. So having the two of you associated with BKP will ensure we remain a living legacy for years to come, leaving our mark in the history books. We don't normally allow sophomores, but you'd be an exception.

"Then there's the issue of getting you coupled up with someone. I'll have to do a little digging in the gossip and chatter, but I think Alexander Fitzgerald might be up for grabs." She reached for my hair and pushed it around a bit, eyeing my face. "I think with a little work and some training, you'd make such a little hottie. Do you wear much makeup at all? Some light contouring could make all the difference and make those blue eyes pop. Right, girls?"

Again, they all nodded in agreement with her, creeping me out. It was like I was in a horror movie about a cult.

If one thing terrified me, it was cults. And I was sitting right in front of one.

Wait.

Did she just say her boyfriend was Brent Vaughn? Panic

attack incoming because there went my stomach right out of my ass.

Kelly half-watched me from afar, leaving me to deal with these vultures on my own. Hell, James didn't look like he wanted to intervene with Sloane. Kelly looked amused while she leaned against the wall, typing away on her phone. Her attention was on something else, but I was sure she'd want to hear what this was all about later.

For a chill girl, she was *very* interested in learning all the gossip and secrets.

"Anyway," she continued, "you need to rush with us. It will rebrand you away from that piece of shit, Garrett, and his family. Did you hear his father was being investigated? They're going to be blacklisted for, probably, ever, and you do *not* need to be anywhere near that dumpster fire. Did you know that they were shady?"

Everyone leaned in simultaneously, eager to hear my response.

"As everyone knows, I've kept my head down. I was oblivious to a lot, and I thought he was just being nice to me. We met over the summer and went on dates and stuff, but we never talked about family business. Do you think he knew who I was?" I was genuinely curious. She seemed to be on top of the latest information. I just got the feeling Sloane was nosy.

The girl directly to her right gasped. "Of course he did. I bet he *stalked* you before approaching you! He's barely holding on to a spot in the top ten. His family has been declining year after year, and I'm not surprised at all by their downfall. I bet you he wanted to step up his family's reputation by canoodling with you!"

I scoffed. "Stalked me? Really?"

They nodded in unison. The precision of these girls was better than that of any synchronized swimming team I'd ever seen.

"He totally did," Sloane said. "A rebrand is necessary. Then, we'll get you linked up with a squeaky-clean boy, stat." She clapped her hands, and a few girls produced their phones, showing me pictures of what I could only assume were the guys they wanted to push on me. "Penn. Calvin. Alexander. They are top ten boys and likely to be single as of right now, per our sources. I can have the girls do more recon on them, but they're solid options. I would say to go for the number one, but he's mine."

Holding in my facial expressions was so hard that I opted for biting my tongue as hard as I could. What would she do to me if she found out that not only did I sleep with Brent, but that he was pursuing me endlessly? *Don't forget you gave him your V card, you dumbass.*

Another girl clapped briskly. "We need to find out who's single and set her up on dates. Immediately."

More freaky nodding in sync. So, so freaky.

"We will be your new guide in all things wealthy and elite. You need to learn the ropes of how our society works, as you *obviously* have no clue about the social etiquette that comes with being who you are. We are having a party tonight for those who can afford it, and you will be there to show your face. I can work on clearing the air and your name for you—my family has all the connections, of course. It's the perks of being a Whitmore. I can start and end people, and I will be right by your side, helping you out."

So, this was being elite. Also, who the fuck are the Whitmores?

She patted my knee. "Don't worry about the problem families, either. Their spawn won't be in attendance. You can bring along your little friend as a courtesy." She gave another hair flip so she could flick her gaze to Kelly, who was still leaning on the wall, paying us no mind.

I nodded, knowing that attendance was probably mandatory. Getting on her bad side right off the bat didn't sound like a good idea. "And my bodyguard."

"Duh! Give me your phone." She opened her hand, expecting it. Obligingly, I handed it over. She took it and scrolled faster than I'd seen Kelly flipping through her phone. She took a selfie and then handed it back. "I put my info in your phone for quick access to me. I don't hand out my number to just *anyone*, but I trust you with it. I texted myself, so I have yours too." She flicked her wrist, and the entire group stood up with her. "We'll see you tonight! I am *so* happy I caught you before the party. Don't worry, babe. You are in good hands with me."

That was a lot of speak with nothing of real substance having being said. She struck me as the type to hold a firm grip on her place in the world, fearing that she might lose it at any moment. Whatever just happened, it left me dumbfounded that people could act like that.

Kelly appeared in front of me, snickering. "What was all that?"

"A lot of nothing. One thing's for certain: Sloane just told me that Brent is her boyfriend."

She stiffened. "We're *so* fucked, aren't we? I mean, *you* definitely are."

I had a feeling I would be doing a lot of mental facepalming this semester. "*We* definitely are. She invited us to an exclusive party for rich people and, in the same breath, tried to set me up with three different guys."

My phone dinged with a message. It held the complete list that she mentioned. "Check this out. It's a list of the 'top families' that Sloane is oddly obsessed with."

"Wait." She grabbed my phone from me. "You're number three. No wonder she's obsessed with you now. And her so-called boyfriend is number one. Are you surprised that she's trying to claim him as hers? Huh. Looks like I'm number five."

"Oh no."

"What?"

"Sloane is going to hate you."

She turned my phone around. "She's sixth."

20

Fallon

"What are these documents, even?"

Tucked away in my room with James, he had files and documents out on display. My brain was spinning with words that sounded too business-y for my experience—well, lack of experience. The folders were full, and I was expected to start learning how to read documents like these as CEO.

"In this folder we have our financial documents. This is the profit and loss statement, and we read it to understand our operational efficiency. This one… Are you okay?"

He must have seen my eyes glazing over and the words flying over my head. "I think I need to get a notebook for this. A big one."

"This is why Mr. Evans wants you to be a business major. It's not out of malice, but for your benefit." He kept a level head amidst all this mess. After all, I was paying him, right?

"So… you're my bodyguard *and* my tutor?"

"In a way. So, this one—write this down—is the balance sheet. This details assets, liability, and equity, so you can understand the financial health of Montgomery Group."

Scribbling away, I was determined to truly learn the material. My mother left this to me, and I wanted to ensure her work didn't go to waste. An entire company would be at my mercy, and as a result, employees who relied on the company to feed and clothe their families would be affected. It was a big responsibility to uphold when I was barely in my twenties, and it was not the ideal situation. Everyone was doing their best.

My phone rang, and I was oddly happy that it was Evans, taking me away from my brain turning into soup. "Hello, Evans. Yes, I am learning and reviewing, and yes, I will comply with your demands."

A pause filled the receiver before he responded. "Good to hear. We will be tackling your PR *nightmare* here, but you will need media training. Expect someone by to get you started, and for now, rely on James for guidance. He is your encyclopedia." He paused again, leaving me nervous about what came next. "Do I need to tell you the obvious regarding the boy, or will you make good choices until you are in the boardroom this weekend?"

"When will I be needed?" I sighed.

"Sunday. Expect your Sundays to be booked from here on out. I am pleased to hear of your steps forward despite this dramatic scenario." The line went dead.

"Fuck you, too."

James pursed his lips. "Are we okay to continue?"

"I need a snack first."

Food wasn't an option because as soon as I made it to the living room, someone knocked on the front door. I ripped it open, my patience for the day wearing thin. So much so that I was surprised I didn't rip the door off its hinges.

Of course, it was Garrett at my house. Awesome. He stood there, taken aback that I was so aggressive. "Bad time?"

"Garrett," I sighed. "Unfortunately, you cannot be here and right now, it's best that we don't speak to each other." I caught James out of the corner of my eye as he entered the living room, back in bodyguard mode. "My company is having a PR nightmare. I have a lot of employees to think about right now." I shooed him. "Please. Maybe another time, but not right now."

James was there behind me, ready for anything.

Garrett looked angry. His fists were balled up, and his jaw was clenched. "Fine, but we *will* have a chat about this later. You can't say no forever, and you need to hear what I have to say."

My bodyguard stepped into his view and crossed his arms, silently telling him to get lost or get hurt. He got the hint because he backed away, stomping through my front yard.

Geez, did I even know this guy?

"I'll answer the door from now on," James said, leaving no room for pushback.

"Babe, you sounded like a *boss* just now," Kelly called from the kitchen, holding the leftover box from last night.

That box was calling my name. "Thanks. I am over it for today. I don't want to go to this damn party, learn these damn business documents, or do anything else. But what choice do I realistically have? Everything is happening at the same time. Give me some of that damned cold pizza."

She whipped out some coffee and set the table for us, leaving space for James if he chose to join us. I wondered what he thought about being a bodyguard for a girl like me and what he thought of the antics that went on. *Oh, to be a semi-silent observer.*

"This is *sex* pizza, now."

I groaned. "How is it that I forgot about that?" *Liar.*

"Damn, it was that bad?"

Avoiding her gaze—and James's—I bit into my pizza. *No, it was so great I could do it again despite being sore.* "We're not getting into it. What I will say is that I don't think he sees me like a normal guy would. I think I just gave it up with the worst possible choice."

"Being horny will do that to a girl. No sparks with Garrett?"

Were there even sparks with Brent, or was he just hot and the pheromones got to me? Garrett felt like a safe choice, but based on what everyone was telling me, it seemed that *not* sleeping with him was the smartest thing I'd done in a while. He never got pushy with it and in hindsight, it made sense that his motives could have been something else entirely.

I took a lazy bite of pizza. "Getting into bed never really

came up much. He wasn't pushy about it, and we seemed... surface level? I don't know how to explain it, but I think what some people are saying makes sense."

"Not that it matters now, but he wasn't the one. Don't be so quick to believe what other people are saying just yet. In this world, everything is like an onion. Layers upon layers, just like I wish this pizza had."

She was right. It didn't matter anymore. The drama was already spread all over the internet and probably made it to the freaking news, *and* I slept with Brent after telling myself for so long that I wanted to do it with *The One* one day.

"Snack time," James interrupted.

I got up from the table. "I guess I need to at least finish a bit of this work before getting ready for the party."

Financial documents were officially noted. The documents contained sensitive information, but I had to see what the company reviews on a regular basis in order to lead effectively as CEO. My notebook would be filled before the end of the month. Budget reports outlined projected expenses and revenues for upcoming projects. Investment portfolios informed leadership on investment opportunities.

My brain was soup. How long before it dripped out of my ears?

But at least I looked pretty despite everything getting worse. *Everything gets messier before you can clean it.* I kept that in the back of my mind as I mentally prepared myself while Kelly applied my armor for the night: a full face of makeup and a dress that screamed *I am Fallon Montgomery.*

"So, you like him?" Kelly asked while she focused on my eyeliner.

"Pass."

"Oh, girl." She laughed. "It's going to get *so* much worse for you if you act like this after a hookup. But sure. I'll finish getting you ready for this shitshow of a party."

Let's get this shit storm started.

The primary party was being held at a neighboring fraternity.

The *after* party was at Sloane's sorority house. What would happen at either party was anyone's guess.

The boys must have paid an arm and a leg to get their place decorated because no group of college dudes could decorate to that calibre. From the outside, the party screamed Halloween in a low key way. The darker colors and themed decor made it clear that everyone was ready for fall and itching to go all out ghoul. Pumpkins manifested everywhere, darker colors adorned the decor, and attendees wore masks and costumes.

"I didn't think Halloween started this early with anyone but us." We stood at the edge of the driveway, and I didn't feel like I wanted to go in.

Halloween may actually be terrifying this year.

"It's September now. Anything after July is free game." She nudged me forward as a drunk person in a sheet danced by, holding a bottle of something.

I pouted at her. "My brain hasn't even registered that it's September. We should have dressed up."

"We're hot nonetheless!"

"We could have been a couple of naughty nuns." I winked.

"Ha! Very sacrilegious. Let's drink and dance and hope no one bothers you until it's time to move on to the next venue."

We followed the stream of people inside to whoever was serving drinks and snacks. There were a few familiar faces, but I never clocked them as the top families. Unless... that was reserved for the afterparty.

The snack tables were full, and that was my first stop. I needed *something* other than sex pizza to sustain me for the rest of the night. Especially if people were going to be throwing drinks into our hands left and right.

Avoiding people was also my goal.

"Come on, you can't hide in here forever."

She dragged me into the main room to the bar, where more familiar faces began to appear. Sloane. Her groupies. Shane.

Brent.

"Yeah, no. I'm going back to the other room before those

people see me." I tugged on her arm, but she wasn't budging. For how small she was, the girl was as strong as a brick house. She had strength from how many pancakes she ate.

I pleaded with her using my eyes.

She shook her head. "There is no hiding for you anymore. You said so yourself not that long ago. These are the people you are most likely going to have to see and deal with for the rest of your life, from the circle you were born into. One way or another, you have to face the music and live by the nepo baby rules. Trust me. I've thought about it, and I've resigned myself to the fact that no matter how much I avoid my father, I can't escape him or this life. So, get in there and kick some ass."

In many ways, she was right. She grew up with more knowledge than I had and never told me too much because my mom had died, and she was more concerned with being there for me. She also never told me too much about her family's expectations, other than that her dad disapproved of most of what she looked like or was interested in. Despite this, she was still aware of the societal expectations in our echelon and the etiquette that was required.

A drink was placed in my hand as she linked arms with me, leading me straight into the lion's den.

21

Brent

My heart skipped a beat.

Why it was doing that, I had no idea.

I'd seen her around campus a few times last year, trying to lie low. That blonde hair and those blue eyes drew me in like a moth to a flame. The way she viewed the world was pure and good.

This year, she was becoming tainted, and I wanted to prevent it from happening as much as I physically could. Being in her bed and watching her sleeping face was as close to heaven as I would ever get—God was sending me to hell for sure. The scrunch between her eyebrows when she looked at me—full of animosity and curiosity at the same time—was gone, and her expression looked so innocent.

So sweet.

The anxiety of seeing her and Sloane in the same room rushed over me, no matter how much I tried to push it down. Keeping my cool would be next to impossible. I was truly fucked by how my body responded to Fallon being near me while having Sloane in the same vicinity.

"Babe!" She snapped her fingers in front of my face. "Did you hear what I said, or did you take drugs from the back room or something?"

It was laughable that she thought I would stoop so low as to take drugs. She really thought that little of me. It was between that and how she treated me like a dog.

I pretended to pick some lint off my shirt to avoid her dagger like eyes. She thought of me as her property, too. We hooked up, sure.

But, babe? *No way.*

Swigging my whiskey from my flask, I tuned out whatever else she was going on about. That high-pitched voice felt even more shrill when I simply didn't care anymore. "Stop calling me babe."

More whining. "I can't help it!"

Considering she's the one who told me our hookups were noncommittal, I should have known better before sticking my dick in crazy. She never minded what I did outside of her, but laying her stakes on me in public was far beyond *noncommittal,* if you asked me.

A sleek black dress and a face so done up that it looked ready for the red carpet were calling to me. I excused myself while Sloane was distracted by some groupie fawning over her. The girl that I spent the night with pulled me in like a magnet. I was the moon that circled her.

And she looked just as gorgeous now as she had when she tried to make herself unattractive in stained sweatpants. I shook my head at the thoughts as Josh called out my name. Approaching her directly when I still wanted more was a dangerous game to play, given the uproar that would be caused by the whiny little devil herself.

If she wanted to kill Fallon, she'd try.

"Josh." I reciprocated his fist bump and checked out the group of guys prepping a pool table for a round of games. "What's the wager tonight, boys?"

"Info we have on the families involved. Loser spills. We have whistleblowers here tonight, and it's going to make things interesting, to say the least." Neatly done blond hair came into view after I heard him. Alexander Fitzgerald.

I hated that dude's guts.

"Ah, a wager I can get in on. Though I keep my hands clean… unlike some people." I threw on my nonchalant face, scanning the group of guys to see who I could get a rise out of.

Playing poker was fun. Threatening people, even more so.

"Fuck yeah, man! That's what I'm talking about. Let's play ball—er, pool!" Josh was tipsy as shit, but he was here for a good time. His family was nowhere near wealthy anymore, and he was just happy to be here, not serving drinks at the bar for once.

"Tell us, Vaughn," Alexander said. "Do you have any dirty details on that Garrett? None of the football team showed up, like the *fucking* cowards they are." He downed his drink and threw the empty cup on the floor, spitting for emphasis. "My parents are looking for any and all minute details they can use to help the prosecution. High profile case and all."

Yeah, yeah. We *loved* hearing about his family's legal legacy whenever he was around. He wouldn't shut up about it wherever he went. Sure, his family had been here for generations, but mine had too. Our families never had any beef between them, but after the incident, we almost did. On top of all that, the guy just rubbed me the wrong way.

Alexander had to have been a sociopath, honestly.

I shrugged. "I'm sorry, did I lose a game? I have information, but someone's going to have to beat it out of me."

They all leaned in.

I took a slow swig from my flask before tucking it back into my jacket.

"What're you all looking at? You want to hear all about how I live across the street from his little girlfriend or something?" *I'm going to need more alcohol for this.*

Josh perked up. "We live across the street from her? I might need to make a trip up the street to offer a shoulder to cry on. She's a hottie."

That pissed me off enough to beat the shit out of him, friends or not. The thought of anyone touching her like that pissed me off. She was *mine*.

215

"No, you little *gnat*. She's from a prominent family here. If anyone is going to be introduced to her, it's going to be me. I already have it in the works that she's going to be mine. She'll be sure to be interested in my services." A twisted grin spread across Alexander's face.

Great. Maybe I *should* have done drugs. At least I'd be able to fucking deal with all this talk about the girl that was *mine* and would not be touched by the likes of these fucks. *Sorry, not sorry, Josh.*

But I made a move that I would regret. "Have at it; she seems uptight from what I've seen of her. She's over there if you want to get your head bitten off."

He clapped me on the shoulder, handed me the pool cue, and walked in her direction. I dug my own grave with that one, and I wasn't sure I'd let him live through the night if he put his grubby hands on her.

Someone needed to bring another round of drinks. I needed to be drunk for this.

"Alright, boys. Who's ready to play pool?"

Taking the first shot, I broke the balls and pocketed two.

Someone piped up. "So, do we know for sure that Garrett's family is guilty of what's rumored? We only have one family identified, and sometimes we like to gang up and take out the weaker dog. There's more than one family getting destroyed at any moment, and we need to find out who they are—if that's even happening."

I handed off the pool cue, observing the conversation. Keeping my mouth shut about important information was my main goal. Finding out what other people knew was the second step. Anything I heard at either party was to be immediately reported to the Dictator as soon as possible. Full write up.

"A guy in my class ran out as soon as the text dropped."

"And who was that?"

The cue came back to me, and I took my shot while listening carefully.

"Oh gosh, uh, was his name *Pencil*? No, that's not a name.

Pens and pencils... Oh! Penn. Is that a name?" He sounded very drunk, but Penn was most definitely a name. Penn was a top family, reigning over whatever they wanted to. They were a political family with an affinity for insider trading.

"Penn Windsor? Money laundering for sure if they're not scrutinized for their love of the stock market."

Yep, just like I said. It was plausible that they could have been taken down, too. Bradford's family operated in finance, and they could have held hands and reigned in the cash. There were large rings and smaller rings operating in dirty business.

My family kept it in the family. Until Maria Montgomery entered the stage.

A group of people caught my eye from where I stood. Fallon, Sloane, Kelly, and Alexander were all together in one little hushed conversation. Sloane was gesturing between Alexander and Fallon, clearly introducing the two. I wasn't aware that Fallon and Sloane were acquainted, and that made everything even more complicated. But more than that, what the fuck was she doing?

Matchmaking and vying to maintain her family's status.

Sloane was obsessed with this little fucking list she had compiled of the wealthiest families who attended WBU. I still remember the day she beelined her ass over to me to let me know that I was number one on the list. She was obviously trying to cement her place in the world by sleeping with me and being seen with me, but I was too stupid to see it. Getting my dick wet at the time was more important than anything she was saying.

At least she shut up when it was in her mouth.

Focus!

Alexander smiled at Fallon and shook her hand. It was creepy. He motioned to her, and she handed over her phone. This bastard was trying to get her number, and she didn't even have mine in her phone!

Kelly looked between all three of them, critiquing and criticizing everything with her arms crossed. As she should. A guy appeared behind the group and tapped her on the shoulder, pulling her away from the other three. Great, Fallon was alone with the sharks, and I was nowhere to help.

"Brent, what do you think?"

I blinked and refocused on the group. "Sorry, what?"

"What's your opinion on Shane Jones?"

"Who the fuck is that?" I could have sworn I heard that name somewhere.

A few chuckles erupted around the table. "Get your head out of your ass, Vaughn. He's the campus dealer, bro. Sources say his family went bankrupt or some shit."

That was a name to add to the list in the files. Especially if he was close enough to what was mine. Reaper and the boys could do some recon for me on that.

I took my next shot. "If I want drugs, I'm not going to some shitty campus dealer. I have respectable *men* for that. Everything is speculation right now, but I wouldn't say I'd be surprised."

A voice that sounded like nails on a chalkboard chimed out behind me. "Babe!"

Fuck me in the ass with a cactus.

"I'll be back, guys." The table gave me some extra sexual remarks as I backed away, ready to rip my ears off my head if she used that tone of voice again.

"Stop fucking calling me that. What do you want?"

"Come on, I'll show you." She grabbed my hand and pulled me right to who she'd been talking to.

Alexander winked at me as Fallon looked up, startled to see me. The girl I just slept with, cuddled all night, and stayed for breakfast with was being dangled in front of some other man right in front of me. I looked her over, giving nothing away about my thoughts, and stayed casual.

I nodded at him. "Alexander."

"Brent! My man!" He raised his glass at me. "Thanks for the nudge on getting me this beauty."

Cringe. *Don't express shit, Brent.*

Her eyebrow perked at his statement. She was wondering

what the hell he was talking about and why I told him to take a shot at her.

"Brent, baby, I'm helping *the* Fallon Montgomery. She came to me for help because of that trashy Bradford family legal drama. I figured I should introduce her to some top-ten boys to remake her image and induct her into our world. Aren't I doing so good with helping her?"

"Mhm." I'm sure she did *not* seek out Sloane, of all people, for help.

"*Aaand* since we will all be at the afterparty, I'm excited to see the budding romance between two powerful families. He's second, she's third, and I will be named the matchmaker at their wedding. Ah! It's all so exciting."

Sloane was fucking insane.

Fallon kept her mouth shut. *Good girl.*

Alexander turned to her, running his nasty hands through her hair to brush it back. "Want to go somewhere private to talk, or shall we save that for the afterparty? I have a contact who will be bringing some pretty white lines to the *exclusive* VIP gathering."

My fists itched to hit him until his brains were splattered on the floor.

She perked her lips into a grin that looked genuine. "I think I can wait for the afterparty. I just got here and need to loosen up first."

Oh, Blondie, you have no idea how deep in shit you are. The elite's kids and their friends partied, took drugs, and fucked one another at those parties. Literal elite orgies. The guys, I'm sure, took full advantage of hopped-up girls who wouldn't say anything anyway.

Sloane checked her phone. "My house is opening in an hour if anyone wants to get there early to start their party fun. Brent, let's go." That purr in her voice might have convinced me in the past, but I didn't trust Alexander for a moment with what was mine.

No way in hell would I let him get her alone.

"Yeah, no. I'm going to head back to the guys." I avoided eye contact with Fallon.

"Ugh, you're no fun, but that's okay." She put her hands on me. "You can just stay over with me later. Anyway, have you ever met Fallon?"

I glanced at her for a second, more regret building in my bones. There was also the issue of not trying to lick her entire body with just my eyes. "Nope," I said, emphasizing the "p," and it hurt me to know this was in her best interest. "Which is surprising because her name is everywhere now. Did you even go to this school last year?"

"I did." She had that adorable sour tone to her voice again. "Did you?"

I crossed my arms and stood taller. "Guess you really did live under a rock like they say."

She suppressed a scoff and turned her attention back to Sloane. "I'm going to head off and have some fun with my friends before the afterparty."

"Your friend who slinked off with her beau, Shane? They might want some alone time." Sloane wiggled her shoulders at her like they were brand new best friends. "I'm sure Alexander can help you party with your friends. He's quite the gentleman."

"At your service. C'mon, let's go have some fun."

I didn't want to interject, but I felt I had to. "Shane as in Shane Jones?"

"That's her boyfriend."

God, Blondie looked so good while she had that sour attitude with me.

"One of the guys at the pool table said some *interesting* things about him and his family. They think he's got something to do with the shit—could be just rumors though. Might want to keep your entire house clean if I were you."

"Then I do need to find her." The gears in her brain were turning, and she likely thought everything was turning into a giant conspiracy around her.

Watching the innocence in her eyes start to fade was going to break my heart.

"Heard he sells shitty drugs on campus."

Sloane looked excited with the new information presented to her. "What a layer to add to the story! A drug dealer could be a fun twist. I should talk to my parents this weekend to see what's going on in our circles…"

I had to make some quick moves to get people to move the way I wanted them to. Fallon was going to hate me, but what I did now was all for her.

"Sloane, why don't you go and round up the important people for the afterparty so we can get things started early? You can do more sleuthing, and we can continue this discussion there." I grabbed her by the waist and gave her a bland kiss that I hoped Fallon could see through. Whether or not she hated me, I would keep her safe under the wing of my grandfather.

My kiss earned a giggle from the whiner, and she moved quickly to oblige me.

Alexander was hauling Fallon off in some random direction while looking at her like a hungry animal.

My night was fucked.

22

Fallon

I regretted sleeping with him.

Like I knew I would.

Whatever. I needed to find Kelly. Hearing those things about Shane needed to be cleared up—and quickly. She had only been gone for a few minutes, and I hoped she hadn't gone far. That Alexander guy was following me as I broke away from the group and headed off in the direction I saw her go.

This guy was a fucking creep. He was trying to undress me with his eyes the entire time, and there was a sinister undertone in his gaze that said he'd do it whether I wanted my clothes to come off or not.

No, thank you.

There were many levels of drunk people around me as I pushed past them all to find the path Kelly may have taken. Maybe upstairs, if they wanted to go somewhere to make out or hook up. *Or do fucking drugs!* I checked my peripheral to see if I'd lost Alexander in the crowd and almost fell over in relief upon realizing he wasn't near me. That was the last thing I needed—being in a dark room, trapped alone with one of the wealthiest kids in the nation, unafraid behind the shield of his daddy's money.

There were a lot of doors to check, but I started on them

anyway. She had to be here somewhere. Door number one opened to reveal three people naked in the act, completely unaware that I'd even opened it. *Gross*, and not Kelly. Door number two was locked; I knocked for a response. Nothing. The next door was a few steps ahead, but someone quickly came up behind me.

"Blondie," the voice whispered.

I didn't know whether I should be relieved it was him or not.

"Oh, why don't you go fuck your *girlfriend*?" My steps hastened so I could stay away from him and continue my search.

Behind the next door were a couple of people who had passed out naked. Again, *gross*. Where the fuck was I?

"Hey," Brent growled, grabbing my wrist. "I'm here to *help* you."

I snatched my wrist back from him and turned around without a response to keep looking on my own. Fuck his help. Fuck him.

"Fuck." The rooms upstairs showed nothing, and I stomped down the hallway to look for her downstairs. She had to be somewhere.

"Fallon."

I sidestepped him. "No."

He moved to block me and easily evaded my attempt to shove him away. I didn't want to be anywhere near him because I felt icky. Everything felt icky. I wanted to find Kelly and just get out of here, even for a few minutes to breathe before we had to trudge on with the rest of the night. I didn't want to be at a stupid party or afterparty, and I sure as hell didn't want to be *the* Fallon Montgomery.

My wrists were trapped in his grip. He bent down to meet my eyes. "Let. Me. Help. You."

"No." I thrashed against his grip.

He didn't budge.

Stupid man strength.

"Are you mad at me?" His tone was teasing, and his expression became dangerous.

"Brent. So help me God, let me go *right now*." I used as much force as I could to yank my hands downward to get him to release me. No one would put their hands on me *ever* again.

He released and showed me his hands. "Fine. Now what?"

Anger grew inside me. He acted like he didn't know me, for sure. That made sense, considering we were dealing with much more than just a simple hookup. Being seen with him moments after the tabloid drama with Garrett was not something I wanted, anyway. But kissing her in front of me was such a brutal move. It showed that he really didn't care as he said he did.

"Find Kelly. Get to the next stupid fucking party. That's it. You want to help? That's *all* I want from you and nothing more." I pushed past him to get downstairs and out to the backyard.

The sea of people awaited me, and keeping my head down was going to be an impossible task. I didn't want them to see me and act like a bunch of starved piranhas, but it was inevitable, given that my face was embedded in their minds in the current climate. Phones were out, with a few people snapping pictures and calling things out to me. Those pictures would end up on social media, on some random headline, and worst of all, on Evans's desk.

Ignoring them and their chatter, I started texting Kelly.

ME:

Kel we need to get to afterparty now

Keeping the screen on, I breached the back door and stepped onto the porch. My eyes were peeled for her wild brown hair and her usual standout outfit.

"Circle of life. Or whatever they say." Brent's voice invaded my space again. He flicked open his cigarette case and offered me one. Just like that first night.

Part of me wondered if any of these things would have happened if I had never got on that stupid motorcycle with him. Never talked to him, even. Better yet, I wished I had never even glanced in his stupid direction.

"Don't ignore me when I'm standing right in front of you," he said.

I stared at the cigarette hanging out of his mouth. How could he be so chill about everything all the time? The constant of something insane happening must be a regular occurrence for these people.

"I'm not here to be chummy with you."

"Not what you said when—"

"Stop."

My phone buzzed. Thank God.

KELLY:

where u at? ill meet u

ME:

back porch come alone plz

KELLY:

okayyyyyy weirdo

Brent let out a puff of smoke, looking at me expectantly. "So?"

"She's coming out. She's found. You can go now." It was tempting to shoo him away, but that might be seen as me being playful or as an invitation. There was no way I was in the mood for him, and it showed.

He snatched my phone from my hands and held it out of my reach. With the one hand he held high above me, he typed something while I began to reach for it. Still typing, he used his free hand to push my head away until he finished.

All while balancing that stupid cigarette in his mouth. "Ah, much better," he said, handing my phone back.

I glared at him. My screen was back on the home page, and all apps were closed, so I didn't know what he was doing. "What did you do?"

"Since another man wants what's *mine*, I figured the least you could do was let me have your phone number, and you can call me when you need me to crash another date." He loosely pulled the cigarette from his mouth, flicking the ash from the end.

"You deserve *nothing* from me," I huffed.

He smiled. "You're so fucking cute when you're mad."

I crossed my arms to put a barrier between us. "You're clearly with Sloane, and—"

"No," he said firmly. He came too close to me, and I could hear his breathing again. "I have no desire to be with her. She's clung to me for a long time because she likes my last name." His eyes flickered and darkened, looming over me. "Blondie, are you jealous?"

He almost entranced me, but I took a large step back from him. From that magnetic pull. "I'm not answering your questions."

"I have my answer."

The back door opened, and Kelly stepped out. "What's with the creepy 'come alone' message, and what has you sending it?"

Brent leaned onto the paneling on the back of the house, flicking his cigarette ash again. "Want to let us in on the secret about your boy toy?"

She looked between us, caught red-handed. So, she knew about Shane and his extracurricular activities. And she was okay with that? I thought I knew everything about her, but it turns out that I didn't. Was her meet-cute with him even real, or was she seeking him out for what he could provide?

The constant conspiracy revelations were getting to me.

"What do you mean?"

He chuckled. "The fact that he's *allegedly* a drug peddler for the kids on campus. Know anything about that or why he's doing it?"

Brent seemed to have an interrogation tactic because I would have come out swinging with all the information I had. He tried to draw it out of her, so she had to come clean instead of allowing us to sit in false knowledge. It was about finding out what they knew first, and I saved that information in my mental notebook for later.

Look, Evans, I'm learning, you prick.

She looked guilty. "What's wrong with being a little... entrepreneurial?"

"This isn't funny, Kel. Everything is a mess with all the little stories popping up in the news."

"Okay, yes. He does deal, but it's not for some weird reason like you'd think."

Brent's eyes met mine. The look told me that things were getting serious. "I think the three of us should get to the afterparty and find somewhere more private to chat. We need to get our stories straight on what we've heard and what we know."

Kelly let out a resigned sigh. "Did something happen?"

Thud!

Just as Kelly spoke, a body hit—well, *splat*—on the concrete just before the pool.

I thought I was going to be sick on the porch. His limbs were...crumbled. Blood started pooling beneath him, and that empty gaze in his eyes...

Oh God, is he...dead?

Brent quickly grabbed both of us by our arms and led us around the side of the house with a swiftness that made it seem like he may have dealt with a few *too* many death emergencies before. There was no way I was going to recover from this.

No one was freaking out.

"Keep moving. Walk faster." He kept his voice whisper quiet as he shoved us forward.

My life was turning into something horrifying. The image of the guy lying there, broken and dead. Should I have called an ambulance? Should I have assumed he was dead? There was no real way to know. Cops would be all over it, investigating and letting people know if he was dead or alive.

Just another PR nightmare to add to the list.

His arms were draped over both of us as if he were flirting, guiding us away from the crowd for some alone time. It was a smart move. It made me suspicious of what else Brent knew—or had experienced—as part of the insane "Nepo Baby Club." We slowed to a casual stroll, trying to appear unaware that there was a—*potentially*— dead guy in the backyard.

"I shouldn't have opened my mouth," Kelly muttered.

Meanwhile, I kept silent, flicking Brent's arm off me. What was I supposed to say? She just made a terribly morbid joke after seeing that guy firsthand. He looked so... contorted.

Just breathe. All you can do is breathe right now.

Noticing my hand was being held, I tried to focus on the feeling. Everything started to feel far away, blurry. Like I was slipping away from reality. There was no way that happened, right? No, definitely not.

"Do you two know what really goes on with the wealthiest families?"

It was Brent's hand I was holding. I didn't want to be holding his hand.

"Some of it. Not like I'm in the biggest of the circles." Kelly's voice was far away.

His skin was warm and soft, though.

"You've been using drugs, then?"

There was a callus on the palm of his hand.

"Fallon?" His voice also sounded far away.

He was looking down at me from quite a height. *Was I on the ground?*

"Hey." He bent down and pulled my hand back into his, but I yanked it away.

I shook my head, and things came back into focus. Kind of. *Focus.* "Kelly's doing drugs? Like more than weed?"

"Chill. Most people try something at some point." He looked back at Kelly standing behind him. "For right now, you know nothing. My best bet is that this gets tied up with a nice bow as an accidental death, and no one will be the wiser. I've seen it happen more than once."

I've seen it happen...

So it *was* a normal occurrence. Lovely. I just experienced my first wave of shock and disassociation, and I wasn't sure if I was quite back yet. The next party awaited us, and I was on the ground, trying not to die. Throwing up was a better option than feeling disconnected from reality. My head was spinning, and I tried to reconnect with my body, with anything. I felt the concrete under my hands; it was cool to the touch. The night air had a slight edge to it. Grounding. I was coming back down. *Maybe.*

Freak outs could come later. It was time to stand up and finish the night. *If my legs didn't feel like boneless jelly blobs, maybe.*

Beta Kappa Pi—"BKP," as everyone referred to it—had a line up at the door. The exclusive party was ready early, per Brent's request. Someone was at the front with a tablet, checking names. The party was for the people on the list only.

We lined up at the end of the line like it was a nightclub. A hand brushed the small of my back—Brent and his antics.

Only it wasn't him.

"Hey, beautiful."

Alexander. He towered over me, stooping down to kiss the top of my head like we were cozier than it seemed. Even though we just met each other.

"Oh, hi." I leaned out of his grasp and linked arms with Kelly.

He tried to place his hands on me again, reaching for *other* parts of me while I leaned farther away from him. No dice. He pulled me closer to him, holding me like we were a couple or something. "Don't be so shy, baby girl. We'll get to know each other just fine tonight."

Ew. There was vomit coming for me at some point during the night. I felt it building up.

As we moved through the line rather quickly, he held onto me with a firm grip. The struggle in front of everyone wasn't worth it. From what everyone told me, it was a game of staying in line and playing chess instead of checkers.

I suck at chess.

Kelly eyed us with confusion but said nothing. She also knew not to stir the pot. Brent, on the other hand, was attempting to avoid looking at us. There would be daggers in his eyes despite tonguing Sloane in front of me.

If I weren't so uncomfortable, I'd say it was worth it to see him jealous.

The guy with the tablet put a purple wristband on me. Alexander told me it was to mark my prestige among the party's peasants. The importance of prestige and money was becoming clearer to me as the days went by. Money and power ruled it all, but you weren't allowed to say it out loud.

The rules weren't meant to be spoken.

I spotted a few girls spinning from the ceiling on aerial silks. They looked like hired professionals with their well-practiced and elegant moves—like ballet in the sky. Other girls walked around with hors d'oeuvres in bunny costumes, their bodies almost bare and their faces covered. Guys in top-of-the-line tuxedos carried trays filled with drinks and *other* items. I didn't have to wager a guess about what those were.

On top of that, security guards were posted everywhere.

Mine was hidden for the night. A large man following me around instead of hiding out in the shadows might make me stick out more than I wanted to. He promised I'd be safe, but our definitions might have differed.

"I'm game to start this party right." Alexander's hands gripped tighter on my arms.

Too tight. I couldn't force him to let go. The vomit monster was threatening me again, and I needed to keep my wits about me.

Dinging rang out across the party, and in unison, everyone pulled out their phones.

UNKNOWN:

Party foul?

Attached to the text was a picture of the body I had seen. He was dead on the ground, and the flash from the picture made him look even worse. My ears started ringing like a bomb had gone off. The disassociation threatened to take me again. *Not yet.*

"Good riddance! Let's party!" The crowd in the room cheered, and the music thumped even louder. Laughs and smiles were all around, and there wasn't a care in the world.

It was as if I had witnessed a scene from a horror movie, and I might just be the main character. What would a character in my position do?

She wouldn't be flailing and dissociating. She'd be doing her damnedest to keep her shit together. *To fit in.*

Kelly looked uncomfortable for the first time tonight, like the bad news had finally hit her. She rubbed her arm and forced herself not to fidget with the news. She took most things in stride, but I didn't take her for having a flippant attitude like the rest of these rich assholes. Brent slinked off in some random direction.

"Don't worry"—Alexander patted my head and stroked my hair—"we have no connection to any of that. All I have to do is hand over my card, and we'll be left alone. Why don't we blow off some steam and do some dancing to loosen you up?" He showed no emotion about the *dead* person at a party he was just at. *No conscience, either.*

I needed to get rid of this guy. He struck me as the type not to ask for consent. "I'll be with Kelly for a bit." I tried to keep my tone sweet, smiling at him. How convincing it was, I couldn't be sure.

As expected, he brushed off my objection like a seasoned, sleazy used-car salesman. "Baby, give me just a few minutes of your time. I promise I'll make them worth it—I want to get to know the future Mrs. Fitzgerald better." He raised my hand to his nasty lips and placed a kiss on it.

Gross. "I didn't think I'd get a marriage proposal right off the bat."

Kelly pretended she didn't hear a single thing and interjected that she was taking me to the bar to loosen me up first, and that I'd be better in a bit.

"That dude is a fucking freak," she murmured in my ear as she pulled me away from him.

"Observation or experience?"

"Both. Come on."

Both?

Conversations and eerie laughter swirled around us as we moved through the crowd. No one cared about the tragic ending to someone's life. It was like they were *celebrating* it.

"Think we should send flowers? Or would a gift card be better?"

"...and you know how it works. Money talks and dead men don't..."

"...hope no one else opens their mouth. Don't they know better than..."

Giggles and crunches from food swirled in my ears, and my body threatened me once again. It would either be vomiting or passing out. Kelly gripped my hand tighter because she had heard it all, too. Everyone here knew something, one way or another. I was horribly out of the loop and wondered what my mother knew—or thought—about this life that she failed to at least *warn* me about. She must have had a lot of trust in me before she died. *Hope you still have it up there, Mom, because I have no idea what I'm doing.*

"Money talks and dead men don't" played in a loop in my head.

Adrenaline had been pumping through my veins since I stepped foot into the frat party, and it showed no signs of slowing down; I needed food. The table in front of me boasted a lot of carbs, and I had a feeling I'd burned through whatever energy I had left. I nabbed a bunch of snacks.

I kept my voice low. "You heard the same things, right?"

She nodded, her eyes scanning the crowd. Her arms were comfortably crossed over her stomach as she surveyed the scene. "Mhm. Keep your toes out of the water—piranhas everywhere."

Understanding began to come to me. If I wanted to stay above water, I would have to take her advice in unconventional ways. Last semester, she encouraged me to branch out, and I knew this wasn't what she meant by that, but I needed to take the advice regardless. "I need to start swimming with them."

She raised an eyebrow. "What are you thinking?"

"The things I heard—I need to know what's going on. I'm tired of feeling like a child."

The crowd was still laughing and cheering over a dead potential whistleblower's kid. Whatever food I managed to eat wanted to resurface. We pretended to mingle while keeping our eyes and ears open to where certain people with specific wristband colors started to migrate. They looked to be heading toward a door in the back, guarded by two large, imposing men. Guards. Someone approached them and showed their wristband to be let in.

I had the most prestigious one. Purple.

I bet I could get in.

"More exclusive area?" she whispered.

"Where we find secrets," I replied.

We beelined for the door and were let in with no hassle. *Purple wristband.*

The atmosphere inside was alien to that of the party. The noise was almost nonexistent—like the walls were designed for it. No flashy lights or loud music. Just clusters of people engaged in hushed conversation, and a woman playing the harp in the corner.

She looked like a prisoner over there.

I looked around and saw secrets, business, and lies in the mouths of everyone.

More snippets of conversations wafted by as we waded through the tables and made our way to the bar.

"...he's worried about shipments..."

"...no more loose ends tonight..."

"...the scandal needs to be tempered down. Fitzgerald..."

My heart pounded with anxiety during the conversations. It felt like I wasn't supposed to be here, and everyone would stand up and point me out. Like a nightmare. They'd point me out as an outsider and throw me off the building next.

I wasn't supposed to be here. I could feel it.

Kelly elbowed me cautiously, nodding over to the corner. Brent was speaking with someone across the room.

"Drinks," I whispered and turned my attention to the men manning the... stations of sorts.

I wondered what Brent would be discussing in a place like this. He was number one, after all, and his grandfather was the top businessman in the country. You didn't get there without being in places like this and working with other top dogs. You *also* didn't get there by being a stand-up person, ready to make a difference in the ways a commoner would expect. You got there by dealing in money, power—*blood*.

"Champagne?" The man behind the bar offered a glass to each of us, his hands covered in white gloves. "We also have something stronger."

The man at the second station gestured to his *bar* of sorts. Trays of drugs. Casually displayed for all to use at their convenience. No way this was happening.

Holding my flute, I smiled and politely declined.

"What the fuck do I do?" I kept my voice as low as humanly possible, hoping to avoid any eyes that came my way.

She smoothed out my skirt, looking unbothered. "Drink and observe. The best thing is to watch quietly without drawing attention to yourself."

This was a whole new side to the girl I had known for a large chunk of my life. She was prudent despite her playful side, but she must have had her fair share of secrets based on how I've seen her behave. Her silence spoke volumes to me now. Our bond seemed able to withstand most things, but I sent up a silent prayer that it would survive *anything*.

We drank in silence, observing, until Brent inevitably left his conversation and made his way over to us. He accepted a champagne and tucked a packet of something from the table into his pocket.

"Enjoying the party?" He took a sip of his drink.

Despite the chaotic events, I felt a sense of relief having two familiar people next to me. "Mhm."

I couldn't exactly say I was enjoying the party, right?

"I realized something earlier. You were kept out of things for a reason, but you're in it now." He kept his voice hushed enough that I could barely make out what he was saying.

What the hell did that mean? What reason was he talking about?

Reading my facial expression, he shook his head and smiled. "Not here. You two staying out of trouble?"

"Why would we get into trouble?" Jokester Kelly was back.

"Double trouble, then. Fallon, I'd like to discuss some business with you when you have a chance. My people tell me that you're being groomed for your leadership position. Our families have a longstanding… relationship. I'd like to keep it"— he looked me up and down like we were back in the bedroom again—"*strong*."

Taking a swig of my drink to clear my throat, I grumbled at him. "I have a meeting with one of *my* people coming up about current events. I'll inquire about your request with him."

"I look forward to it. Shall I have our schedules lined up?" The look on his face said he was enjoying this forced polite interaction. I wanted to punch the look right off it.

"Sounds great, Mr. Vaughn. I should probably find my way home now since I have an early morning." I raised my glass to him and turned back to Kelly.

"Did you just—never mind. I have something I need to do before we can be on our way home. Meet me right outside the front door in twenty."

Something she needed to do? With whom?

"I'll be leaving this *wonderful* room and rejoining the party until then," I said, inching my way to the door to get the hell out of the uber VIP area.

The outside party jolted me awake as I stepped out. Geez, that room *was* soundproof. I was relieved to be back in the main area. *Never thought I'd say that.* We parted ways, and I marched my hungry ass back to where the food was. My small purse was calling me to squirrel away some extras for later.

Say what you want about rich people; they have good snacks.

"You're a slippery one, aren't you, baby girl?" He snatched my wrist with even greater force this time. His eyes looked a bit glazed over from whatever drugs he had taken, and I genuinely feared for my safety.

Alexander. His swagger didn't compare to Brent's; he wasn't as practiced at it. He was the *daddy will sue* type if he didn't get what he wanted—and those guys never carried much charm.

I used my free hand to pop some fruit into my mouth and looked down at my trapped arm. "Right now? Not really."

His smile grew pitch black. "I could change that, you know." He brushed a strand of hair behind my ear. "You and I could be a power couple. Take the world by storm. My soon-to-be power, along with your company, would give us something Chamberlain Industries could never have."

Got it. Money and power were what all these people liked to play with. I smiled at him as sickly sweet as I could manage. "Then you'd have to woo me properly. I've heard you're quite the gentleman, but I'm not seeing it."

He released my hand and relaxed his shoulders by an inch. A small lowering of his guard. "Why didn't you just say so, baby girl?"

"I just did." Feigning boredom, I popped another snack into my mouth. If I wanted to make it out of this, I needed to come up with a winning strategy. Because I had to face the fact that his type was willing to kill for what they wanted.

Note to self: Figure out what a winning strategy is if you're a million steps behind everyone else.

"I love a challenge. Go ahead and play hard to get." His words sounded more sinister than any movie I'd ever seen. They sounded cruel.

"Well, it was wonderful to meet you tonight. I have an important event I cannot miss." I nodded politely and excused myself, being careful not to full on sprint in the opposite direction from him.

The guy was a lunatic, and the asylum was looking for him.

Kelly headed to the front door at the same time as I did. A good sign that it was time to get the hell out of here and back home, where I could pretend I was safe.

Outside, I almost collapsed to the ground from the weight lifting off me. Kelly pulled out snacks and handed me cheese and crackers wrapped in a napkin. *Food, my favorite.*

My phone pinged.

WORLD'S HOTTEST BASEBALL PLAYER:

hey blondie

Awesome, I forgot all about that. Brent stole my phone, gave himself my number, *and* gave himself a stupid name. Before I could reply, another message came through.

UNKNOWN:

see you soon baby girl

Great. I sighed and swiped out of my messages because I was not going to deal with either of them.

Kelly looked pensive during the drive back. The driver hopefully enjoyed having us as calm passengers. Who knew what the poor rideshare drivers had to deal with on and near campus, alongside the wealthiest kids in the country?

I was just looking forward to being in bed and blissfully knocked out, trying to rid my mind of the garbage swirling in my head. That was the hope, anyway. Sleep might not want me as much as I wanted it.

"Sit down." Kelly motioned to the couch after I kicked my shoes off.

"Okay..."

"I need to ask for your discretion."

My eyes narrowed. "Like an NDA type thing?"

She nodded. "Pinky promise me this does *not* leave this room."

We linked pinkies and sealed the deal.

"I know why that guy died."

23

Fallon

"What do you mean you know why he died?" I wasn't sure if she was trying to play a sick joke on me or if she was being serious.

"A few times when I was around my dad, I heard some things. Crazy things."

It tracked. She clearly knew more than I did. Her actions after what we witnessed—and what I wanted to forget—struck me as strange. Just like Brent. They were both around their families before Willow Bay and learned so much more about the life we lived than I did.

And honestly? My mom was an asshole for not telling me.

"There are families here who will kill you for one thing or another. I watched some scary men threaten some people, their families, and their kids if they didn't cooperate—by listening, observing, and reporting back to them. We deal in more than just regular business contracts. I kept my mouth shut so *I* wouldn't be threatened by my own dad."

"I don't understand. What motivations are there for killing each other?"

She slumped into the couch. "How do you stay above the law? How do two people keep a secret? *Threats*, or if one of them is dead. The connections run deep and wildly far. If I was blacklisted, for instance, I wouldn't be able to show my face in public, let alone get a job as a grocery bagger. It's the same thing that made Mafias so successful back in the day. We just run them publicly."

From what I gathered, multiple things needed to happen at once to maintain power. Building a relationship with trusted allies who support you and your goals is essential for maintaining a strong foundation. These families remained close-knit for a reason. Keeping and expanding resources held power in multiple facets. If you had enough money, you could change the laws to your advantage through lobbying. How else would some of these big names remain at the top? The political advantage was second to none. Then there was the threat of retaliation. If you and your allies are threatened, you band together to eliminate or contain those threats.

And those were just *some* of the rules they played by.

I breathed out after letting my thoughts run wild. "So, they were asked to be what, moles?"

"Eyes. Ears. Silence. Encouragement. Those are the four tiers they want. Otherwise, you'd be useless."

"Encouragement to do what?" *Did I even want to know?*

"Eliminate threats."

They *killed* after being threatened themselves? I had to take a moment to look away from her. The twists and turns just kept coming, and I still needed to vomit. The standard was, what, killing? Was everyone guilty of something? Was blackmail the standard? Threatening someone's life and then turning them to killing someone else felt like a made-up story, but if it was in the name of self-preservation, I wouldn't know what I would do in their position.

If all of this was true, I needed to get far, *far* away from people like Alexander who would *kill me* for turning him down. Sloane appeared too obsessed with what she was into, which made me wonder if she was also acting out of self-preservation.

Would I be capable of killing someone?

Was everyone scared for their lives?

That text was right… *Let the games begin.*

She waited for a few minutes before continuing. "I never wanted this life either, you know. We were born into it and it's what our parents are handing down to us. Extreme wealth and notoriety above all others don't come without a cost. It means the devil is constantly knocking at your door."

It felt like she was trying to tell me something other than what she'd said out loud. My stomach was still threatening me—

Not anymore.

I threw up all over the dining room floor. While it was nice that I felt a major relief from my nausea, I was deeply upset that I couldn't make it to the sink or bathroom to toss my cookies.

"Jesus Christ! Are you good?" She made a mad dash for the bleach and some towels.

"Actually. I'm a lot better now." My eyes were out of focus, but I excused myself to take a long, hot shower in an attempt to feel something.

I towel dried my hair and padded out into the living room after trying to burn myself back into reality, where Kelly was watching a movie—well, texting while a movie was on. "You know what I need right now?"

"What?"

"To cash in on a promise that I think you'll also enjoy."

Did I want to call Brent? *No.* Did I want to see Brent? Also, *No.*

But I did—I picked up the phone and dialed.

One ring.

Two rings.

"Hello?" He sounded amazed that I called him so soon.

"So… I need to cash in on that delivery promise right now."

Grunting came from the other line. "Like, right now?"

"What are you doing?"

"Nothing, Blondie. I'll be over in… an hour. Tops. See you soon." *Click.*

Kelly pursed her lips, wondering what the hell I was doing. "Delivery promise?"

I laid myself out on the couch. "Food." After everything that had happened—throwing up in the kitchen and my mental breakdown in the shower—I needed proper food. It was the least I could do for myself.

"I know you've been through a lot, babe. I've always been curious about you not sharing much about your mom's business, but then I realized you weren't told the same things we were as kids. Your mom was a great woman, but she did you a disservice by not telling you that you're one of the richest girls in the country. And when she passed, I didn't know all that you had gone through at your aunt's house. I just wanted to be there for you as a friend."

There were certain demons I never wanted to talk about with other people. Aunt Sylvia was one of them. The abuse, the occasional drunken beating, the constant projection of jealousy toward my mom were her shitty coping mechanisms for not being successful like her sister. No one but me was included in my mother's legacy.

My mother hated her family from what I gathered. She never talked about them much, but I got the gist that she wasn't treated well. With her mounting success, her five siblings attempted to come around and cozy up to her when she became the family's "golden child" instead of the black sheep.

She turned them all down.

I remember the stories my mother told me about when she was a kid. It was like she was a success from birth, despite what her family felt about her. She started making cookies for money to pay for an item she wanted. Then, she moved on to simple services like cleaning and pet sitting. It was a story I couldn't live up to because everything was handed to me.

A go-getter who took no shit from anyone? I was not her.

Cancer dragged her down in the end. Far too early. I was eternally grateful for everything she gave me, but I wasn't sure she'd made the right choice. Did she really think I was capable of handling what the world would throw at me? If she did, I needed answers to my burning questions.

She wasn't here to give them to me, so I hoped to God that I could find the answers within the company she left me.

Kelly was silent as the TV played in the background. I searched her expression to see if something else might be hiding deep down. There must have been signs I missed if she was able to hide so much within herself. Just like Brent, she was too calm and collected for my growing anxiety.

Speaking of the devil, he knocked on my door right on time.

He was on the porch holding two very large bags full of the diner food he promised—*pinky* promised—to deliver. I couldn't contain my happy dance when I saw the bags.

"Wearing that *and* dancing for me? It must be my lucky night." He kicked his shoes off and stepped into the living room.

"Woah, who said you were staying?"

"Hey, now. I went all the way over there and back to get all of this for you. I think I deserve to eat some food, too."

Kelly looked up from her phone. "Brent for the second day in a row?"

I looked him up and down, biting my lip. "Fine. No funny business, though! "

He chuckled and kissed my forehead.

This fucking guy.

He leaned down to me and dropped his voice to a whisper. "I take your business *very* seriously." His eyes scanned my body with a look that said he was hungry for more.

Grabbing the bags from him, I ignored his comment and dragged them to the kitchen. I was absolutely famished from not eating enough and then throwing up. Today was shit and I was not going to process it—Evans might have ideas for therapy later.

Therapy sounded like a solid option.

But who did one talk to about witnessing a murder? Were there elite therapists? I wouldn't know if I could even trust another living soul enough to tell them without developing even more paranoia. Nothing would ever feel normal.

"How's my favorite waitress?" I asked.

"She wondered if you were my girlfriend. So, I told her yes." He sat down with the same confidence and nonchalance as he typically did. It wasn't *technically* normal to be that chill, but who was I to say anything? "Also, did you know your bodyguard dude is camped out in front of your house all by himself?"

"He does that sometimes. Wait. Did you just say you told Martha that I was your girlfriend?"

Kelly came out of the kitchen with silverware and plates. "Does this mean you two are official and Garrett is nixed?"

"No," I said.

"Yes," Brent said at the same time.

She was doing a terrible job of trying not to laugh at him for injecting himself into my life. "That clears *everything* up. You two are something else."

I looked him dead in the eyes. "I hate you."

"That's not what you were saying last night." He casually started eating his food after looking at me again with that same expression. *Hungry.*

Being casual was not what I expected. My brain felt broken. Everything still felt just out of reach. "I need the both of you to explain just what in the hell is going on. Also, why are you two so chill after watching someone die? This has to be a normal occurrence if you two are as cool as cucumbers, despite my attempts to keep my composure, while I can't help but feel nauseous in the kitchen."

My world was turned upside down. My virginity gone just a day before, by the guy sitting in front of me—whom I didn't even know that well. My best friend, whom I'd known for years, was suddenly telling me that she knew a lot more than I did, essentially spilling secrets. I didn't know how to cope with those two things, let alone with murderers running rampant and kids willing to sell each other out. Did I even know who I was at this point? There were so many questions for my mom, and I wished she could have given me something to answer them with, but that was a long journey I had to trek on my own.

Was running away an option?

"I think you need to sit down and chill for a bit. You don't need all the answers in one day, and you're not looking like you're dealing with it well. Did she say she *threw up in the kitchen*?" Brent looked at Kelly to verify what I said like he didn't believe me, but it was true.

"Yup. Right there."

He shoved some food in his mouth and scooted to his right a bit. Of course, he would be that dramatic about vomit but *not* about death.

While he might have been right about not needing all the answers in one go, I felt too far behind to care about it. If I was already becoming a mess, why not rip the whole band-aid off and tell me that I needed to start killing people or something? It felt like a not-so-secret society.

"Fal?" Kelly's voice yanked me out of my thoughts. "Did you hear me?"

I shook my head, physically trying to shake my brains out. Maybe they'd fall out of my nose—or ears. "No... sorry." I weakly took a plate from her, focusing on a piece of pie that I wanted.

"What were you doing when I called you?" I glanced at Brent shoveling food into his mouth like he hadn't eaten in weeks.

He shrugged, unbothered by my question. "What do you mean?"

Way to play it off.

"Just what I said." I put my fork down. "I heard grunting or something from your end."

Exposing that sharp jawline of his, he tilted his head to the side and gave me a bored look. "I'll tell you *if* you tell me that you're mine."

I scowled at him and looked back to my plate, where I could distract myself with pie. "No." Blueberry pie. My favorite.

"Fine," he said with food in his mouth. "You're mine, and I was handing someone's ass to him."

I guessed he was answering for me then. *Yeah, no.* Kelly

247

glanced at me over the breakfast food piled onto her plate, daring me to continue the banter.

"Care to elaborate on the latter?" I wasn't going to address his claim to me, but I *would* pry into what trouble he was getting into *this* time. The man got into fights as if it were his day job.

He scoffed at me, a smirk playing on his lips as he sat back and crossed his arms. His blue eyes flashed with intensity. "Can you tell me you're mine?"

"Possessive much?"

"Yes, I am. I will admit to everyone in this room that I want you to be *mine*. You didn't seem to have a problem with it earlier..." He leaned back over the table with his eyebrows raised playfully, eating more food, his eyes locked on mine.

I laughed. "The only people here are Kelly and me."

He held his phone up like a trophy, his eyes flickering with mischief as he accepted an unspoken dare. "I will publish it to the media unless you say something nice to me."

A part of me wondered if he would actually do it. He seemed like the type. I played along with him, not wanting to test anything else that might give Evans a heart attack. "You have a nice butt."

Kelly laughed.

"Hmm. I'll take it. Look at you being such a good girl. Now"—his eyes darkened, grin widening—"you said you want answers? I can give you some, but... you need to take the news easily. Finish your pie so you'll be comfortable."

He wanted me to comply with his every demand. *Asshole.* It was hard to take him seriously with how aloof he was. I never thought he'd be the type to be so playful. He was blunt, intense, distant, and above all, a major playboy. What was his angle? I wasn't keen to trust him—or Kelly, for that matter. Both of the people sitting in front of me had secrets beyond my wildest imagination, and I wasn't sure how much *news* I could handle.

Paranoia seeped into my bones. The danger on—and off—campus was enough to make someone feel as though they were losing their mind. I was handed this world on a silver platter, and I had no idea how to navigate it. What would come next? I worried that I would become a target in my naivety, an open target for someone trying to take me down for not being deeply entrenched in the depths of criminal business practices.

Was this how the wealthy lived? Beyond the law? The government?

"Business isn't black and white. That's what you get for tonight. Stick with me and I'll keep you safe." He refocused on the food, piling more onto his plate for a second round. "Can I stay again? I'll behave." His question was directed at Kelly, not me.

She chewed while pretending to ponder the question. "Hmm." Rubbing her chin, she played into the joke. "Maybe I should ask my mom if you can stay; I'm not sure if she likes me having boys over. What do you think, Mom?" She smiled at me. *Both of them are assholes, my God.*

"You two are ridiculous. Both of you do whatever you want."

He leapt to his feet with an evil grin spread across his face as he strode to the kitchen. Opening the fridge and rummaging around, you'd think Brent owned the place. My house was *not* his place to pretend to be this comfortable. The fridge was also not his to rummage through.

Kelly also stood, stretching out her limbs with a yawn. "You two don't moan too loud today. I'm going to call it a night. Brent, thanks for the food," she said, leaning over to place a kiss on the top of my head, wrapping an arm around me in a hug. "Love you."

"Love you too, dude," I replied, looking up at her. She had a sad smile, her eyes full of an unspoken apology.

I'd known her long enough to recognize her facial expressions and body language as well as I spoke English, but there seemed to be something deeper beneath the surface that made me feel uneasy. My best friend was entangled for far longer in a world that she didn't seem to want to be a part of any more than I did. Protecting her felt like my duty, but I failed us both by being blissfully unaware of the elite system. I wished I knew what she went through behind the curtain. I wished I knew more entirely to keep us both safe.

After she padded away down the hallway, Brent returned to the table with *my* jug of orange juice. He made himself so comfortable in my house that I wondered if he'd ever leave at this point.

"I hope you're not too comfortable. Why do you want to stay here anyway?" Maybe I was curious; maybe I was looking for validation. Or I was just trying to understand what was wrong with his noggin that made him think he could be a regular guest.

"Two reasons. One: we have real business to get to. Two: I wanted to see you." He plopped down after pouring two cups of OJ for us.

I wanted to get the business out of the way. In over my head, he might have more insights to offer me. "Start with number one."

He shifted in his seat and rubbed the back of his hand before relaxing and sitting back with his cup. "My grandfather wants me to bring you in to bring you up to speed on the partnership he had with your mother. The group you have running things right now has made major disruptions to what was an otherwise smooth process, and he doesn't want to lose any more time. He's old, cranky, and has even less patience since he crossed over into his sixties."

Everyone talked about the relationship he had with my mother, and I wanted to know more about it, but that question would be better suited for Augustus himself.

I crossed my legs, unsure of what to do with myself or how to respond. The table between us was great to have as a space, especially since I needed major distance from everything right now. My heart rate spiked with anxiety from revelation after revelation, and coming to terms with what my mother was involved in was not something I wanted to deal with, like, ever.

The lump in my throat, paired with the thundering heartbeat in my chest, wouldn't allow me to squeak anything out.

His eyes softened with concern as he dropped his smile to a

thin line. He saw how truly beneath the water I was, trying to swim in the deep end without a single swimming lesson. My inexperience wasn't limited to my sex life; it was in *everything*.

"My grandfather and I run a large-scale operation in the black market. Arms, drugs, shit like that. Your properties across the globe serve as meeting points and safe houses. My grandfather expects complete cooperation."

24

Brent

God, I loved punching men in the face.

I gripped him by his collar and pummeled him over and over with my right, ringed hand. The sound of my fist connecting with someone's face made my world slip away into temporary bliss. Blood on my hands gave me a high that nothing else could compare to.

He also deserved it for trying to fuck over the family business. While the Dictator was a pain in my ass and got on my nerves far too much, he granted me the serenity of violence inflicted upon others every now and then.

This time, we had a thief in our ranks, stealing some of the product after a delivery from overseas. That wouldn't fly, seeing as we ran a tight ship.

"I'm sorry, boss!" he yelled in pain, giving me spikes of excitement with every punch I laid on him.

"No. You're. Not." Each punch perfectly marked each word. Throwing him to the ground, blood smeared across his face, I growled, "You're sorry you got caught."

I held him down with my boot, spitting on him for good measure.

My phone started ringing in my back pocket. I checked the screen to see who was calling me at this hour.

Incoming call: Blondie

"Sit still, this is an important phone call." I dug my boot in deeper.

I answered, blood smearing on my phone as I swiped. "Hello?" My voice was a light, excited purr in response to her choice to call me. Thank God I put my number in her phone.

Her voice was on edge, but still so sweet to hear. "Hey, so I need to cash in that delivery promise right now."

The idiot under my boot squirmed as he tried to escape from beneath me. I bent down and pressed my knee into his chest— we weren't done here. "Like, right now?"

A moment of silence filled her end of the call. Was she going to retract? "What are you doing?"

Ah, I made too much noise with the little idiot. "Nothing, Blondie. I'll be over with your delivery in…" I checked the time while covering his mouth. No way I'd let him interrupt my girl finally reaching out to me for once. "An hour, tops. See you soon."

I hung up quickly and smacked him across the face.

Dropping my voice to a sinister growl, I leaned further into him, grabbing his cheeks. "Tonight is the luckiest night of your pathetic fucking life. If I *ever* see your ugly face again, a beating will be the least of your worries. *Capisci?*"

He nodded, fear in his eyes.

"Good, good." I released his face, giving it a light but forceful slap. "Don't make me regret this, or you'll have an immediate appointment to meet your maker."

Trying not to sprint to my bike, knowing I was on the clock, I didn't want her to wait too long and change her mind. Not when I was making so much progress with her.

She was going to be mine.

Ding!

The door to the diner opened, announcing my arrival. I broke far too many traffic laws to get here, get her food, and get back on time.

Martha quickly made her way around the counter, looking

around me. "Where's the girl? Brent, so help me, if you scared away the first girl I got to meet… Is that blood on your ear?" She went from wagging her finger at me to cleaning the blood off my ear.

I didn't have much time to clean up.

Martha was the woman who raised me. When my mother handed me over to the Dictator, he hired anyone who dared to try to calm my wild nature. He didn't have time for it himself. I couldn't blame him—running the conglomerate didn't leave time to look at a child more than once a week, let alone raise one.

I never knew if she had met my mother before she killed herself, but I never dared to ask. I accepted my life for what it was—shitty. Plus, opening up about mommy problems? *No thanks.*

I held up my hands. "Chill, *Mom.* She's the one who sent me here! Don't worry about the blood."

Her shoulders relaxed while she cleaned me up, her smile returning. "Oh! I am so glad. The one girl I ever met and then she's gone instantly? I would beat you silly if you did that to me; my old heart couldn't take it," she said, gripping her chest in her typical dramatics.

She was the only one who could draw a smile out of me. "She's not going anywhere, Martha. Anyway," I held up my box. "I need this stuffed to the brim with whatever she ordered last time."

Giddy as could be, she took the box. "I love a girl who can eat. Tell me about her while they cook up the food."

We spent a few minutes—like a mother and son—catching up and talking about Fallon. Martha never saw me with girls; I never stuck around long enough to learn their names most of the time. But Fallon? I knew from the moment I first saw her that I would pursue her until I died. She was the flame, and I was the moth.

But getting attached to my grandfather's business partner's daughter? Not my plans, but she was sure to be stuck with me forever.

What I loved the most was how she pretended to hate me. The disgusted looks she gave me made my dick hard. Her little suspicious glances she threw up to hide her attraction only made me want to throw her down and have my way with her more. She was conflicted in her feelings, that much was clear. Unlike the other girls who threw themselves at me left and right, Fallon had an innate distrust of me and wanted to run the other way.

Good thing I was willing to give chase to her. That goody little two shoes.

"Here's the food, sweetheart!" Martha emerged from the kitchen, placing the box on the counter.

I fished out a few hundreds and left them for her.

Why I needed to pay when I owned the place? Eh, it made me feel normal.

I showed up to Fallon's house five minutes past the hour. There was no way I'd be late and have her change her mind.

Convincing her to let me in wouldn't be terribly difficult, but I wanted her to want me there just as badly as I wanted to be there. The girl kept me on my toes.

Kelly went to bed, leaving just the two of us sitting at the table after a strange interaction between them. I didn't plan on leaving tonight—not that she had the option. I wanted to feel the softness of her skin all over again, no matter what it took.

There was also a need to make her aware of the Dictator's plans and how she'd be involved.

See? I can do business too.

From what I remembered, her mother was a force to be reckoned with, and my grandfather took an interest in her ferocity. Something I could see developing in Fallon. Maria came from absolutely nothing and had the vision and willpower to make it happen. A *brutal woman*, some called her.

Which is exactly what my grandfather wanted—brutality in the form of a gorgeous woman to take the world by storm. She made connections quickly and could sell ice to a penguin if given the chance. So, my grandfather created some opportunities for her and watched her run straight to the top.

Under one condition: she needed to help him with the black-market deals by being a pretty face that no one would question. She did, and she did it well.

My grandfather wouldn't accept anything less from her daughter.

Her throat bobbed, and I could see some fear in her eyes. She was in an ocean without a boat.

How she softened me like this, I'd never know. "My grandfather and I run a large-scale operation in the black market. Arms, drugs, shit like that. Your properties across the globe serve as meeting points and safe houses. My grandfather expects complete cooperation."

She shook her head, partly confused and partly horrified. The welcome party for the elites and how we ran the world must have felt like a bullet to the chest. From the little information I had about her and her mother's relationship, it appeared her mother shielded her too much from the shitshow that was the top one percent.

One didn't get rich and stay clean at the same time. If you believed that, you'd be a fool.

"I don't…" she trailed off. Her face said horrified, while her body slumped into a hopeless pile in her chair.

Hopefully, she didn't puke again.

"I know," I replied, voice softening further. "But it's better you find out now so you can prepare yourself for what comes next. Leadership." I stood up to gather the food and put it in the fridge. No cleaning for her while her worldview kept crumbling.

She stood when I did, her legs shaky as she tried to find her footing. "Is it bad that I keep feeling like something horrible is about to happen at any moment?"

I pondered that while sealing up the food and placing it all in the fridge. "I think I would say that's a normal response. If you weren't, I'd say you fit right in with the rest of us. Paranoia is a natural feeling, and a lot of people feel it. My grandfather gets paranoid. Granted, it's in a different way."

"And what's your motive for being here? Why are you here?"

Her questions made me stop and look at her. Why she consumed my thoughts would be a better question. Why was I drawn to her, wanting her to drag me under with her?

"It's in both of our best interests that I help you," I said quietly, closing the fridge.

"What about before the scandal crap?"

"What about it? I told you before that you're different and I liked it. What's so difficult about me being interested in you for more than one reason?"

She approached me, big blue eyes staring up at me. They had a sheen across them—sadness glazing them over. Her brows furrowed while her mind worked, but her face held the most innocent thinking expression. I almost melted into the floor.

Laying a hand on my chest, breathing deeply, she spoke softly. "You're Brent Vaughn."

I gripped her wrist and pressed her hand harder into my chest. "And you're Fallon Montgomery," I teased, lowering myself closer to her.

"What makes the most prolific bad boy interested in me? Why do you like me?" Her fingers ever so gently squeezed in response to me pressing her hand further into my chest.

Grab my heart. Take it.

I brought my hand up to sweep some of her hair away before cupping her face. "I like you, Blondie, because I love challenges and things I don't deserve. You're such a hard one to get to pay attention to me. I like it."

Her lips parted in disbelief. A small breath escaped them, and a light turned on behind her eyes. She had a life to her that I wanted to feel, to explore. She seemed so much more alive than anyone else I'd ever met.

"I, uh—" she stuttered, trying to look away. I held her hand firmly in place on my chest.

"What?" I tilted my head to follow where her eyes drifted to, wanting to hold her gaze. "Talk to me. If you don't want to talk, I can think of something else we can do with our mouths."

She dropped her eyes to the floor, but I refused to let her look away. Grabbing her chin, I forced her to look back up at me.

"I don't want either of those," she said, her voice barely a whisper.

"Such a little liar." I dipped my face to hers and met her lips with mine. The way her hand gripped my shirt told me everything I needed to know about what she wanted.

Fuck, her lips are so soft.

Until she pulled away. "Isn't this a conflict of interest?"

Growing impatient with her clothes still being on her body, I slipped her up and over my shoulder, carrying her down to her bedroom. I'd never get tired of doing it, even when she beat on my back with her fists the whole way while she told me she hated me and to put her down.

Fat chance.

Locking the bedroom door, I tossed her onto the bed. Her eyes were wide in disbelief, and her mouth was agape. "Wh— what are you doing?"

I grinned, climbing onto the bed and prowling towards her. "Whatever I want. Just like you told me to do."

She backed away from me. "That's not what I meant."

"That's what you said." Grabbing her legs, I yanked her back to me. "Don't say things so carelessly, babe. What was it you said last time? I want more?"

Completely underneath me, she squirmed under my touch. So cute. So innocent.

Her breathing sped up, hitching in the most adorable way. "Brent..."

"Yes?" I kissed her neck while my hands re-explored her body. I wanted to memorize every inch and feel her soft skin until the end of time.

Goosebumps spread across her skin as her back arched. "I-I..." she squeaked.

Sitting back, I pulled my shirt off, reveling in how she drank up my body with her eyes. She laid there, speechless, while her gaze drifted down to my pants. Her throat bobbed while she took in the bulge that formed in my pants. I grabbed her hands and placed them on my belt. "Take this belt off for me, Blondie."

She bit her lip, unsure of what to do. Those vibrant eyes met mine with a spark of desire, and she held my gaze while slowly undoing my belt. Pulling it free, she tossed it aside and unbuttoned my jeans, slowly lowering the zipper.

My pulse raced, each breath shallow and quick, and an insatiable hunger for her touch consumed me. Shoving my pants to the ground, my dick was readily apparent in my boxers. I watched curiously as she hesitated to reach for it.

Trying to control my urges, I whispered, "Don't be shy."

Her hand steadied and gripped my cock through my boxers, and I swore I could have come right then and there out of pure excitement. Releasing a low moan, she drew her eyes back up to mine. "Is it okay if I don't know what to do?"

Fuck.

"What is it you want to do?" It was incredibly hard to focus with her grasping my cock and looking at me with those innocent doe eyes.

Grabbing the waistband of my boxers, she pulled them down to reveal what was underneath—my cock fully hard with need for her. She replaced her hand and started stroking it.

"Mhm," I groaned. My legs threatened to give out while standing there.

She tucked her hair behind her ears and looked ready to open her mouth for me. *God, what that mouth must feel like.* "Can I..." she trailed off, looking intimidated by the size.

"Just tell me what you want," I gritted through my teeth. I *needed* her so badly that I was about to throw her down and take her until we both became puddles on the floor.

She kept stroking me as she stood, her eyes playing a dangerous game with me. Our mouths crashed together, and I groaned into her mouth—her hand stroking me was far too much of a tease. A small moan rolled from her lips and into the kiss before she shoved me onto the bed.

"I want you to lie there," she said as she straddled me, coming back to plant her mouth on mine again.

Fully clothed, she taunted me with the way her hips moved over me. The confidence she had grew with my responses to her touching me, and I could tell she was working up the nerve to use her mouth.

I gently gripped her by the hair, holding her face back from mine. "Are you working up the nerve to use your mouth, Blondie?"

A sheepish smile formed on her lips—those soft lips.

Fuck, I couldn't help myself.

"Go ahead. Use your mouth for me." I released her hair, and another adorable squeak came from her.

How I wanted to fuck that throat of hers.

She balanced herself so that her mouth was so, so close to my cock. I waited impatiently before she opened wide and took my entire cock into it. A guttural groan of relief escaped me when she embraced me completely.

"Just like that," I moaned, slowly guiding her head movements.

She gripped the base with her hand and added a stroking motion while she bobbed her head up and down. *What a fucking natural.*

And how I couldn't wait to be inside her again, pounding those sounds out of her, making her scream my name.

With her newfound confidence from listening to my moans of approval, she furrowed her eyebrows in cute determination to make me come for her. Just like I'd done to her.

"Yes, baby, just like that." I stroked her hair, keeping up the praise.

Thinking back to when I was balls deep inside her, eating her out, and even just touching her, I felt the build-up coming. That mouth was doing otherworldly things to me while I watched her with sweetly fierce determination to make me feel good.

My core tightened and I felt it coming. "Fallon... Fuck. I'm going to come for you," I breathed heavily, the words sounding more like throaty murmurs. I reached the edge and tipped right over it, my hot cum releasing into her mouth.

Oh, fuck me. She swallowed all of my cum before coming up for air.

A wave of relaxation washed over my body before she crawled up and laid next to me, perfectly nestled between my arm and chest.

Those tantalizing eyes searched my face for something, and I gently caressed her cheek. Feeling completely at ease, I lightly pressed my lips to the top of her head.

Was it bad I wanted to lie like this forever?

Her hand drew small circles across my chest and I watched with a smile as her cute little brain churned through a whirlwind of thoughts. "What's on your mind?"

A small huff of air slipped from her mouth. "Lots of things, but I don't know what to make of anything."

I absently played with a few strands of hair. "What things?"

A mild look of embarrassment played across her face. "Well, you're you."

And I was utterly obsessed with her. "Yes, I am me. Are you talking about me wanting *you*?"

"I just..." She searched for the words while continuing to glide her fingers along my stomach. "...didn't think I'd carelessly—"

"Sleep with someone like me?" I finished her sentence for her since we both knew what she wanted to say. "If it makes you feel any better, I thought you hated me."

"I *do* hate you."

No, you don't.

She sighed. "Are you a murderer?"

Well, that was a change of pace. "I prefer beating people to a pulp if that's what you mean."

"That doesn't answer my question."

"You have a lot of questions," I sighed.

Readjusting so I could better see her face and pull her closer to me, I brought my lips to hers and wrapped my leg around her. All I could think about was falling asleep and slipping into a blissful unconsciousness that I desperately needed with my obsession in my arms.

"Brent?" Her breath was warm on my chest.

"Yes?"

"I'm not sure what I should do."

Squeezing her a bit tighter, I said, "Go to sleep, you can worry tomorrow."

Laying there in silence, I held her until she fell into a deep sleep. The fully relaxed version of her face made me feel a little more at peace, when any other time, I'd be wide awake and worried about shit on my side of the world. I felt like I could stay wrapped up with her forever, letting her be my calm until the end of time.

Distantly, I heard my phone buzzing from wherever I had tossed it in the room when I brought Fallon in to distract her. I slowly peeled myself away from her, being careful as not to wake the sleeping beauty, and went to check it.

My relaxed contentment ended just like that because Sloane had called more than ten times. *So much for being relaxed.*

Making my way quietly down the hallway and into the living room, I answered, pretending to have just woken up. "Hello?"

Fuck, my whispers sound loud.

"Where are you?"

"Sleeping," I said curtly.

"You're not home or at the fraternity!"

I pulled the phone away from the screeching voice and rubbed my hand over my face. She was seeking me out at any location she knew I'd be? "No. What do you want?"

She let out a horrid sound. "I haven't seen you, like, all day!"

God help me. "Sloane. Stop. For the love of all that is fucking holy, knock this shit off. It's not cute nor is it endearing. We've been nothing but hookups, and I'm over it."

"Oh! So you're fucking cheating on me?! We will just see

about that. When I find out who the skank you're sleeping with is, I—"

I cut her off. "We are not together. Stop calling me."

"Where. Are. You?" I could literally picture how she was standing just from her tone.

The urge to bang my head against the wall was growing. "You're becoming obsessive. Lose my number."

She faked a sob. "Brent!"

"Find another rich man to cling to," I said, ending the call.

I turned to find Kelly, intently listening to me in front of the fridge, arms crossed.

"Hey." I waved.

"Mhm. Hey, yourself. I only have one thing to say." She approached me, lowered her voice, and put her finger on my chest, staring up at me from about a foot away. "I better not hear about her being put on Sloane's hit list through the fucking grapevine, do you hear me? If anything goes fucking wrong and she gets put into danger, I will not hesitate to put a fucking bullet in your head myself."

25

Fallon

My plans for a normal life went out the window. I wanted to come out of my hermit hole and have a great semester, but that opportunity was long gone, and I didn't know what to make of it.

Trying to forget most of what had been going on, I took a shower, letting the warm water and steam consume me from the inside out. Brent was fast asleep in my bed. Kelly was in the kitchen preparing leftovers from last night.

Why was my life so fucking strange?

I asked for *normal* different—not this shit!

Using my loofah, I tried to scrub it all away to no avail. The soap cleaned my skin, sure, but it didn't clear my mind of the absolute shit show that was unfolding.

My mental inventory of events was overwhelming. Getting a boyfriend over the summer was my first step toward feeling normal during my sophomore year—going on dates like regular people gave me hope. Somewhere along those lines, Brent decided to rain on my parade with *hail*, like the reckless asshole he was.

Don't even get me started on those fucking texts, the scandal, and the dirty business practices of the elitist assholes who tried to run the world like they were Illuminati wannabes.

I could handle the boy problems. But the other stuff? Nope.

Groups and cliques around us were imploding at insane rates, their facades of niceties crumbling like a decaying building on its last leg. I watched someone get murdered in real time, for God's sake.

The VIP room with the underground, shady deals was my new life. They expected me to play along or die.

My Titanic hit the iceberg; I was sinking. My stomach felt like it was playing jump rope inside me due to the anxiety I had.

My company provides locations for black market operations. The implications of that were insane!

Oh yeah, and the weird fucking texts I kept getting. *What the fuck, right?*

Alexander was a complete fucking weirdo and probably had plans to force me into having sex with him. He seemed like the type.

And there's my stomach acid in the tub.

My skin was rubbed raw by the thoughts stirring in my mind. The water turned cold from how long I stood under the stream—my skin became pruny. Maybe I could drown myself in the hot tub later.

I tiptoed around my room in nothing but a towel because I forgot to get a change of clothes before jumping into scalding hot water, too excited to bathe all the nasty thoughts *and* Brent off of me.

Stupid, stupid girl. You fell into his trap again.

By the time I had oversized clothes on that covered more than everything, Brent stirred in my bed. *I need to wash those sheets immediately.*

"Too bad you're not still naked," he yawned.

"I'm heading out after breakfast. I have a meeting at Montgomery Group." I kept my voice soft so he couldn't hear the trepidation in it. He didn't deserve to get that from me. I was just a fun time for him and a business deal for Chamberlain Industries.

"Let them know you've been formally invited to the

compound with the head of Chamberlain Industries to spearhead conversations about the business partnership." He stretched out and planted his feet on the ground. Some time during the night, his boxers found their way back onto his body.

I grunted in agreement and left the room to let him do whatever he wanted to do. He had no bearing on my life, and he could see himself out.

Ew, he was probably going to use my shower.

"Morning!" I entered the kitchen, fussing with my oversized clothes. Maybe I went too big, but I wasn't going to chance another change with *him* in my house. No way.

She carefully laid out a buffet of whatever we had in the fridge on the kitchen island. I wanted to feast with how empty my stomach felt after throwing up in the shower, hoping it would stay down this time. Hashbrowns and bacon felt like the safest options for my first plate.

"Ready to grab today by the balls?" Loading up her plate, Kelly flashed me a smile. Too calm, too unbothered. It freaked me out.

Suspicion grew with everyone I was around.

Before I could make her suspicious of *me*, I grabbed a breakfast sausage and bit into it, smiling back. "Yup. I may not know what's going on, but sounds like a plan."

Brent emerged from my room looking as if he had never fallen asleep. Freshly cleaned and put together, it was easy to put last night behind me. "I should keep extra clothes here if I'm going to be staying over." He looked down at his clothes. They didn't even look like second-day wear.

Kelly snorted. "You live across the street."

He loaded up a plate and plopped down at the table with the same casualness that Kelly and I had while living here. Like he was a current resident at my house. What an asshole. It took only two days for him to become casual roommate level at my house.

"James will be picking me up to go to the office today." I looked over at Kelly dumping ketchup on her hashbrowns and tried pretending last night never happened. Everyone at the table knew and didn't talk about it while I silently finished most of my plate, praying that my phone would ring to save me from this awkward breakfast.

Brent winked at me over his food and my phone buzzed.

UNKNOWN:

Secrets spilled create a stain just like blood

Well, that wasn't ominous at all.

Incoming Call: Evans

"Looks like that's me," I said, standing to grab my purse and bolt out of the house. "Hello?"

"Your car is waiting. James and an associate will escort you." *Click.*

I held the phone out in front of my face. "Nice to talk to you too," I replied to no one, closing the front door and escaping the events of yesterday and into the events that awaited.

"Hello, Miss Montgomery," a man at the door greeted, opening it up for me. He offered to take my coat and purse for me, but I opted to keep everything on me. No way I'd trust anyone for a while—even with just my coat.

A few men walked around me, making me feel like I had the freaking Secret Service at my disposal. Boarding the elevator, they circled around me in a protective manner. The upcoming CEO deserved protection, after all.

That's why I had James stationed with me day and night, occasionally swapping out with someone else for around the clock surveillance.

They escorted me to the boardroom, which was filled with men in expensive suits, and stood in a strict line outside the door. Hands at the ready in front of them and eyes forward—it was kind of cool but a bit off-putting.

"Miss Montgomery," Evans said, holding his arms out, walking towards me to greet me in a hug. "You look wonderful! Look at how much you've grown up."

Very different from when he was on the phone. I scanned the room, and everyone was looking at me and only me. "Um, thanks."

Mr. Evans, CFO of Montgomery Group, shifted around some power due to the lack of a CEO, was acting CEO in preparation for my arrival. My birthright, as they said. I was set to take over at twenty-one, but why I wasn't aware of things earlier or brought around, say, when I was eighteen, made *no* sense. The reasoning behind the unfolding plot just wasn't connecting.

Instead of being brought in, I rotted away at my aunt's house, waiting until she violently kicked me out.

"Since we are all here today, I'd like to honor your mother's memory. Her leadership and ferocity have shaped this company into the powerhouse it is today. Without her, we'd all be out of a job."

All the men nodded in response.

I tried to shove down the lump forming in my throat as everyone bowed their heads to show respect. Maybe today was a bad day to realize that I needed to grieve my mother properly. I never visited her—at least, not yet.

She was waiting for me to come talk to her.

A few beats later, he spoke up again. "First steps as our upcoming CEO! We have a crucial meeting to schedule with you and Augustus Vaughn, head of Chamberlain Industries. I know he will want an immediate audience after hearing the news that you will be acting in certain roles, mostly learning, until your full succession as CEO of Montgomery Group."

I raised an eyebrow. "What shall this meeting entail?"

Someone at the overly large table leaned forward. "Vaughn is looking to expand into some of our prime real estate holdings. A very *game changing* partnership for us moving forward." Real subtle. He was insinuating what I already knew in the least conspicuous manner—I'd seen toddlers do a better job.

So, he knew. Now, who else?

My eyes glanced across the room and settled back on Evans as he spoke up. "That is Mr. Caldwell, legal counsel."

"I see," I said, my mind racing in anticipation of the major life change I was in for. "Will there be coaching for this meeting, or will I be showing up with my pants down?"

He slipped and a small smile appeared on his lips, appearing as if he were proud of me for starting off strong. "From what we've seen, he's grown less patient over time but is still a shrewd businessman with... unconventional tactics. He's likely to gauge your resolve."

Unconventional tactics? Could these guys be any less obvious? I wondered when I would have the opportunity to talk about it or if it's an *everyone knows but doesn't say* type of ordeal. *Who did I ask about the rules of the game?*

"Your mother always stood firm in her ground during talks with Vaughn," Legal Counsel Man chimed back in. I already forgot his name. "He's likely to expect the same from you as her successor—and daughter. They had a fruitful relationship that we continued to manage over the last handful of years, but it's time for you to come into play."

A metric ton of weight settled onto my shoulders. The overviews and tutoring that James provided began to make sense in my mind, and I was ready to use them. "Understood. I'd like a full briefing on our holdings, recent acquisitions, and any history between our two companies."

The men around the table looked at each other before shuffling to pull out their tablets and computers, seemingly ready to dive into the details. Or childproof them.

If I were going to be the CEO of Montgomery Group, I needed to be fully educated enough to hold any secrets above other people's heads, on top of understanding the intricate inner workings of my company.

This was my new normal, and as much as I wanted to fight it, I had to be prepared for whatever would come my way. The company became clearer to me through my continual readings, and Augustus Vaughn most likely expected another Maria.

Mr. Legal Counsel exchanged a knowing glance with Evans and I could easily read into what it meant. Again, these men sucked at subtlety. "Before we head into the meeting with the details you've requested, I would like to speak on a *private* legal matter with you."

Evans nodded at him. "If I could have non-essential personnel leave the room for this."

I tried to pay attention to body language to pick up on some cues. A few seemed relieved to put away their belongings and exit the room, while others appeared completely unbothered by the request.

Sitting in my chair and inspecting my manicure, I hoped to mimic the unbothered look. "I'm here and now most of the board has been kicked out."

Legal Counsel and Evans took their places on either side of me while I sat at the head of the table. They each pulled out their tablets, looking hesitant to start speaking.

They didn't know I knew that they knew.

What a fun predicament.

"Your mother and Mr. Vaughn—"

I cut him off. "My mother supplied properties for Chamberlain Industries to operate in drugs and arms overseas, and sometimes in the country."

Both of them went wide eyed. They must have assumed I knew nothing and wanted to ease me into it. Evans coughed a bit from hearing me speak so bluntly. "Well, yes. For this meeting, it is imperative that you approach it with caution and avoid plain speaking. He may assume you are aware of former— and current—arrangements and speak in a vague manner to avoid suspicion."

I cut back in. "He probably just expects a carbon copy of my mother. From what everyone *keeps* telling me, she was ferocious, no? I get that I'm green behind the ears because she never disclosed anything to me, but that's not an answer we can get from her now, is it? So, stop treating me like a baby and tell me—*in plain speak*—everything about their relationship."

The people closest to me kept me ignorant for so long, like I'd never find out the reality of the shit the wealthy got into. What the *elites* got into. What I wanted to know was *why* I was kept in the dark.

There was no way anyone in this world was clean, and I had to swallow the pill that my mother was one of them. And that truth was going to be revealed through my ever-increasing involvement.

Both men were so unsettled by my brazen speech as if they'd never seen my mother. I've seen the stuff about my mom. *Brutal businesswoman.* Given that I was dreadfully behind in my knowledge and needed to learn everything about my world, this was not the time to be unsettled.

"There are a few details Mr. Caldwell and I need to discuss before the board returns."

Mr. Legal Counsel, AKA Mr. Caldwell, cleared his throat. "I have been your mother's legal counsel for what seems an eternity. When she first got started, Mr. Vaughn offered her whatever she wanted in exchange for the temporary usage of certain properties at preorganized dates and times. This kept things under wraps while forming a strong bond between the two and creating a god-like level above their competitors and just about everyone else. The two weren't on top for no reason. When he offered her this proposal, she took it with *no* hesitation."

I shook my head, wondering what made her say yes to something like this. "Why didn't she just say no and start a company like everyone else?"

Evans shifted in his seat and fidgeted with his hands. "Well, Augustus Vaughn technically gave your mother a leg up in her world to build an empire. How else could a woman with a background like hers become one of the wealthiest women in the world so quickly? She wanted that for herself, and she took that offer without hesitation. He saw what she could become and how it could be mutually beneficial."

Brent's grandfather was the devil my mother made a deal with. He dragged her into a criminal underworld, dangling success in front of her like a carrot. I wondered if Brent would try the same with me—unless he already was.

I drummed my fingers on the table in anxiety and anticipation. My heart thumped, and I was becoming flustered. "Leg up—what do you mean by that?"

"Opportunities. Connections. Cash flow," Caldwell replied. What it *takes* to be the one percent of the one percent is what she had, and he provided her with every *resource* to achieve it. She was wonderfully poised, a classy woman with a great mind for business. That's what drew Mr. Vaughn to offer her such a deal, which is no easy feat considering he holds a monopoly on much of the world. He knew she could handle matters with a bright smile on her face while remaining ever discreet about it all."

But she was a kind, loving woman... There was no way my mother was the type of person everyone kept describing. Then again, I didn't know her before I was born. She was thirty-seven when she had me—thirty-seven long years as a woman without a child, but with a vision for the future.

She just lived a double life with me.

"All of this," I breathed in, "was before she had me?"

"She started kicking up dust in the business world the day she turned twenty-one."

Just like she willed me to do as her dying wish. Was she emulating her own life in mine with her plans? It felt weird to put that on your own daughter, but it seemed I might not have known her as well as I thought.

I resigned from learning any more until a later date. My head was spinning, and throwing up again was not in my plans. Getting caught up with current events in the company was more imperative and felt more normal than talks about criminal enterprises and deals with the devil.

The suits flowed back into the room, settling comfortably into their seats again. Adjusting ties, sitting back in chairs, and getting ready for important matters.

"We are at a pivotal moment in the company," Evans said from the projector screen at the opposite side of the room. "Our top priority is easing Miss Montgomery into her leadership position and continuing on with our company mission: Connecting discerning clients with unique properties and exceeding expectations—every time."

A manila envelope was handed to me ceremoniously. "A write up for you, Miss Montgomery. This outlines our most current events, important relationships held, market trend research, and other key details I felt were important for you to browse at your convenience."

I swallowed the uncertainty in my throat. "Thank you, Mr..."

"Jones. Executive Director at your service."

I nodded and tucked the envelope into my lap while feeling eyes on me. What secrets I could find inside this envelope had me in no rush to find out. James would take me over it later.

Evans ran the meeting. We covered current and future marketing trends in luxury real estate, our experiences with consumers, key demographic shifts in certain countries that present opportunities, upcoming government regulations and changes, how the company will continue to move forward with these factors in mind, and political situations in specific countries to be aware of.

I took explicit notes like I was in school.

What the hell was my mom doing at twenty-one where she could have handled all this?

26

Fallon

"Why aren't you wearing your Sharks outfit?" Kelly pranced out of the hallway, fiddling with an earring while she looked like the epitome of school spirit.

I, however, laid comatose on the couch in my pajamas and hadn't moved for probably four hours. "I don't want to go," I groaned as I looked to the ceiling as if there was a god up there willing to offer me guidance in my life.

She smacked the top of my head. "Today is the big football game!"

"Ow! I don't want to go and see anyone. Garrett is playing, and I abruptly broke up with him and slammed the door in his face. I can't imagine he has fuzzy feelings for me. Even worse, he's become the center of the rumors along with those other kids associated with the disgraced families. Don't you read the news?" I stood up to shuffle over to the kitchen to attempt to eat something after skipping breakfast.

Nausea was hitting.

She followed behind me, fussing with my clothes, trying to pull off my pajamas. "The news is for losers, and Garrett won't even see you. He's going to be playing football! I also heard that after the game, a few people are going a few towns over for a pretty sick fall festival."

I smacked her hand away when she tried to undress me. "Parties are not my jam. Tried it and I'm over it. *Especially* with what's been going on lately. The mass texts are getting super weird. Who is sending them?"

"What mass texts?"

Closing the cupboard with my hands full of candy, I nodded over to the table. "Check my phone. Haven't you been getting them?"

She shot me a concerned look. "Um, no."

Unlocking my phone, she scrolled through the messages, her face growing more and more concerned. She looked freaked out by the time she glanced back up at me.

There were three sent after the one I knew she had received.

> Secrets spilled create a stain just like blood.
>
> The stakes in the game have never been higher.
>
> Who will be the first to squeal?

Her mouth hung open in shock, staring at my phone. "Fal, did you just *assume* these were mass texts? I think you might have a stalker or something."

I shrugged. "I guess so. If it was just sent to me, they clearly didn't make it obvious enough. Do you think they're being sent to specific people now?"

Trying to maintain my composure, I pretended they weren't sent only to me. I already had enough paranoia about the death of a supposed whistleblower, being stalked by Alexander, and questioning Brent's motives. Oh, and Kelly being suspicious as hell.

She had been sneaking out, not knowing that I knew she was doing something in secret. Sure, she went out to parties and bumped coke sometimes with that boyfriend of hers, but even *she* had been acting odd lately.

And it wasn't because of drugs.

Maybe she knew who could have been behind these

messages. They were ambiguous enough, and she *worked* in this field. She had to have some idea of something—not that she would tell me.

She shifted uncomfortably. "It's a possibility, but I don't think you should shrug this off just yet. Maybe I can talk to—"

I held up a hand to stop her, "I don't want to think about it. I will get ready for the stupid football game if it means we don't have to talk about it."

Going to this football game was going to make me sick. I looked around at everyone mindlessly sitting in the bleachers or in line to buy snacks, and couldn't help but feel queasy about it. My gummy worms wanted to crawl back up. Life seemed to go on as if nothing were happening.

Kelly and I wore coordinating Sharks outfits that gave me a sense of blending into the crowd, sporting the home team. Girls were dressed like different versions of the cheerleaders—some more *spirited* than others.

We opted for miniskirts and barely-there crop tops with the word *Sharks* across our chests. The teal green and white outfits said, *we love our football team* and that we hoped to take home a win.

I felt naked; making it home alive and not frozen to death would be a win for me.

Kelly leaned over to whisper to me, "Sloane incoming."

Great. Brent's *girlfriend* coming over to schmooze with us again.

"Hi girls." She waved at us, a posse following closely behind her. "Cute outfits! Do you like mine?" She did a twirl while her group clapped for her in the background.

I'm not sure she was wearing much of anything to comment on. Her teal sequined shorts could pass as underwear, and her white top shoved her boobs together, begging for attention.

I smiled warmly. "You look amazing as always, Sloane. Excited for the game?"

She rolled her eyes and flicked her wrist. "Who cares about

the game! I'm trying to take home a hunky man tonight." She giggled.

Kelly quirked an eyebrow. "Your beau?"

"I could never get him to be exclusive. I'll have to take what I can get from a man like that, but I do adore him." She scooted away from her groupies and toward us. "Between us, I've been trying to get him off of me for a while. He's *very* needy."

Feigning surprise, I tried to step on Kelly's foot to get her to help me out. "Wow, didn't take him for that type. Very much playboy vibes from that one."

"Sure, he sleeps around with the occasional *skank*," she whispered, eyeing me up and down, "but he always comes crawling back to me." Backing up to her regular position in her group, she said, "We're going to get some snacks! See you girls later."

And just like that, she was gone after blowing us a kiss.

Kelly and I shared a look of disturbance.

"What the hell was that about?" I asked. She'd looked... off, but shrugged off the comments.

"Dude, I don't know. That girl is mental."

I tried not to laugh. "I went from virgin to skank in a few weeks. I'll take it."

"Such a dirty skank, you are." She chuckled. "Want to get a pretzel and soda and get ready for kickoff?"

We settled into our seats with our snacks and drinks, getting ready to watch *the* game of the season. We would be close to making it to the championship game if we could secure tonight's win.

Our sports teams boasted some truly amazing athletes. With our scholarship program for the truly elite athletes, we claimed some of the best players in all collegiate sports. It was one of the main reasons Willow Bay offered up full ride sports scholarships for the best athletes. They couldn't miss an opportunity to go to the richest college in the country and brush shoulders with people who could skyrocket their careers and lives.

If they wanted to pay the price for fame, like we paid the price for our wealth.

I never knew much about football, or sports in general, but at least I knew what a touchdown was. When our side of the crowd cheered, Kelly and I followed suit—hollering like avid sports fans.

Some of the players looked extremely athletic, and after college football, they were a shoo-in to get a spot on the pro football team of their dreams.

Some tackles and hits looked brutal, and I couldn't help but wonder how bad injuries could get on the field.

As the ball went back and forth and opposing sides tackled each other and referees blew their whistles, we made it to the final stretch of the game. I understood how you could get sucked into a game because I was on the edge of my seat.

Tied.

The away team called for a timeout.

"What do you think is going to happen?" Kelly asked, shoveling popcorn into her mouth like it was a feature film.

"Not sure, but I'm not a football buff."

The bleachers beside us squeaked as someone approached and leaned into my ear. "We'll win. We didn't pay shit loads of money to lose."

Alexander.

"Yeah, I'm sure the sports equipment we use costs a pretty penny," I said, nonchalantly leaning away from his hot breath. He was persistent, and not in a good way.

Kelly looked up at him and waved. "Hey."

"Hey," he replied, still looking at me. "You two going to the festival tonight? A big group of us are going, and I was hoping to get some alone time with you, baby girl."

I shot a glance over at Kelly. "Not sure yet."

He gripped my wrist. "I'll give you a ride. I'll find you after the game."

I yanked my hand away. "No need. We'll see you there," I said with a tight smile.

He patted my head and stalked away.

Those looks he had were wasted on his corrupt soul—tall, blonde, and handsome, sullied by daddy's money and deals with the devil.

Time out was over before I could digest Alexander's odd interaction. The man had a vibe that told you to bring a rape whistle if he came around, but I was so far into the iceberg that no one would care if I used one.

Just a handful of seconds were left on the clock as the boys lined up face-to-face for their last play of the game.

The ball snapped, and our team sent it flying across the field as all the team members sprinted, dodged, and tackled their way down the field.

A swift catch by one of our teammates and he was off to the end zone to score a touchdown.

That's it, we won!

Kelly and I stood to cheer for the win with the rest of the bleachers in a victory chant while the player danced his heart out inside the endzone.

We watched the bustle of people moving from the bleachers while teams huddled in both defeat and victory. Kelly turned to me. "Do you think what that creep said is true?"

I shrugged, finishing off my pretzel. "At this point, why wouldn't it be? You've seen what certain assets open you up to. Plus, we have guys who have been working their tails off to get into pro teams. Let at least those ones have the win."

"Huh," she said, "I didn't think about it, really. Guess there is no fair fight in this world."

No fair fight indeed.

We filed out onto the field to exit the football arena, locked arm in arm as always, and I caught something in my peripheral vision.

A football player ran toward us.

He stopped in front of us and removed his helmet. Garrett. "Fallon! You came to my game?"

"It's a sporting event for the school." I tried to get Kelly to tug me along, but we were stuck under prying eyes trying to discern the drama.

"I still haven't had a chance to talk to you about anything." He moved closer, reaching out for me.

I tried to push his hand down. "Look, not here." My eyes darted back and forth trying to gauge the amount of attention that was on us.

He evaded my swat to his hand and grabbed my wrist, pleading with his eyes. "Then come on, we can go talk privately."

Unlatching from Kelly's arm, I tried to pry his hand off me. "No, Garrett. I told you we were over, and I cannot talk to you."

He ignored me and continued to pull me along. First, it was Alexander, now Garrett. *When will it end?* Last semester was so much easier...

Kelly tried to stop us, but got tangled up in the rubberneckers and groups of people who were just trying to get out of the stadium. I was on my own, Garrett dragging me away.

We got down the field where a few players mingled, and he released me from his grip. "Good. Now we're alone."

I promptly smacked him across the face. "You do not get to ignore me and drag me off like that."

A shocked look colored the rest of his face while my handprint left a nice red patch. "What the hell, Fal?"

"*Why the hell* are you causing a scene like this?"

He gripped my arms, his eyes frantically searching mine. "Fallon, I have been trying to tell you what is going on and that I had *nothing* to do with it."

I shook his hands off my arms and took a step back, holding my arms across my body in a protective stance. "We cannot be seen together, no matter the circumstances." I turned my head and started to walk away to leave him standing there.

But the motherfucker gripped my wrist again.

"Hey," a voice came from behind. "Is there a problem over here?"

Garrett's eyes nearly popped out of his head. "What are you doing here, man?"

"Not much," the voice said coolly, a tone I recognized well. "Just wondering why you're hassling a pretty girl when it's obvious she wants to leave."

"U-uh," Garrett stuttered. "You know how it is with girlfriends, man. They get mad at you."

Brent came into view, arms crossed. "Yeah, man. I know how it is."

Garrett's face relaxed into a grin, thinking he could talk his way out of this. "Then you don't mind giving us some space to talk?"

A chuckle came from deep in Brent's chest, dark and dangerous. "Yeah, dude. I mind," he growled, his eyes darkening with a predatory glare.

I watched as Garrett began to grow weary, more fearful of Brent. Was it wrong that I found Brent's intimidation factor kind of... hot? Garrett threw his hands up like he was facing down a wild animal. "Whoa. I was just talking to her, Brent. She's my girl—"

Before I could blink, Brent's fist connected with Garrett's face in a satisfying *thwack*. I backpedaled, eyes darting around as guys materialized out of thin air, drawn to the smell of rising testosterone levels and impending violence like sharks to chum.

Lots of footballers en route. Both teams.

It was a veritable buffet of football players because both teams were piling in. The North Ridge Panthers, looking lost and confused, glanced around like they'd stumbled into the wrong field. Suddenly, one of them started hollering at our team, accusing us of cheating our way to victory.

Oh, sweet baby Jesus. This was about to turn into an all-out *Friday Night Lights* meets *Fight Club* brawl.

I tried to catch a glimpse of Brent, but he'd chased Garrett—about twenty feet away from the brawl in front of me—and tackled him to the ground. He was on top of him, landing punch after punch with a sickening smile across his face. He was a shark, and he smelled blood.

That man can throw down, good heavens.

Backing away into some semblance of shadows to try and stay out of view, I watched in a mix of horror and awe at how men could just... punch and kick the crap out of each other. It was equal parts terrifying and mesmerizing, like a car crash you couldn't look away from.

Kelly would be eating popcorn. Shit, right. I needed to find Kelly.

My options were to stay in the corner in a safe-ish manner or run past the brawl in search of Kelly. The timing to find my fight-or-flight response was happening, and my body chose the third option—freeze. I planned on staying in the corner until someone came to collect me.

A few staff members, referees, and faculty came to break up the fight, claiming it was started by the away team. They weren't technically wrong, but they weren't right, either. Brent had to be pulled off Garrett by three large men before his jacket was straightened out for him, and one of the men pointed away from Garrett.

I was still in my corner, hidden from view.

He stormed over to me, blood on his knuckles and a drop of blood leaking from his split lip. His eyes burned with his unleashed fury as he closed the distance between us. "What did he say to you? Did he do anything to you?" he asked, searching for any reason to go back and kill Garrett.

"I-I don't think so," I forced my words out, blinking up at him. *Was I hurt?*

Without waiting for an answer, he gently took my hand and lifted it to inspect my wrist. There were clear marks on it from being gripped so many times over the course of about an hour from two separate men.

His jaw tightened, his nostrils flared, and the look in his eyes darkened into something feral. "Did he do this to you?" His words were clipped, he could barely contain his rage.

"M-my wrist was grabbed… I, uh, there were two of them," I managed to spit out, my voice trembling as my mind spun in a loop. Everything swirled together, and I could hardly tell which way was up.

"Two?" he growled. "Who is the other one?"

My face was blank when I looked up at him. "Alexander Fitzgerald."

"Why are you talking to Alexander?"

I gulped, feeling small under his gaze as he tried to soften his eyes on me. "Sloane kept trying to push him on me, and now he won't leave me alone."

If he clenched his jaw any harder, his teeth would surely shatter. "I'm so sick and tired of that girl." His voice was a low growl before his tone softened as he turned his attention to me. "You," he murmured, moving his fingers through my hair in a way that felt halfway between soothing me and taming the frazzled mess it had become, "don't need to worry your pretty little head about Alexander."

He started rubbing my arms down gently in slow, deliberate strokes. "What are you doing?" I asked, my voice barely above a whisper.

"Calming your nerves," he said, his lips quirking into a small smirk. "You look like a baby deer caught in headlights, Blondie." He leaned in and pressed a soft kiss to my hairline.

I flinched back instinctively, making him pause.

"What's the matter?" His hands hovered just above my arms like he wasn't sure if he should let go or hold on tighter.

I shook my head, trying to clear my head. "Nothing, sorry. I need to, uh, find Kelly. We're supposed to go to the festival together." Patting my pockets frantically until I found my phone, I fumbled to send Kelly a text.

The screen lit up with multiple messages:

KELLY:

where are u?????

I can't find u!!

UNKNOWN:

baby girl, I'm waiting for you

KELLY:

where did he take you??

My stomach dropped. Deleting Alexander's previous text thread hadn't stopped him from texting me again. I considered blocking him, but who knew what that might provoke. The second anonymous text I got drained the blood right out of my body.

UNKNOWN:

dirty little secrets...

A picture of Garrett and me on a date was underneath that second unknown text. Along with a picture of Brent and me.

My hands trembled as I turned the phone and shoved it into Brent, showing him the messages.

His eyes darkened as he scrolled. "How long have you been getting messages like this?"

"I'm not sure," I admitted, my voice barely above a whisper. "I thought they were mass texts until just now. One is Alexander. Sloane made me give him my number, but I deleted the first texts before his messages made me hurl. But the other one..." My hands were slightly shaking, and I felt like I was working up a cold sweat.

Who was watching me? What did they want? Another mystery to add to the already tangled web of situations I kept finding myself in.

I tried to close my eyes and breathe slowly, but it felt like it just made it worse. There was someone specifically seeking me out, sending me messages, and I was stupid enough to think it was just mass texts being sent out.

This couldn't be happening to me... I felt the sudden urge to puke again. Bending over, I knew it wouldn't come, but I needed my head between my legs for the nausea.

"I'll help you find Kelly." He held onto my arm to steady me.

I held up my hand, breathing heavily. "Don't. I'd rather not be seen with you and have your girlfriend gunning for me too. There are too many people who want to see me fall right now before I take over my company." God, this nausea was killing me.

Tucking my phone to my chest, I tried to stand up to move past him but was stuck behind his arm.

He rubbed his free hand across his face, a little bit of blood smearing from the cut on his lip. "You don't need to worry about her or anyone else for that matter. I can handle it."

"You should also clean up your hands and face. Probably before you see anyone else."

His face softened further, and he moved in far too close to me. His eyes were still wild, and his jaw muscles flickered with his thoughts. A hand came up to my face while he leaned over me, his arm resting above my head. "I should."

My eyes flicked down before I could look at his mouth. "Yeah, you should."

"Mhm." His lips brushed mine.

I obliged his mouth with mine, tasting the coppery flavor of his blood on my tongue. *What am I doing?*

"Uh, guys?" Kelly's voice made Brent stiffen and turn to face her. "What the *hell* happened to your face?"

27

Fallon

"So… what happened?" Kelly shut the door to her car.

We decided to go to the festival after all. I wanted to go and have fun despite the chaos swirling around. Dodging Alexander would be a challenge, though.

I bit my lip and played with my hands. "A lot happened."

"Clearly," she scoffed. "I see you getting dragged away by Garrett, and then come find you kissing Brent with a bunch of dudes in the background stomping each other out."

Clicking the lock button on her key fob, we went to stand in line at the entrance booth for the festival.

"Things are a bit weird," I admitted as the employee put on my wristband.

"At least he's hot, right?" She chuckled.

I rolled my eyes and grasped her hand, swinging our arms as we walked through the gate.

The festival was beautiful. Cold air wrapped around me, carrying the smell of smoke, cinnamon, and wood intermingling, making Halloween feel even closer. Traditional fall festival booths were scattered around, a corn maze boasted a few acres of confusion, and there were plenty of snacks to try.

"Step right up!" a voice called from a game booth. Rows of toys hung from the top, tempting everyone to try their luck at a rigged game. A guy tossed ring after ring with a girl by his side and a group of people around him, all hoping he would land the perfect shot. They cheered as he won a large teddy bear and handed it over to the ecstatic girl.

Other groups crowded around as some worked with determination, their brows furrowed, using miniature saws for pumpkin carving, creating the best designs to take home with them. Nearby, a squealing group of people gathered around barrels filled with water, apple bobbing. Each person had someone bent over the edge, desperately trying to catch an apple with their teeth.

Looking around, I took a deep breath and released it. This was a *normal* fall festival, filled with laughter and smiles. The weight of everything in my life wouldn't completely dissolve, but I could enjoy the views—even if just for a moment.

"I totally want to get my palm read. Oh! Or some Tarot cards," Kelly squealed, pointing to a sign depicting a hand. *The festival psychic.*

"With my luck," I sighed, "they would tell me that I'm going to die tomorrow or something."

She wiggled her eyebrows at me. "Or... they could tell you that Brent is going to bang you into next week."

"Eww." I playfully smacked at her.

The festival around me *was* a nice distraction, but I couldn't help the plaguing thoughts that lingered in the back of my mind. Getting sent creepy texts and pictures of someone watching me? *No, thank you.* I couldn't quite understand what the goal was— unless it was to unsettle me. If that was the case, mission accomplished.

And who knew how many pictures they had of me?

I kept looking over my shoulder, wondering when Alexander would strike and try to kidnap me. He was far too rich to worry about the consequences, and I had a feeling he'd already gone too far with others before. His brazen confidence was startling, and I didn't want to see what would happen if he got angry.

Kelly finally decided on getting her palm read, and I trailed behind her into the tent, brushing past layers of velvet curtains and soft cotton drapes.

The room was stunning, adorned with intricate tapestries, crystals, and antique brass trinkets that caught the flickering candlelight. It felt like stepping into another world.

Sitting at the table, a woman summoned us with a graceful wave. "Come, darlings. Let Madame Dira see what your future holds. Who is first?"

"Me!" Kelly raised her hand.

"Tell me, are we doing palms or tarot?"

As if her question changed the entire ambiance of the room, the flickering candles cast shadows that danced across her face. The air was thick with the scent of incense, curling into tendrils around us.

Kelly plopped herself into the velvet chair and extended her hand, palm up. "Palm first for us, then we'd love to do a card reading."

"Of course, my dear," she whispered in the small space. Taking hold of Kelly's hand with her own, weathered with age, she grazed her fingers across Kelly's palm. "Oh yes. This line here? This is your lifeline..." She paused dramatically, eyes flicking up to Kelly's. "How old are you, dear?"

"Twenty..."

"Well, this line here has a shadow crossing it." Her eyes flicked to each of us, crafting an aura of intrigue. It was a great party trick. "You've an important decision ahead that will determine the course of the rest of your life. I see great darkness in one of the paths. The other will be brighter despite it being fueled by great loss."

The way she spoke sent a chill down my spine and Kelly shifted uncomfortably in her seat. Clearly, she wasn't expecting that type of reading. "What about my love life?" She tried to put up a smile.

Madame Dina readjusted Kelly's hand in hers and traced a delicate line with a pointed crystal. "This line here shows you're bound to experience times of extreme loss and heartbreak. This chain pattern can mean many things—feeling trapped or desperate..." Her gaze shifted from Kelly to me, her eyes dark. "Unless you choose the right path forward."

This was Kelly's idea, not mine. I pursed my lips and glanced around the room, focusing on the flickering candles and intricate tapestries instead of Madame Dina's ominous words.

With a sudden bang, Madame Dina slapped her hands on the table, making both Kelly and me jump. "You, girl! Sit in this chair. Palms first."

"I, uh, okay." I scrambled to exchange spots with Kelly, both of us looking like nervous wrecks.

She grabbed my hand with a bit of force and dragged it under the light. "Both of you have many challenges you must face. Your lifeline shows many paths forward, but they are all clouded in darkness. You are twenty as well?"

I swallowed the lump in my throat, trying not to let my facial expressions give away my anxiety. "Yes, Madame."

"Good. Good. And this love line..." She traced it with her crystal, sending shivers down my spine. "...is very strange. It starts here"—she pointed to the beginning of the line—"and breaks into parts here."

"W-what does that mean?"

"Truly, I don't know. You have many difficult choices ahead."

She released my hand and clapped twice. "Now! Tarot cards. Both of you, sit."

What I assumed was hocus pocus, she laid out cards on the table with practiced precision, telling us about our strong bond of friendship in the past. That could have easily been guessed by looking at the two of us. We operated like sisters.

She slowly flipped over the card that was supposed to reveal our present. The dramatics were freaking me out.

"You two have secrets held back from one another." She clicked her tongue and looked at each of us, feeling like she was staring into our souls. "Depending on how you handle this, your future card may change."

She waited before flipping the last card—for a more dramatic effect, maybe?

I looked at Kelly. "Are we supposed to tell our secrets now? Or do we—"

"Hush, girl. Madame is speaking with the spirits." Her eyes were tightly closed before flipping over the last card. "Oh."

"Oh?" Kelly and I echoed in unison, leaning forward to get a better look.

I looked at the card. Why was there a *death* card? *Oh, no. I'm going to die tomorrow for real.* My mind raced with every way I could die.

I tried to remind myself that this was a party trick of a card game. Madame Dina was probably just playing up the drama for entertainment. But as I sat there, staring at that skeletal figure on the *Death card*, I couldn't shake the feeling that something big was coming. Something that would change everything.

"Ah, the Death card," she murmured, her fingers lightly brushing the corner. "Do not fear it, my dears. This is not *necessarily* a harbinger of doom, but a powerful symbol of transformation and rebirth. To move forward, you must let go of the past."

That sounded like code for *I'm going to die.* I glanced at Kelly, but her expression was unreadable. I, on the other hand, was ready to bolt from the tent and never look back. *Forget the festival!* I planned to invest a *lot* of money in bubble wrap and hazmat suits.

"For you, this card suggests a time of great transition. Seems like you two should settle up on your secrets if you'd like to keep each other." She shuffled the cards back into the deck and shooed us away. "Go now, I must rest. You two have *a lot* to discuss with one another."

Almost stumbling out of the tent, Kelly and I shared uneasy glances.

"Maybe that wasn't a good idea," she said, rubbing her arm nervously.

"No shit. I'm already freaked out enough as is." I mimicked

her movements, feeling the goosebumps that formed on my arm. "That lady gave me the heebie jeebies."

A hand grabbed me from behind and I pulled back, yelping.

"Woah, it's just me!" Brent exclaimed, looking startled along with me and Kelly. He searched our faces for what had freaked us out.

"Brent!" Sloane sauntered over, purring at him in her typical sultry voice with her swaying hips. She demanded attention and an audience wherever she went.

Good God, would she ever leave us alone for more than two seconds? She was always somewhere, lurking.

She didn't seem to have a giant posse with her this time around and changed into more appropriate attire for the festival. Kelly and I had the same idea with stopping at home before driving over. While it covered more, appropriate may not have been the best term. A mini skirt with a cropped sweater didn't look warm enough for the ever-cooling evening.

I choked back a laugh, thinking about whether she'd find one of her minions later and steal their clothes.

Brent didn't look like he was having any of it. "Sloane, I'm busy. I already told you I don't want to see you anymore." He turned back to us, ignoring her pleading eyes.

She stuck out her bottom lip, pouting in a particular manner that felt a little devious. *Good ploy, I'll admit.* "Baby, I told you I was sorry. What business do you have with Fallon anyway?" A look of curiosity crept onto her face.

"Business that is none of yours. It's between our families, *not* yours." His voice was cut and harsh, but I could only guess how many times he had told her to get off his back.

She stamped her foot, furrowing her brows like a toddler. "Don't be rude. Can we all go to the corn maze? I'll invite Alexander too." She pulled out her phone and zoomed through it with her thumbs before any of us could stop her.

God dammit.

"Not necessary." Brent clicked the power button on her phone to turn the screen off. "I was just leaving."

Her face lit up. "Then I'll go with you."

"*You* could go into the maze with Alexander," Kelly muttered under her breath.

I didn't want anyone to go into the maze with me. Actually, I preferred not to go at all. Kelly and I didn't officially plan to navigate the corn maze or take a chance on getting lost forever.

"Anyway"—I took a step backward, pulling Kelly with me—"thanks for the business update, Brent. I'll see you in the boardroom."

It looked like we were *sprinting* to the corn maze after all. Without extra people. Getting lost in the dark was bad enough without cutthroat assholes following along with us. I wanted to be far enough away from them so I could breathe.

"Let's get in there before anyone sees where the hell we went," Kelly whispered.

The employee handed us two glow sticks and a guide to help us make it out. How would we make it out with only a couple of glow sticks? He had to be kidding.

"Just glow sticks?" I asked, holding up my pathetic excuse for a light.

He didn't look entertained, glaring at me. "That's it. Either go in or don't."

Kelly tugged me along into the entrance. We stepped into the dark, tall cornfield. The leaves and debris crunched under our feet as we slowly moved deeper into the first corridor, away from the noise of the festival goers. It felt colder away from everyone, and an eerie silence slowly overtook us with each step away from the grounds. We cracked our shitty glow sticks and held them up to the guide.

"Step one: 'Find your footing with the crows,'" Kelly whispered. "Does that mean we have to find something crow-related?"

I kept my voice as low as possible as I whispered, "I think it means we should find a scarecrow. I could be wrong, but the first checkpoint has to be close. Does it say anything else?"

She held the glow stick out, squinting at the paper. "Yeah, step two." She giggled.

"Let's look for a scarecrow first."

We slowly crunched our way to a fork in the road. The first decision to be made. One would lead us ahead, and the other would bring us to the scarecrow.

The only sounds I could hear were our footsteps, the whisper of the wind, and distantly, the rumblings of the festival. If there were other people in the maze, they were eerily silent.

I didn't know if that was comforting or scary.

"Which way do we go?" I asked Kelly.

She looked around, pointed left, and we continued to find out if the direction was correct. We only had a flimsy piece of paper and the faint glow of our cracked glow sticks to get us through.

A gust of wind picked up, shaking the leaves around us. I jumped slightly at the noise and grabbed Kelly's arm. She pulled out her phone in a *fuck it* moment—the glow sticks didn't really do anything for visibility.

"I think I see something." She pulled at my hand to get me to move faster with her. "Is that a scarecrow?"

It sure looked like one. "I think so. What is step two?"

Kelly fumbled with the paper, shaking it out and holding it under her phone's light. "Step two says, 'Follow the lantern.'"

I looked around, not seeing anything around us but cornstalks and the sad, slumped figure of the scarecrow. "What does that mean?"

"Is he pointing anywhere?"

I pointed her flashlight up at him and sure enough there was an extended arm pointing vaguely into the darkness. "That way," I said, pointing in the same direction.

While we trekked in the direction the scarecrow pointed, I didn't know whether to ask about what Madame Dina had said or not. She clearly had a reaction to the *secrets are being held back from one another* line. We already discussed some secrets on Kelly's end, but were those the full extent of them?

"That reading sounded like a bunch of hocus pocus," she whispered as if she was on the same train of thought as me. Her voice sounded on edge as if the thought had been plaguing her more than it did me.

"I told you," I giggled.

The quiet rustling was interrupted by the sounds of stomping somewhere in the maze. I clapped a hand over my mouth and exchanged a worried look with Kelly. Those footsteps didn't sound like they belonged to someone enjoying a fun night out in a corn maze game.

Time to find the lantern and quickly. She grabbed my hand and clicked off her flashlight, bringing us back to the glow-stick-only approach. It wasn't my first choice, but keeping low visibility meant we had less chance of being seen.

I brought my voice as low as it could go. "I think I see light shining through over there. We could cut through."

As quietly as possible, we pushed our way through the corn, taking a shortcut to reach the lantern. When it came into view, we knelt to use its light to read the guide.

"It says 'Avoid the...' as step three," Kelly murmured, squinting at the paper under the lantern's glow.

"Avoid the what...?" I leaned in to get a better look at the guide. It didn't tell us what to avoid at all. *Well, that's* super *helpful.* "What's after that?"

"'Enter the ring of stone.'"

Great. We were officially lost forever.

"Whatever, let's take the most logical path forward. There are three paths here. One of them takes us back, and the other takes us forward."

We stood with only our glow sticks as our weapons and our only hope. The stomping had stopped, but whoever it was had to still be out there, lurking. Maybe they were just pissed they got lost? That thought brought little comfort to my nerves.

"Baby girl..." A man's voice called out, low and taunting.

My stomach dropped. *Alexander.*

"Pick one and run," I hissed to Kelly.

She chose the center path after I grabbed her hand and we sprinted in, feet crunching the fallen leaves in rapid succession. My breath came fast and shallow, my heartbeat pounding so loudly it drowned out everything else. Alexander was in the maze, and he was looking for me.

We came to another decision—left or right. Kelly didn't hesitate as she led us to the right, keeping her steps as light as possible while we made a run for it. I scrambled to keep up without stomping the hell out of the ground behind her.

"Baby girl," he called out at a distance, "I know you're in here. Come out, come out wherever you are."

We hit a dead end. "Fuck," I whispered.

Kelly didn't miss a beat. "Let's go through it."

We heard him steadily walking around at that point, so the only option was to cheat the maze. A quick push through the corn led us to a corridor going left or right. We'd cut through the maze twice already, and there was no time to try to figure out which way was right or wrong.

All we could do was move.

Rushing down the left part of the corridor, we came to a massive pumpkin in the way. "Is that in the guide at all?"

She looked down with her pathetic glow stick, scanning the guide quickly to find anything about a pumpkin. "Step six says, 'Leave me on your doorstep and I will guide the way.'"

"That sounds good enough to me." I held up the glow stick to see if our pumpkin friend was carved. His face stared back at us, its jagged grin pointing to the right. "Score, his face points that way. Let's go."

We froze, holding our breath at the sound of the rustling of corn. Soft footsteps sounded like they were right on the other side of the corridor wall.

Crunch. Crunch. Crunch.

No voice accompanied the footsteps. I pointed in the direction we needed to go, and we set off slowly, trying to match our footsteps to the sound of the wind picking up leaves and shaking the corn to mask them.

Once we rounded a corner, she held up the guide to try to figure out where we would go next. "'There must be a sacrifice' is what it says."

I looked at the paper to verify. What kind of sacrifice? If that meant splitting up, I would die.

I took a deep breath before concluding it meant splitting up. "So, we split up and meet back up here when we find out which way leads us forward," I said, steeling myself to prepare for an even worse end to the night.

"Count to one hundred and then make your way back here. It should give us enough time to figure it out before he finds us."

I nodded, heading down the path to the left.

One, two, three...

With only my fading glow stick, I hoped I had enough time to attempt to figure out what a "sacrifice" meant and get back to Kelly. The path I took was zany, with multiple turns and only one path forward. It felt like a good sign that it led on for so long, but when I came to another break in the path, I wasn't so sure.

I chose the path to the left first, looking back to make sure I'd remember which one I came from.

Twenty, twenty-one, twenty-two...

Dead end after three turns.

I retraced my steps to try the path on the right. This one felt just as long as the path I took to get in here. Trying to stay on the balls of my feet to minimize noise, I heard more footsteps and the rustling of the cornstalks. Was he also cutting through?

Holding my breath, I tried to time my steps with his to mask my movements. It was hard to hear with my heart rate thumping in my ears and throughout my entire body. Sounds started to feel distorted.

I'm going to get caught, and he's going to kill me or something.

Seventy-five, seventy-six, seventy-seven...

The countdown in my head felt like a ticking time bomb.

"Baby girl, I know you're in here. I saw you come in." He

meandered around a bit more, crunching as he went, wondering where I'd gone.

I didn't think I had time to figure out the maze, but there was no place to hide from him. He sounded a little way off from me, but one wrong move and he would cut through to come find me. And if he found me, I wouldn't be able to get away this time.

"Over here!" Kelly called, making a distraction.

He made his way over in her direction while I tried to match my footsteps with his toward the other path to see if it was a dead end. I chanced pulling out my phone and using the light to look around, scanning the entire area for a clue that it was the right direction. What did sacrifice mean?

Oh. A ritual circle.

Duh.

If I were going to make it out of here with Kelly, I'd need to think quickly to get her over here. I set my glow stick on the circle to mark the spot and looked around to find a few rocks to throw for distractions.

"Where is she?" Alexander's voice came from a closer distance this time.

"She was right here... We split up, but this maze is, well, a maze." I heard a touch of humor in her voice. Ever the expert liar to get herself out of trouble.

I found two decent-sized rocks and chucked them over the corn, praying I wouldn't accidentally hit anyone. The first landed with a loud thud, and Alexander shifted towards the sound. "I think I heard her. You go that way." *Good, good.*

I threw the second just a little bit off from the first and he stopped to listen and cut through some of the corn to try to find me, moving away from me.

Ninety, ninety-one, ninety-two...

With my feet trained on his step pattern, I quickly retraced my steps and peeked around the corner to see Kelly standing still, holding her chest. I motioned for her to come, and we quickly made our way back to my glow stick, Alexander walking around in the distance still calling for me. If I had known this would have been a horror maze, I wouldn't have come in.

I dared a whisper. "Next step?"

We looked over the guide. The final step read, *Don't mind the ghosts.* We exchanged a shrug and tiptoed to the next stage of the maze, desperate to get the hell out of there.

28

Fallon

We split up again.
And again.
And again.
Getting out of this fucking maze was a nightmare.
My phone buzzed.

KELLY:

> I found the end!!!

"Score!" I said.

"Score, indeed," a voice said from behind me.

I looked up at a large, imposing figure before me. I typed an *SOS* and hit send before clicking my screen off and backing away to run, hoping I could remember which split Kelly ran off into.

He let out a deep, wicked laugh that made me want to gag. "Now, now, little girl. Where do you think you're going?"

"I'm leaving the maze," I whispered back, slowly continuing to back away from him.

His legs were longer and caught up to me quickly, grabbing me by the hair. "You aren't going anywhere." His features were dark, almost black with a soulless expression.

I let out a small yelp in pain from him gripping my hair. "Let go."

"No. You keep escaping my grip, and I don't care to give chase any longer."

He kept hold of my hair and planted his mouth onto mine, forcing a grossly wet kiss. It wasn't like anything else I'd experienced; it felt all wrong. He forced his tongue into my mouth, letting it flop around like a dying fish.

Pushing on his chest, I tried to force him away from me. No dice; he outweighed me by a good seventy or more pounds.

Forcing me to step backwards, my back connected with a pole of sorts, trapping me between a literal rock and a hard place. "Stop it." I tried to wiggle away from him to run.

He gripped me even harder, digging his fingers into my skin. "No chance, sweetheart. You're mine. Didn't I tell you that?" He lifted my shirt, exposing my stomach. "Look how soft your skin is. I can't wait to dig in," he growled.

God, I hoped Kelly would be looking for me. *Did my text even send?*

"Get off of me, Alexander," I said, smacking at his hands. What good that would do, I didn't know. I had to try something, anything.

"You keep slipping away from me. It hurts my feelings," he breathed against my neck, his voice low and chilling. Before I could react, his teeth sank into my skin. "We're meant to be together, baby girl."

"Ow! Get OFF!" I stamped on his foot, getting him to release me from his grip, and bolted, holding onto my neck where he bit me. I couldn't tell if it was saliva or blood on my fingers, and I didn't care to find out.

I heard his heavy footsteps pounding on the ground behind me, getting closer with each second that I tried to run. I was far too short to outrun him.

Turning each corner I met, I kept going until I hit a dead end. *Well, time to go through,* I thought while pushing aside the corn, the stalks scratching at my arms and face. The stalks sounded so loud as I pressed through them and out into the other side, leaping back into a sprint.

Hoping I was getting toward the end, I chanced to look back but ran headfirst into a hard body. "Oh God, so sorry," I muttered, trying to sidestep and continue running, still holding my neck like I was preventing myself from bleeding out.

"Jesus Christ, Blondie."

I froze for half a second, looking up in disbelief. "Brent?"

"Kelly found me at the exit and said you sent an SOS. She said Alexander was in here being a fucking freak, per usual."

I gripped his arm, my eyes wide in fear. "Brent, he tried to…"

"Not one more word if he's going to make it out of here alive tonight." His voice dropped to a low rumble, daring someone to try him. Even in the darkness, I felt his face getting that dangerous look to it. "Why are you holding your neck like that?"

"Don't beat up anyone else today, Jesus. Just get me out of here."

I turned at the sound of heavy footsteps crushing leaves, dirt, and gravel beneath them as he almost reached us. "No way you get away that easy, baby girl." Alexander's voice was closer now.

"*Baby girl?*" Brent said teasingly.

"Ok, fine. Kill him."

That was all he needed to hear. The moment Alexander broke through the wall of corn, Brent pounced like a cheetah chasing its prey. It was terrifying—*and oddly hot*—to see him sprint full force, closing the distance in seconds.

Alexander had no chance to see him coming before he was tackled to the ground.

"What the fuck, bro!" He struggled underneath Brent straddling him, laying into him with his fists. "Get off me," he muttered.

"Get off you?" A sickening laugh escaped Brent's chest, his fists still going.

They rolled and Alexander took his best shot to get a hit in, missing and hitting the ground. Brent rolled off of him, effortlessly getting back to his feet and throwing his jacket in my direction. "Cover yourself up, Blondie. The exit is just behind you to the right."

He motioned for Alexander to approach with his hands, taunting him. *Playing* with him.

Unleashing the predator that lay just beneath the surface.

I covered myself up in his jacket and rushed down to the end of the maze where I saw Kelly waiting nervously.

"Fal!"

"Let's get out of here." I hurried toward her.

She caught me mid-sprint, wrapping an arm around me as we rushed to her car, the sounds of the fight, the festival, and the horrors fading behind us. The sooner I was home, the better. Kelly put the car in drive, sparing occasional glances at me on the way home.

Neither of us knew what to say, but we both understood.

At home on the couch, I was wrapped in a blanket and served bottomless hot chocolate while we watched *fictional* scary movies.

"Another movie?" Kelly flipped around with the remote, looking for another horror to watch.

"No way, I need to go to bed. I've got another briefing tomorrow to prepare for Brent's grandfather. I don't know how my mom did it," I said, sinking further into the couch.

Turning off the television, she looked at me with curiosity. "So, you're getting into two relationships with Brent. A *very* personal one and a professional one. Can't wait to see how that turns out."

Could the couch have been a cliff to roll off of? That sounded nice.

"I'm not dealing with this. Goodnight." I stomped off into my room.

Flicking on the lights, I expected a boogeyman to be in my

room. *Nothing.* Unless you counted the weird sounds from outside the window. I pulled the curtains back an inch to peer out into the night.

Tap. Tap.

Were those... pebbles?

I slowly opened the window.

"Fallon, I need to talk to you," the voice said from below my window.

"Jesus Christ, Garrett," I breathed, gripping my chest. My anxiety would be the death of me. *Were heart attacks from anxiety a thing?*

"Meet me in your backyard?" His voice sounded desperate.

I shifted slightly. Kelly was still awake and there was no way to get out there covertly. Not that I wanted to; I felt like I didn't know this guy to the full extent. He could have been trying to lure me outside for who knows what.

"Can't. Kelly is still awake. You can talk here if it's that important," I whispered.

He let out a huff. "Okay, well. For one, you didn't have to sic Brent on me. What is up with you two? He's with Sloane and she's not a very... amicable person."

I rolled my eyes. Was he being serious right now? "Next question," I said flatly.

"Huh, as soon as I'm out of the picture... Anyway, I need to clear up some of these allegations. The Fitzgerald family is running amok and acting like a Mafia right now with some other families. The reason families like mine are being caught up in cases is that someone's daddy calls the shots and doesn't like it when people don't act like his little worker bees."

To be honest, that tracked. Alexander had this aura about him that screamed *I'm a piece of shit and my daddy allows it* and it made me sick.

"Okay? Doesn't change that I can't be seen with you. My advisors aren't too thrilled with us being dragged into your guys' drama." I glanced around, wondering what else was lurking out there.

He grunted and I could tell a frown had formed on his face. "Your family has been involved with this shit for longer than you might think. I'm at the center of this drama spreading around campus because my dad wasn't abiding by some secret group rule. But from what my family's advisors and legal counsel are saying, there's some stuff your mom was involved in that relates to a lot of what's happening."

Great, another mystery.

Thanks, Mom. Could have used a heads up, you know! I silently scolded her in my head as if she could hear me.

Okay, I was tired of the vagueness from everyone. "So, why are only a few families going down?"

"It's all to do with the top ten and the group at the very top. You've seen the list? Those ten run a lot of shit, Fallon. Sloane's family keeps tabs and track of everyone, organizing shit. Your *friend* is in the family of blackmailers. I'm surprised you didn't know that by now with your association with Vaughn. Also, tell him not to attack me again. Shit hurts." He rubbed his face. and in the shadows, it looked like he would have a nice shiner on his eye for a while.

I bit the inside of my cheek, unsure of how to respond. "How can I trust what you're saying? I've been told things about you using me for protection from the fallout. So how do I know this isn't a ploy? That you aren't being paid for something?"

He groaned. "Why would I come here after you got my ass handed to me? I still give a shit about you, you know. Even if we never made things official."

A small pang in my chest left me feeling confused. I didn't know anything, and I had very little information to go off of in all the situations I found myself in. I was drowning with sharks —while bleeding.

Garrett seemed kind and caring, and none of our interactions ever gave me red flags. But then again, he could be a great actor like the rest of them.

On the other hand… his family was going down.

I didn't know what to think. These kids around me turned on each other in the name of self-preservation. Nothing made sense.

"I don't know," I whispered, putting my forehead to the window. "I just don't know anything."

He got closer to the window. "I won't lie and say I didn't know exactly who you were before we met, and that a lot of the rumors aren't my fault. I feel like a lot of this is my fault. But the charges, the feds, and the other families gunning for us aren't. Those are all the doings of the other parents around us, and we *all* are cannon fodder for each other to use in their wars. The only problem is that some families aren't scared of getting their kids dragged in, or worse."

My eyes flicked up to him. "What do you mean 'or worse'?"

"The kid who died? You think that was an accident? Whatever the reports say, it's a lie. He was killed in the war zone that all our parents have created. None of us are safe—you especially. Your mom died a while ago, and the predators have been circling, sharpening their nails in preparation for you. You're about to be dragged into shit you can't come back from."

He tried to get even closer to the window, but a bush was in his way. "Fallon, you cannot trust anyone from the top ten. Look what they did to me."

My eyes dropped to my hands. "I'm one of them though..."

His hands gripped the ledge of my open window, his brown eyes coming into better view. His face looked worse in the light, and it would look even worse later. I also couldn't help but feel like there was something *behind* his words. "You can't trust any of them. If something happens to me, I can at least say I tried to warn you."

I pinched my eyebrows together. "What the hell would happen to you?"

"For exposing the truth? A lot. I'm a dead man walking. Don't play their games."

And with that, he stalked off into the night.

Exposing the truth? What was he about to do?

29

Brent

"Jesus! I'm done. I'm done!" Alexander yelled from underneath me, pathetically throwing punches that wouldn't land. I rolled off him and stood, dusting the dirt and leaves off me.

I pointed a finger down at him. "Don't fucking touch her, man."

He stood up, shaking off dirt and leaves from his nice white shirt. "I thought *Sloane* was yours, dude! Don't attack me for wanting a nice piece of ass."

I gave him another shove. "Don't fucking spook her. I have her meeting with my fucking grandfather this week, and I can't have her backing out of a *really* important fucking deal because you fucking *raped* her. Don't fucking touch her. I will kill you; consequences be damned."

He ruffled his hair, shaping it back into place. "Someone is getting *possessive* lately. What's Sloane going to think? She's not one to take lightly to that type of competition. Not to mention what she'd do to that little girl? I think I can safely put stakes on Fallon—that girl is such a fucking tease."

I balled up my fists. I swore he was asking for another hit to the face. "No word of this to anyone, you understand me? I *will* kill you myself."

He laughed as I turned on my heel and made my way out of the maze. *Fucking arrogant prick.*

Riding fast enough to outrun my thoughts on the highway, I headed towards the Dictator's compound. Getting ahead of Alexander was my top priority.

Of course, he wanted to lay claim to her as soon as her status came out. He was obsessed with beating me, being the top dog, and being a fucking dick in general. When he was told no, he became a brute with his daddy backing him up to get whatever it was that he wanted.

It was always that way.

We had our fair share of competitions, but I wouldn't let him take what was mine. He hated losing to me; I was simply faster, better than he'd ever been, and he hated it. He hated me. Ever since I separated myself from his side, it was every man for himself.

And I sure as hell wouldn't let him get to Fallon first. He would ruin her.

Slamming the front doors open, I trudged through the foyer on a mission. My rage was hot in my blood, reaching its boiling point.

"Brent, welcome sir I—"

"Grandfather. Now," I growled to the butler.

"Of course, Mr. Vaughn. Right this way," his tone softened, not willing to provoke my anger. He'd seen plenty of my outbursts that sent men to the hospital, and today was no different.

If he touched her, I would sever his hands and make him eat them.

My grandfather sighed, knowing full well I was about to irritate him. "What now, boy?"

I couldn't help my tone, even knowing he may hit me for it. "Alexander Fitzgerald is trying to spook the Montgomery heir."

"Pray, tell, what are you on about?"

Letting out a restless breath, I continued, "Ever since the news came out about her, he's been relentless in pursuit of her, and I'm convinced he's trying to sabotage the relationship between our families."

He sat back in his chair, a contemplative look on his face as he lit up a cigar. "Since when were you two at odds with one another? I seem to recall a time when you both were glued together, running amok and getting into petty crimes together. Is this a little dick measuring game between the two of you?"

I tried to calm myself, flicking an invisible piece of lint off my shoulder. "When it comes to business, I have no friends. I sure as hell don't need him and his daddy getting into our affairs."

With a flick of his wrist, an employee appeared at his side, bringing him an ashtray and a glass of liquor. "Tell me more about the sabotage, then. As I'm aware, this family of theirs seems to be tearing at the seams, grasping at straws. The investigation seems to have spooked some amongst the top of the food chain. Whistleblowers are willing to come out and speak about things they've witnessed, and I worry the Wilder family cannot keep up with their end of the bargain to silence them."

Tapping my foot impatiently, I chose my words carefully. "Which is exactly why the Montgomery heir needs to be… reined in a direction. *Quickly*."

His eyes flashed something dangerous before taking another puff of his cigar, smoke curling around him. "Does she show signs of not wanting to deal as her mother did?"

The question threw me off guard. Did she? What was she going to do? Was she briefed properly by her company? Was I fucking things up? Rubbing the back of my head to compose myself, feigning a yawn, I replied, "As far as I can tell, no. If she keeps being pursued by Alexander…"

He held his hand up. "I got it. Don't worry about him. I also have your next assignment of employees to deal with. Don't come back until it's finished. Dismissed."

His employee handed me an envelope and ushered me out of my grandfather's office. Another round of employee management meetings to go.

I couldn't wait to take my anger out on some of them.

30

Fallon

School was awkward.

Evans demanded heavier security measures after I alerted him about Alexander's attack on me at the fall festival and his attempt to push himself onto me. I could still taste his disgusting spit, no matter how much I brushed my teeth or washed my mouth.

He also told me that that family is a nightmare of brutalities and advised me to steer clear of Alexander if I could help it. The whispers through the grapevine have not been *so great*. Someone's family has been working to destroy anyone trying to blow the whistle on business plans amidst the ongoing investigation.

I assumed it was either Sloane's or Alexander's, since they were the top contenders for wanting more power for themselves. Alexander wanted ties to my family—merging an international luxury real estate business with the most powerful attorneys in the country was a surefire way to stay on top. Sloane's family sought connections with the biggest, most powerful conglomerate ever known to man—the benefits were endless for anyone who hitched themselves to their train.

Brent's family and mine were *supposedly* safe from the investigation, with the amount of hush money being paid out to the government, cops, and lawyers crawling around threatening a federal indictment.

It was a great time—*not*.

Sloane kept trying to get me to come over to her house after the festival, and I couldn't bring myself to even respond to her. She was a scary broad, and her family hosted the meetings for everyone to participate in activities I couldn't bring myself to attend. Sooner or later, I'd have to oblige for fear of what would happen if I didn't play nice.

Since she couldn't get me to respond, she decided to bomb Kelly's phone, asking when we were coming by for a girls' day.

I tried to stay in bed, but responsibilities called, and I had one final briefing before the dreaded meeting with Augustus Vaughn. James came in to show me documents and make sure I was at least eating.

The documents went straight over my head, and I couldn't muster much of an appetite.

I needed to have my head on straight.

Leaving my class for the day, I cringed at the thought of the walk across campus with my own personal security to keep me *safe* from the dangers that may be lurking in every corner. *The perks of being me, I guess.*

The guy who came with James didn't talk much.

"Care for lunch, James?" I shot out into the silence of our walk.

He grumbled, "We should get to the office, Miss Montgomery."

"Fast food?"

"We can pick something up, if you'd like."

"What's your favorite?" I tried making conversation. I didn't have many people I could just chit-chat with that I positively trusted, so my guards got the short end of the stick from me bugging them with small talk.

He seemed to ponder over it. James towered over me at six foot five and had an imposing, broad figure. "Burgers."

"So, we're getting burgers for lunch!" I almost fist pumped at the excitement of having some nice, greasy food in my stomach.

James smiled at me. The other one never expressed much and always refused to come inside, even as the nights kept getting colder. Too professional, but at least I had eyes on the outside of my house around the clock.

Successfully conning them into lunch with me, we ate in near silence in the car. I blurted out a few things to which James responded, and the other one didn't bat an eye at. He also didn't agree to eat with us.

"Do you like your job?" I asked.

"Some days," he replied quietly, finishing up his food and discarding it into the bag. "Time to go."

He started up the engine, and we were off for me to face my fate.

Dreading the rest of my life, I wondered how many situations I would find myself in. The CEO of my mother's company was a large task she left, and I was horrified to know what would happen to me if I didn't follow her footsteps closely.

I barely knew the footsteps she laid out for me to follow.

The creepy texts seemed to be on pause. Kelly started looking into it and promised to keep me updated on what she found out. Everything was moving quickly, and the paranoia was starting to creep in again. I needed to know where the closest garbage can was in case I was going to throw up.

What if people found out I slept with Brent? What would that do to our companies?

What would Alexander do? He sent me a strange text this morning asking to take me on a date, but I hadn't replied to him. He freaked me out too much. His family was full of powerful, brutal people who held sway over law enforcement. Not comforting.

I felt like I was in the eye of the storm for a brief reprieve, but the winds were going to start picking up again soon.

With the building in view, a pit formed in my stomach. I wanted to jump out of the car and die.

All right, let's put on our big girl pants and do this shit. I already shed my virginity to the bad boy on campus. I can do whatever at this point.

The room was filled with those on a *need-to-know* basis only.

I sighed defeatedly and plopped into my seat. "Alright, boys, let's get this over with."

The chatter stopped at the sound of my voice.

"Just like her mom," one of them mused.

I could only dream of her footsteps being that easy to follow, but she accomplished this at my age. I could figure out how to get it done with a little help. All of this was going to be my new normal, no matter how much I kicked, screamed, or cried about it.

I took a deep breath, firming myself to speak. "Evans, I need you to brief me quickly on the decisions that my mom made. I need to make decisions like her. I don't have her experience, but I need to make sure things run smoothly and that no one can catch me off guard. I'm going to tell you all, I am completely scared shitless, and I need your help. I am all-in because I have been drowning with the sharks."

Mr. Caldwell smiled. "Don't worry, Miss Montgomery. You're more like her than you know. We all have the company to worry about, and we will be with you every step of the way."

The meeting started with a brief overview of some operations that were being orchestrated between the Montgomery business and the Vaughn empire. They needed new locations to hold goods, and we were on our way to acquiring them in secluded spots.

Who knew I'd go from not knowing what sex with a real guy was like to learning how to organize black market transactions within a couple of weeks?

Evans turned his attention to me. "When dealing with Vaughn, be sure not to let him see you bleeding. He is a brutal man and will not take things easy on you for your ignorance of the business. He wants to resume as if you were Maria herself. I'm sure he plans on handing the operation to that fiend of a grandson as soon as he gets a handle on him and his… defiant ways."

Well, that piqued my interest. "You mean the one I go to school with?"

"Yes. He's a troublesome one, but not someone to worry about as with Alexander. No rape cases pushed under the rug for him. Girls seem to flock to that one." He tapped his tablet, strumming his fingers across the black screen. "You have met him, yes?"

Yep. Sure did. Especially when he was…

Focus!

"If you mean watching him pummel any other guy in his sights, sure. Anything to note?" I tried to act casual, but my intrusive thoughts might have been getting the best of me.

Tapping his chin and opening his tablet to scroll through some information, he replied, "Where the Fitzgerald child has had to cover sexual harassment, the Vaughn grandson has had triple that in assault cases. He's volatile, unpredictable, and erratic. If he were normal, he'd be on death row by now. For now, he joins his grandfather's 'cleaners' in the family business, until he is deemed ready for leadership."

I opened my mouth to speak, but closed it out of uncertainty. Trying to formulate my thoughts, I asked, "How do you know this much about *their* company?"

"When you have such close contact between families *and* companies, it's hard not to know what's going on in each of them. Whatever happens here, I'm sure Vaughn has his ways of knowing."

Did that mean he knew what we were up against? He had to.

"Wait. What are cleaners, and what does until he is deemed 'ready' for leadership mean?"

His lips pressed into a thin line as he contemplated his next words before offering a smile meant to disarm me. "In the nicest way I can say this, they *clean up* those who are a liability."

"So, murder," I blurted, my thoughts running out of my mouth before I could catch them.

"Well… sometimes, yes."

I scanned the room of men; my eyes must have looked wild. Why *not* murder? They were already into the black market and illegal trading.

But Brent murdering people?

Was there no hope of normalcy?

With the new information in mind, I swallowed the pill of reality. It was a large dose that sent shockwaves through my entire being. Accepting this new reality was going to be a tough hill to climb.

"Does he join them voluntarily? Wait, don't answer that." I held my hand up, trying not to physically clutch my pearls. "Let's get back to dealing with Augustus. What will this meeting be like, and how do I act?"

Another man piped in. "Your mother was an expert when dealing with him. He practically groomed her and expected nothing but the best out of her every performance. A mentor to your mother, they held a very particular bond of close associates."

He mentored my mother and taught her everything she knew, but I was left to flounder until she died. Was I supposed to catch on or what?

"So, why didn't he reach out sooner when she died?" My bluntness would be the death of me.

"Well, he did. While you were sequestered with that atrocious woman who gave everyone lip when we all reached out," Mr. Caldwell butted in.

I wracked my brain to try to remember anything from Sylvia's hell hole that would trigger a memory of any of this. As far as I knew, I was kept in the dark about most things, and she never paid me any mind outside of her proclivities. I was told to sit down, shut up, go to school, and mind my business.

Anything else would get me corporal punishment.

No letters came that I knew of. I never did much outside of school besides talk to Kelly. I lived in my bedroom for most of those years—doing homework or reading just to avoid her—

before I was ousted and able to access some of my inheritance money to buy a house.

I even rummaged through memories of her abuse to try to search for clues. No dice.

"I never got anything," I finally admitted into the silence. "What did she say to everyone?"

"Mostly excuses," Evans said. "That you were grieving, didn't want to take messages, or that you were out with friends, and that being underage made her your legal caretaker. She threatened multiple lawyers on us, claiming you made that call and wanted to be left alone."

I balled my fists on the table, trying not to slam them in frustration. First, she abuses me. Then, isolates me. "She neglected... to relay that information to me."

"Well, we have signed documents from you verifying certain details."

That time, I did slam my fists into the table. "Show me the fucking papers, Evans."

All eyes were fixed on me, some wide in surprise. A timid, soft-spoken girl like me finally snapping. Whatever Sylvia pulled was going to put her at the top of my hit list.

He did as I asked and pulled up a folder, sharing the screen to the projector in the room. There were multitudes of documents spanning the years I was with her with multiple statements and agreements.

The first was a no-contact request due to grieving the loss of my mother, Maria. It clearly stated I was unable to coherently think or communicate while I dealt with the tragedy of her passing after years of watching her slowly die. I never wrote that, but my signature was expertly forged with the guardian's signature beneath mine.

"Evans... I didn't write these."

He didn't show signs of any emotion or thought. His game face was on. "These were produced by a lawyer from within the company. He claimed to have met with you over each and every letter, statement, or agreement that was relayed to us. Multiple have corroborated that story."

From the texts to the vague comments made by everyone, this felt like it made sense.

Feeling a bit chaotic, I pulled out my phone.

Here goes nothing.

> we have rats in the ranks and they've been crawling around for years. Need help.

I shot off the text, wondering what my life would turn into after it went out.

Feeling an inch of relief from sending the message, I looked out at everyone spread around me, waiting for either instruction or what I would say next. "Then we have rats that need to be trapped. These"—I motioned to the screen and stood—"are not mine. I've never seen them. The options are that I was either coerced under the influence to sign these, or they've been forged. Neither are great options, but whatever you all agreed to within some of these is null and void and I want Sylvia to answer for her actions."

The men looked around, wondering what scheme we'd been pulled into. For all we knew, Sylvia could have signed the company away from underneath me. The money-hungry bitch who loathed my mother for building herself up from the dirt had tricks at play.

I stood near the projection, tapping my foot as I looked through the letters and contracts sent using my name. Some approved monetary requests for her. Others were contracts signed for benefits that lasted well past guardianship period after I turned eighteen. She'd planned and plotted against me while I was under her care.

But why?

Did she really hate my mother that much? Mom never told me much about her family, to the point that I never knew them personally or interacted with them outside of occasional necessary associations. Whatever my remaining family had planned, it was all in the name of undermining my mother's legacy. It made me wonder what fights she had that kept me in the dark for so long. Hiding me away was smart, but telling me nothing left me wide open.

"Give me a list of every person who approved, viewed, or even touched these documents. They undermined my mother and they're done. If any of you in this room are on this list, I will personally kill you myself for putting this company at risk."

With my arms crossed at the head of the table, I searched the expressions of the men before me, wondering if any of them knew anything about this. There would be a reckoning.

Evans cleared his throat, clearly surprised by my death threat. "I'll have that list to you by end of day and you'll have beefed up security for a few days."

I nodded, holding onto my last scrap of composure.

31

Fallon

Just pretend everything is normal for one night.

I didn't even want to celebrate Halloween this year. My life felt like a fucking horror movie. Costumes would be scarier since I knew the monsters that lurked underneath them.

Kelly picked out costumes for us while I tried to hide away in my room, hoping she'd forget I was there. It was no use because she barged in with her eyes covered. "Are you decent? Is there a naked man in here?"

"Ha, ha, very funny. I want nothing to do with him," I lied. I sent him that text yesterday.

And he never replied. *Go figure.* He only wanted anything to do with me when it benefited him or his dick. I was such an idiot.

"Well, he's going to want everything to do with you when he sees you in this!" She pulled out an outfit from behind her.

I groaned at the lack of material on the hangers. "What are those?"

"Sexy devils," she said, throwing one at me.

I held up the small piece of red fabric, wondering how I would even fit into that thing. "Tell me this is a joke. I can't go out in public with my ass and boobs showing at the same time.

This is a thong! Where are the straps? Why do you do this to me?"

She giggled and flopped on the bed, pulling a couple of packages out of her hoodie pocket. "These are the stockings to hold your butt cheeks in."

Hold my butt cheeks in... "There's no way I'm wearing this."

My thoughts were racing with the boardroom briefing. Not only was I supposed to be prepped for my meeting with Augustus Vaughn, I also had to deal with the fact that my abuser had been trying to take everything out from under me for years. How was I supposed to juggle a meeting about illegal business ventures and a greasy family member wanting a piece of the pie that wasn't theirs?

There were too many documents forged in my name to even attempt to go through in a single day. Evans had a preliminary list of employees involved in dealing with Sylvia—they had meetings and secret dealings. Her pockets were consistently lined with money; she also had multiple sketchy boyfriends she went out with. Who they were, I didn't know. Those men could have been heavily involved in her schemes, or worse, leading her down this dangerous path to wealth because she was so blinded by dollar signs.

Augustus expected me to be my mother, just as he mentored her to be. It was probably the assumption that she filled me in before she died, but she didn't, and I had no letters or documents from her to help me out. Brent's warnings and the board had to be enough.

I felt nauseous again.

"Hello?" Kelly waved a hand in front of my face, trying to snap me out of my trance. "Are you putting these on or no?"

With a sigh, I snatched the stockings from her hand, feeling the silky fabric slip through my fingers. I could already sense the thrill of another reckless decision washing over me. But if I was going down, I was going down in style. I had the perfect touch to add to the already daring outfit waiting for me in my closet.

She scrolled through her phone while I slipped into the

stockings, shimmying them up my thighs and butt. How women used to wear these daily back in the day was beyond me. *True boss babes*. I hastily grabbed the barely-there bodysuit and pulled it over my chest, zipping it up my back—though it barely made it halfway.

"Okay," I muttered, leaping into my closet for the final *pièce de résistance*.

As I rummaged through the hangers, I brushed past Brent's jacket—secretly wanting to burn it—and found what I was looking for.

I grabbed what I'd really been looking for: a floor-length sheer robe in a perfect red, the kind that whispered danger with every flutter of its fabric. Along with it, the matching red heels that promised to make even walking feel like a power play.

Making haste before Kelly noticed, I slipped into the robe, letting it glide over the bodysuit, its sheer material teasing just enough while covering nothing. I told myself if I was doing this, *I was fucking doing this*.

"Kel," I called out, poking my head from behind the closet door, keeping the rest of me hidden for maximum effect. "Mind giving me a once-over? Just wanna make sure I look halfway decent."

Her eyes flicked up, glistening with excitement. "Yes, show me!"

Her jaw fell to the floor when I slowly stepped out, donned in all red. A small twirl in a circle made her jump up and let out a scream.

"Oh. My. God!" She clapped both hands over her mouth to prevent herself from screaming again. "You're a... I don't know! A fucking goddess. Holy shit."

I looked down, swirling the material between my fingers. "It works?"

Slapping my arm with half anger, half laughter, she said, "Girl! You're going to kill it. Let me get your horns and pitchfork so people know you're there to lead them back to hell with you when they inevitably follow you out of that party."

I laughed, but deep down, I knew this was one of those bad decisions I'd regret by morning. I was sure of it—I was regretting a lot of things the mornings after. Brent would be in attendance at the party; they were celebrating the upcoming baseball game along with getting ready for Halloween.

Despite texting him for help, I didn't want to see him. Things were too complicated for me. He wasn't just the toxic playboy everyone whispered about; he was something *darker*, more dangerous. The man was judge, jury, and executioner in his world of underground dealings, and I had willingly stepped right into the middle of it.

But why me? What drew him to me in the first place? His family business and its relationship with mine felt like the perfect reason to string me along to make sure things went smoothly. If he took over his company, hitching himself to me even closer than his grandfather was to my mom made perfect sense. It was all just business.

Garrett had known who I was all along; yet he claimed his intentions were pure. He never told me he knew what my inheritance was and that pissed me off. It felt like everyone had a hidden agenda these days, and I was the one walking blindfolded into the fire.

Then there was the issue of the conspiracy to take the company out from under me, pulling the rug out from under me and sending me crashing to the ground. Whoever was involved, it was a long con that had been carefully plotted, and I was desperately trying to catch up. Five years behind, and now everything—me, the company, my future—was dangling by a thread.

I couldn't shake the anxiety that constantly gnawed at my core, making me feel as if everyone around me was in on a secret I wasn't privy to. They've been in the loop while I've been blissfully ignorant, waiting for a group of thieves to steal it all away, leaving me in the wreckage I could have never seen coming.

The frat house was alive with flashing lights, smoke

machines, and costumed students. Skeletons, witches, clowns, and more laughed, drank, and danced under the all too spooky lights. The party flickered with warning signs I refused to acknowledge.

As we walked up the pathway, a few mummies chased each other around with rolls of toilet paper, throwing streamers and squirting silly string everywhere.

All eyes turned to Kelly and me as we walked, almost dazed, to the entrance, heels clicking with each step. My costume was tight to my body and exposed me to everyone, but I made a last-minute decision to add a red masquerade mask to add an extra layer between me and them.

A hint of hiding the storm brewing.

Inside, the party was alive. Laughs, drinks, and dancing galore. We moved through the foyer desperately seeking our first drink to take the edge off, to numb me just enough to pretend to be normal. Like they all pretended to be.

"What drinks you have back there?" I asked the literal Joker manning the bar.

He made a flourishing movement with his hands and laughed maniacally. "A drink for everyone, my dear."

"Eh, just give me something strong, Mister J." I turned to Kelly as he hopped away to concoct something. "I feel like everyone is staring."

A giggle escaped her bright red lips while she adjusted her horns. "It's because you're hot and mysterious, dear. Enjoy it for a while and let's get your mind off of everything for just one night."

Before I could respond, cheering began in the front room as a crowd formed. "*Sharks! Sharks!*" they yelled. We peered into the room to see what all the fuss was about, and a gap in the crowd showed the baseball team.

Their uniforms were dirty, covered in fake blood, and they each sported different kinds of masks. Half masks, full-head silicone masks, and classic Halloween movie masks. A horror-themed baseball team.

And there goes the hoard of girls.

I rolled my eyes and accepted my drink from the clown behind the bar, taking a nice long swig to burn my throat—and my jealousy.

"Remind me never to swoon over a male." I offered my drink to Kelly.

She took a swig of it, hissing with the intensity of the burn. "Is this straight alcohol?"

"I told him to make it strong. He must have made me the Lucifer special," I said, throwing the rest of the drink down and holding up my cup, signaling for another round.

She eyed me up and down, crossing her arms and tapping her pitchfork to her shoulder. "Uh, did something happen that I don't know about?"

Letting out a breath of frustration, I gave her a defeated look. "I'm just tired of feeling a hundred steps behind others. Getting kicked down the stairs to the reality of everything has been jarring. I learned some new info on our *friend,* Brent, and my trust levels are low. Being involved in certain things feels against my moral code."

My eyes grazed back over to the team when I caught his name on the back of his jersey. Of course he wore *that* mask. I shook my head as Kelly rubbed my arm trying to comfort me in my mental anguish. "Things are complicated," she cooed, "but things will be good. I'm here with you, and I'm not going anywhere. Our friendship is real and as solid as bedrock—or diamonds or something. It's unbreakable and I'm sorry this has been happening. If I could change anything…"

I grabbed her hand and squeezed it, feeling temporarily comforted by her touch. She was my best friend in the whole world. Secrets or not. "Love you," I said, kissing the back of her hand.

"Then let's party!" She raised her drink in a toast before taking a long swig of it. I followed suit, downing the rest and tossing it to the bar. The alcohol was warm as it slid down my throat, quickly fusing with the beat of the music that thudded through the house, shaking the walls and vibrating under my heels.

I let out a heavy breath, forcing a smile as Kelly pulled me onto the dance floor.

Just for tonight. Forget about everything for a little while.

I pushed the creeping anxiety down, forcing it to fade—even if just for a few hours. I focused on the warm hum of alcohol seeping into my veins and the thumping music around me.

Kelly grabbed my hand and spun me around as onlookers watched the devil twins getting lost in the moment amongst a crowd of dancing bodies. The beat wrapped around everyone, with the fog machines creating a thick haze across the room. I focused on the beats to ground my heart and forced my nerves to play pretend.

But then I saw him.

A baseball uniform-wearing figure at the edge of the crowd, semi-hidden behind a group of dancing students. A girl desperately trying to get his attention. His face was fully pointed in my direction, hidden behind the bloodied ghost mask.

For a moment, I felt the old paranoia creeping back in. The doubts. The uncertainty. But I bundled it back up and shoved it down. I wasn't going to let him get in my head.

Tonight was about feeling normal for once amidst the chaos that erupted around me like a volcano.

He stepped forward, fixated on me as he parted through the crowd. The air became thicker than the fog with tension as he made his way closer to me. I tried to pretend I didn't notice by twirling with Kelly and swaying to the beat. I knew he could feel my pulse quickening with each step he took in my direction, how my skin tingled with awareness of him.

I couldn't escape him.

He was behind me, close enough that I could feel the heat of his body. Those hands of his hovered over my hips, teasing me with his presence. Even covered by a mask, I could see the coy grin playing on his lips. I fought an arch in my back as I caught my breath in my throat, he brought the mask dangerously close, grazing my ear.

"Dance with me." He had a low, sultry tone, commanding a dance with me.

I couldn't say anything—I didn't trust the adrenaline in my veins. I let him move closer, his hands snaking low on my hips in a firm grip, our bodies syncing up. I felt the magnetic pull between us once more, just like when he was in my bedroom.

The scent of him—a mix of leather, smoke, and something uniquely Brent—filled my senses. Despite everything, I couldn't help but lean into it. I hated myself for it, wanting to tell him no.

I hated how easily he affected me. How easily he made me forget the darkness with a single touch or the way he gripped my hips.

"Why are you doing this?" I whispered low enough so only the two of us could hear. It was heavier in meaning. Why me? Why did I get dragged into this mess? Why did he make me feel things I didn't want to?

His hands dragged upwards, grazing across my stomach as we swayed. I fought back a shiver from his touch, the feeling of his body on mine, the way his hands moved on my naked body clear as day in my mind. "I can't help myself with you."

I let him sway with me a moment longer, feeling the blissful buzz of the alcohol shoo away my clarity of mind.

But reality had other plans.

"I got your message," he breathed, low and soothing, while his hands roamed my body to the rhythm of the music. "Want to chat by the bar?"

Yes, get me out of here. I nodded before he took my hand and led me away from the group of moving bodies to a more secluded spot. Kelly was still having a blast, feeling herself on the dance floor and letting her inhibitions fall away.

"There's some super screwed up crap happening," I groaned when he brought me to a corner void of people. His body closed in on me, one hand going to the wall as he grazed the other up my side.

His breathing was heavy behind the mask, his chest rising and falling from dancing a while. "Before we get into it, I want to let you know that you look so fucking incredible. God…" his voice was so low, almost possessive while he searched for words. "You are an *absolutely* stunning woman."

I felt the heat in my veins rise up my neck and into my cheeks. "Anyway," I diverted the conversation, "when I texted you, I'd learned that there's been background sabotage that would affect both of us."

"How so?" his body language never shifted, making it look like we were regular party goers—drinking and flirting.

Trying to keep my composure, I continued, "When my mom died, I was sent to live with her sister, Sylvia. She'd been plotting to destroy my mother's work by forging documents. When I was sent there, she forged a letter from me claiming I only wanted messages to go through her. Which isn't true."

His hand firmed up a bit at my side as some of my words sank in. Sabotage never made it very conducive to be horny. "How many documents?"

"Too many to go over in a single day. Here's the kicker," I breathed, hoping he'd know what to do. "She had help from people inside the group. Lawyers. Employees. Higher ups. They'd all been plotting to rip the Montgomery Group to shreds and probably stage a hostile takeover when I turned twenty-one. I'm betting they didn't expect me to find out this early because it gave me a heads up about what's to come next year."

From his silence behind the mask, I could see the strain in his body as he digested the information. "How much time do we feasibly have?"

"My birthday is April nineteenth. Honestly, I'm surprised you didn't know my birthday already. Maybe six months before the world comes crashing down." I looked down at my feet, observing my ridiculous outfit. I felt bare and out in the open.

His hand softened and started making soothing circles on my stomach. A comforting gesture even though I felt anything but. "We have time. We can fix this mess, but we'll have to work quickly. I can brief The Dictator before your meeting with him, though... I'm surprised he's not aware already. If he is, he's never mentioned it to me."

It was an interesting thought. Evans told me that our families knew things going on in the background, and with that comment, I didn't know what to make of it.

An angry face caught the corner of my eye as she made her way over to the both of us hiding in the corner.

"Brent, baby," she cooed, "what are you doing with—" she stopped in her tracks.

Yep, she knew it was me. *Not good.*

"Fallon?" Her voice was a mix of shock and disbelief. "What are you doing with *my* man?"

He shook his head, annoyed. "I'm not your boyfriend. I've literally broken up with you—what—five times now?"

Her eyes were locked with mine, full of jealousy and something else I couldn't quite place. "I thought we were friends, Fallon. You used me to get to my man. Alexander is going to be gutted when he finds out." She made a move to go for her phone.

I stiffened, slapping his hand away, unsure of how to respond to that.

Brent turned to face her, his frame towering over her as she was forced to tilt her head upward. "Sloane, go back to the party. I'm not doing this with you."

Sloane's lips curled into a tight, horrifying grin as she focused her face back to me. "You have *no* idea who you're messing with, Montgomery. Brent's been mine long before you ever showed up. You're probably fun and all..." She tapped her finger to her lips, eyeing me up and down. "...but you'll be just another passing phase for him. Isn't that right, baby?"

Um, ouch?

All I could do was roll my eyes at the ridiculousness that my life had become. At least petty drama felt a bit normal outside of the hostile takeovers and illegal activity.

"That's enough," he said, body tightening up. He pointed

back to the party. "Go play your games somewhere else. I'm tired of you interrupting me and acting like I'm a fucking dog. It's over. Finished. We're done."

For some reason, that gave her a giddy smile. "Don't say I didn't warn you," she said in a sing song tone and skipping away, freaking me the fuck out.

Ripping off his mask, he brought his face close to mine. "I'll handle this." And he crashed his lips into mine.

Somewhere, deep down, I knew I couldn't run from the truth forever despite not being able to trust anyone around me. Not from the secrets. Not from Brent. And not from the storm that was about to tear my life apart.

32

Brent

Her lips were on mine.

Fuck, if only she knew how much I loved that mouth of hers.

She tasted like a whiskey mix, and the scent of her perfume sent me over the edge.

I wanted her, on the wall at this party.

Unfortunately, that would have to wait. No matter how much her breath hitching made me want to push even further, to throw her over my shoulder and carry her up those stairs, and have my way with her again and again.

For now, a kiss would have to hold me over until I could get her all alone again and bury myself inside her.

She pulled away from me, breathless and dazed. With my hands on her waist, I steadied her against the wall as she looked me up and down with those big doe eyes.

"I'm a little buzzed," she admitted.

"I can taste that," I purred back. I'd love to taste something else, too.

A heavy sigh escaped her perfectly red lips. "I was supposed to have fun tonight, but it seems everywhere I turn..."

Shushing her and playing with a strand of her hair, I placed a kiss to her forehead. "Don't worry about it. You focus on having fun. I'll deal with everything else. Sloane. The rats. All of it."

Kelly approached with an incredulous look on her face. "Are you two done sucking face? There's a costume competition and I'm going to enter Fallon."

I released Fallon from my grip, ushering her to Kelly. "Be my guest. I have business to attend to," I said, turning around and covering my face back up before stalking out of the room.

Time to go to work.

Making record time, I needed to work quickly before I approached my grandfather. He was very particular in his dealings with me. If I didn't come back with a job well done, I may as well not come back at all. So, I would take care of our problems before announcing another.

A much larger problem.

I found it odd that he didn't know about snakes in the grass, unless he was playing his old tricks again. Nevertheless, *odd*.

The envelope contained two profiles: Mario and Nicholas.

Mario had worked for my grandfather for about ten years and had gotten complacent. He let things slip to the point that he was ignoring theft, amongst other things. Growing soft after ten years was what my grandfather loathed about him. He had two choices: Fix himself quickly or let me fix him permanently.

Nicholas, on the other hand, was set to die tonight. He was someone Mario had *forgotten* to report for theft. He stole drugs from a drop-off location and sold them on the streets to line his own pockets. Too bad our hearty paychecks weren't enough for him.

I called up a few available men to group up with for the long night ahead.

Dave, John, and Reaper. Some of the best cleaners we'd probably ever had. Reaper was a bit of an oddball, demanding to be called death's name. Thank God he didn't ask to be called Lucifer. That would have been awkward.

Heading out with Lucifer tonight, hehe.

The Dictator asked Mario and Nicholas to be near for some sort of meeting; I just hoped they weren't runners.

It made things messy.

"Hiya, boss." Reaper saluted me with his typical greeting, wearing his favorite black riding gloves, as always.

"Reaper." I nodded.

Dave and John eyed him standing there. For such brutal men, they were awkward.

I tossed the profiles down on the table beside me. "Here are the two men. Nicholas isn't to leave alive. Mario is… either, or. You boys can take your pick or flip a coin—I don't care."

They read over the profiles for a moment, memorizing the faces of the men they were about to brutalize.

I continued, "They're supposedly at one of our places a bit north. I suspect Nicky boy to be a runner type. Do your due diligence for twenty minutes before we split. We need this handled before morning."

Folding my arms, I watched them scramble to work with the time we had left to verify the locations of the men. Making the mistake of thinking I had more time with this task before Fallon dropped her bombshell on me, I needed extra hands on deck to ensure the smooth completion of another task from my grandfather.

His tasks were endless, and my participation in the business was strictly cleaning. I had to earn my way into the formal business, and it didn't help that we had to keep covering up assault cases and domestic disputes.

I just fucking loved a good fight to get me going.

John broke the silence about ten minutes in. "I'm showing Mario at the place on Eighth Avenue, but Nicholas is nowhere to be found."

"Grab your party supplies, they both die tonight." I grabbed my helmet and let them pile into the car. We'd meet up eventually. I had an interrogation deal with first, then I'd hand him over to the wolves to be torn apart limb by limb.

Bursting through the door, I came face to face with Mario. "Mario, Mario, Mario." I clicked my tongue at him. "We have some business to attend to tonight, and I'm going to need you to be cooperative."

My walking in scared him. He was wide-eyed with fear, his hands gripping the chair. "What kind of business, M-mister Vaughn?"

"Oh please"—I rolled my eyes—"my grandfather's name is Mister Vaughn. He sent me here to ask you a few questions." I dropped my duffel bag to the floor, pulling out some ropes as my eyes remained locked with his.

His panic levels were rising, his chest rising and falling quickly. "I didn't do nothing!" He looked left and right as if anyone would be there to help him.

A cruel laugh came from my throat. "Oh, Mario..." I started tying a few preliminary knots absentmindedly while he watched and looked for an escape. "We both know you did. Now, you'll answer my questions if you know what's good for you."

His hands were visibly shaking as I approached and booted him in the chest, sending him flying backwards out of the chair. He screamed. I laughed. The chair collapsed into a few pieces on the ground and Mario was gasping for air, gripping his chest in pain.

I crouched down next to him. "Still going to play dumb? Or can we have a civilized conversation?"

Grabbing his arms and tying them together, he begged me to stop whatever I was doing. "Boss, what is this about?"

"Complacency," I replied simply, continuing to tie him up. "The type that leads us to be very, very disappointed."

Realization washed over his face that we knew what a shit job he'd been doing when it came to the deliveries and organization of the trade. "It can't be that bad. We've been doing great overseas with no issues!"

My hand itched, so I punched him in the face. "I'm going to ask you a series of questions about Nicky boy, and you will answer honestly and with as much detail as you can. Otherwise, my men will come in and rip you apart—piece by piece."

His chubby little face squished under my fingers as I gripped his head and forced him—tied up—into a non-broken chair. It was tempting to put my boot to his chest again, but I had other tools at my disposal for extracting information.

"I'll tell you anything, boss," his voice quivering while I flicked open a knife.

I started cleaning my fingernails with the knife, casually sitting in front of him. "Did you know Nicholas was stealing from us?" My eyes were trained on him, piercing into his soul. My knife casually pointed in his direction.

"I-I…"

"Ah, ah," I warned. "I'll know if you're lying."

"I thought he just took a little for himself to sample." He flinched after responding, bracing for impact.

"Wrong answer," I growled, stabbing my knife into his left thigh. "The truth will set you free, my dear Mario. How many times did you look the other way?"

"Ah! I, uh—" He was breathing heavy, the pain of the knife distracting him from a formal train of thought. I pushed it a little, for fun. He cried out, "Ah! I haven't—I mean, I've been looking away for…" He clenched his teeth, gritting through the pain. "…somewhere like two years."

"Why?" I ripped out the knife, relishing in the sweetly sick sound it made.

Another scream, mixed with an adrenaline-fueled giggle, escaped him. "Nothin' was going wrong. I figured…"

"You could go lax on us? Wrong answer." I swiftly reached over to break a finger—or two. Not my fault he clenched his fingers together. "Where's Nicky?"

"I don't know! Ow!"

My patience was wearing thin. "Wrong answer," I said with a wicked laugh, stabbing his other thigh.

"Boss?"

I turned to see Dave entering ahead of the other two, a hint of curiosity on his face. They all held their cleaning supplies and would most definitely be using them.

Motioning to the man in the chair with the knife sticking out of his leg, I gave a smile. "Oh hey, Davey. I was just asking our friend Mario here where we could find Nicky. It's important we find him tonight."

Through his panting and bleeding, Mario looked to the three men that strolled into our little interrogation with pleading eyes. "Please, please! I'll tell you everything you want to know!" He shook his tied-up hands, shifting the chair around a bit.

Kicking him in the shin, I asked, "Then why were you making it so difficult?"

"Boss, just use his phone," John piped up.

I nodded to them to search his belongings. Reaper pulled out his toys to play with after rolling out a plastic sheet next to me, standing over Mario waiting to play with him.

Mario shook even more, making me wonder if he would go into shock soon. "Nicholas has been dealing with some bad people, okay? Bad! They'll kill me!"

Rolling my eyes, I grabbed him by the hair, forcing him to look at me. "I'll kill you, shitface."

"Heh, yeah. Shitface," Reaper taunted.

"Look. These guys are fucking scary, and Nicholas started letting them skim a little from our drop locations for some extra cash." His breathing was jagged and rough. I needed to staunch the bleeding to keep him awake a little longer. Stabbing people was tricky. The wrong spot made for too much blood loss.

Stupid motherfucker couldn't have just answered my questions?

"I have his messages, boss." Dave held up the phone. "Looks like Nicky boy split and he's heading out of the country."

Open palmed, I smacked Mario in the face as hard as I could. "You are so fucking lucky I need you alive right now."

33

Fallon

"And the winner of best costume goes to..." He opened the envelope to read the name. "...Fallon Montgomery for being *the hottest devil this campus has ever seen*. Seriously, it says that."

The crowd roared to life as I was led forward to the DJ to accept my prize—a bottle of whiskey and a Halloween figurine trophy.

So much for a low profile.

"You're hot!" A bunch of guys yelled from the crowd.

I took my prizes and tried to scurry off the stage before the DJ stopped me. "No way! You're due obligatory pictures now. Everyone line up!"

The first person came up to me to take a picture together.

Sloane.

"Hey, bestie!" She threw her arm around my shoulder, sending a wave of nervous energy down my body. Her lips dipped close to my ear as we took a few pictures, a vicious grin apparent in her voice. "I hope you know what you're doing. The games have just begun."

Smiling through her threats, I made it through the next twenty minutes with groups of guys wanting pictures with *the hottest devil on campus* before Kelly finally saved my ass.

"Look." She showed me her phone full of cash deposits. "We've got lunch money for forever now."

I laughed, knowing she'd been up to something. "Were you secretly charging for pics?"

"Duh!" She flipped her hair. "There's money galore on campus, and now we have lunch paid for a year in advance."

The party raged on, and I found myself losing steam as I grew more nervous about the meeting with Augustus the next morning. That nagging feeling creeping back into my chest that something was horribly wrong reignited my paranoia. Drinking more wouldn't solve the issue.

"I'm gonna head home," I said to Kelly. "Are you staying?"

She shook her head, giving me a sweet smile. "Nah. Let's go."

Good, because I needed to throw up.

The next morning, after retching over the toilet all night, I tried to mentally prepare myself for the day, but my phone buzzed with yet another new headline:

Breaking News: Another Accidental Death on Willow Bay's Campus. Should College Parties Avoid Alcohol?

The notification flickered across my screen, sending me back to the threat from Sloane.

The games have just begun.

And the series of creepy texts that came to my phone—some with knowledge of Brent and me.

It made sense, really.

I wasn't just living through a bad soap opera; I was trapped in one.

Kelly ambled softly into the kitchen in her disheveled pajamas and messy hair while she stretched her arms in a yawn. "Hey girl! Breakfast? I'll make bacon and omelets."

"Check this out," I said, extending my phone to her. "This is right after Sloane threatened me last night."

She pursed her lips, opening the fridge to pull out ingredients. "This scandal has everyone on their toes, especially since a bunch of these rich assholes are turning on each other. It's giving Mafia, if I'm being honest."

"The one percent of the one percent just acts like this?" I couldn't fathom how the top did all that they did. It felt soulless, like they'd signed their souls away in exchange for power and money.

There was a separate set of rules by which we lived. Yes, *we*. The government worked for us, law enforcement was merely a bill to pay, and doing what you wanted wasn't just a fantasy. It horrified me. I could get away with so much without suffering anything other than a fake slap on the wrist.

And it made me angry at my mother for keeping me boxed up like she did. Kelly knew the reality, Brent knew the reality, and everyone around me was in the loop while I stood on the outside like an actual child begging for porridge.

Kelly stood at the stove prepping breakfast, keeping a bit too silent for my comfort. Was the news affecting her? Or were there other things going on that she was keeping close to her chest?

"I have that meeting with Augustus today," I injected into the silence.

She cracked an egg into a bowl. "Today's a big day. You think you're ready?"

I'd forgotten to mention to he what I'd learned about Sylvia. I wasn't sure if I wanted to. Based on what I learned about her involvement and her knowledge of certain extracurriculars by way of her father—whom I didn't know if she still spoke to—I was not in a very sharing mood.

More secrets to hold that would tear us apart, according to Madame Dina.

I nodded, offering up a smile as I poured orange juice. Looks like we both had our secrets. "I've been briefed again and again since Evans started dragging me in early. James has been filling me in on details when he comes inside, too. I wasn't technically supposed to be involved until I was twenty-one, but I'm happy I started now. It'll make things easier."

She flipped the omelet, the spatula scraping the pan—the only sound between us while she pondered what I had said. "How come you've not been involved even earlier? Like when you were eighteen?"

"Good question," I said. An answer we had yet to fully investigate, and not something I wanted to ponder out loud.

Sylvia had been doing a lot of damage, and I had six short months to figure out how to stop it. Six months to flail around.

"Well, I'm off on a date after breakfast," she said, breaking up my train of thought by dishing up two plates with omelets, bacon, and toast.

The silence between us was less than comfortable, filled with words that needed to be said but wouldn't be. It made me think that the fortune teller may have been right in her prediction.

There were many dark paths that lay ahead of us.

"What're you planning to do on your date?" I poked around with my fork, hoping to break the weird silence.

She clicked her tongue. "He wants to go golfing and then lunch at his family's old country club. He has no idea I'm about to wallop him with a good game of golf."

"Ever the athletic prowess, and I didn't know Shane was part of a country club," I said with a mouth full of food. "I, on the other hand, have a date with a very old man. "

"Eww! Make sure he leaves you all his money, though," she snorted, avoiding the topic of Shane. She was usually very talkative about her male ventures.

"Very funny."

The compound for the Vaughn residence was intimidating. It was Mafia style. An empire dressed as a mansion. The scale of every building had me holding my breath as I stepped out of the car. *So, this is what wealth looks like.* The compound sprawled in front of me like a small city—straight out of a movie, where power dripped from every corner. Every shadow spoke of the control the Vaughn's held.

The landscaping was so immaculate, it felt unnatural. The hedges were trimmed with near-robotic precision, the grass was a healthy green and perfectly even, and rows of flowers framed every edge and pathway. It was beautiful in a terrifying way—demanding respect, intolerant of mistakes.

Inside, classic architecture and warm colorings spoke to an old yet inspired design. Dark wood lined everything, and every surface was comprised of leather or true velvet. Each room I came into seemed to watch me, judging my every movement.

Augustus Vaughn knew style and oozed with it.

I bet he had his own swagger, too.

I tried to focus on the intricate details of the decor to steady myself and familiarize myself with my surroundings, but this wasn't a house or even a mansion. This was a fortress. A statement.

"Welcome, Miss Montgomery. Shall I take your coat?" A man at the door opened and ushered me in, leading me through the foyer.

I may as well cooperate. "Sure, thank you." I plastered a sickly-sweet smile to my lips, hoping to feign niceties.

"Yes, right this way. The Vaughn men shall be waiting for you inside."

"...Men?"

"Yes." He smiled, gesturing to the staircase. "Augustus and his grandson, the heir to the empire. Now, allow me to escort you to the sitting room."

Fuck.

Trying not to trip up the stairs, I gripped the railing to steady my entire body as I followed him up to my doom. I should have known Brent would be involved, but I let my naïveté get the better of me.

Everyone else was always a step ahead of me, leaving me to flounder and drown in the deep end.

"Hello, Miss Montgomery," he said. "I've been looking forward to this day for a while. Please, sit."

I bowed my head in a small greeting, giving the hint that I was cooperative and willing to listen. *Just as I was told*. Why none of my men were here with me was frustrating. I only had my one lone security guard on standby, a hallway away.

Feeling disadvantaged, I took the chair he gestured to. It was terribly close to Brent. His gaze flickered over my entire body, and I tried to cool myself down as the heat rose to my neck. The last I'd seen him I was semi-drunk and ready to strip my clothes off for him again.

And again.

"It's my pleasure to meet with you, Mr. Vaughn."

"Oh please," he scoffed. "Call me Augustus. I remember when you were just a mere babe clinging to your mother. You've grown into a beautiful young woman and let me extend my condolences for the passing of your mother."

Grief crept into my chest. So many times I've heard condolences for my mother, who'd been gone for five years. "Thank you, Augustus." I mustered a small smile, hand going to my chest to grip my heart.

He shuffled some papers around. "Let's cut to the chase. Your mother and I had a... particular agreement regarding the usage of some higher-end overseas properties. I would have loved to have coordinated this earlier with you, say, when you were eighteen. But here we are, and I'd like to not waste any more time."

Was I supposed to mention that the reach outs he made were usurped by Sylvia? Did he know about that? How would I even broach that subject? Maybe it was best left for another day, or a private conversation with my team. "I am aware of and have been filled in on the details of this working relationship. I am here as a formality to discuss the continuation of this relationship, which will continue as it has with me as the operating CEO in charge. There will be no hiccups or slowdowns with your needs."

A devilish smile appeared on his face, reminding me of Brent. They were related, surely. "So glad to hear you've been raised the Montgomery *and* Vaughn way. Your mother and I had close discourse as partners of sorts. I would like to start bringing you into joint meetings to reinforce our ventures."

With all the prep I'd done, I would have assumed this meeting would have been trickier. Given everything I'd been told about the relationship between him and my mother... it had seemed quite informal. I wondered if he saw me as her reincarnate.

"I'm happy to assist where needed. I do need to preemptively let you know that I am still a novice in my current standing. Things may be a learning curve for me."

I glanced over to see Brent looking completely uninterested and uninspired by our current conversation. His eyes were focused on... my legs? Whatever he was thinking, I didn't need to know about it. Just looking at him gave me unnecessary heat in regions of my body that shouldn't be hot—especially in front of his grandfather.

"Anything to say, boy?" Augustus challenged him. His shift in tone from me to Brent was apparent. Grace to distaste.

"My current job title doesn't allow me to speak on these matters," he said. Brent's tone was also different, making me wonder the dynamic between the two.

Where my mom treated me kindly, it seemed Brent received the opposite entirely. Was he not in the same boat as I was? Learning the CEO ways of his large conglomerate? The way he spoke was like he'd been banished.

We *almost* had something in common.

I swore I saw Augustus roll his eyes. "You will soon be head of this company, as you are my sole heir. Consider yourself in the same shoes as Miss Montgomery, effective immediately. Your current position is still in effect, as you work well there. However"—he stood, lighting a cigar and dismissing his man-in-wait from behind him—"you two must get to know each other. As you are both the future of this entire enterprise. Both companies are intertwined, you see."

My hands faltered a bit with confusion. Was he saying that we were to work together? "I'm a little lost."

Also, no way! I *just* told myself that I wanted nothing to do with this playboy!

The smoke plumed, a scent of vanilla and tobacco filling my senses. It was a calming sensation—which is why I assumed he lit it up in the first place.

He found his words after a few puffs and some vague hand gestures. "You two are assigned together as business associates of sorts. Brent will be in a similar position as you—learning how to be a proper CEO. I will be the guide based on the experience that your mother and I bring."

Brent tapped his foot in frustration. "Sounds like a merger is in order, then, sir."

Taking small strides around the room in thought, a smile on his face, I could tell he'd been brewing a plan of his own. "Not out of the question entirely, boy. We'll talk when Miss Montgomery's taken her rightful place at the head of the table."

A merger? Was that the long game here?

Brent's eyes met mine, and I held my breath for a showdown between them. "Tentative position accepted. What's the next step?"

The build-up for this meeting with Augustus Vaughn was the worst part of it all. When he dealt with others, he seemed to be brutal and calculating. He was sharp for an older man.

What I didn't expect was for him to be soft with me and treat me well, even though that's how it seemed he treated my mother throughout their working relationship. I wondered what it was like for the two of them to work together.

What did she say about me to him?

Had I met Brent before? As a baby or something?

Augustus broke up my thoughts with two words. "Cleaning house."

34
Fallon

I think I've lost my mind.

I sat in the back of the car with my face in my hands, resting my elbows on my knees.

"How did everything get so fucked!" I huffed.

This year turned into something I never asked for. My mom was dead, and I couldn't even grieve her five years later. In a matter of weeks, my worldview had been shattered into unfixable pieces.

James, the security guard and driver, squeaked the leather seat as he turned. "Fast food?" His voice was tentative as he spoke, unsure how to help in a situation where I wasn't in danger, just frustrated.

Knuckles rapped on his window before I could agree to be swept off my feet by a good order of French fries.

Oh no. James rolled down the window enough for me to see who was outside.

"May I speak with Miss Montgomery a moment?"

I shook my head at James.

"The lady said no," he translated.

He sighed. "Let me in the car, Blondie. We need to chat."

I leaned back in my seat to cross my arms. "Stop calling me Blondie, and no we don't."

"We work together," he argued.

For the umpteenth time around him, I rolled my eyes, over his antics. "No, we don't."

"Well, sure, not as a couple—at least not at the moment. Professionally? Yeah, we do babe." I didn't even have to look at him to see his aloof expression with that cocky grin on his face.

Maybe I could start punching men in the face like he did. Could be cathartic.

I turned my head back and firmed my gaze at him through the window. "No."

"No? Should I go back and tell my grandfather that—"

"James," I sighed.

He understood and clicked the unlock button on his door. Brent wasted no breaths climbing into the back with me.

The space was too small as he slid in next to me. "Aren't you staying for cocktail hour?"

"No."

He smiled, and his voice reflected it. "How many times are you going to tell me no?"

I smacked his hand away before he could twirl my hair around in his fingers as he did when he toyed with me. "However many I want. Why? You gonna *clean* me about it?"

Understanding flickered in his face, eyebrows doing their thinking thing before he rubbed the back of his head. "I told you things are *complicated*."

"Complicated? Killing people is that complicated?" I scoffed, shifting my body further away from him. "Just fuck off. I am in no mood for you right now."

What was I in the mood for? A redo on life? My mom to come back from the grave? A burger? A moment of fucking silence, maybe?

I closed my eyes and took a deep breath in through my nose, releasing it out of my mouth. A calming technique my mother used.

It helps release the stress, she used to say to me.

He moved to face me, eyes searching my face for something.

His expression was far too soft for my comfort. "Blondie," he breathed, "look at me, please."

No. I kept my eyes firmly set out of the window, looking at a neatly kept garden bed full of multicolored flowers getting ready to die for the winter. They looked how I felt—droopy and sad.

"Miss Montgomery?" James peered into the backseat.

"Just start driving. You know where to take me," I replied flatly.

The car ride was silent outside of the low music that circulated and the hum of the engine. I felt Brent's gaze on me the entire time. James flicked his gaze at us in the back seat a few times along the way.

It was safe to say the drive was awkward. We pulled into the same burger joint I'd asked to be taken to before, and I dreaded having any further conversation with Brent.

"Can we talk?" he asked.

I shrugged. "Go ahead. James, can you get me what I had last time?" I ignored Brent's gaze.

He looked between us two. "Anything for...?"

Brent gestured vaguely. "Whatever she's getting. On me." He tossed his wallet into the front seat, turning his entire body toward me. "Blondie, look at me."

What would I even say to him? My head hurt and I wanted to throw up again. Life still didn't feel real enough to comprehend and I hoped to wake up from this nightmare that was my life. Pinching myself wasn't helping at all.

"I don't want to." My voice was small, and my eyes threatened me with tears if I didn't calm down quickly.

"I understand this is a lot for you, but I need you to let me in so I can help you. There are things we need to talk about so you are aware and can be prepared. The last thing I want is for you to be blindsided again. Our companies work in tandem, and I can protect you."

Protection. That didn't feel like a word I was familiar with. "Sheltered" and "ignorant" felt more my speed.

"How are you supposed to protect me when it feels like

everyone else is ready to jump at me with claws? Before I was even aware of what I inherited, other people were miles ahead of me to take what I had. You can't undo years of dominoes falling."

James cut the tension with two bags of food. *My savior.* The smell improved my nausea, and I didn't even realize that my stomach was as hungry as it was. Eating was hard after all the shit hitting the fan. And that body on the ground...

"Miss Montgomery?"

My eyes refocused on James, who was staring at me with a fatherly type of concern. The only other person who looked at me like that was Kelly. She became concerned when I didn't act like myself—lately, that was quite often. She didn't know what to make of my headspace. When I lacked a normal appetite, she tried to get me to eat or to watch a movie. Despite her attempts to help me, I couldn't shake the feeling of strangeness around her—she'd been acting odd lately.

Homework felt too weird to complete when I was dealing with people recklessly killing each other and snitching to their handlers.

"Are you alright?"

He was still there in the front seat trying to hand me my portion of the food order. I wanted to take it, but my hands wouldn't move. My stomach didn't feel quite right again.

The door opened automatically. My body knew what it needed to do. I was by the side of the car, dry heaving again. Throwing up was becoming normal, and I was sure I needed medication of some sort for the mental breakdowns that felt never-ending.

James was there. Brent was there. Someone was holding my hair and rubbing my back. Tears flowed freely, and I couldn't throw up no matter how desperately I wanted to. It was all stomach acid and spit. God, it hurt.

"I think I'm hungry now."

❧

My bed was cozy as James went on about basic business topics and how to read certain documents. He knew I wasn't paying much attention, but he also knew that I needed some form of distraction for my aching and broken mind.

I threw up when I got home. Brent and Kelly chatted about who knows what when I passed out from throwing up. James sat with the other guy outside for a bit while I was taking a disassociation-induced nap after cleaning myself up.

"…to find financial irregularities."

Like I said, I wasn't paying much attention.

"Can you repeat that last statement?" I was staring at the ceiling, lost in my thoughts.

"Learning to understand quarterly reports and the balance sheets will help if you are looking to find financial irregularities."

"Has anyone been keeping track of those documents? I think I want the name of the person who handles reports like these. They may be connected to the people who had a hand in trying to destroy my mother's legacy."

He looked surprised, almost. Like the documents he talked about were in the hands of someone capable. But, from what I've learned lately, no one was to be trusted. My guard would be up and strong around everyone who wasn't me.

"Mr. Evans would have the name of anyone handling finances. It may be more than one person, and if you're correct in your assumptions, it would be tearing down the company leadership and putting it back together. A feat in itself—outside of keeping daily operations going."

If the financial portion of the company was being handled by those wanting to do us dirty, I didn't want to know who else was inside the walls that had sledgehammers waiting to tear down the walls. Another worry to add to the list.

I sighed and resigned myself to not getting distracted like I needed to be. "I think our tutoring session is over. This has been enlightening, and you've helped me tremendously, but I'm getting overwhelmed again, and I don't think I have another dry heaving session in me tonight."

A sad smile came over his face. Since being assigned to me, I think he started understanding how dreadfully ignorant I was. It was like seeing someone transferred into an alternate reality—and that reality was a horror movie—floundering until the killer finally stabbed them to death. "I understand. I'll let Mr. Vaughn know."

"Brent or Augustus?"

"The one patiently waiting for you to let him in."

Oh, don't tell me that James is going soft for Brent now. "I don't think that's the best idea."

"Then I'll let you kick him out yourself. He won't leave if I tell him to."

He was right. Brent was stubborn and wouldn't leave if I told him to either.

Not two seconds after James left, Brent was leaning in my doorway. "Feeling any better? I bought some anti-nausea meds while you were out cold." He shook the bottle at me.

I held my hand out for them, silently agreeing to let him in.

"No sour words for me?"

"I think someone who deals with the financial documents has been working to undermine the company and help take it from me." He deserved to have his questions ignored—we had bigger problems to deal with.

He laid next to me. "Then I'll find out who it is and deal with them. You need a solid night of sleep. And maybe a doctor?"

So casual. He offered to kill someone just like that and told me to kick back and relax like I asked him to take out the trash bin. It's like it didn't register that it was killing someone for him —it was just a simple bag of trash going out to the curb.

"Don't mind my nausea; I've always had a visceral reaction to anxiety. Back to the topic: You'll find these people all in one night and solve my problems within twelve hours?"

"I would do it in ten minutes if you asked me to."

I scoffed. "That's a little unrealistic, don't you think?"

Next to me, he trailed his fingers up and down my arm. When he got this close, he was always so touchy. I couldn't think of a time when he was this close that he wasn't trying to connect his fingers to my skin in some way.

He flipped onto his side and played with my hair. "For you? Never."

"What else did you need to tell me?"

He kissed my head. "It can wait a few more hours since you're telling me you don't need a doctor."

I was too tired to fight. Food wasn't staying down, and my brain was tired. "Why are you here?"

"Because you don't seem to have any other friends." Why he always needed to poke fun would never make sense—the situation we were in didn't need shitty jokes.

"What makes you think you're my friend?"

The dim light made him look softer than he was. Shadows were cast in just the right places, making him look comfortable for a change. His eyes were trained on my face, which made me question if I looked like a complete wreck, and his thumb gently stroked my cheek in soft swipes. "I don't want to be your friend."

"Good."

"Why're you asking so many questions?"

Because I can't make sense of anything around me. Because he appeared in my life out of nowhere and I couldn't understand why. Because my brain was going in a million different directions, and I needed to be distracted.

"So, you'll answer them. How come we were assigned together?"

"Fate, probably." His eyes looked sleepy even though I knew he was wide awake.

"Are you taking over your company soon, too?"

He sighed and kissed my forehead. "I don't know. Sometimes he has plans that I'm not aware of and have to fly by the seat of my pants."

"How long have you been killing people for?"

"What made you think it's someone in your finance department?"

A lot of things did. The letters that were signed, making her my guardian and forging my name, took legal people to handle. Staging a hostile takeover would mean making deals that required money. If that was the route being taken, based on my —limited—knowledge, it would be a perfect coup set up to make a few unseen tweaks to steal it from under me.

How would she take over if I became the legal owner now, though? We needed to work quickly and have the succession begin immediately. *But the will states twenty-one...* The puzzle of my mother's timing confused the shit out of me. Why wouldn't there be a clause for early succession?

I sighed and leaned into him more, letting him wrap his arms around me. While it felt nice, I shouldn't have gotten used to things like him touching or holding me. Sex wasn't going to breach its way into my mind. "A lot of things. It made sense when I thought about it."

"What else are you thinking about?"

"That we should keep our relationship to strictly business."

"This is considered a business conversation," he countered, leaning into me more. He wasn't planning on letting me go any time soon.

I had to rip the bandage off. "I don't want a romantic relationship with you."

"That's too bad."

"What about Sloane?" She was still deep in the back of my mind, her threats making me wonder how far she would go because of Brent. She threatened me twice in one night. If she knew earlier, that means her *skank* comment at the game was directed at me specifically.

From what I gathered, her family held the same power as any of the other leaders in the elite world. They organized people together, meaning they could organize them apart.

"Don't worry about her. In fact, don't say her name ever again. I want to forget she exists for just two seconds."

The more I wondered, the more I worried. If connections meant everything to her, securing a relationship with him would mean a lot for her. The money, the power, and the strange bragging rights she wanted to have so badly. I didn't want to be mixed up in something else when threats loomed over my head from every other angle. She had the power to try to kill me—or to try to push me somewhere.

Like with Alexander. If she pushed me that way, what was in it for her?

"She claims to be your girlfriend and threatened me. How could I not be concerned? My company is slipping away from me when I barely know how to read a damned budget report. Not to mention the weird threats and ominous messages I get."

His eyes shot fully open. "Why did you not think to tell me?"

"I told Kelly. She said she was going to sleuth about. It doesn't concern you."

"It does after today. Blondie, whatever you think you want to do, you're not going to get rid of me. Our fates are tied together, and they have been since we were born. Your mother tied her company to my grandfather's ship. That means that you and I will *always* be tied together."

I regretted speaking. "I don't want to be tied to you!"

"I want to be tied up with you forever. If I sink to the bottom of the ocean, it better be because you dragged me there yourself. Drown me, Blondie, because I don't want it any other way."

My heart rate sped up, and he knew it. He knew when my body reacted to him because he reveled in it. My body betrayed me every time—I just preferred to blame him for it.

"You barely even know me."

"Then give me more of you."

"I... can't."

He played with my hair again, kissing the side of my face and pulling his body closer. The pull between us was purely lust. No way I would like someone like him. A killer. A ruthless man trained by someone who clung to the top via illegal means.

"Then let me find it." His hands moved to my body, spreading across my stomach and gripping my sides.

"You won't," I breathed. His scent overwhelmed me and sent me somewhere else. The back of his bike. On the porch, smoking. In the diner, eating food. In my bed where he—

Our lips met, and I knew it was another mistake. For him, it was just sex. For me, it would have to be just a distraction. Because after tonight, I would need to cut any and all romantic ties.

We were assigned to work together. Just business. Nothing beyond that could happen.

"We can't, Brent. Our comp—"

He covered my mouth with his hand and shushed me. "None of these words need to come out of your mouth. The only thing I want to hear is you moaning my name and forgetting everything else; let me be a terrible distraction. Your terrible decision."

Just a terrible decision between business partners.

Before I knew it, our clothes were off, and he was on top of me again. His hands trailed down my body with the confidence of the secret knowledge he had about it. Those hands have been here before.

And before that, his small touches were memorizing my skin.

"There are people here," I whispered.

"I don't care. Everyone will know that you're mine eventually."

His mouth trailed down my chest and toward my navel, placing kisses on every inch like he hadn't seen my body in decades.

"But—"

"Then you better be quiet."

With a desperate quickness, he gripped my legs again to settle in between my thighs.

"Brent."

"Blondie. My sweet, sweet Blondie." He bit down softly on the inside of my thigh. "I could eat you for breakfast, lunch, and dinner."

My back did that automatic arching thing again, drowning out the sounds my mind made. The outside world felt far away, but in our little bubble, it wasn't far away. It just faded into the distance to keep me sheltered from how it broke me down piece by piece. He found each piece and kissed it.

"We can't."

"We can. Don't worry about anything outside of this room. You're here with me, and I'm a hell of a lot scarier." He sank a finger into me, watching for my reaction.

If things could only be as simple as sex.

When he knew he found the right spot, he added a second finger, pushing into me with slow and steady movements. I felt myself relaxing and grinding my hips into his rhythm.

"That's it. Just like this?"

He knew it was. He just wanted to hear me say it. "Yes," I breathed. "Just like that."

Keeping the pace, he growled with need before clasping his mouth onto my clit. He sucked and he licked until my eyes rolled back into my head and I just about shouted his name.

I gripped the sheets around me, hoping I could hold on for dear life as the orgasm built up inside me. "Fuck," I groaned. It was right there, and he was hitting it over, and over, and over…

My orgasm quickly overwhelmed me, sending shockwaves through me. A rush of relaxation and ecstasy ran through me. He took that as a sign of victory and kept going, urging my spasming body to take just a little bit more.

At this rate, he seemed to be down there for more of his enjoyment than mine. "Have I ever told you how delicious you are?"

"Probably twice already." I was panting, and my mind wasn't formulating words or thoughts properly. His tactics on distracting me *might* have been working.

He chuckled, skimming his lips over my skin. Each time they made contact was a jolt of electricity to my already sensitive body. "I'll have to keep reminding you."

Crawling up to meet my eyes, his mouth never left my skin.

He caressed every part of me like he'd never see it again. Like it was his last meal before execution. Skin to skin, his body and hands were glued to me.

I felt relaxed enough to melt into the bed.

"Blondie?"

"Yeah?"

"Have I ever told you how soft your skin is?"

I scoffed at him. The niceties were getting ridiculous. "Is this just a compliment session or something?"

Fingers trailed up my stomach and circled around my nipples, giving me a shiver down my spine. "It could be if you want it to be. I would worship your feet if you'd let me."

This guy was something else. Every time I thought I would know what he'd do or say, he did or said something that made me question what the hell was rolling through his mind.

"Uh. No feet stuff. Unless it's strictly a foot massage with no sexual undertones."

He kissed me. Soft and slow. "Whatever you want," he whispered into my mouth.

My hands found his body this time. Feeling the muscles in his arms to his shoulders as I held on, lest I slip away from this moment. He had muscles in all the right places, and his physique could make a blind woman swoon.

I pushed him over and climbed on top. "I want something like this."

"Be on top, then. Use me however you'd like to. I'm all yours." He gripped my hips, guiding me closer and closer.

There was no hesitation this time. I guided his cock right where I wanted it to go, sliding it inside me. Since that first time, I got curious about more. A needed distraction. Something simple.

It was simple to have sex with him. Maybe later it wouldn't be. For now, it was.

I controlled the pace from above him, letting his cock slide in and out how I wanted it. The full feeling when he was deep inside had me begging for more.

"Just like that," he cooed. "Look at you on top of me. Such a beautiful sight."

Our lips met when I leaned over, him taking over the thrusting and holding onto my hips as he kept up the pace. "You feel so good," I mumbled in between kisses.

The pace quickened, and he was pounding inside of me quicker, faster. My God, it was so good I never wanted it to end. I wanted to be wrapped up in this bedroom forever just letting him fuck me over and over again. Being drunk on this feeling could last forever.

He swiped my hair away from my face to look into the depths of my soul while he was inside of me. His eyes were a pool of intensity with our bodies connected. I'd never seen him look so serious, so calm, and yet so at ease in the same moment. It was like he was enjoying it so much more than I was.

Slamming into me again, his hands gripped tighter. "Where do you want it?"

"Want what?" He was already inside of me, there was perfect.

He grunted, his hands holding even tighter. Kisses furious. "Where do you want me to come, Blondie. Tell me."

"I don't care."

"Then I'm about to come inside you."

Another new feeling. He was pulsing inside of me for the first time, and my sensitivity level was maxed out. We both moaned while he came, and I knew it would be the end of me. The end of everything. A few times of sex with him had become addictive.

Too addictive for me to let it keep happening. A distraction was nice, but this couldn't continue. We were business partners, and this complicated an already messy situation.

Plus, my bodyguard *probably* just heard me have sex. That's awesome.

Brent kissed me again, not wanting to let go. He held onto me as I laid on his chest, his heartbeat started slowing down to a normal rhythm. We laid like that for too long because my eyes threatened to close on me for the night.

"Brent?"

"Yeah?"

"I think you should go."

He held on tighter. "I don't want to."

Sleep would have been easy to drift off into with him, but I couldn't let this go any further. My heart needed to be guarded. Sleeping with him was a mistake. I wanted it to be as simple as liking a man and deciding to go all the way, but that wasn't where I was.

Our companies were linked, and that made whatever we were doing complicated enough. Couple that with the current climate of the situation? A ticking time bomb. We still had to figure out who was behind the series of creepy texts and if Alexander would be back with a vengeance. All of that was far too complicated if I got dragged into anything to do with Brent outside of a professional relationship.

He didn't seem to believe me when I told him I wanted him to go, but he left without a fuss—bad sign. Something told me he would give me the win for now, but that he'd be back and with a vengeance. Nothing would *reaaallly* keep him away for long. He would be back.

The door shut behind him, and tears flowed freely. The distraction wasn't enough to keep my spiraling mental state at bay.

Or my bout of nausea.

My phone buzzed, but I was too sick to see who it was. It was probably Brent, and I had no energy to deal with that.

So, I cried until I fell asleep on the bathroom floor.

35

Brent

One Week Later

"What's got you looking uglier than usual, boss?" Reaper was munching on trail mix while we waited yet again to see what the hell was going on with Jason Haines and his associates.

The last we heard, there was trouble in paradise, and his company was flailing and at risk. Nothing lasted long when you start trying to fuck over the one who gave you your leg up in the world. Never look a gift horse in the mouth—especially if that person was Augustus Vaughn and you wanted to steal business away from him. He would gut you or ensure that someone else did.

I gritted my teeth and accepted the packet of trail mix from him while there was no activity, and we were out here with our thumbs up our asses. "Nothing."

He chuckled. "Woman problems, I get it. Don't need to tell me twice."

"Just shut up and tell me what you heard last from the higher ups."

"Last I heard, you *were* a higher up after that little meeting with your girlfriend."

If she was my girlfriend, she wouldn't have kicked me out so easily. That would change sooner rather than later, but I decided it was best not to push my luck. Her mental state was in no working order, and watching her break and shatter within a couple of days was the worst thing I'd ever seen. It was like telling a little kid Santa didn't exist anymore. All the life and brightness I saw in her that first night was dimmed and darkened by the people I knew would do that to her.

"She's not my girlfriend. She's my business partner and nothing else. And yes. You're right. The Dictator wants me to start taking on some leadership shit for only God knows why. Something tells me he needs the extra cover for something, *or* that something so big is coming that it could implode the world. Whatever it is, he has his plans about it." I shoved trail mix into my mouth and looked back through my rangefinder.

Reaper was manning a rifle tonight. From what we saw last time, we might have to use it. I just hoped his marksmanship was different from his hacking and slashing.

"How's Davey?"

"Stop sending him porn videos. He's not into the weird shit you send him."

The trail mix crunched in his mouth. "Oh, come on. An all-dude orgy ain't *that* bad. I'm sure he'd love to participate."

Some days, I didn't know what I'd do with this guy. The masks were weird enough.

"What's the news with that execution? Did we find out who that driver was or why the men were executed so inexplicably?" It perplexed me, and I needed to know what was going on.

"From what I hear, Jason has issues maintaining his people, and we're here to find out what his course of action is. Mr. Vaughn is very interested in the business practices of the man trying to steal some of his overseas partners in the weapons trade. It's hard enough getting quality shit, we don't need some butthurt kid ruining it for an entire industry by being careless."

The black market always had new people popping up, trying to take out their competition. No one dared to try to take out Chamberlain Industries and preferred to work with us rather than against us. It worked out better that way. My great-great-great-grandfather was quite the businessman, from stories I was told.

Arthur Vaughn and his associates formed a group with other founding businessmen like the Rockefellers and original politicians who shaped the country. When they stemmed away from oil and railroads, they set up trade agreements and thus started their under the table dealings around the world.

Flash forward to today, we ran an unstoppable conglomerate that was near impenetrable. The squeaky wheel in our wagon was the Montgomery Group, and it had been since Maria died. My theory was that Jason wanted to poke us enough and break enough spokes to take over where she left off.

That original group? They eventually let in more families as time went on. Those were the families we dealt with on a regular. Call it a secret society if you want to, but it came with a lot of shit. Lots of rules to abide by, and they were ever changing and nuanced as fuck. I wanted to burn it all to the ground.

But the hitch in that plan was Fallon, the heir to a company that was teetering. What a mess that girl found herself in.

She had no idea.

"There's some movement up ahead. Try not to shoot anyone at random." I pulled up the view as the SUV approached.

"I count two armed men. *Super* tactical, and I bet they feel badass with all that gear. Too bad I could put a bullet in their brains. You say the word and I'll drop 'em."

They rolled up and exited the vehicle. I couldn't make out if Jason was among the men or not. They were smart; I gave them that. Everyone did their best to cover their faces with hats or hoods knowing that meeting in secret never meant you were alone.

"Do you have a solid visual or identification?"

"One is a woman, and they're calling her boss."

"Is this a new group? Are you sure we've been following the right trails with Jason?"

He hushed me so he could hear better.

We sat in silence while we both observed what we could of the conversation. There was a woman there from the looks of it. What women did we know who played in the black-market game with Jason's minions? I didn't have the slightest idea on who she could be.

Unless Jason hired a front woman. Which was entirely possible. No one batted eyes at them. A savvy woman could take everything from you and you'd thank her for it. If I were him, I'd do it in a heartbeat, considering there were eyes all over him and his operations.

Everyone wanted a piece of the illegal pie when they thought they could get away with it. Unless you were in the big boy club run by the top families, you'd never be safe.

The boys in the club weren't even safe from each other.

And if you were an outsider like Jason? A tough game to play when it's rigged against you.

"We need ID on who that woman is. Body language tells me that she's calling the shots in this meeting. This is Haines' meeting because they're talking about his specific deals. The big deal in Russia? Yeah, that's what they're talking about. Guns and munitions being brought back to undermine the Vaughns."

Because of our flighty boy, Nicholas, that deal was still going through. *When I get my hands on him...*

I snapped some pictures of everyone in the group, and luckily, no one was dropped in the same way as last time. Everything was just a *normal* conversation. A normal day of black-market dealings and under the table operations—a regular Tuesday.

We watched until everyone dispersed, Reaper looking upset he couldn't shoot anyone. I had bits and pieces of information to report back, and braced myself for the ride back to meet my grandfather.

≈

380

Inside the poker room, I waited until I was needed, listening to the intricacies of *business*.

"Haines is planning to offer a better deal to the Russians than we were. Considering he's going through a neighboring country, the prices are higher crossing more borders. It can't be that lucrative."

"Who needs lucrative when you're trying to get one over on your biggest competition?"

"What about our Moldova contact?"

Many hands were trying to get into the cookie jar lately, and people were scrambling to get a hold of their own operations. The drugs coming from the Middle East slowed by the loss of properties and contacts in the surrounding areas. Washing money in the UAE had to be transferred over to Switzerland for similar reasons.

It was a tight ship to maintain with the teetering Montgomery Group. Whoever controlled the company would be directly impacting most of the deals.

"Has anyone contacted Russia to offer a bounty on Haines?"

"You'd probably want to offer the same in Venezuela. One of ours split and is hiding out somewhere. Get his name and picture out—and offer a nice cash prize to whoever delivers him first."

Cigar smoke and corruption were contained within the safe confines of the poker room in our compound. The biggest names in the world came to play to maintain a stranglehold on the globe.

And I was just a busboy at the restaurant.

"More liquor, boy." The Dictator held up his glass, signaling for me to do my duty.

Just continue taking orders.

I've been in these rooms for a while and had a working knowledge of how things operated, *and* had the confidence that I could contribute positively to the conversations and operations. He just didn't want me to do so.

Like how I knew Romania was always willing to negotiate

better terms to outshine the Balkan territories. No one gave them any mind despite them having better access to arms to move out, and an easier time doing so. The government was cooperative—for money. Other places required some form of clandestine operations.

"We have information on Jason Haines letting a woman lead his operation." Reaper busted into the room with a file. "But I have suspicions that it's something else."

The Dictator looked surprised to see him waltz into the room so carelessly, but he shouldn't have been. Reaper was a wild card, and he wore a cover that showed none of his face, with an expensive suit to boot. The rest of the men turned to see what was going on.

"Do tell." He puffed his cigar and kicked his feet up.

The file was opened and spread out across the poker table in a way that said *fuck your poker game*, and Dave came in behind him—face uncovered. "We've been trailing this deal for a while. Each time, this same woman has been there doing the deals. One of the times we staked them out, she executed Haines's drivers like it was nothing and replaced them with other men. We still have a missing Nicholas who is currently out of the country with insider information about our operations."

Everyone leaned over the table to take a look at the file.

Dave continued where Reaper left off. "We spotted Haines last night. He's hiding out and keeping his head low with only two men by his side. It smells fishy considering the large name he's made for himself over the last eight years. This woman has been seen with him for the last five years or so and is increasingly poking her head out as the timeline continues."

Interesting. She wasn't a frontwoman. Was she his girlfriend that, what, overtook him? *A cunning woman, I tell you.*

"Has our favorite vermin finally found himself in a predicament?"

"It would seem so," Dave confirmed.

36

Fallon

UNKNOWN:

> I need to speak with you regarding an important matter with your company.

I stared at the text for the last week, unsure of what I should do. The creepy texts needed to end, and I had enough to fill up a scrapbook to commemorate my sophomore year as the worst year yet. I wondered when the other shoe would drop.

Whatever. It could wait until after breakfast.

"Where's Kelly?" I asked James.

"She left pretty early and returned only a little while ago."

"Have you slept?"

"Not in my job description."

Fair enough.

The fridge was fully restocked at some point, and for that, I was grateful. Whoever it was left my favorite foods. There were packages of sour gummy worms on the counter, along with a few other goodies I loved. Breakfast was about to commence, and I hoped I wouldn't throw it all up.

I clicked on the TV to do some light watching while I cooked, and a breaking news story was the first thing that came up. *Just another day in Willow Bay.*

"College student Shane Jones was found recently deceased of an alleged drug overdose late last night when a couple, out for a walk, discovered him face down in the Bay. Please be aware that these images may be disturbing to some audiences."

Kelly's boyfriend found dead from an overdose? That was something I wasn't expecting to hear this morning. Part of me felt like it was related, but there was so much going on in this area that it could be an isolated event.

I didn't think that it was.

Pictures flashed across the screen showing a blurred out Shane face down in the bay. All I could think of was when that guy fell from the third-story window and hit the ground. The sickening sound he made when he hit the cement played in a loop in my mind.

James was in the kitchen cleaning up the glass and juice that I had dropped on the floor before I even realized I'd dropped it. "Don't move. I'm going to clean up this glass before you step around with your bare feet."

I didn't even hear it shatter. "I'm so sorry!"

"No, no. *Don't* move."

People seemed to be dropping like flies. There was no way Shane's death was a coincidence, considering he had been the topic of conversation not long ago. Kelly started dating him, and everything seemed fine to me. If he was dealing or using drugs, there should have been some indication of either option.

Right?

Aside from Kelly smoking occasional weed, bumping coke, and going to parties—where they obviously had *more* drugs— she never seemed the type to get involved in the world of *hard* drugs or dealing like that. She never showed signs—

"Miss Montgomery? You can move now."

Everything had been cleaned up, and I'd missed that too. Jesus, I needed to see a therapist or something. My brain wasn't being very nice to me, and the dissociation was getting a little too much to handle after days of constant beating and trauma.

"Do you think that's connected?" I pointed to the screen

where they were still talking about Shane's death and taking interviews from the two people who discovered him.

He seated me at the table and tended to the skillet, making me the breakfast I had planned on making for myself. "You'll find connections everywhere you look. What you need to do is focus on what's within your control."

What a levelheaded response. James looked older, and his demeanor never changed. He was calm, cool, collected, and ready to do just about anything I needed from him. Within the company, he must have seen a lot of things over the course of his tenure, and I had no desire to know about them. *Maybe later.*

"Then we should continue tutoring?"

Kelly stretched and yawned as she made her way out of the hallway and into the kitchen. "James! You're making breakfast? What an angel."

"Long night?" I clicked the TV off so she didn't see what was playing. With the info she dropped on me about her family, I wanted to see how she played her cards.

"Very."

My heart rate shot up and I tried to keep cool. "What did you get into?"

"A few parties and some drinks. Nothing crazy." She sat down at the table and crossed her legs in the chair. "Are you and Brent official yet?"

James coughed from the cooking station.

"Not talking about it. How's Shane?"

She fidgeted, barely maintaining her usual composure. "I, uh, didn't see him much last night. He went off with his buddies, and I stayed to drink and party."

Yeah. I was starting to become suspicious of my best friend—I couldn't quite shake the feeling that she knew more than she was letting on. Not with that body language, anyway.

"She was off quickly after breakfast," I mused into my notebook as James continued his lecture about the company's paperwork.

He turned the TV back on, knowing I wasn't listening to him anyway. A lawyer was on there, speaking to the public about the recent events and how there would be crackdowns on the college parties happening.

"I will be giving my full legal aid to the city so we can find the people drugging and poisoning our children. There will be change!" He shook his fist in the air before leaving the podium.

The crowd was murmuring and asking questions.

"Mr. Fitzgerald! Are you concerned with your own son's safety, given recent events?"

"My son, Alexander Fitzgerald, is a stand-up young man and will be keeping his ears to the ground so we can punish the criminals who are responsible for the rise in crime in Willow Bay. No further questions."

He left and my jaw was on the floor. No way Alexander's father was just on TV lecturing good people about there being a slew of criminals in our wake. There was nothing common about the crimes going on at the school. We all knew the rules of the game.

Well, the ones in the right tax brackets knew the rules of the game.

"I knew it! Everything in this stupid fucking town is connected, and something is in the middle of all of it."

"Yes. It's your company."

"Wait, what?"

My company was at the epicenter of everything? If that were the case, then there would be hordes of people gunning for me. Anyone who wanted more power and more resources, not just in our country but globally. It made sense. The luxury real estate company that did deals across the globe would have others foaming at the mouth to have that kind of reach. Augustus had deals with us that allowed his black market trade to operate seamlessly—our properties gave him the perfect cover, and all business expenses looked legitimate.

If Shane died because of it, where did he fit in, and what did Kelly know about it?

Buzz!

UNKNOWN:

No good drug dealer takes the fall. Too bad his plans were already set in motion. Who will be the first to break?

If I was holding out hope that things weren't connected, it all shattered immediately. What exactly the fuck was going on, and what could I do to figure it out before the timer ran out?

37

Brent

"Who's the girl that just left your girlfriend's house?"

Reaper and I were posted up, eating lunch and casually watching footage from the front of Fallon's house. The security cameras I planted when she kicked me out should have been installed long before then, but they were up now, and I could see anything that happened in and around her house.

She was not doing so great this morning. Her bodyguard had to help her avoid another mental breakdown after Kelly left. If she couldn't get a handle on things quickly, my grandfather would probably take measures of his own. Securing the company was the first item on his list of priorities, and she needed to be on board with everything. Despite claiming that things would resume as normal, he was an impatient man and always willing to change course.

If the course change meant I could be around her more, I'd be happy.

"Her roommate and best friend, Kelly Wilder."

He contemplated that while crunching down on his chips. "I think I've seen her a few times. The video doesn't zoom in all the way, but that's the troublemaker I was telling you about a few months ago. Butchered my surveillance, we lost the guy, and then he wound up dead."

When she said she had rats, I didn't think she was living with them, too. Stupid me for not thinking to install cameras two years ago when they moved in, I guessed.

"If that's the case, I need eyes on her or some form of surveillance. Get a few of our tails to see what she's up to and what trouble she's been getting herself into. I'll need to report that to the Dictator."

Speaking of, he was waiting for us in his office upstairs.

"Boy."

"Hello, sir."

Reaper plopped down in the chair across the room, holding a cat like a football.

"What do you make of the situation with Haines?" Lighting up the cigar, he leaned back in his chair and awaited my response.

"I think we are underutilizing Romania." I poured a drink for him and then for myself, positioning myself across from his desk. He wants to know what the future CEO thinks of business, and I planned to let him know that I've been paying attention all these years while he used me as an attack dog.

"What does Romania have?" A coy smile played on his mouth and dared me to speak up and play like one of the big boys.

"A willingness to cooperate for the right price. Better arms available than our current resources. The Slavic countries have been stingy lately from higher demand in the current climate, but with Romania, we'd have open, air-free trade with the government. A foot in the door to practice legitimate business outside of arms deals."

We sat there staring each other down for a while, and he nodded his head after thinking about it for long enough. The air felt stale with sweet tobacco, and the silence grew uncomfortable.

"Thank you for speaking plainly. I will consider your opinions. What I want to tell you now is of great importance. With the intel we have now, and your great work putting together pieces of the puzzle for me, it's obvious that my suspicions are correct. The Montgomery Group is in great peril due to a lack of leadership for the past five years."

Not to mention his getting older, but I wasn't going to be the one to tell him that. Any chances I had of taking over the company would be over if I mentioned how old he was. Last guy who showed concern about him being older left with a broken leg. And I was pretty sure Reaper might have been the one to carry out my beating since the old man didn't have his cane with him.

In no way would I risk *Death* himself beating me to a pulp.

"Her board of directors, I assume, did a terrible job." Since when did he stock his office with gin? That shit was disgusting.

"Evans is a good team player; he just fails at leadership. The entire company is going to need an overhaul."

If I were to wager a guess, he had a plan brewing in that cold mind of his. What that plan was wouldn't be revealed until it was time to take action.

If you share your plans with those around you too soon, it gives them time to make a move against you. Always operate as if nothing will change, and then, when it does, no one can stop you from implementing a plan that cannot be stopped. The game of chess isn't just a game; it's your war strategy.

It worked well for him. No one had been able to cross him yet, and he remained on top, just as his father had before him. He must have wondered if his company would die with him before I came along like a baby left on his doorstep. Some days, he acted as if it would, even with me around. Other days, he spoke in almost code about how I needed to be prepared for certain situations. No one ever got a real read on my grandfather. His late wife might have, but she died long ago.

"We'd need to make one quickly with the vultures circling the Montgomery girl waiting to attack at any moment."

He waved off my comment. "Always operate…"

"…as if nothing will change."

"Good boy." He slapped the table and stood. Pacing around the room and contemplating.

The only read I was ever able to get on him was when he paced his office in deep thought. Things would get tense, and he would pace—that's how I knew things would happen shortly after. He never had a poker tell, but he never got up from the table and walked around when he played.

"We have intel on the Wilder heir," Reaper butt in. He was impatient to share because he wanted to go home and drink himself to death with however many cats he picked up this week.

The Dictator stopped. "Do tell."

He relayed the story of when he saw her causing a ruckus before the guy we trailed ended up dead. He didn't mention how he thought it was her in the security footage, but knowing him, he probably identified her correctly.

Reaper wasn't the type you doubted if you wanted to stay alive.

"So, no one thought to remove her with our current issues with that family?" His anger spiked, and maybe he'd find something to beat us both with.

"You told me to stay *away* from her until you assigned us together. I can't keep up with you, old man!"

Yeah, that did it. He chucked his glass at me, and it hit me in the face.

I couldn't wait to be out of this fucking school. A handful of days later, proudly displaying my newly cut-up face and a developing black eye, I sat at the bar at the latest stupid fucking party I'd been dragged into. Most of these parties weren't for fun—working for the Dictator never really ended, and I was on the clock twenty-four seven.

"Hey baby, what happened to your face?" *Not this girl again.*

There was always an angle with her. She wouldn't take the hint to leave me the fuck alone. *Lucky me.*

Knocking back my drink, I looked over at her. The absence of her minions meant she had something up her sleeve. "Haven't looked in a mirror lately, so I wouldn't know."

"Let me guess… you were defending my honor?" Her finger swirled around on my forearm and trailed up to my shoulder. "So sweet of you. I can give you a massage upstairs as a thank you, if you'd like."

"Nah." I shrugged her off and signaled for another round.

She sat on the stool next to me and played with her hair. It wasn't anything like Fallon's—it was brunette, highlighted to get as close to blonde as she could while still clinging to her brunette status. "You can't keep telling me no, Brent. Bad things will happen if you do that."

"Can you cut to the chase already? I'm tired of your games."

Ever since she had a lingering suspicion that I was on my way out, she decided to get dirty and mean. The threats did nothing to me, but she decided to drag Fallon into the mix, and that's where I drew the line. She could throw whatever she wanted at me because I knew nothing would happen beyond her temper tantrums. If it was Fallon she was after, there was a good chance she knew she could get me to bend the knee if she tried hard enough.

"You and I are meant to end up together. You know, the power couple of the century." She fiddled with the straw in her drink, batting her eyelashes at me.

How many times would I have to tell her that wasn't cute? It was annoying.

"If I were meant to end up with someone, it's not you."

"I could kill her, you know." Such a casual tone for such a serious threat.

My patience wore thin. "Pray, tell, how would you do that?"

She could kill Fallon, in theory. It would be harder to pull off than just killing some random kid or someone without a high-profile name or company. Fallon was a target for more than one person; adding Sloane to that cohort didn't make a huge difference. I had my suspicions she would try to take out her romantic competition, but to do it for that sole purpose? No way. There had to be a larger carrot dangling in front of her if she wanted to kill what was mine.

Playing with a stemmed cherry, she let out a laugh. "She's so fragile that a shorter list would be what *wouldn't* kill her. Plus"— she brushed her hand across mine—"half the fun is watching you unable to do anything about it. In every scenario I've played in my mind, you come running back to me, begging me to take you back." That was the Sloane I knew. The evil, conniving one.

Everyone saw her as the bubbly socialite, meeting everyone and shaking hands. She got to know everyone, and there was a reason for it. Underneath the pink was a dark and twisted core that knew the secrets of many of the students around. She played the role of the big sister well, getting people to spill their guts in the form of the biggest secrets, which she then turned over in exchange for something else—her place at the table.

If you wanted to remain in our world, you needed to abide by the rules and make yourself irreplaceable.

"You're playing on thin ice right now. You think because you haven't been touched thus far that you're untouchable. Let's see how far you get throwing stones in your glass house."

I needed all hands on deck if the world was coming for what was *mine*.

38

Fallon

"Executive summary?" I held up the packet James had dropped onto my bed while I was pretending to be normal and studying for an upcoming test. It was strange to think I was still pretending to be a normal college student. At least I had the last few weeks to hold onto what I considered normal before my classes changed.

Cellular biology is so simple compared to my life.

While I was relieved to have had Thanksgiving break to sleep and gorge myself, I wasn't happy about Kelly disappearing. What happened to a girls' trip? On top of that, she was gone the last week, too. Whatever she was in, she was in deep.

He sat in the reading chair across the room. "This document outlines your path to leadership, giving you important information in short summary format."

Evans. That man was up my ass every other day about something or other. Now, I had a document "outlining my path to leadership." Flipping through the pages, I saw timelines, responsibilities, and expectations. And those were just the first few pages. *Very on brand.*

"And here I thought my homework was almost done for the night."

"Sorry to be the bearer of bad news, but I do come with good news." A paper bag containing my favorite fast food was held proudly in his hands. I had to have been growing on him—even just a little bit.

"Simultaneously bringing the worst and best news at the same time. You're really something, James."

Opening the bag, I saw that he got himself food, too. While I still didn't have many friends, James could be considered a friend in my life. Even if he was on my payroll.

"We have a meeting at the office in New York tomorrow. Mr. Evans wants to find a loophole for a power transfer quickly and will be outlining that to preface the meeting."

Nothing would get in the way of me and my food. The meetings were boring business things and high-level overviews of the company. This would change the scene of how I interact within every meeting with the board. They would expect me to make executive decisions that affected the entire company and *all* the employees.

No pressure for a twenty-year-old, right?

"I'll need a shower to clear my thoughts." I eyed the door, and he took the hint to leave.

There was a clicking sound coming from the bathroom.

Scratch that, the window.

"Fal!"

"Garrett? What the hell are you doing here again? You need to stop this."

He seemed desperate. "You're in danger. I'm hearing things, and your head is up on the chopping block for your company."

"And what? You want to protect me this time, or do you want a piece of the pie too?"

"My dad *just* went to jail. He wasn't going to get dirty with the other families, and they destroyed mine. More will be dropping if they don't get in line. My family was a warning. You need to be careful around Brent. His grandfather is at the top and is a brutal man. I don't know if you can tell, but Brent is pretty… cunning and brutal himself."

Brent told me he wanted to help and protect me, but that

could have also been a ploy. With how tied our families were, if mine went down, what would happen to theirs? They had a vested interest in keeping Montgomery Group afloat for their own interests. Unless… they wanted to integrate Montgomery Group into their conglomerate.

"I don't think it's Brent who's my biggest worry at the moment."

"The Whitmore family wants in with Chamberlain Industries. You pose a direct threat to them getting in with the Vaughns. Sloane wants a marriage into that family."

Great. A man I didn't even want was causing girl drama with me. If the extent of my problems was a girl wanting a guy I didn't want, that would have been the easiest time of my life. Instead, I was dealing with powerful families and the girl who wanted Brent—both of whom were capable of killing me.

"Where do you fit in?" Garrett's place in the world confused me. First, he was a football player. Then, his family was toppling like dominoes. Now? He was a desperate man who seemed to know more than he let on.

"Keeping my head low. I'm leaving the college and staying away; I don't think this will blow over anytime soon. I wanted to give you a heads up because I *do* care about you, despite what you believe or have heard about me. It wasn't 'all a ploy' like you think. I'll be working on figuring out where I go from here— I have some help."

My chest tightened. It made me feel guilty for tossing him to the side if what he said was true. If he was interested in me for more than my status, I kicked him to the curb during the worst time in his life. But the rules we had to follow would forbid it unless I wanted to suffer the same fate as him. Because his family wanted to rise above the nastiness, they were being punished in true Mafia style takedown. If you didn't follow the rules, you couldn't play the game.

Unspoken.

Unwritten.

And yet, we were still beholden to them.

I couldn't trust anyone in this world.

So, I settled on watching shit television and eating sour gummy worms on the couch after bidding *goodbye for now* to Garrett. My pitiful "at least be safe for Christmas" could have been the last thing I ever said to him.

Kelly waltzed through the door like nothing had ever happened. "How was school this week?"

"How was your impromptu vacation?" Was I a bit sour? Maybe. She ditched me for *Thanksgiving* and then acted like she didn't abandon me. I even wondered if Christmas would be off the table.

What Garrett said earlier played in my mind with how she went missing over the week. I didn't believe that it was a vacation, but I was happy to not have her looking over my shoulder while I was learning with James and whoever else Evans sent over to pull me forward in my knowledge. I was not up to speed, but each day I got better.

She sighed. "Wonderful. I really needed to decompress and spend some days at the spa."

Wasn't she just at a spa?

"I'm heading to the baseball game tonight. You coming?"

That caught her attention. "Did you also go and schmooze at the parties while I was gone, too? You are becoming a social butterfly. I would *love* to go to the game with you and watch your boyfriend wipe the floor with their competition."

While schmoozing wasn't the exact term I would have used, she was correct in her guess of going to a couple of parties to play nice and pretend I was playing with the rest of them. Montgomery Group needed to have a presentation of the upcoming strength—they all wanted my company and had potentially put me on a platter. Sloane was playing nice in front of others, telling them all about how I was joining her sorority, but I saw the look in her eyes when she spoke to me in passing.

Alexander was another pile of problems. He wanted to dance and drink and go to the back rooms. Avoiding him was a full-time job. I obliged a few dances and drinks to make nice, but he was always asking for more and more. There was only so long I could go before he forced something.

And Brent wasn't there at any of them. At least, not that I could see. My only protection was James or someone else assigned to me. *Could they even prevent some of the things that may happen to me?*

I distracted myself with schoolwork, studying my own company, and staring into the abyss. The unknown text I got remained unanswered.

"He's not my boyfriend. Are you feeling better after the news?" The news of Shane. She never really addressed it when the news came out, but that was yet another secret we kept from each other.

She plopped down with a cup of coffee and kicked her feet up. "It doesn't feel real yet, you know? I tried to come to terms with it this week, but I couldn't get myself to do it. We spent a lot of time together, and I liked him, but he had secrets of his own."

The secret iceberg strikes again.

"It'll be weird dating someone again, I bet."

She shifted in her seat. "Yeah, it will." She wasn't able to keep her full composure this time.

We got dressed for the game in silence. Silence wasn't common in our house, but with all the things unsaid, there wasn't much we *could* say to make things feel like they used to.

When we showed up on campus, the lights were bright against the faded sky. Everyone was excited to see the Sharks take home another victory, sealing us with a winning streak to party about until summertime. Crowds formed around the players as they made their way out for their warm-ups.

And there was Brent Vaughn, dark star of the baseball team, eating up all the attention. It felt like a repeat of the last time I saw him garner the attention from the girls, but this time, everyone wanted a handshake or a high five from him to bring home the win they knew he could secure with the team.

He searched across the sea of people before him, looking for something—or someone. I wanted to say that he was looking for Sloane, but I didn't think it was likely. He was looking for *me* because I hadn't reached out since I kicked him out of my house after we had sex. When I asked for space, I didn't think he would be the type to give it.

I caught sight of Sloane sauntering out there to see him. She wanted me to see her parading him around like he was a prize. Just an object for her to use in whatever manner she desired. Leaning into him, she planted a kiss on his cheek and whispered something in his ear. A gross feeling settled into the bottom of my stomach watching the two.

We stood in line for gross stadium food like we did at every other game we went to. Pretzels and nachos sounded not all that bad, but maybe tossing in a corn dog would mix it up a bit. "I think I want to stuff myself with nasty baseball food."

"When else would you want a corn dog?"

I held out my plate to her when the order came back. "Hold this while I use the restroom?"

The mirror caught my eye when I entered, and with the new skills I had, I went to ensure my eyeliner and mascara were still intact.

"...we used to be friends! Can't you do me, like, a *tiny* favor?" Was that Sloane's voice?

"Absolutely not. She's—" Someone started the hand dryer, cutting off Kelly's response. I ran into a stall closer to the exit to see what I could make out.

"...and we haven't been friends since middle school."

Kelly and Sloane... were friends? *Consider the plot thickened.*

"I bet my father could offer yours something he can't refuse..." Yeah, that was definitely Sloane talking to Kelly. *What the hell is she talking about their dads for?*

More hand drying interrupted my listening. Can't these people just walk out with wet hands like normal people?

"...it's in your job description. Just tell me what happens. Kisses!"

I didn't hear anything else after that. If they were working together—Kelly seeming apprehensive about it—did it have something to do with me? At the party, Kelly called Sloane some names. Of course there was a history there.

Quick to finish up, I made it back out to her, pretending to have fixed my face up a bit.

She looked incredibly guilty.

"What's up?" I smiled. "Did they forget your mustard or something?"

Avoiding eye contact, she muttered, "Something like that."

The game played and dragged on after we made it back to our seats. We were up points, but that never meant much because there was plenty of time to even out the score or pull one up on us. I hated to admit it, but sports were growing on me. The anticipation. The fanfare. All of it was fun to get into, and we had great teams at the school.

Football might be a sore spot for a while.

"I know the game is basically over," Kelly started, looking over at me, but not *truly* looking at me, "but I'm hungry again. Do you want to come get another crappy pretzel with me?"

The look on her face made the hair on the back of my neck stand straight up. Alarms were going off all over my body. If there wasn't someone threatening us with a gun, I'd be surprised.

Agreeing felt like a bad idea, but I did it anyway.

My gut feeling was right when Alexander popped into my field of view and he grabbed me, dragging me into a private bathroom. Kelly was nowhere to be seen.

"Hey, baby girl." He planted sloppy open-mouthed kisses on my neck and it felt like a dead fish was attached to my skin. I wouldn't have been surprised if he *was* a dead fish.

I shoved but he didn't budge. "What the fuck are you doing, Alexander?"

Scary blue eyes met mine. "You didn't think I would just accept your teasing forever, did you? You're mine, and it's time you start acting like it. We're going to be the next power couple, baby."

My hands were pinned above my head while his free hand lifted my shirt to get a better view of what was underneath. "Stop that," I hissed.

"Hush. I'm taking a look at what's mine. I heard that *Vaughn* bastard stained you, so I want to see where I can erase him off your skin." That didn't sound any kind of good.

If there was a good time to throw up, it was while Alexander was trying to grope me in the bathroom, locked away from everyone else who could see—and potentially hear from the crowd being too excited over the game. *It's my unlucky day.*

"No one has a claim over me but myself." I stomped on his foot to get him off of me, but that was *also* no dice.

He slapped me across the face, and it landed with a nice, crisp smacking sound. I would be red any moment, and I was pissed that he'd ruined my makeup for the evening. There was no way to wiggle out of his death grip on my wrists above my head. I was trapped with a rapist.

"I didn't know you had such a temper, little girl. You're going to be tied to me for the rest of your pathetic little life. I made sure of that." My shirt went up and tied around my wrists while he ogled my body.

"Pray tell, how am I going to be tied to your sorry ass?" If I was going to be stuck here and prodded, I might as well get information while I could. Everything felt like it was slipping away again. I felt sick.

His hand grabbed my bra and shoved it away from my boobs. "The deal is done. You may as well enjoy what I'm giving you. No one likes an ungrateful brat."

The deal was done? What the hell was he on about?

"There's no deal if I didn't sign any paperwork. You know just as well as I do that's the facts of deals and contracts."

The smile on his face turned dark. "And you, my beautiful flower, have no idea what I'm capable of. Now hush and show me how much you want to please me."

Teeth grazing over my skin, the feeling of throwing up wasn't quite coming to me. I wanted so desperately to projectile vomit on this sick fuck. Bracing for whatever he wanted to do, I held my breath when he clamped his mouth over my nipple.

No way this was happening.

Knocks started on the bathroom door. "Open up!"

"Ocupado, my guy!"

He continued banging on the door. It got louder and louder until it stopped. Maybe they gave up.

Alexander turned back to me. "Where were we?"

Click! The lock opened, and the man busted through the door, locking it again behind him.

"Miss Montgomery is coming with me." He blocked the door and crossed his arms. "You're in deep shit now."

I covered my bare chest as well as I could when Alexander released me from his grip to threaten this guy with whatever money his daddy had. It happened quickly. The man took Alexander in a move that had him yelping from how his arm was held and expelled him from the restroom, locking himself in with me again.

Me with no shirt on.

"Who the hell are you?" I backed into the wall again.

He turned around, continuing to block the door. "Go ahead and make yourself presentable. My name is Dave, and I work for Mr. Vaughn."

"This is what I get for dismissing my bodyguard for an evening."

"He should have never agreed to it. If I hadn't been watching, who knows what may have happened to you. Are you decent?"

"How do I know you are who you say you are?" I sorted out my shirt and any sanity I had left in this world.

I heard him chuckle from where he stood. Good to know he thought this was funny. "You're learning a bit more lately, aren't you? Good to know. Mr. Vaughn was worried you'd run into trouble and sent me out to keep an eye on you."

Sounded like Brent.

I patted myself, realizing that Kelly had my bag and my

phone. There was no way to call for help, even if I had the chance to. An ugly feeling crept up inside me and it made me wonder if I had just been set up by my best friend.

She spoke to Sloane earlier about how they used to be friends, and I realized there was *no* soul I could trust in the world. If my closest ally was plotting against me, what hope was there for anything? Nothing was safe. Nothing was sacred. At this rate, I believed she killed her own boyfriend. Nothing made sense.

The crowd cheered outside, signaling the Sharks had won the game, while I stood in the bathroom—a mess—after being betrayed, assaulted, and left for dead in a sea of sharks, all hungry to eat my sinking boat as it plunged to the bottom. Dave escorted me out of the restroom after giving me a hoodie to wear, along with his sunglasses to hide my face. The sick bastard hit me hard enough to leave a lasting mark, so I kept my head down while we moved through the complex to get me home.

Screw my belongings. Screw my keys. Screw it all because I was being moved around like someone's pawn, and I was tired of it.

∾

"Do you need a bath?" James was tending to my face while Dave sat in the living room. "I shouldn't have let you dismiss me, but with other security… It'll never happen again. You have my word, and you're stuck with me until I take my last breath."

"That's romantic, James, but don't feel bad. It was my order that you take a day off."

Dave scoffed at the two of us. It was all too clear from his attitude—and affinity for a leather jacket—that he was one of Brent's men. He was judgmental and rude—the requirements of working with Brent. He pulled a package out of his jacket and placed it on the table. "From that no-good friend of yours."

My phone and my wallet.

"What do you mean that no-good friend of mine?"

"Stupid girl. Do you even know who the Wilder family is?"

I didn't. James threw him a look that said *don't even right now.* James seemed to know what he was on about, and I was left out of the loop like I usually was.

"The Wilder family is responsible for reporting back to their side of the group—and they play both sides every time until they decide where to place their bets. They also *directly* silence those who get in the way of progress. It makes sense why she wouldn't have told you. I wonder what information she was feeding her daddy while she lived here all this time."

Anger warmed my skin, and I set my jaw. "*You* don't get to make assumptions about my best friend like that. I'm going to run a bath. You two can *fuck* each other for all I care right now. *Don't* bother me."

Stomping down the hall, I slammed and locked the door so I could take a bath in peace. Kelly was gone, and she'd left my things with Dave. Where would she have gone that she couldn't give me my things or offer me an explanation for what happened earlier with Alexander? Or why she looked so guilty when she got back? It could have been a simple conversation for her to explain herself and rectify things. If she was in danger and was being threatened, would she come back to explain? People killed each other over almost nothing in our world, and I wanted to at least give her the opportunity to explain.

She held secrets for a reason, but I needed to know what for. The warm bath soothed my aching body, helping me breathe and think. I wanted to lay in it for an eternity so I never had to deal with any of the drama or death again.

Then, my phone rang.

"Hello?"

"Fallon Montgomery?"

"Wrong number, sorry."

"Wait! My name is Jason Haines and I'm calling about your company. Your aunt Sylvia fucked me over and she's coming for you next."

"How did you get this number?"

I was tempted to drown myself right then and there at the mention of Sylvia. Never did I think I would hear that name again. She booted me out without so much much as a *sayonara*.

"I've had you under surveillance since you were eighteen. I've always known what you were up to, but I don't anymore. Can we meet privately?"

What?! "You just admitted to *stalking* me, and now you're asking me to meet you privately. You must be out of your damn mind if you think I'd agree to that."

My bath became *not* so relaxing. I was naked, and some man on the phone just admitted to surveilling me. A growing concern I had was how many people had seen me naked. Were there cameras in my house? *Oh my God, I'm spiraling again.*

"I'm willing to meet at the Vaughn compound."

Of course he was. "What the hell do the Vaughns have to do with this? Tell me what the *fuck* you know about my aunt."

"She's my—well, was—girlfriend."

"My aunt is your ex-girlfriend," I repeated, disbelief dripped from my tone. This had to be a joke or something. Someone would pop out and tell me it was a funny joke they were playing on me. The nightmare couldn't be real. She was supposed to be long gone, far away where she couldn't contact me anymore.

"Yes, and she plans to usurp your company just like she did with mine. I'm in hiding and I at least want someone else to have warning before that ruthless woman gets the chance to get her claws into something else." He sounded genuine, desperate. Like a man who had just lost everything, but I knew I couldn't trust what was being presented to me.

"Fine, but we're doing this *my* way."

39

Brent

She pissed me off.

Not only did she kick me out of her room after we slept together, she *still* refused to call me. Business partners, my ass. *I want everything.* She was mine.

My security was following Fallon around everywhere. I had constant updates on movements in and around her house. She became a little pet of sorts once I found out Sloane was gunning for her head. Nothing would slip out of my sight, and Reaper would see to anyone's death if they so much as tried to touch a hair on her perfect little head.

"Ready for tonight?" Dave tucked his holster into his waistband and inspected his gun. He would be watching Fallon wherever she went since she was coming to the game without her regular bodyguard.

Yeah, we heard that conversation.

"The win is already in the bag. Too many people paid off the officials and coaches. Willow Bay wins by default this year. I *love* it when sports betting gets rigged." I grabbed my bag full of sports gear from the table.

My men would have to have fun without me while I played in the *big* game.

"Too bad I can't bet on you losing," Reaper muttered, kicking his feet up onto the table.

He had been in a bad mood for days, and I didn't dare poke him when he was mad. Whatever was going on in his personal life made him more short-tempered than normal. He didn't even send me pictures of random cats over the last week.

"What's the news on Whitmore? She's a loose cannon gunning for the heir of the Montgomery Group. We all need to be on high alert any time Fallon steps out of her home."

I started tracking Sloane's movements, careful not to let her know I was doing it. She probably assumed I would be keeping an eye on her, but that's what she wanted me to do—as in, on my own. My men were on her, and if she had been aware of that, she'd be pissed. We had to be careful with all the other families, who were at each other's throats.

There was a rift bigger than the San Andreas fault line happening. The elites were turning on one another in anticipation of attempting to snatch the Montgomery Group out from under Fallon and up their power over the black market. Everyone wanted it. Whoever had control over the properties that Chamberlain Industries utilized to keep our operations on top would shoot us in the foot, causing a major shift in how things operated.

It would be chaos.

For now, it was crabs in a bucket.

I just had to stay ahead of them all and ensure Fallon rose to the top—even if it killed me. We were sitting ducks if she lost everything. Urgency was of the essence.

"Your scorned ex has been talking a lot of shit lately. Also, in secret meetings with that Fitzgerald kid."

After he killed that kid in cold blood, I left him to his own devices. The event that separated us was when we were still pretty young. I was a violent guy myself, but that fuck was ready to kill anyone at any time. Sure, I could have said something, but what was there to be done? The Dictator would have shrugged me off again without listening to me, and his father would have threatened me in some way.

I kept my distance, but if he came anywhere near my Blondie, I'd have no issue with putting him into the grave. While we were both violent, his violence was senseless and protected by big shot lawyer daddy. Of which, I'd have to deal with his father. I settled on having to kill the entire family if I needed to. I didn't care.

"If he so much as touches her, he dies. I don't care how it happens, but he's done for. Dave, you keep eyes on Fallon. Reaper, you do what it is you do best outside of the sports complex. I have two other men patrolling around. And, Reaper, please keep your earpiece on if you can help it." Tossing on my jersey, we were out.

Just one more game, I told myself.

"I'll be out of reach until the game is over. Watch her like a hawk and don't let shit happen to her. Who knows how many knives are out with not that long to go until her birthday. Protect her like she's me and don't worry about me. I can take care of myself out there. She can't."

They all nodded in silent agreement with me. I felt like I was pleading with them, but she was at the center of everything. *Fuck it*, she was *my* fucking everything the first time she looked into my soul.

Every fucking laugh. Every judgmental look. Her hesitation with me made me want to enter her walls. Watching her hope in humanity falter made me sick. I wanted the lights in her eyes to stay as bright as the moonlight on a full moon. She was the moon in my night sky. She was the sun of my summer.

Whatever she did to me, I never wanted it to end, and I would go to the ends of this earth to grovel for her to simply *look* at me.

"One more game," I whispered. Tossing my duffel over my shoulder, I made my way down the corridor, leaving it in their hands while I went to play a rigged game of fucking baseball.

"She's waiting for you," Reaper nodded to me when I entered the empty locker room.

Sloane played dirtier than I thought she would, with her *good luck playing a rigged game* whispered into my ear. She planned it all. Every ingredient would be tossed into her fucked-up cake she was baking: schemes to get rid of Fallon and force my hand. Anything it took to bring me to my knees and make me give up.

I'd rather die first.

There were hired men from every fucking possible side at the game, keeping tabs on everyone there. Every family was on high alert, and Sloane hired as many men as possible—her men replaced the stadium security *and* staff. We got played.

Alexander thrusted himself at Fallon to distract her. He wanted to play for keeps and power. The plan for him was to, what, get a chunk of her company? Get into the circle being created by the Whitmore family? If only my grandfather had told me more, I'd be better prepared to do whatever it took to protect not only Chamberlain but also Fallon. She was integral to his plan—he just had his stupid fucking rules of not acting until the last minute.

But I didn't think he had any more moves to play. He was testing me to see what would happen. He was playing a fucking game with *all* of us. If he *wasn't* actively fucking dying, I wouldn't have a clue what he was doing. What was the goddamned play?

"What did Dave say?"

"Not much. He got her out in time and she's at home right now. Your grandfather requests your presence."

I threw my shoes across the locker room with as much force as I could. "Fuck his requests. What I'm concerned about is what the *fuck* happened to *my* woman! He can sit and fucking wither away and die in his office for all I fucking care. Get your shit, we're going."

Fuck him and fuck his requests. Whatever he had could wait for

416

all I cared. He could have been dying in the hospital with the biggest company secret, and I wouldn't have shown up.

Reaper took my keys and drove us back, muttering something about how dangerous I was when I was angry. I didn't care. I'd commit every felony known to man if it meant I could get to her. Nothing, and I meant nothing, could ever stop me.

I just about ripped the door from its hinges when we arrived. I wanted to know where she was immediately.

"She's relaxing in her room," James, her good-for-nothing bodyguard announced.

I ignored him. "Dave. Status?"

"You know most of the details. Found her half-naked, locked in a bathroom with that mouth-breather, Fitzgerald."

Without thinking, I clocked James in the jaw. Reaper grabbed me and pulled me back before I could execute his ass. "You fucker," I hissed. "Dave, why weren't you on top of her? I'm going to fucking kill all of you!"

"Simply stated: We were undermanned for this." He was no less guilty than James in my eyes for letting it happen, and I itched to beat the shit out of them both.

"All of you were in charge while I was in that *fucking game*, playing along with the fucked up world we're in! I want extra men on her at *all* times. Never less than three. I can't trust a fucking soul here. You're all dead men walking. Do you fucking hear me? Dead men!" I shot daggers at her so-called bodyguard while Reaper gripped the shit out of me. "Get off me. I want to go fucking talk to her." I thrashed against the hold he had on me.

Dave cleared his throat.

"Brent?"

She looked so beautiful in her pajamas. The last time I'd seen her felt like a lifetime ago. My body went limp at the sight of her, and I swore to myself that I wasn't falling that hard for this girl, but I was.

"Blondie," was all I could say when she took my breath away.

Reaper let me go, and I ran to her and tossed her over my shoulder. She started beating my back just like she usually did, demanding to be let down. We spun in a circle before I gently set her down. I checked her body and looked for signs of damage.

My eyes landed on her face. Bruising formed. Gingerly, I brought my fingers up to check the swelling; I needed to feel her skin. "Who did this to you?"

Her eyes fell to the ground. "Alexander."

I pulled her into me, the smell of her wet hair calming my nerves. She always used light floral scents, and I loved how she smelled. I wanted her to consume me with flowers. "I will never let that piece of shit lay another hand on you. If I do, you can kill me yourself for failing to protect you. *Never* again."

"It's fine," she mumbled. She looked embarrassed to be held like this in front of everyone. Not that it mattered who saw us at this point. The world was going to know that she was mine, and I would kill them for so much as thinking about her the wrong way.

Was it bad that I wanted my lips over every square inch of her body, relieving her of the memories of when I wasn't there for her? I dragged her down the hallway so I could have her alone, even if only for a few moments.

Behind her door, I couldn't help but kiss the top of her head and hold her close to me again. Somewhere between when I told myself I wouldn't get attached to her and now, she took my heart and held it inside her, and she didn't even know that she had.

She probably didn't even like me.

"Tell me what happened. Whatever you want me to know." I sat her down on her bed and knelt before her on the floor, giving her the full vantage point over me.

I played with her hands between us, massaging the fingers one by one while she stared at me, unable to form the words she wanted to speak. "It wasn't fun, and I know you want to hear about it so you can go on your typical rampage, but..." she bit her lip and looked down at me before her.

"But, what?" Placing her hand in my palms, I raised it up to my lips. If all I would ever get again was the pleasure of kissing her hands, I'd take it.

"I got a phone call."

"From whom?"

She didn't reply. Her mind was racing; I saw it from the little scrunch between her eyebrows. The gears were always turning in that mind of hers. How badly I wanted to know what she was thinking, yet I waited.

I waited when she kicked me out and told me we could never be anything. I waited for her to kick that *boyfriend* to the curb. Hell, I even waited for her to get on my bike. I've never waited for a girl before, but she made me weak in the knees from day one. She was a beautiful siren, and I'd let her drag me down and kill me.

"Why did you leave?" she breathed out.

"What do you mean?"

She let out a defeated sigh. "I kicked you out, and you left."

"You think I really went anywhere?" Maybe she did like me.

"Do you know a man named Jason Haines?"

I blinked. "How do *you* know him?"

She pulled out her phone and showed me a text message. "I never responded to this, and then he called me. He told me something about my aunt and demanded we meet privately."

So, Jason was gunning for her company after all. He was very low key, keeping his head down so he could work to undermine us and spearhead the black-market dealings. With her mom's—now her—company, he would soar above us and stomp us into the dust.

"How did he get your information?"

"That's the weird part. He claimed he and my aunt have been basically stalking me for years."

To get ahead in the game. To take over before she had the opportunity to. How long was Jason lying in wait to rip the carpet out from under her, from me? He hated my grandfather so much that he played by the same rules.

Never make a move unless you're ready for action.

All those rats we tracked down…

"All of that aside, why would he be calling you to tell you this? Wouldn't that just alert you to his plan?" *Color me confused,* but that gave her the opportunity to *plan* for their takeover.

She hadn't pulled her hands away from mine. Instead, she was stroking my fingers. "He said that my aunt took everything from him and that he was calling me for help." She let out a small laugh while she continued playing with my hands. "Which is funny because he was there plotting against me with her, and now he wants me to take pity on him."

"Look at my Blondie turning into such a business savant."

"Don't be condescending."

I kissed her hand in apology, looking up at her, hoping she knew I was serious. She learned a lot over such a short period of time. With her birthday beginning to loom over us, a sharper edge was forming in her. A proper, cunning businesswoman was emerging, and I loved it.

"I wouldn't dream of it, babe."

She rolled her eyes at me, and I relished it. I wanted her rolling her eyes, fighting me, telling me to get lost. That's how I knew she was in there and that she was fighting. She was full of life. I wanted nothing more than to continue to see her like that.

"I just don't understand how my aunt took his company from him."

"Love makes you blind." I'd let her take whatever she wanted without even batting an eye. I'd let her strip me of it all, and I'd offer my freshly cut-out heart as a final gift. "We do need to get this information to the guys so they can start planning. My grandfather needs to know about your aunt so we can take countermeasures against them and prevent a takeover and losing everything we have."

I also loved saying *we* to her.

"If what I suspect is true, not much will prevent her from taking Montgomery Group," she whispered.

"What do you mean by that?"

40

Fallon

I woke up at three in the morning with Brent holding onto me as if I would slip out of his grasp. My nightmares were getting worse, and I unlocked a new fear—sexual assault. Not to mention stalking and being watched without my knowledge. All of it freaked me out, and sleep didn't come easily when you were on edge and freaked out most of the time.

Luckily, I didn't throw up and felt like having a snack. Brent didn't budge as I slipped out of bed and made my way to the kitchen.

That man from earlier who was holding onto Brent was still here. He was wearing a pink ski mask?

"Uh, hi." I waved. I glanced over at what he was doing, and he was watching cat videos and drinking with his feet up on the coffee table. "I'm Fallon."

"Reaper," he grunted and put in a headphone under his mask.

Guess I interrupted something important. He was in my house, the least he could do was be respectful or say something to me. He was worse than Brent and looked three times as odd. Who covered their face like that?

"Do you like pink?" I sat down with a box of Chinese leftovers that James had brought for me. Craving lo mein when I felt like crap was my go-to. If I could hold my food down, this would bode well.

He didn't respond.

I threw a roll of paper towels at him, and he caught them midair. "I'm watching something. You don't have to be so annoying so early in the morning."

"Do you want any food?" *Anything to make this interaction less odd, actually.*

He sighed, took out his earbud, and made his way over to me. There was attitude in the way he walked. It was like he was a petulant child in a grown man's body.

I handed him a plate. "Thanks," he grumbled.

"Does anyone see your face and live?"

"No."

"Is that why they call you Reaper?"

He took the stack of napkins from my hand. It was funny watching him eat through a mask. "They call me Reaper because that's what I'm good at."

"How long have you worked for the Vaughns?" I didn't know why I was interrogating the brooding, large man whose face I couldn't see, but I had bad nightmares and needed a distraction. Brent was knocked out cold. The least I could do was get to know the people that would be around me the majority of the time.

"Long time, little girl." He scooped piles of food out of the containers and onto the plate without so much as a glance in my direction.

What a peculiar human. "Does that mean you're old?"

"Old enough. Why do you ask so many questions? Eat your food."

I heard a faint *meow* from the corner of the living room and a small, grey cat came out from hiding and pranced its way over to us.

"When did *that* get here?"

"That's Pumpkin. I found her stuck in a pumpkin patch and took her home."

If Pumpkin lived at his house, it made no sense as to why she was at my house. "Why is she here?"

He shrugged and continued eating. Pumpkin jumped into his lap and laid down to take a nap after he gave her a piece of meat from his plate. Who knew scary looking men had affinities for little kittens? They looked happy together.

"She likes to travel, and I figured you might like her. What's got you up so early?"

Shoving food around on my plate with my fork, I rested my chin in my hand. That was a great question. "I couldn't sleep, and Brent snores."

"Good to know. I'll write that down for our next meeting. *Snores.* Do you need pills to sleep? I have great ones for insomnia. They're called melatonin."

Brent really should have warned me about this guy. Not only was he... strange, but he also had a curious sense of humor. I never thought someone could be this dry but so witty at the same time. And he liked cats.

What did this guy get into in his free time?

"Do you always wear this pink ski mask?"

"Do you always ask a lot of questions?" His eyes flicked to mine as he ate—*through the mouth hole in his mask.* He had thick eyebrows and haunting green eyes.

"Sorry," I grumbled.

"Here's a sight I never thought I'd see." Brent was in the hallway, leaning against the wall.

Reaper grunted again. "Your girlfriend is chatty."

"Why don't you come back to bed, babe?"

They were both so casual about everything. But, with what I could only assume they saw on a regular basis, what I was going through was probably a walk in the park for them. Brent and his men were out torturing and killing people in their line of work and organizing illicit trades; a straightforward situation like mine had to be easy.

He was also back to calling me *babe* again.

"I can't sleep. I have a meeting with Evans today and there's just too much going on in my mind right now."

I didn't know what to expect from going to New York. The meetings became need-to-know only after Evans pulled certain people out of the company. Cleaning house was going to be messy, and the fallout would be insane. We had rats in the legal team who worked in tandem with my aunt to give her certain rights to what was mine, using documents that were signed and forged in my name.

Before I turned eighteen, she was my legal guardian and signed everything as such. We combed through the documents, and she forged agreements in my name that allowed her to make decisions through lawyers until I was twenty-one. That meant she had secret plans to pull the company out from under me on my birthday.

Evans would have questions to answer regarding how this happened under his watch, as well as the names of those who may have seen those documents or allowed this to occur. Augustus Vaughn was right about cleaning house.

How much death would come from those words, time would only tell.

Brent lightly rubbed my shoulders and played with my hair. "How about a movie? We have time to kill, and I hate to see you miss out on sleep."

"Actually, since you're both here…"

Reaper gave me a look of annoyance. He didn't like to be bothered by the looks of it.

"What is it?"

"I'm about to find out how many people have been secretly working behind my back to pull the rug out from under the company. Why they wanted to ruin the company makes no sense to me since everyone gets paid well and the company is a successful one."

Brent looked at me with pity. "It's always about money and power. You'll never see a relaxing day in our world. We handle backstabbers daily, and it's because someone offers them more than what they're getting. Greed is a nasty thing. So is envy over those who have more than you."

"Says the uber rich guy."

"Don't call the kettle black, *pot*. If I get to a point where I run my grandfather's conglomerate, I'm not planning to be a stuck-up asshole about it. What I won't accept are those with unending greed that jeopardize other people."

"I suppose."

"What type of leader do you plan to be? You're set to inherit one of the top companies that is built on luxury. You service uber rich guys like me."

Fine, he had a point. There was no denying that I was born into this and now had to wrestle with my morals surrounding the elite. I *was* the elite. It didn't feel like it, but it was true, and this part of society was nothing like the others. Endless money created more than simple first-world problems.

We had a hand in shaping the entire world.

"I never thought about the whole me being a leader part."

He stroked my hair and planted a kiss on my head. "So, let's sit and watch a movie. We have to get you through the worst of it before then."

I fell asleep during the movie, and James coming in around seven woke me back up. Brent wasn't on the couch with me, but I was silently grateful that no one saw me sleeping curled up with him. I still wanted to keep my distance from him romantically. Business had to come first, and we couldn't complicate things by getting our personal lives twisted up in the height of this situation.

The trip to New York was lonely and long. James was silent. I figured he had nothing to say; he probably didn't want to freak me out or put me on edge. It was still early in the day, and the lobby to the offices was a deserted wasteland. No hustle and bustle yet.

"Miss Montgomery." The doorman nodded at me.

"Good morning."

The elevator dinged, sending off alarms in my body and

spiking my adrenaline again. If the elevator could crash and send me to my death, that would have been preferable.

"Evans." I nodded, walking into the boardroom. Not many men were in attendance.

"Miss Montgomery." He set down an envelope. "I've come with news today. We are aware of documents withheld from company knowledge."

I sat in the chair at the head of the table. *My* place at the table. "Jason Haines called me. He told me that Sylvia Montgomery has usurped a certain amount of power out from under him. Now, she's coming for me."

"Your new associate will be joining us." The door opened to reveal Brent, Reaper, and Dave in suits.

Reaper was wearing a skull mask. *Could be fitting.*

Brent took a seat to my right. "As Miss Montgomery said, Jason Haines has been a thorn in the Vaughns' side for quite some time. He now seeks pity from the very hand he burned many years ago. This is a long and quite bitter tale of jealousy.

"You see, Jason Haines was not picked as a mentee in favor of Maria Montgomery. He didn't like a powerful woman who was smarter than him getting a one-up over him in our world. Like a spoiled child, he did not accept the offer from my grandfather and set out to compete with him instead. A while later, he meets a woman by the name of Sylvia Montgomery, who has the drive to destroy her sister's life's work. Once her sister dies, she takes to enacting her revenge on her niece, the sole heir of Montgomery Group. Jason, believing he is in bed with an ally, discovers that he is not. Back to square one, he crawls back, asking for crumbs from the table."

The puzzle pieces made sense. I only saw them from one side —Sylvia's side—and what she wanted me to see. How was I blind for so many years to her antics?

"Since this involves both of us," Dave cut in. "We are going in on a joint effort. Our department has the skills necessary to rip weeds out by their roots. Unfortunately, the garden is overrun, and it may take some time. Evans, you have had close dealings with Augustus and should be up to speed on plans."

The relationship between Montgomery Group and Chamberlain Industries ran so deep that someone looking too hard wouldn't be able to distinguish where one ended and the other began. My mother left me with a very confusing situation to manage, but I didn't think she could foresee this type of betrayal and plotting against me. She also didn't know that her sister was going to gain guardianship over me. Sylvia volunteered.

Now we know why.

"While we work on the legal nightmare, you all have the list of those who are suspicious characters from this company. I bid you well in your endeavors. Miss Montgomery, I assume you are up to speed with current events of the company's high-level overviews this week?"

"Yes," I replied, hoping I could hold an aura of assuredness. "My birthday is around the corner, and I am looking forward to the transition. Media training has reached out, and we will begin our efforts to make me not so... me." My heart was running wild. Things were happening quickly, and I was still sorely unprepared for it all.

The press coverage of a CEO transition was scary. The news about my movements and how I ran a company would be brutal —my life scrutinized at every turn. It would be an endless twenty-four-hour news cycle, and I would be the star of it in my role. If Brent could do it, I could too, *right*?

"Good. I have some meetings to attend to. Mr. Caldwell will be going over some details on legal issues with you all and... other pertinent information you should know. None of that leaves this room." He exited swiftly and left us to our devices.

Dave pulled out a device from his bag and set it on the table.

I raised an eyebrow at him.

"This secures the room. Feel free to speak plainly."

Reaper set a knife on the table. "This *also* secures the room."

Brent tore open the envelope with his own knife, cutting it

with precision in anticipation of what he would find within the pages. I hoped the list wasn't long, but that was just a pipe dream. There was a chess game afoot, and we were catching up to speed. The papers were spread out, featuring profiles of each person deemed suspicious.

"This is the list of everyone potentially involved?" He looked to me.

"From the last time I spoke to him, he was developing a list of everyone who had authorization to access documents pertaining to what Sylvia might be planning. Some of these people dealt directly with the paperwork she moved back and forth between herself and the company. Lots of documents with my forged signature. I'm hoping we have a thumb drive with the documents along with these names. James, do you have that?"

"I will by end of day."

"Good," I noted. "This has been a plan in motion since my mother died. Maybe even before. This has been *years* of work. She kept me quiet in her home until I was eighteen, and she still has certain powers over me until I'm twenty-one. Transitioning myself to CEO will be a feat if we can do it."

Brent pondered that while browsing the profiles and handing them off to his two men. The gears in his head were turning over the information, formulating a plan of attack. "I'm still trying to find the connection to everything at large. Nothing is an isolated event."

"What do you mean?"

"There's been infighting for years. I assumed it was because of your company becoming weaker before you took over, but something else has to be going on."

Reaper laughed at that. "Nothing classic interrogation can't fix. Look at all the toys we have to beat on until we figure it out."

"How do we figure out where to start?"

Brent placed his hand over mine. "Welcome to my sect of the world, Blondie. This is where we excel. You won't have to worry about a thing because we will figure this out."

I worried that we wouldn't be able to figure things out. I

hadn't seen or heard from *her*, and things just felt *off*. There was a feeling of a tipping point in my bones that kept me on edge. My sleep deteriorated, and I was plagued by anxiety. Not to mention, my skin crawled at the thought of someone touching me who didn't deserve to, and another person admitting to surveilling me without my knowledge for years.

Paranoia wasn't exactly the word I'd use to describe how I felt.

"I *need* to be involved. You can't kick me out now."

His men looked to him for guidance and opinions. A small blonde girl was telling them she would be involved when they went out to do what they do. The *cleaning* work.

Brent didn't look like he wanted to agree with my being involved, but what other choice did he have?

They had an entire silent conversation amongst themselves while I waited for someone to respond. I couldn't help but wish Kelly was with me.

Mr. Caldwell cleared his throat to interrupt. "Let's go over a few key legal details before you all get trigger happy. For one, I know nothing about what you all are about to do. Two, Fallon has legal bindings over her head until she is twenty-one. This document here outlines your guardianship with your aunt."

"Then, it's true. She really is planning to steal everything. No work on her end, just greed. Just a jealous woman with a plot to steal. Even if she gets everything she wanted, she wouldn't know what to do with it anyway."

A saddened nod. "She may bring the end of a lot of things if she were to succeed. Here. This is the guardianship outline. This was hard to dig up, and no one would have even known about it since it's a private legal matter. What else she did outside of this I *can* dig up, but it looks like she's heading towards stealing ownership."

"How could she steal ownership if it's clearly outlined that I take over at twenty-one?" My mother had a legal savant write her will. The thing appeared ironclad, but again, I knew nothing of our world and how dirty one could get in order to get a leg up on someone else.

"There are a few ways in which your allies at the company wouldn't have known, and we need to prepare for *any* option." Mr. Caldwell added.

Business, in the way my aunt was using it, was not in my training materials. I barely understood the basics of the company and legal documents. How was I to understand the loopholes that she could have used?

I looked around the room and saw the small circle of people who were my supposed allies. Brent posed himself as my ally, but how did I know he wasn't planning something of his own? Mr. Caldwell could be a huge liar himself. Nothing felt safe. I felt unprotected.

"What's the most likely scenario you can think of?" My hands shook as I fidgeted with them under the table. Anxiety seeped out of every pore in my body.

"The most likely? Proxy vote manipulation or amended bylaws. Or both. We don't know how many allies she has within the companies or how deep her plan spans. With her working with others who have a vested interest in bringing down the control Montgomery Group has, she could have multiple contingencies."

Well, fuck.

"That thing really secures what we say in here?" I gestured to the box on the table.

Dave nodded.

I looked at Brent. "I'm going to need you to teach me how to kill people."

41

Brent

She was glued to her phone texting Kelly for what seemed like forever. Seeing her heartbroken over whatever scenarios she'd made up in her mind tore at my own heart—she was desperate for a reply from her only trusted ally. *So she believed.*

Kelly left and went MIA after Fallon was attacked by that fuckwad. He was the first on my hit list. I didn't care how I killed him, I just knew I would take full pleasure in removing the scum that touched *my* woman from this earth. He should have been eliminated years ago; I was just too complacent.

From the moment I first laid eyes on her, I was hers. She just didn't know it.

And it killed me to watch her suffer in the days that followed, clouded in deep depression. She sat in the big chair in her living room, unable to muster an appetite or the desire to take a shower. I took care of her for two straight days while she called out sick from classes.

The front door opened to reveal Reaper walking in with a large bag. He tried to make her talk to him, but she was never in the mood for his antics. She did like Pumpkin, though. "I come with snacks," he announced, holding up the bag.

She gave him a sideways glance from her spot petting the cat.

"What is it?" I stood up from my spot on the couch, watching her stare at her phone, uninterested in her favorite movies.

"Frozen yogurt. I made them give me containers of the toppings, too. They kind of just gave me whatever I wanted." He set them down on the counter and put his hands on his hips to survey his loot.

I sighed. "Did you think the mask may have given them the idea that you were there to rob them?"

"No. Why would a masked man rob a frozen yogurt place?"

He had a point.

"Blondie, you want any?"

She shrugged.

"I'll take that as a yes. Come sit your cute ass at the table." I dished up what Reaper brought back and set out the toppings for her.

He nodded in the direction of the backyard. Great hinting skills, that one.

I closed the door behind us and looked back at her, looking longingly at the table. Maybe she'd eat something.

"I followed that friend of hers."

"And?"

"I don't want to give any definitive statements, but she's the Wilder heir. You tell me."

"They're the ones responsible for a *lot* of trouble over the last decade. They do what we do at a high level. What's to say they didn't plant her in Fallon's life? Everyone knew Maria was sick, and it would be a perfectly executed plan to keep tabs on her. It doesn't make sense how it fits in with her aunt, though."

He shook his head and sat in a chair. "Many things can be true at the same time. What we need to know are the intentions of people. She met with the Whitmore girl, and I broke off from there to see her meeting with the Fitzgerald boy."

"What do Kelly, Sloane, and Alexander all have in common?" I mused, wracking my brain for a centralized connection. "I know multiple families would want to see ours go down, but what is their play? Sylvia is trying to take over Montgomery

Group and just fucked over Jason Haines. There are other pieces to the puzzle that I'm just not seeing."

The code names fit. "Rose" and "Rabbit." What I didn't understand yet were "Garden" and "Stick." Where was said garden, and what was said stick? Did my grandfather know more than he let on?

Messing with the zipper on his jacket, he seemed to be done with the conversation. He was never one for a long conversation. Unless there was action, Reaper got bored quickly.

Sylvia fucked over Jason—which he deserved. She took everything from him, and I needed to know how she did that. And *who* helped her.

"We're going to have to talk to Jason for his side of the story."

"Mr. Vaughn is going to hate that idea."

"No word about Wilder to Fallon. She's fucked up enough as is."

He made a zipper motion with his hands over his mouth and made his way back into the house where Fallon had dished herself. *Good girl.*

"This is coconut," she said. "It's one of my favorites. Thanks, Reaper."

He sat down next to her. "If it wasn't, I would be back there now, blowing up the place for giving me the wrong flavor."

I should have given him more direct orders to avoid freaking her out in general.

I watched her sift through the toppings, memorizing her choices to learn more about her in a non-creepy way. Simple observation. She liked sprinkles, cookie dough bits, and peanut butter chunks. She ate carefully, watching the two of us sitting at the table with her.

"Are you two going to join me, or am I supposed to eat this all by myself?" She cocked an eyebrow at me, a glimpse of her coming back out of her depressed shell.

Grabbing my own, I dished up the same thing she did. I wanted to test the flavor combinations.

"I think I need to leave my hole," she sighed.

Thank God. She was starting to leave a large dent in that chair.

"You also asked about how to kill people." I pulled the spoon out of my mouth and pointed it in her direction. "How are you supposed to do that from your chair?"

"Don't antagonize me, Vaughn. My best friend is missing, the world is on fire, and I can't keep my stomach out of my mouth. Have some empathy." Her blue eyes lit up while she ripped into me, and I relished in it. The spark behind her eyes would come back eventually. She took another bite, and I could see the sass re-enter her body.

"Don't hate me 'cause it's true." I flashed a smile at her, and she looked like she wanted to throw something at me.

Good. Get feisty.

"You're such an asshole."

"But I'm *your* asshole."

"No. You're my... associate."

"I could be down for some roleplay. I hear you have a wonderful boardroom we could use."

Her mouth fell open, and she threw a spoon at me. Reaper watched comfortably from his side of the table. He enjoyed dinner and a show while watching her attack me. Her face curled into a slight grimace—it looked far better than a droopy, depressed expression.

Was it bad my dick could get hard with her hating me like this? She was so full of spite and anger; I couldn't wait to let her take it out on me. Let her use her frustration on my dick? *God, yes.*

"You're so gross."

"Thank you."

"We have a visit to pay to someone later tonight," Reaper cut in.

Fallon looked to me expectantly. "Can I go?"

"Only if you wash your hair."

She chucked a full container of gummy worms at me.

∾

Dave threw down the profile of a man who worked in the legal department. His immediate supervisor was Mr. Caldwell, the lawyer from the boardroom who didn't rub me the right way. Everyone was suspicious at that company, and I couldn't trust anyone who was around Fallon. If he handed us these profiles and tried to send us on a wild goose chase, we'd be fucked.

Time was ticking until Fallon's birthday.

"What do we have on him outside of his ability to access legal documents that *may* have come across his desk? Evans said there were personal legal matters that would have zero eyes from anyone in the company."

I was still missing something. It was going to cost me everything.

Dave awaited orders from me. He wasn't one to formulate opinions. He pointed and I said shoot was his job title. Reaper knew more because he'd been with us a long time—I heard he was freshly out of the military not long before we took him into our company. I was young.

Reaper was the one to respond. "Mr. Vaughn authorized whatever means necessary to do what we need to do. He has a lot of interest in preserving the Montgomery Group. Chamberlain Industries depends on it."

"So, we just grab this guy and terrorize him with no way to know anything?"

"You can use me," Fallon piped in.

"Fallon, you are out of the question. You're here by the grace of God right now."

She picked up the file from the table and flipped through it. "There's no notes. Just his picture and what he does at my company."

"Standard practice. We ask no questions and bring knives." Reaper brandished his KA-Bar from his vest and picked at his nails with the tip.

Gawking at him, she turned back to me. "Then how do we broach this without alarming those who might be watching?

Jason told me he has been surveilling me for years. Who knows who may be watching me now?"

"Since you're so smart," Dave cut in, "what do you suppose we do now?"

She rubbed her face, clearly torn. With years in this world, I had become numb to what she was dealing with. I was pretty trigger happy myself.

"I don't know. I just have a feeling we shouldn't be going in with so little information."

"Boss, we have to make a move—quickly."

"Look, Blondie. We have to make our moves. There's no time for a jury deliberation here."

"Time's up. Let's move."

We arrived at the Montgomery Group field office, where Allen was supposedly working late into the evening. I could smell the anxiety coming from Fallon while she fidgeted with her jewelry.

A big, bald fucking slob sat there while some poor woman was sucking him off.

Yeah, I would kill him just for putting this woman through that.

Reaper burst through the door. "Allen? Is that you? Are you cheating on me?"

Jesus Christ, Reaper.

Allen shoved the girl off of him and stood up with his hands up, dick still out. The sight of a fat man, sweaty with his dick hanging out like that was enough to give me nightmares for the rest of my life.

The girl scrambled out, holding her dress up to her body.

"Get out of here, girl. This is my man," he mocked.

"Wh-what do you want? I'll give you anything you want. My wallet is in my briefcase."

"Your boss has some questions about this. It's an HR nightmare in here," I called out. I nodded to Dave who stomped over and set Allen down in his chair, covering up the unsightly scene we had walked into.

"At least I feel better about interrogating him," she whispered in my ear.

He was still stunned, with his hands up in the air, while Fallon came out from behind me. "Hi, Allen. I have a couple of questions for you. Well, we do." She gestured to the group of well-armed men backing her up, ready for whatever the night would bring.

"M-miss Montgomery. You aren't set to take role until—"

"I know. And I think you know that's why we're here. I wasn't sure about coming to see you earlier, but I think my apprehensions have been put to bed. Can you answer something? Do you *know* why I'm here to visit you tonight?"

He shook in the chair a bit. His thoughts crossed his face in a series of expressions. The answer took root in him as he surveyed us all. Mostly Reaper. "She'll know you're here!"

"Pray tell, who is this mythical 'she' you're talking about?"

Dave finished tying Allen to the chair and opened his duffel bag of toys. A clear sheet was spread on the ground. *Cleanup*. Something I hoped she wouldn't have to see.

"Rabbit! Haines is gone and she's ruthless!"

"Tell me more." Reaper set his boot on his thigh and pretended to be patient and awaiting an answer. Allen looked at him in horror. "Because if she's ruthless, then I'm the devil."

"Are you talking about Sylvia? Taller. Brown hair. Hazel eyes. Drinks a lot and likes to get violent when she does?" Fallon's face became serious. When she spoke of her aunt, she got a look in her eyes—a certain calmness. The kind of look that told me Blondie would be the one to take her aunt out without a second thought. And, damn, if that didn't make me secretly proud.

Our little kidnappee was breathing heavily and sweat dripped from his greasy nose. His head was slick with sweat, and his lips started to tremble. "Sounds like her."

Reaper stabbed him in the leg and Fallon's face about turned green. She gave a small flinch as the blade pierced his skin and forced him to scream in pain.

"No time for fucking games. Tell me what you know, and

441

your death will come easy. I won't ask again." He ripped the knife out and started cleaning it with a cloth.

She swallowed hard. "Just tell me one thing: Is she planning on stealing the seat from me, or is someone else plotting to topple the company completely?"

"She's got a contract over you. I don't know what. I wasn't in that meeting." He stopped to take a breath, and Reaper slapped him across the face. "I was there to grant her guardianship over you and change your requirements for succession."

Change the requirements for succession? If Sylvia had a contract over Fallon, what was it for, and who was it with? I had my ideas, but hoped we could find solid answers here.

"How many times was my signature forged?"

I watched her anger grow like she was siphoning it from the ground. Her jaw was set and the hands she held behind her back balled into fists. I knew this was personal for her, but having your own family member abuse you, plot your demise, and try to steal from your dead mom was another level of fucked up family drama.

"Too many to count, too many loopholes to get it overturned or reviewed by a judge. We had multiple sign offs for you to be able to fight it in court."

"What's the fucking *point* of all this?"

Shit, if she had a gun, she might have just pulled the trigger.

"What's the point of anything? Money. Power. Whatever vice floats your boat." He spit blood from his mouth to his left. He was clearly tired. "She never gave a why. She just went to work at taking your inheritance. I don't get paid enough to care."

"Do we have all the answers we need?" Dave gestured to the sheet on the ground, eager to get on with his portion of events.

"Your birthday won't matter. She'll take you down for this. Dead or alive, I'm compromised because she has eyes and ears everywhere with the power she stole from Haines."

Fallon held up a finger. "How did she steal from him?"

Allen sighed as blood kept dripping from his wound into the

puddle below him. "Sex. Secret deals with other big families. You."

"Me?"

"I don't have all the details. I'm just one man."

I couldn't risk my protective position of her. Gesturing to Reaper, I made hand signals for him to search the place.

"Don't worry," I said, pulling Fallon back to my side. "I can figure those out."

His eyes got bigger when he finally focused on my face. "The Vaughns? Ha! You have no idea what's coming because all you big families are all the same. Money. Power. Greed. It blinds you."

I smiled. "You're the same, too. How far did greed get you? What families?"

He shook his head. "I don't know. Above my pay grade. Whatever you can find in my files is all I know. It's bigger than Haines and his *Rabbit*. You're up on the chopping block, kid."

Pulling Fallon behind me, I turned and plugged her ears, holding her head to my chest while Dave took care of it.

Some men at the end of the line looked like Allen. His face was pensive, wondering if what he'd done was worth it, but also accepting of his fate. This world never lets you out alive. Others that I've seen stayed haughty until the life drained from their eyes.

He heaved Allen onto the sheet without so much as a fight and tied a zip tie around his neck. Suffocation wasn't messy, and gunshots were far too loud. He wrapped him up and surveyed the heavy man he'd have to drag out of here shortly.

"Boss, there's *a lot* of files."

"Search them all. There's gotta be something about what he said in here," I said, tugging Fallon out into the night.

42

Fallon

The Week After Christmas

There would be *no* end in sight for my insomnia and nausea. The internet would say I'm either pregnant or dying. I was neither. The third option? Traumatized.

Reality wasn't far away anymore. It was all too real and too close for comfort.

I still saw—and heard—that poor schmuck hit the ground. The concrete by the pool slowly becoming covered in blood. The whispers about him afterward fueled my insomnia day in and day out. Murdered in cold blood for *allegedly* seeing and saying things he wasn't supposed to.

My second dead body was the man I interrogated and ultimately killed by proxy. He was in *my* company, and he betrayed *me*, my *dead* mother, and *my* company. The sound of the knife stabbing into his leg echoed on repeat like a busted record. Brent tried to save me from the sight of him in the sheet, but I looked at him nonetheless. Asphyxiated, he turned blue underneath the clear sheet. They didn't hide him well enough from me.

I sat numb on the bathroom floor for a while.

The knocks on the door wouldn't end.

Knock, knock. "You've been in there for twelve hours. You have to come out at some point—even for some water."

He was right. I looked at my empty water bottle that I hadn't bothered to refill. Instead, I locked myself in overnight and took what sleep the bathroom floor would give me. It wasn't much, but I'd take what I could get.

Knock, knock. "Are you even alive in there?"

I heard faint whispering behind the door, and someone was fiddling with the doorknob. The lock wasn't an impossible task to pick. The key was even above the doorframe. They probably didn't want to bother me until morning.

When I didn't come out, they started knocking.

A new, twisted part of myself wondered if they thought I killed myself in here.

What would they do if I did?

The door opened, but I didn't turn to see who had come in. It wasn't Kelly; she had been gone for a while, and we all knew why. All my texts went unread and unanswered. What I wanted to know was why this was happening and what was going on with her. I saw the suspicion on everyone's faces when she was brought up, or when they knew I was searching for any sign of life.

There were only four regular people who frequented my house: Dave, Brent, Reaper, and James. None of them knew what to do with me, how to help me cope, or come to terms with my new reality.

I thought fighting dirty business was the worst of it, but I felt like I was dealing with some secret society. In a sense, I was. I never knew about the international black market trade deals or how close to home they were.

"She's alive," Reaper announced.

I looked at him from the floor, curled up in a fetal position. Must have been a sight to behold.

"Two more rats are gone. You can stop throwing up now." He left the bathroom, muttering about how it was a bad idea to involve me to Brent.

446

Dave concurred in the hallway.

They'd been hardened from their years of working like this. It made me scared that I would end up that way.

What I'd give to have things like they were a few short months ago. Or even to have had a normal Christmas. I never put up a tree, watched cheesy movies, or did presents. I simply pretended it didn't exist.

"Blondie, have you showered yet?"

I didn't respond.

Instead of antagonizing me again, he entered the bathroom and closed the door behind him. He knelt down and slowly stroked my hair.

"Can I run you a bath?"

No words would form for me to accept or decline. The water was turned on, and the rushing of water sounded like a waterfall escape.

He left and came back with items I'd need for bathing. Along with bath salts and a candle—I assumed for calming me.

"Come on, let's get you cleaned up."

Two hands scooped me up off the ground, and I was cradled to Brent's chest. His heartbeat was an even, calming tempo. He placed a kiss on my head as he sat me down on the edge of the tub.

Silently, he stripped me out of my clothes and kissed each of my shoulders before helping me into the warm water.

I looked around and noticed he had added bubbles.

He carefully placed a candle in the corner of the tub and lit it. The flame flickered to life; it was one of my favorite candles, and I'd bought backups to stash in my closet to keep Kelly from stealing them all. Water rushed over my hair as I sat there, holding my knees to my chest.

Shampoo was scrubbed into my scalp and rinsed.

Then, conditioned and combed.

Soap was scrubbed into my back.

"How's my Blondie doing?" He kissed my shoulder again.

"Feeling more clean." I managed a small smile through my fog.

His hands were gentle as he continued to clean me up. If I let him, he probably would have brushed my teeth for me.

"Question for a question?" he asked, scrubbing one of my arms with a loofah.

I scoffed at him. How was he trying to play these games with everything going on? "What kind of questions?"

"Easy ones. What's your favorite color? If you tell me it's pink, I'll be excited that my guess was correct." He handed me a toothbrush.

"I like pink, but my favorite is the deep purple of a sunset. What's *your* favorite color, big, bad Brent Vaughn? Black?"

He swapped arms to scrub and placed a kiss on my hand. "The golden light that reflects off your hair in the sun. The bright blue of your eyes when you tell me you hate me. The soft pink of your lips before you kiss me. And my number one? The reddish tint of your cheeks when you're so close to me that you can't help but blush."

My mouth fell open, and toothpaste dripped out. "That's not something I'd expect you to say."

"What did you expect?"

"The black of your motorcycle."

He splashed me, and I flicked water back at him. For someone so serious and so bad boy-ish, he had some soft spots hiding under there.

"You used your question. It's my turn." I looked around the bathroom where he had brought in the pajamas he knew I'd want to wear. My favorite candle he knew I'd want to use. He added bubbles and salt to my bath to help me relax.

"Why do you hate waffles so much?"

He would turn down waffles every time they were available, saying that he hated them with a passion. I never knew anyone to have something against food like that—unless it was Brussels sprouts or cooked spinach.

He took my leg in his hand, scrubbing it starting at my foot.

"When I was a kid, I refused to let my babysitters cook for me. It got so bad that I wasn't eating what anyone else would make, so I started trying to cook in the middle of the night because I was so hungry. I attempted to make myself waffles and burned them every time. I continued to make them because it was the only thing I knew to do, and so I ate burned waffles at one in the morning for months.

"Then my grandfather hired Miss Martha, and she *really* gave me the what for. But instead of forcing me to eat what she made, she taught me how to make pancakes. Little by little, I started trusting her enough to make me small items, so long as she promised me she would never make me waffles ever again. The burnt taste is etched in my brain, and I will never eat another waffle again. I'd probably puke like you." He teased me with a smile on the last part, rinsing off the loofah in the water.

"I'd be traumatized by waffles too. I also didn't realize Martha was a longtime person in your life."

His eyes fell to the water after finishing with my legs. I'd never seen that look on his face before. He had a mix of sadness and introspection on his face, which he never showed. "She took care of me like a mother. My grandfather told me about my mom's suicide before I stopped eating, and he could see what it did to me. So, like any good mother would, Miss Martha took me in as her own and raised me until I became a hellion who wouldn't listen to her—like any son would."

Miss Martha *was* his mother. And he brought me around to her diner for our first *date*? It made sense to me why she was so shocked to see him with a girl. That was her *son*, and he brought along a girl to basically meet his mother on a first date. Did she even know that I had just met him that night?

He changed subjects. "The water is getting cold. Do you want me to help you out and into your pajamas?"

I wanted to tell him *no* and to leave the bathroom—out of my own depression so I could be alone—but it was futile since he'd sneak in and fall asleep with me later.

I nodded.

Pulling the drain on the tub, he lifted me out of the water and into a towel. I wrapped my hair after he sat me back down on the edge and waited for him to retrieve my warm clothes.

The oversized sweater was the first to come. He slipped it over my toweled head and pulled each of my arms through after making sure they were dry. He got down on his knees to help me into the oversized shorts.

My heart was in my throat. He undressed, bathed, and dressed me again. "Give me your feet so I can make sure you're warm enough for bed."

He looked up at me, wondering what I was doing.

Before I knew what I was doing, I kissed him.

And he kissed me back.

"I thought you said we couldn't," he whispered into my mouth.

My core heated up instinctively around him. I didn't know why I couldn't rip myself from this man's body, but all I knew was that I wanted him again.

"We can't," I breathed.

Our mouths never parted.

"Definitely." His kisses became urgent.

His hands found their way up my sweater, gripping onto my sides.

"Nope."

My legs wrapped around his waist.

"We're just associates." He used my own words against me.

Teeth grazed my neck.

"Strictly business." Who was I kidding? Would it ever be *just* business with him?

He picked me up and pushed his way into my bedroom, hands firmly grasping my ass while our tongues danced together in a full-blown make out session.

I ripped the towel from my hair before he threw me onto the bed and started pulling off his shirt. The want in his eyes while he took in the raw version of me was more intense than it had ever been. I was the moon in his sky.

"If you kick me out again tonight, the next place I'm coming for you is bending you over that big shiny table in your boardroom. Then your big CEO desk. Then in the lobby where everyone can see you trying to deny that you're mine."

Wetness pooled between my legs at his threat. I bit my lip and shivered from the thought of him fucking me over and over again. It might have been winter, but my room was fully heated, and every word of his made my goosebumps form and intensify.

"I'm not yours. We're just associates." I spread my legs open for him to get a full view of me.

He bent down with no hesitation and licked me up and down. "You say you're not mine, but how's it you drip for me and me alone?" He snaked his hands under me and yanked me by my thighs to him.

Half moaning, half yelping, I knew I was done for.

He licked. He kissed. He sucked. He drove me wild without even giving me so much as a finger to enjoy.

He pulled me even closer. "You say you're not mine, but I'm the only one to ever touch you. To taste you. To fuck you."

I was speechless. He was claiming me as his, but we were working together. Everything was so complicated.

"Tell me it's not true, Blondie."

I met his gaze hesitantly. His eyes dared me to tell him no one more time. If I did, he'd just prove to me that he was right. If I told him I was his, it would be my undoing. I kept silent.

Eyes wild with the fire that burned within him, he crawled up and positioned himself above me. His gaze softened just by a hair as he took in my face and kissed my forehead.

"Tell me something."

"What?"

"Anything," he whispered.

"Thank you."

"Don't thank me yet."

He slipped out of the rest of his clothes and lined himself up with my entrance. The tip slid up and down, and my hips followed, silently begging him to be inside me. He cocked his head and smiled at me, knowing full well what I wanted.

"Put it in," I groaned.

"Ask me nicely." Another graze upward.

"Please," I gritted, "put it in."

He wasted no time pushing his cock completely into me and we both sighed in relief. Small, slow thrusts started us off with him still on top of me. Moving my legs, he wrapped them around his waist. "Do you know what you do to me?"

I panted, trying to keep pulling him in. The way he felt made me feel feral. "I think I can relate."

In response, he thrust into me harder, letting me feel the entire size of his cock before thrusting again. "Do you? Because I imagine being inside of you for the better part of my day. Associate or not, I'm addicted, and I won't stop."

"Then don't."

As if that was some magical phrase, it set him off. He thrusted harder into me and moved his hand down to place his thumb over my clit. "I won't stop until you've at least given me a puddle. Until you come so hard for me that your little legs shake for me again. Until I've satisfied myself with drinking you up."

He traced circles until he watched me react to every movement he made, learning my body in every position he possibly could. Massaging my clit as he thrust into me was another new for me. He knew that. He wanted me to come with him inside me this time.

Fuck, I definitely would. He knew everything because it had only been him. He learned my body quickly and used it as a weapon, forcing moans from me and building up my orgasm to a point where I couldn't take it anymore.

It was faster this time. Stroking my clit and thrusting into me was a double whammy that I wouldn't come back from. The heat and electricity built up to my climax.

"I'm gonna—fuck!" The pulsating was filled up by his cock

buried deep inside me and he watched me, knowing that I was coming. His eyes flickered, telling me he felt my orgasm.

"Yes, baby. *Yes*. Come all over my cock. That's it... just like that." He kept on with his thumb on my clit. "Fuck, yes. I feel your pussy pulsing on me."

Was it possible to bottle up this intense orgasm feeling? Because holy shit, I thought I exploded into a million pieces. He shattered me over and over, and he had no plans of stopping.

He slowed his thrusting just a little, savoring the feeling of my walls throbbing around him. If I didn't know any better, I would have thought he was trying to kill me with pleasure.

"Fuck. Brent!"

"Yes, baby. Let it all out. Scream my name. Look how wet you got for me."

He maneuvered me face down after my legs failed, propping me up on a pillow. My ass was on full display in the air. I felt myself dripping down my leg before he lapped it up and spread me open like he was going to feast on me.

I whimpered. "Brent."

Sucking on my clit, he moaned, and it sent electricity through me. I was so fucking sensitive it wasn't even funny. Never in my life did I think *this* is what sex would feel like.

"I need another one, Blondie. Will you come for me again?"

Again?

No response was necessary because he curled two fingers inside of me, pressing right where he knew I would respond. Since my legs were useless, I had to sit there and take it. His fingers thrusted in and out right where he knew it would bring me back to my boiling point before using his mouth on my clit again.

"Just one more," he cooed.

It was easy to get me there a second time with his expert hands. And that fucking mouth. I should have known from that cocky ass smile that he'd have me orgasming far too quickly for my own good.

I bit down on the pillow as the wave hit me, groaning

something completely incoherent into it. My body gave up completely because I slumped over like I had been hit by a train.

A sexy train?

Clearly, my mind was useless at this point, and I felt like I was vibrating.

"Goddamn," I muttered and flopped myself over. My chest was heaving like I had run a marathon, and he was smiling at me. "What?"

"Just you." He smoothed out my hair and laid next to me. "I may have imagined bending you over that desk, though."

"If we can pull off my transition to CEO, sure." I slapped at him playfully.

His thumb grazed my bottom lip. "If that's all it took, I'll get you ownership of any company you want. You name it and I'll make it happen. *If* I can fuck you in your office."

I let him cozy up next to me; it's not like I was going anywhere. He wore me out in the best ways. He pulled me to his chest and put his lips to the top of my head.

We sank into the bed together, and I sighed.

"What's rolling around in that head of yours?"

"I just don't know what I do from here."

He pulled me as close as I could get. "Sleep. Continue as normal and stick to the plan until we can figure it all out."

43

Fallon

Three Months to Fallon's Birthday

"I'm happy you decided to meet."

I took a sip of my coffee, crossing my legs. Unsure of how it would go, all I could do was my best. "We won't have much time today," I admitted, staring at the box on the table.

This secures the room echoed in my mind. I snagged one of my own and never let Brent know what I was up to. It was chess, not checkers.

He had his plans, so I had mine.

"Let's get down to brass tacks, then. You have a relationship I envy, and I spent half a decade of my life being drained by your aunt. We can help each other."

I didn't know much about Jason Haines, but my first impression led me to understand why Augustus Vaughn chose my mother over him. He was a needy man who acted like the world owed him something—his body language even suggested as much.

No one owed you anything. That truth was hard to learn in this world.

"Why did my aunt turn on you?" I kept my expression

neutral, not wanting him to see anything other than what I wanted him to.

"Greed and her unrelenting vendetta against you and your mother. I was happy to partner up with her because I wanted to get back at the Vaughn family for turning me away all those years ago, but your family has a way of conning me out of everything."

That was an insinuation, and the way he was looking at me told me my distrust was a mutual feeling.

I perked an eyebrow over my mug while I took another calculated sip. "It seems we're in the same boat with Sylvia, then. How do we take her down?"

He skipped over the question, probably wanting someone to hear his wails of self-pity first. "I know you didn't know your aunt well, but she is *definitely* the sister of your mother. Don't get me wrong—your mother was much kinder, but they both share the same tenacity."

A thought crossed my mind that I filed away for later. "If we move forward, I'm aware that your loyalties lie with yourself. What other convincing arguments can you make to ensure we have a successful partnership in taking her down?"

"I would get my company back, for one." His jaw ticked with irritation, and I saw the look in his eyes warning me to tread lightly. "Two, we finally end the line of women from your family fucking me over. I'd say, if you help me, we can be amicable."

"Alright, then." I nodded at him, preparing to make a deal with the devil.

My own game of chess had just begun.

44

Brent

Two Months to Fallon's Birthday

"Mister Vaughn." Our doorman opened the door to my office.

"Mister Vaughn is my grandfather. What is it, Frank?"

The door opened to reveal Garrett standing outside my office. "You have a visitor with an urgent request. Shall I let him in?"

The fucker was already here, inside our estate. How much more *let him in* could there be?

Flicking my hand at him, Frank ushered him in and retreated. Someone needed to tell him visitor requests were to be handled at the *entrance* to the property, not at my fucking office.

"How'd you get onto the property, Bradford?"

"I spilled some info they knew you'd want to hear about Fallon."

That *was* a convincing statement. My attention perked up at the mention of her name, despite it coming from this guy's mouth. Why he was here talking about her was my next question.

"So, tell me what you have."

"First," he said, holding up a finger and sitting down in the chair across from me, "I need to tell you that this is big. *Huge,*

461

even. The Fitzgerald family, the Whitmore family, and others want to steal the spotlight. A group effort has been launched to attack families like mine who don't pick sides, and my father is awaiting a prison sentence because of it."

What did I care about his family? There were takedowns on a regular basis in our world, and his family wasn't anything special.

"You're not in our circles anymore, so what the fuck could you know? You were the one cozying up to her before I stepped in. Don't act like it wasn't partly to get in the good graces of the inner circles for your family." I poured myself a drink, kicking my feet up on the table.

God, it felt good to be in charge. *I could get used to it.*

He scoffed. "You—never mind. Believe what you will, but I'm out here fucking hiding from everyone. I'm sticking my damn neck out here for *her* sake now."

The Bradford family had been grasping for straws in recent years, unwilling to play by the unwritten rules of the inner circle. The look on his face told me he was serious, but he could have been playing well. We had our own agreements, but if there was one thing I knew, it was not to trust anything at face value.

"Hiding? Wonderful. If no one knows you're here, I can bury you in my garden, and no one would be the wiser. I suggest getting to the point of your visit." I tipped the glass back, drinking up all the whiskey from my glass. Being in front of the man who got to run around with Fallon in public was testing my patience, no matter what his role was.

"Fine." He crossed his arms and glared at me. "Fitzgerald wants Montgomery. As in *Fallon* Montgomery. Whitmore decided she wanted to meddle to get back at you."

"Tell me something I don't already fucking know, Bradford. *Tick tock.*" Pressing a button on the keypad in my office, I paged for Dave to sit in on my little meeting.

He shifted in his seat, looking at the keypad warily. "Fallon is to be ousted from her company."

"As I said, I already fucking *know*." Standing, I placed my hands on the desk, leaning over to tempt him with my anger issues. Everyone knew I had them; not many were stupid enough to try me. "I am running the Vaughn family, and I know everything about everyone. Tell. Me. Something. I. Don't. Know."

He breathed out. "She's to be contracted to the Fitzgerald company as his *wife*, in order for her company to be spearheaded by some other person who has the authority to do so."

Out of all the rats I took out and files I sifted through, *this* particular piece of information was never revealed.

"Well, now, you're going to tell me exactly how you got this information and who said it. And if I don't believe you"—I looked over to Dave standing at the door—"you don't get to leave. Don't forget what I've done for you, *and* what I'm now doing for your family."

"Give me the status of Wilder."

Reaper sat casually, spread out on a chair with some demon mask on. He adjusted his over the ear headphones as he took a swig from the bottle of rum he had brought in with him.

He burped. "Ah, the troublemaker. I followed that girl around, and she's been a real headache. Her daddy is sending her out to collect intel to use for blackmail. On whom? Don't ask me."

I rubbed the back of my head, hoping to stir up some thoughts. "Her family takes people out. Collecting intel... Are you sure?"

"About as sure as I am that I have a huge dick."

Gross.

"Anyone else drop dead in the last few days? Casualties have been stacking up, and we are close to all the answers on how to handle it and make our moves. The Dictator just got back from Eastern Europe, making some agreements and acquiring some deals for Montgomery Group; he's expecting some answers from us."

Fallon has been pretending that things have been normal with her roommate missing. Well, as normal as she could be, with beefed up security, going to classes like nothing is wrong. Going to the obligatory parties and gatherings, and minding her *p's* and *q's* while observing—and learning.

Our job in our plan was to do our best to prevent any event that could hinder her succession as CEO. Things were running—only somewhat—alright, with efforts from a couple of families launching counterattacks against the split-off groups that were pressing forward to move the company to Sylvia. We were mostly blind when it came to how many moving parts there were.

The insider's circle had a large fissure down the middle. We knew the goal was to implement new leadership, kicking us out of the top.

Crabs in buckets.

"No one of importance to spook the news crews. Out in New York, there's been an uptick, and here in Willow Bay, we have the initial group of college kids that got nixed. That Wilder girl was responsible for that kid bouncing on concrete a while ago and then that staged suicide last week."

I needed another drink. Fallon had been living with the enemy this whole time, while others were concerned about her ex-boyfriend, Garrett. Fallon was adamant that Kelly wouldn't have purposely jeopardized her, but if Kelly was doing her job in the name of self-preservation... True friendships in this world didn't exist—only strategic ones did.

A thought occurred to me. "What about that guy Wilder was seeing earlier in the semester? That drug dealer?"

"No idea."

Nothing was really said when that reject was suddenly dead —he was just written off as a drug peddler and addict. I made a mental note to investigate, but we had more pressing matters with Fallon's birthday coming up than a missing frenemy.

"Follow her and get some of the guys to look into her dead drug dealer boyfriend. Something is fishy there, and it reeks of Wilder."

Leaving him in my office, I climbed the antique stairs that squeaked under each foot. I memorized this house as a toddler, unaware that I'd be grown and conducting business of my own. The dark wood and exquisite craftsmanship became old news to me after years of seeing it. Everything was grand and expertly crafted. A truly traditional mansion with modern day security reinforcements.

I stopped at my grandfather's door, mentally preparing myself for the final countdown to April. Blondie's birthday. The moment of truth. We were so close, yet so far from knowing what would happen.

My knuckles rapped at the door, and I let myself in.

"Brent," he said, lighting up a cigarette.

My name? When did I get upgraded?

"New intel complicating the Montgomery situation. What's the game plan?"

A puff of smoke swirled around his pensive face. I could see that he was having trouble with all the problems piling up around us. Whatever plans he was preparing might have a slim chance of success.

He always had a contingency, though.

"Continue as normal." His voice was softer today. Less angry.

The lines on his face were deeper than usual, and he looked like he hadn't slept in days. His age showed. To top it all off, he was smoking a cigarette instead of his signature cigar, and there were no bottles of alcohol in sight.

Something was off.

"We are also working on cleaning up house at the Montgomery Group. We have men combing through the company looking for any overlooked details. Legal documents undermining Fallon have been planted for years. We need to figure out loopholes." The squeak of the leather chair beneath me was the loudest sound in the room as I leaned forward.

He was staring at an old picture on the wall. Pictures of the past. The easier days to stay on top. "Tell me about the girl."

"Sir?"

"Tell me about *her*. What is she like?"

I wasn't sure what to say. My mouth hung open slightly. "She's, uh, nice. A bit green behind the ears but has a tenacious spirit."

"Is she ready?" His eyes met mine, and I knew what he was asking.

"She will be. Initial shock has worn off, and she's continuing as normal."

Preparing myself for what I knew was coming next, I pulled out my flask and took a swig.

"I see her as my own, you know. Her mother was family to me. Imagine my surprise at the enigma of her not wanting to bring that little girl around, *but* she had her own reasoning for things, as I have mine. Some days I wonder if I did the same for you as Maria did for her, if you'd be a different man."

Another pause. Was he telling me the regrets of his past now? We've never had a conversation like this—at least none I could remember. The fucker had to be dying or something to be talking like this.

I waited silently for him to continue. Interrupting him was asking for a death sentence.

He sighed. "I don't think you'd be able to handle the company is my point. What we do is a balancing act—the line between life and death. Maria is—*was*—our family, and that girl is the next generation. The future of everything that's been built over generations. We've grown so large, and only with the right leaders can we keep it."

Lighting up my own cigarette, I settled into the chair again, wondering where the conversation was headed. If he was announcing his death, I'd be shocked. If he was telling me that I'm the next generation to lead his company, I wouldn't believe

466

him. Considering how he told me I was worth less than shit in the yard, it would be a cold day in hell.

"Look, boy, you've been picking up the ropes like I knew you would. You've been in every room learning every perspective." Extinguishing his cigarette, he folded his hands on the table. "Are you going to be ready to take all of this over?"

"As in after college?"

"It might be sooner than you'd think. College doesn't teach you jack shit, and you know it. It's not like you went there to learn anyway. Once that girl hits twenty-one, all hell is going to break loose, and a stupid little university for rich brats isn't going to matter. You're not going back after this semester."

That's not what I expected.

Leave school? Stop playing baseball? Legitimately join the company for more than optics?

"I don't have much left, and I enjoy baseball."

"Fucking hire your own team in the backyard, then! Your team doesn't even play fair since we pay for the results anyway. The only people who have benefited from that university are the scholarship recipients. The rest of 'em are just playing Barbie dream house, and that includes *you*." He looked like he was about to fish around for a bottle of something when he brought out a small, ornate box from his desk. Pulling out a pill, he popped it into his mouth and grabbed another cigarette from his silver case. He lit it up. "If I assume correctly, that girl is just as magnetic as her mother, no?"

"Sir?"

Did he just roll his eyes at me? "I know you've stayed at her house as many nights as she allows. You think your men don't gossip and compare dicks when you're not around?"

I was confused. My grandfather was talking to me like he was interested in my company. He wasn't drinking. His face had expressions on it.

"It's a necessity to ensure—"

"Yeah, yeah." He waved his hand in my direction. "You're all business about it, but you've played the game well. She's in the

467

Vaughn family for more than one reason at this rate. Don't think I don't know the tricks you like to use. At least when she runs, it'll be to us. I expect an easy transition into public leadership for both of you. Connecting our families like this was the smartest thing you could have done for us. *Especially* with my contingency plans."

His *what?*

45

Fallon

One Month to Fallon's Birthday

I tapped my fingers impatiently on the table, staring at the men around me. We'd been ordered to an emergency meeting, and it didn't seem like good news.

"Look, I know everything feels hopeless, and we need to plan for the worst, but we can work with what we've got. Your mother had a will, and we can fight everything until the bitter end. I hope it doesn't come to that."

Evans ruffled his normally well-groomed hair, clearly disturbed by our plans and the sneaking around that wasn't making a dent in Sylvia's scheme.

I made plans of my own in the background. If she stole everything, I would continue to fight, but it would be dirty. The people I had around me could roll in the mud, especially Jason.

"What do we do in the meantime?" I asked.

He shrugged, another abnormal movement for him. "We're working on getting new judges and lawyers to comb through your paperwork. We can go to the media with a scandal like this, but it could destroy Montgomery Group and our clientele. We work in luxury—and sometimes discreet—business. It wouldn't be a good look."

I gritted my teeth. "Which is what she probably planned for, too."

"Exactly"—he tried to compose himself—"but we must push forward and keep up appearances. Try not to lose hope, kid. Your mom has figured her way out of shit situations before. This might be the worst one yet, but keep your chin up."

Everyone sat in their chairs, the tension thick in the air. I couldn't breathe with the amount of anxiety running through my veins.

Tempted to scroll through my phone again and look at the other series of threats and pictures I'd gotten, the trash can across the room looked like an inviting place to be.

The door opened, and a few people strolled in, an air of haughtiness about them. The crowd of men separated to reveal a woman.

Sylvia.

She had the same long brown hair, straightened to match her business attire. Hazel eyes, full of the animosity and hatred I'd experienced for years, pierced into me.

A man to her left set down a few pieces of paper.

"I am happy to announce that I am going to be taking over as the CEO of Montgomery Group. The sole heir is not *qualified* to be successor at this current time." She looked at me, a wicked grin on her face. "But we do wish her well in her studies until she can prepare herself as a *proper* leader."

"The will states—"

She interrupted Evans. "The will is vague at best. I have plenty of lawyers and judges who can attest to this, and that, as her *guardian*, I can continue leading as I have been until she's more… competent."

Saw that coming.

She'd even found the nerve to dress like my mother, and I wouldn't have been at all surprised if she had stolen her clothes from the home that had been left empty all these years. Hell, she probably moved into my mother's house. I didn't live there and couldn't bring myself to return after all these years. The

472

company took care of it, and I bought my own near campus to avoid all those painful feelings.

A finely manicured hand pushed the papers further onto the table. "Effective immediately, *I* am the one in charge. I am your new CEO."

The news went wild with *Sister of deceased CEO comes forward*. Her sob story about how she wanted to take care of me and honor my mother's memory was disturbing. Whatever twisted this woman's mind throughout her entire life made me *almost* pity her.

I clicked off the TV and chucked the remote across the room.

She is disturbed.

Memories of her being drunk and hitting me flooded me all day. Those images were burned into my mind.

My phone buzzed next to me.

UNKNOWN:

What's a girl to do next? We'll be watching.

My ears rang. Knowing that I was continually walking around with not only a target on my back but also eyes watching my every move sent a chill down my spine.

"Who the *hell* are you?" I whispered at the screen. "Why wait so long between texts? I'm going to fucking *kill* you when I find out who you are, you bastard."

Whatever happened next, I had to choose my steps carefully.

46

Fallon

Two Weeks to Fallon's Birthday

My head hurt.

It was my own fault; I drank a little *too* much last night. My thoughts were too loud in the fog of pretending to be normal, day in and day out.

James watched me take shots after I finished writing up an assignment for a stupid class I didn't even want to take anymore, but Brent told me I had to live my life like nothing was wrong. All part of his "plan."

Plan, my ass.

Yet, everything felt wrong. It looked wrong. It even smelled wrong.

A semester I thought would be different was. It was different in all the wrong ways. I just wanted to feel normal again.

But no. I went from being a hermit to becoming famous, the talk of the town, and part of a strange secret conspiracy. My life was a nightmarish series of events, and I had to pretend they were a walk in the park to avoid being eaten alive.

"Fuck, Mom, what do I do?" I whispered into the sink. I braced my hands on the cold granite countertop. "I am so tired, and I could use a little guidance here."

Knock. knock. "Miss Montgomery. I have two deliveries for you."

"Coming!"

I splashed water on my face and toweled off before seeing what he had for me. There was a bouquet of flowers with an envelope and a small box.

"What are those?"

James, ever vigilant after Brent threatened to kill him, opened the envelope before letting me look at the contents.

"Like they'd anthrax me," I scoffed, snatching the paper from him before he opened the box.

> *I hope you have a wonderful birthday, and I'm sorry I won't be there to buy your first legal drink.*
> *Be safe and be careful.*
> *Love you, dude.*

I held it out to him. "This has to be a joke or something, right? Kelly disappears and sends me a letter and flowers telling me she's sorry she can't be here for my birthday instead of just showing her face? I don't believe this for one second." *That, or she had some audacity.* "What's in the box?" We swapped items.

I reopened the box. Inside was a pre-graduation party invitation from Sloane. She was graduating this school year and wanted all of us to know we were going to be celebrating *her* and not the entire class. *How self-absorbed could one girl be?*

"It's just an elaborate party invitation. With pink lace underwear. Super weird. I swear to God this school feels like a cult some days." I threw the underwear at Reaper, who was sitting on the couch playing with Pumpkin.

Brent assigned him to me occasionally, and I wasn't sure if it was to scare me or others. Or both. He kept his distance after I kept refusing to let him in.

"New panties for you, Reap."

Circling into the kitchen, I found coffee prepared and waiting for me. Just how I like it. Again, I liked the perks of being rich, but the rest of the shit that came with it... not so much. If I had to make my own coffee for the rest of my life just to live in peace, I'd take it.

"This invitation says that the party is tonight. Shall I RSVP for you?"

"I have to go," I sighed. "Integrating into the fold this semester has been a success so far, and not going to Sloane's party would be a bad look. Despite what she might have hidden up her sleeve, I have to make nice."

James made breakfast quietly while Pumpkin swirled around my legs, silently asking for attention. No classes for the day meant I could be a hermit before the party and mentally prepare for the business meeting tomorrow. Evans planned to continue as normal and told us to hold on to the hope that the company would be mine on my birthday.

I was caught up with the operations of the business—both the legal side and the non legal side—and hoped to *God* I could transition into the role of CEO, or at least keep everything afloat while I finished school. Sylvia stealing it from us didn't mean I should give up, but it made everything that much more complicated. The guys planned to keep me in the loop about her activity while we worked behind the scenes to figure out our next steps.

"Basic eggs, bacon, and toast today. I hope you don't mind."

Reaper peeked over to see if there was anything for him.

"Reaper?"

"Yes?"

"What's with the mask thing?"

"What's with your face thing?"

Reaper, the scary oddball, never took his masks off. We never questioned it much and probably never should. It was curious, though. I had to try *just once*.

~

"That's this week in operations." James stood from the table to stretch his legs.

James kept me discreetly informed about company operations. Evans held out hope that we could turn this ship around. Plus, the board could work to undermine Sylvia's plan to dismantle the company.

If they were the loyal types.

I had to stay in the loop so we could look for holes to weasel back into, find some way to take down my evil aunt. There had to have been a way, and I just needed to keep looking.

"So, the progression for the developments in Switzerland is going smoothly? I think the marketing team should be doing more for the client experience since we have expanded to some other countries and need to dial in some messaging. The last few months look a little sloppy. With how strong things have gone up until last year, I'd say we're at risk of some poaching."

He rubbed his chin for a moment, taking in my words. "I can pass this along to Evans and the execs since your *external* meeting on your birthday is about *other* topics. You've come a long way this semester, from learning the basics to understanding some nuance in the company."

I closed the file with a thump. "If I'm being candid, the things behind the curtain may be leaking into business as a whole across the board for all these families. Personal vendettas are getting hotter, and regular people can tell something is up. I need to see what the Vaughns have been dealing with topside, too."

Dave entered the room. "You rang? I'm swapping with Reap for babysitting tonight. Mr. Vaughn is excited to see you at the party tonight."

I wasn't excited to see him. Since he took on an even bigger role for his grandfather, I kept him at arm's length. When we fucked that night after he gave me a bath, I promised myself no funny business after that.

A promise I wanted to keep to myself. For my sanity. Even

though I kept breaking it. It never could be that simple with Brent Vaughn, could it?

The look on his face when I told him to leave again sucked. Like, really sucked. But it was better for us both that way.

"I don't want to see him. Tell him to avoid me, will you?"

He chucked a box on the table and laughed. "No can do. One, you're not the one signing my paychecks. Two, I don't care enough to. He sent this."

I opened the box to reveal a golden dress. A floor-length gown with shimmering fabric that would make me stand out, not fit in. That was his message to me: *Stand out and show them who you are.* "He must be out of his mind. I'm *not* wearing this."

Pulling out a cigarette, Dave headed to the porch. He called out, "It's not a request," before closing the door behind him.

My mouth fell open. Brent wasn't serious, *was he*? A full glamor to wear to Sloane's party? If I wasn't on an immediate hit list, I would be in this thing.

I put it on.

The bodice was form fitting and accentuated my body. Beading and sequins were embroidered down to the waistline. Looking in the mirror, I was reminded of the dress I wore to the first party where he put me on his motorcycle. This one was a matured version.

With a full, flared skirt, I felt like I was wearing a waterfall of sunshine. It matched my golden hair.

The back plunged down, and pearls dripped in a line down my back as the only thing that sat across my skin. A full, open back with a line of pearls felt like his style.

But the full open back made me feel like there was an invisible target painted there.

I did my best with makeup after a semester's worth of tutorials and Kelly showing me what to do. Full glam was my armor for the evening.

At the party, my breathing was shallow. If anyone paid attention, they'd see my chest rising and falling irregularly. Fear and anxiety could have been easily smelled on me.

Eyes fell to me, and fake smiles were plastered on faces. With my *continue as normal* orders, I made fake friends all around and even fell into step with Sloane on occasion on campus and at her sorority. Lunches with fake friends and small talk was life for a while.

"Hey, bestie!"

I smiled. "Hi, Sarah. How are your riding lessons?"

She gripped my arm and laced it with hers, handing me a drink. "So great! How are you and *Alexander*?"

"Mm, he's still trying to take me to meet his parents."

Being normal meant letting people think what they wanted about me. I loathed Alexander, but the narrative he and Sloane painted was that I had moved on from Garrett to Alexander.

A narrative that wasn't the *worst* to have since it tied me in with meetings about families linking together and the drugs they passed around. It allowed me to learn about my surroundings without being marked as an enemy. Garrett was nowhere to be found lately, and sometimes I wondered if he was all right.

Never getting an answer on what side he was truly on put me on edge, but if there was no sign, I'm sure that meant he was at least still alive out there.

"Baby girl," a voice cooed from behind me, and a hand firmly gripped my waist. "You look absolutely divine in that dress."

Alexander spun me around and forced my chin up to meet his eyes. A delicate game we have played ever since he assaulted me in the stadium's bathroom. We never spoke of it or talked much at all outside of the public eye, but he and Sloane whispered about me in the back rooms.

Sloane hated me for how Brent pined for my attention. They were back to their classic games of explosive arguments in public. She and her family pushed hard to get her married to him for a stake in Chamberlain Industries, but something told me that Augustus wasn't interested.

And for that, they had tricks up their sleeve to undermine his company.

"Hello, Alexander." I almost spat on him but refrained. Barely.

"I come with good news for both of us. Deals have gone great, and after this semester, we'll be a power couple. I even have a birthday present for you." The smile plastered on his face was sickeningly sweet. There was no chance I wanted to know what his idea of a birthday present was.

Patting his arm and looking for a way out of the exchange, I eyed the bar. "That's sweet of you. I think I'm going to get a drink."

He snatched my arm. "Don't go far, baby girl."

"Wouldn't dream of it." I ripped my hand away and smoothed out my skirt.

"Isn't it my favorite patron! Fallon Montgomery, back again."

"What's up, Mr. J?"

The same guy was always serving drinks at every party I went to. My favorite bartender.

"What can I get you?"

I laughed and sat at the bar. "Give me another one of those blazing nipples. Been thinking about it a lot lately."

Serving me up, I drank my nostalgia in one go, motioning for another.

Lately, I drank a lot. If I was going to upchuck, I had something to blame it on, and alcohol seemed like a fine choice for that.

A familiar perfume wafted around me, and a woman stood next to me, donned in her best attire. She ordered a classic martini and leaned into me. "Did you hear the news?"

"What's that?" I kept my eyes forward, holding the drink in my hand while I leaned up with my back against the bar.

Her hand came into view—her left hand. On it was a beautifully large princess-cut diamond set in a golden band. Her manicured hand was expertly crafted to host such a gorgeous ring. "Brent and I are going to get married."

Not bothering to look at her still, I took a drink of my fourth round. Whiskey. "Congrats. You two will make an excellent pair."

"I'm excited to hear of *your* engagement," she said quietly, sipping from her glass. "You and Alexander will make a wonderful couple."

The party was in full swing around us, bodies swaying to the beat, drinks being passed around, and people with drugs ran up the stairs for their fun times. Those who were invited to the back rooms were already there, doing what they did best. When I finally chanced a glance at Sloane standing next to me, I saw the smug look on her face.

"We'll see," I said, downing the rest of the amber liquid in my glass.

"I hope he was worth the trouble," she whispered. "I told you what your consequences would be, and I'm sad that we couldn't be friends. Our companies could have had beautiful partnerships to span the world. Just think of all the gorgeous trips we could have taken." Her left hand swirled around the edge of the glass while she played a pitiful look on her face.

"I dunno. I think we're about as close as we can get, babe." I smiled, knowing he'd be watching my every move tonight.

"Your aunt sends her regards, by the way. It's wonderful doing business with the CEO of Montgomery Group."

My jaw clenched.

A hand went to her waist, and I was tempted to squeeze my glass until it shattered so I could slice her neck open.

It would solve one problem, at least.

"Why don't you head to the VIP room?" He tapped her back, ushering her away from the two of us.

She smiled. "Of course, baby. Toodles, Fallon. Hope you have a *great* birthday."

I turned away from him, waving for another round of whiskey from the one person I was happy to see—the one manning the drinks. Being drunk was the best option lately. Whatever games he played, I wasn't interested in the details. We were associates, not romantically paired.

"You look lovely tonight," he said, picking up a drink the bartender set out for him.

"Not my choice of evening attire, if I'm being honest. Too gaudy for my tastes." I refused to look him in the eyes.

I broke off all personal relationship with him—too complicated. I told him to leave me alone permanently, unless it was for business. What reason would I have had to be jealous?

"You know she's bluffing, right? She bought her own damn ring to flaunt around. Most people know she's lying through her teeth to get me to bend the knee. Jealous?" He scooted closer, hoping I'd look at him.

"No, and doesn't matter." The alcohol stopped burning my throat weeks ago. I relished how it warmed my veins and put me to sleep after a while.

"You can't ignore me forever, Blondie. Plus, I want to meet the day after your birthday to discuss things between our companies."

Oh, right, he was CEO of Chamberlain Industries. It was blasted all over the news.

Augustus Vaughn concedes international conglomerate, Chamberlain Industries, to his grandson, Brent Vaughn. He says he's excited about the future and trajectory of their multigenerational endeavors.

That headline came as no shock when he told us that Brent was going to take over. It shocked Brent, but not me. Augustus looked like the type to have more than one backup plan.

You didn't get to the top *without* tricks up your sleeve.

"It's not my company," I scoffed.

"That's where you're wrong," he whispered, getting closer.

Damn him for giving me goosebumps.

But what did he know that he wasn't telling me? His stupid little plan was mostly about keeping me in the dark, leaving me to fend for myself—by myself.

"Trust me, we've been working around the clock to figure things out. If there was a play to make, I haven't seen one. Unless you have something you want to tell me?"

He remained silent.

I scoffed and pushed away from the bar. "Thought so."

I was done.

Done with playing nice.

Done with these fake friends.

Done with the parties.

It's time I learn how my mom took over the world.

47

Fallon

Fallon's Birthday

Tucked away in a discreet location, a few trusted men gathered with me for a meeting about what had been going on in the company since Sylvia waltzed in and claimed it all as hers.

"Before we get to chatting, I want to wish a happy birthday to Miss Montgomery. You've come a long way, and you will take the world by storm like your mother did. We are excited to see what you can do." Evans led the secret meeting we were holding.

He offered a small box to me. "As a birthday present, this was released from your mother's will to be given to you today. When you go home, open it. Maybe it will give some insight."

Someone popped open a bottle and passed around glasses for everyone to take a shot with me as a newly donned twenty-one-year-old.

The mood was light despite the dark cloud that loomed overhead. What Sylvia would do, or had done, was on the back of all our minds. Still, we took a day to celebrate my birthday as a final hurrah for how far we had come until we could no longer continue.

"To Fallon!" Mr. Caldwell raised his glass.

"To Fallon!" The rest of them followed.

We drank up.

I kicked my feet up in the chair next to me. "You all have been great. I couldn't have asked for better people to have my back. Despite this being an odd year, thanks for ringing in my birthday with me."

A sudden *boom* near us went off.

Wasn't it too early for thunderstorms? *Odd weather.*

It happened again.

Boom!

"What the fuck?" James stood to investigate, reaching for the gun on his hip.

He became more vigilant than ever around me. Life or death and all.

More commotion came from just outside the doors before they burst open, with masked men wielding handguns rushing in.

"Hands up! This is a robbery!"

Evans stood with his hands up. "Guys, I think—"

Bang!

He went still, and blood seeped from his skull. Stumbling and gurgling, he fell to the floor, eyes going dead.

Fuck!

A couple of our men stood to return fire. It was going to be a bloodbath.

Shots rang out, and I plugged my ears as James pulled me to the ground and back to the wall.

"Get in here." His voice was low before he stood to return fire at the gunfight that broke out in the room.

Crouched in the corner holding my box, he opened a small exit in the wall vent and shoved me through.

He fired a few more shots before his magazine ran out. He dropped the magazine and fished out another. Before he could load it into his gun, a shot hit him in the shoulder, sending him stumbling back.

I looked at him, knowing he'd be a goner if I didn't do something.

"James!" I called out.

Fuck it.

I made my way back into the room where the masked men were taking out my guys one by one, and if I wasn't quick, James would be next.

I grabbed his good arm and pulled him to come with me. He finally got his magazine into the gun, pointing and shooting, nailing two of the guys coming for us. Pulling on him again, we made it into the adjoining room.

He held his bad arm. "The exit is this way. Let's get you out of here. I have somewhere we can go."

Shaking off the gunshot, he held onto me tightly, pulling me through until we were out into the trees.

All our cars were on fire.

What the fuck was happening?

"Come on." He scooped me up and started running.

Happy fucking birthday to me.

Acknowledgments

Eff me, where do I even begin?

My midnight Darlings, all of you have been my whole life and whole heart. Y'all are a gift from above and have been with me patiently waiting for the release of these books. Literally y'all didn't even know if I'd be a good writer and had my back. You guys are literally stuck with me forever now. No escaping the basement.

My multiple beta readers who gave me wonderful feedback and let me know that this book isn't complete shit. I am honored you took a chance on me. I'm keeping you forever.

Savannah, Mallory, Vanessa (my wife), Kayla, Roxana, Courtney, Lindsey, Louisiana (Queen of the Bayou) Alexandra, Canada (muddler and Queen of Canada) Alexandra, Leeanna (Princess Conseula banana hammock), Bailey (the cutie and image of Fallon), Bats & Books, Toni (@sinful_smut_reader), Renisha M (stalker doonut), Kayley (side hoe), Dawn Joles, Robyn, Sam (that random bitch you know), Tashi (tashiis_book-ish_allure), Janissa Peralto, Elizabeth W., Bethany, Dana, Samantha (bound_with_a_kiss), Hope (hopesturningpages), Kat (katrinas_library), and if I missed you, please come scream at me or throw a shoe.

The friends I met along the way:

@betweentheink.co for being such a cutie and making phenomenal items like my logo and letting me be crazy in your inbox. I didn't ruin gummy worms, I swear! I'm so glad I met you and I cannot wait to see your business soar. You *are* the hottest woman alive and my favorite smut peddler. If a reader is reading this, use FAYEHOLLAND10 at checkout LOL.

@daphnewinters.narrator for being the voice of my Fallon and just being such a fun girl to hang out with in the messages. I adore you and I'm so happy we met. I cannot wait to see what trouble we get into in the future.

@thedevilsassistantpa for responding to my wild ass texts and dealing with me calling you. Anyone with their head on straight would be honored to have you as a PA. You're kidnapped forever, sorry.

@glowstonecandle for making such amazing smelling candles for the book and being such a fun friend and reading my wild messages about the scents. I'm obsessed with you.

@inked_edges for making my merch and running such a fun business and making cute lil cartoons when I email you. You rock and I'm so proud of everything you've done.

@mossypaintandprint you were such a joy to work with as an artist for my characters. You've done them so well I can't wait to work with you on more projects. I cannot wait to see your art career grow.

@neptunedesignsl you were also a GEM to work with. Your art is phenomenal! I don't think you could ever get rid of me at this point; you are a genius. You deserve the world and I can't wait to make more covers with you.

@authorshayjinx for being the sweetest person and hyping me up. You do not go unnoticed whatsoever, and I can't wait to see how your career grows. ILY!

The Dark Romance team for giving us a community on the internet to share in our wildest depraved fantasies and being our true selves.

My friends and family who have no fucking idea I wrote THIS book (they know I wrote *a* book). Yeah, they totes aren't seeing this.

Literally everyone I've come across in the book community has been such a wonderful person to me and let me be my true unapologetic self. I doubted myself so much, but everyone who was here along the way that supported me has a special place in my heart.

To anyone who reads this book, whether you loved it or hated it, I am grateful for you taking a chance on me. I am eternally grateful. I am currently crying, so come collect some Faye tears to keep on your shelf.

www.ingramcontent.com/pod-product-compliance
Lightning Source LLC
Chambersburg PA
CBHW032007110726
47901CB00004B/1003